CREEK COUNTRY SAGA

Book 1

The Red Feather

Beneath the Blackberry Moon

APRIL W GARDNER

Big Spring Press

Beneath the Blackberry Moon Part 1: the Red Feather
©2016 by April W Gardner
THIRD EDITION, 2017

Cover design: Roseanna White Designs
Cover model: Anya Bradford
Big Spring Press logo: Karen Gardner

Scripture quotations taken from the King James Version.

Library of Congress Control Number: 2017903465
ISBN-13: 978-1-945831-04-1
ISBN-10: 1-945831-04-9

Published by Big Spring Press
San Antonio, Texas

Printed in the United States of America.

To Jesus Creator.

And to the Mvskokes
who ruled here before us.

MISSISSIPPI
TERRITORY
1811-1817

Coosa
River

Tallapoosa
River

Kossati

Horseshoe
Bend

Tombigbee
River

Alabama
River

Fort
Claiborne

Burnt Corn
Creek

Camp
Crawford/
Ft. Scott

Fort Mims

Mobile

San
Marcos
Negro
Fort

Pensacola

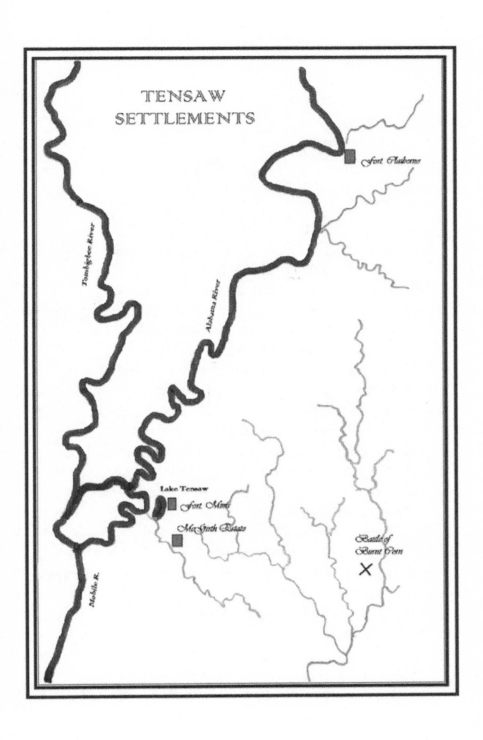

Walk Mindfully Over Southern Soil

Walk mindfully over this good land we call the Deep South.
Picture a million children playing carefree in her sandy soil.
And when you hear the wind moaning
through her tall, gentle pines,
Imagine a million mothers and grandmothers tending gardens
And going about their work
with deft hands and cheerful hearts.
When you see the dark waters of her rivers, creeks, and swamps,
remember a million warriors,
hunting and fishing the bounty
of her forests and streams to feed their families.
And when you gaze at her azure sky, remember the Master of
Breath, who heard the People's prayers for a thousand years . . .
And blessed them abundantly!
The face of the South may be forever changed;
Her First People banished from the land.
But forget not.
The Spirit of the Old Ones is still here, calling their own.
This red clay and sandy white soil we love so well
Will always be Indian soil,
Made sacred for a thousand years by the ashes of the ancestors.

Walk mindfully and remember . . .

epdixon © 2000

Cast of Characters

Wolf Clan
Totka Hadjo (Mad Fire), head of family
White Stone, elder sister to Singing Grass and Totka
Singing Grass, wife of Nokose Fixico
    Children: Fire Maker, Rain Child, Speaks Sweetly
Tall Bull, cousin to White Stone, Singing Grass (and children), and
    Totka
Amadayh, widow
Zachariah McGirth, adopted Wolf

Beaver Clan
Nokose Fixico (Heartless Bear), husband to Singing Grass
    Pawa to Leaping Waters and Long Arrow
Leaping Waters, wife to Tall Bull
Long Arrow, brother to Leaping Waters
Galena McGirth, adopted Beaver
Adela McGirth, adopted Beaver (Copper Woman)
Lillian McGirth, adopted Beaver (Bitter Eyes)

McGirth Family
Zachariah and Galena McGirth
    Daughters: Elizabeth, Adela, Lillian

Other Notable Characters
Gray Hawk, Totka's father
Old Grandfather, Kossati's Beloved Man
Hester, McGirth's servant

Introduction

Today, the southeastern United States is known for cotton, peanuts, country music, and NASCAR. Wind the clock back two hundred years for another world altogether. Expansive longleaf pine forests teemed with wildlife, and among them thrived a powerful and independent nation.

The **Muscogee Indians**, named "Creeks" by the British, once occupied much of the land we now call **Alabama** and Georgia. They were many tribes joined by a confederacy, which consisted of a complex yet efficient government.

Because they adopted many of the colonists' customs, they were considered one of the **Five Civilized Tribes**. This noble and proud people grew in strength and power yet lived in cooperation with white settlers for well over one hundred years.

But the new United States was expanding rapidly, and between the years 1811-1812, the Creek world—political, natural, and spiritual—was turned on its end.

The British, at war with the Americans, forged an alliance with the Upper Creek towns. The Shawnee-Creek warrior, Tecumseh, toured the confederacy, preaching adherence to ancient ways, even if it took engaging in war. The sighting of a comet that stretched clear across the horizon followed on the heels of a yearlong scourge of earthquakes. Both natural phenomena instigated awe and fear in Creek prophets, or "knowers," as well as atypical behavior.

In 1813, Creek country was the decade-old **Mississippi Territory**—the edge of America's vast, untamed frontier—and it beckoned men who desired much, feared little, and respected the land's first inhabitants even less. Greed turned to theft, generosity to hate. Tensions rose and patience dwindled.

Creek factions, red and white, that had for centuries worked together in harmony now found themselves opposed in how best to handle the encroaching whites. The **Red Sticks**, insisting on a return to the **Old Beloved Path**, took up the **red war club** with the British; the **White Sticks**, believing they must adapt or be snuffed out, joined arms with the Americans.

Before long, the inevitable was set into motion.

War.

Dear Reader:

The Red Feather is book one of *Beneath the Blackberry Moon*, the first in a three-part, ongoing romance. If you love sagas that are deep and bold and not afraid to take their time unfolding, this is the one for you.

I've provided maps and a cast of characters in the front and a bold-font glossary throughout for a fuller experience.

Enjoy!

April W. Gardner
www.aprilgardner.com

Chapter I

*F*rom inside the cool, shadowy wood, Totka Lawe squinted into a bright meadow. Its broad sea of undulating bromegrass lay empty. Deceptive. He tuned his senses to the cold fingers of foreboding walking up his spine. His own fingers clenched both the wooden war club tucked into his belt and the lead rope of the packhorse snuffling at his ear.

Go through the meadow or around?

Eight other warriors deliberated beside him, but it was his sister's husband, Nokose, who would have the final say. **Grandmother Sun** neared the end of her trek, bringing to a close the delegation's first day on the return trail to their *talwa*, Kossati, their Upper Creek village. One more sleep in land occupied by whites, followed by another two in Creek country, then home.

Totka swatted a mosquito from his ear and waited for Nokose to speak. Sweat coursed a line from his **roached** hair, over the bare side of his head, and down his neck. He shifted his weight to hide his impatience.

With each passing day, their mission grew more burdensome, their cargo more loathsome. The old wound in Totka's leg throbbed, but he pushed beyond it and centered the load more squarely across his packhorse's flank. The scents of horseflesh and leather failed to soothe him as he flicked glances through the trees.

This was white man's land but only for a little while longer. Soon, the Red Sticks would engage in war, and then, the land would be theirs once again.

At a stirring behind them, Totka stroked the sleek upper limb of his unstrung bow. No smelly, cumbersome musket for him. He peered into the murky shrubs. The darkness that descended held more than night. It seethed with intolerance and distrust so thick it could be measured in every narrowed gaze, in every unspoken word.

Totka no longer questioned whether he'd chosen the correct faction. For better or worse, he'd staked his claim with the Red Sticks. The scarlet feather tied to his hair had sealed it.

All he lacked was another battle, another feat of courage or extraordinary achievement, or another few scalps—from white or red—to adorn the red pole in Kossati's council square. Any one of those would bring his name before the council and, if the spirits wished, earn him higher rank.

The mare tossed her head and sidestepped, shoving him into a thorny bush, then swung back in the opposite direction. Feeding off his nervous handling most likely.

As he extricated himself from the shrub, the hem of his long-shirt snagged on a briar and ripped. Singing Grass, his elder sister, would have choice words for him.

"Ho, ho," he cooed, shadowing the horse's steps. He stroked her sweaty, quivering shoulder, but she stretched and strained against the tether. Head high, she rolled her eyes, revealing the whites, but Totka held firm.

The animal had tested his patience from sunup, and he anticipated hobbling her and brushing the day's dust from his leggings.

At last, Nokose spoke. "We camp there. Strike no fires." He pointed across the pasture toward a dip in the trees that gave promise of running water. Instead of skirting the open expanse, as Totka might have done, Nokose entered its midst at a modest tempo.

Tall Bull exchanged a look with Totka. Sweat rippled on his furrowed brow. "Before this journey is through," he said for Totka alone, "your sister's husband will set us all on the journey to the **darkening land**."

Loyalty blazed a fiery trail over Totka's quick tongue. "Envy has spoiled your judgment, Cousin. Nokose has more knowledge of this region than the rest of us combined."

To prove he trusted his brother-in-law, Totka ushered up a prayer to **Wind Spirit** for invisibility to the white man's eye, then tugged the mare's rope and fell into place behind the third packhorse. As he entered daylight, perspiration moistened his upper lip and seeped into the corner of his eye, burning a trail across his inner lid.

The breeze became a living thing, drying his eyes and thrashing the loose tail of his roach against his back. Ahead, Nokose scraped a blanket of hair from his face only to have it flung back. But Wind Spirit was blowing in from the **East**, the source of all life and success. He told himself it was a good omen.

Above the treetops, a short distance away, rose a single, orderly column of smoke. A white man's cabin no doubt. So close and they, so exposed. Clamping a scathing remark between his teeth, Totka noted their position in the field. Nearly there. He lanced the looming woods with a sharpened gaze and considered the long, cool drink he would take from that stream. Fifty strides more. Forty-nine, forty-eight, forty—

The mare balked, wrenching Totka's joints. He spun and pulled against her as she careened her hindquarters out of line, hooves stamping. A flash of movement an arm's reach to his right caught his peripheral vision. In the same instant, the mare reared, tearing the rope from Totka's sweaty palm.

Under the weight of her burden, she came down hard on her front hooves, one of them wrenching into a rut. With a sickening *pop*, her knee caved. The animal's scream pierced Totka through and all but swallowed the one coming from behind him. As the horse sank to her knees, the pack lurched violently, its bands snapping, its leaden contents disgorging and spilling over the mare's neck and head. Through another shriek and *smack*, her head met the ground.

Totka leapt backward, the iron mudslide nipping at his toes, and collided with the unmistakable hedge of what seemed a woman's soft, yielding body. The feminine cry of alarm confirmed it. In the two breaths it took him to pivot, seize her about the waist, and fling her aside with him, his mind stuttered at the thought of a woman suddenly there where before had been only grass.

They hit the dirt, he on top, she releasing a soft *oomph* in his ear.

Hand on her belly, he pushed off her, eager to free her of him, but a glimpse of her sunset hair stopped him short. This was a white woman, and a good fraction of the Red Sticks' firepower lay exposed at his feet.

Alarm zinged every nerve ending.

The woman lay flat on her back, arms splayed, mouth an oval of surprise.

Had she seen the weapons before Totka knocked her over? If she had, more than one man in the delegation would demand her life, and Totka would be the one expected to take it. But nothing said "guilty" like taking a life. Could he render her unconscious? He could; his elbow was primed for a strike she would not see coming. His muscles bunched for execution, then froze—and if she had seen nothing?

Thinking better of it, he cupped her shoulder with a palm and aligned his weight, ready to pin her when she attempted to rise. He would take his chances.

Eyes wide, she took him in.

He welcomed her scrutiny, so long as she kept the scream in her throat and her eyes on him instead of the tangle of muskets that still tumbled and clattered around the thrashing horse.

He squelched the dread souring his stomach. Killing women was beneath any self-respecting warrior—an unpopular conviction he

14

kept to himself—but if called upon, he would do what he must.

Except for a convulsive swallow, she hadn't stirred since she'd landed. Or uttered a sound. Shock?

He peered behind him.

Several men scrambled to calm the animal. Another tossed a blanket over the spill. Nokose crouched over the horse's throat, knife drawn. Long Arrow, Totka's boyhood friend, locked the horse's head in the crook of his arm. The animal would have to be destroyed.

"Why do you not kill the woman? Or at least blindfold her." Tall Bull, Totka's cousin, stood nearby, observing as Nokose probed the animal's neck for an artery.

"No. Only . . . keep her down and quiet," Nokose said, "until we've cleared the weapons."

Long Arrow spoke softly in the mare's ear as Nokose pierced her hide, drawing another squeal. Blood arched a spurting trail of red across Totka's arm and the woman's chin and forehead.

She blinked fast as though woken from sleep. A sharp intake of breath preceded an equally sharp demand, but Totka's limited English failed him.

"Tell her she is safer where she is," Nokose called. "That she may rise when we are finished collecting the spilled trade goods."

Keeping a watchful eye on her, Totka raised his voice. "Why do *you* not lie to her? You speak her tongue far better than I." Besides, Totka had always been a terrible liar.

"Tell her the word *wait*," Nokose offered.

"Wait?" she repeated, her evergreen eyes sparking.

Totka braced himself for battle, but she was a little thing and would be easy enough to subdue. "She does not approve of your word." He purged the irritation from his tone to avoid agitating the woman further.

Long Arrow chuckled. "Most women do not."

With her first simple attempt to rise, Totka locked his elbow and wagged his head. With her second, he flung a light leg over her abdomen and dispensed a narrow-eyed look of warning. When she spouted a lone, heated word and rammed his thigh with the heels of her hands, he seized her wrists in a loose, single-handed hold and frowned his displeasure.

Her lips stretched into a line before releasing a string of hushed yet adamant words. Blood slithered over her forehead and stained crimson the burnished copper roots of her hair. The overpowering stench of it filled his nostrils and coated the back of his tongue.

She wrinkled her nose and glared at him; he stared back, working to keep his expression unreadable, unruffled. Uncompromising.

Behind him, the sounds of shuffling feet and clinking metal gave him hope he might soon release her. If not, he would have a genuine fight on his hands.

Perhaps she understood **Muskogee**? "Whose woman are you?" he asked in his language. If she'd bound her life to any of the **Creek countrymen** living in Tensaw, there was a chance she'd honed Red Stick sympathies.

Her response was to knee him in the back. The ineffective thump resonated through his chest.

"Woman, stay." These words he knew from a neighboring Scotsman. One, the man used on his wife; the other, on his dog.

She retorted with another set of gibberish. If she would slow down, he might catch — ah! A word he understood, *why*. Although, he had no intention of responding to it. At least not with the truth.

"Nokose, tell me you have those muskets hidden," Totka said.

"Patience. Almost there." Nokose spoke through the huff of labor.

"Why so eager to be free of her?" Tall Bull snorted a laugh. "You are doing fine work handling the woman. Even though you are sorely out of practice."

Totka envisioned the smug satisfaction on his cousin's face. Three **winters** beyond the deed, the man continued to flaunt his theft of Leaping Waters' heart.

"Not a man here will deny I have the more desirable of the two tasks."

"You will eat those words when Nokose tells you to free her of that pretty scalp," Long Arrow said.

Clearly, he did not know the true Nokose. One of the others might be willing to order the woman's death, but not Totka's brother. Nokose was partly responsible for teaching Totka to respect the helpless ones, especially those of the whites who did not understand the way in which Muscogees made war.

The murderous Choctaws, the **Long Hairs**, who'd burned his mother, took the rest of the credit.

Totka shot Long Arrow a smirk. "Not the most challenging way to take hair."

Tall Bull, who busied himself strapping several firearms to the burgeoning pack of another of the horses, glanced Totka's direction. "There is little honor in war with the whites, no matter their sex. The men fight like women and die with fear in their eyes. Better to slit her throat and be done with it. Now, later." He shrugged. "Either way, it will happen."

An angry fire lit within Totka. If his thieving cousin tried it, he'd better look to his own throat. Not bothering to snuff out his anger, Totka studied the wisp of a woman in his charge: blood-splattered skin, hair wild and aflame about her head, pulse erratic at her throat, breast rising and falling in short, rapid succession, apron askew. Quite the vision. One he would be loath to destroy.

Through tense lips, she blew at the hair strewn across her mouth. It fluttered upward but fell straight back. Utterly disarrayed, she eyed him with focused, unblinking composure, as though she guarded a secret he wished to know. And he did. What thoughts traipsed behind those bright eyes?

If she became aware they discussed her scalp, would her self-possession hold? At what point would she turn into a sniveling muddle? They all did, these white women. This one must be close to shattering; although, the blood painting her face gave her an unconquerable air.

"War paint," he murmured. At the ridiculous notion, an unbidden smile rose to his lips. He banished it, but not before her line of sight skipped to his mouth where it lingered several beats longer than expected.

There was no way this woman—*any* woman—under these circumstances would cater to physical attraction. When her eyes returned to his as steady and hard as before, his theory proved correct. But it was too late. He'd already catered to it himself, and in a flash, she appeared cast in an altogether different light.

His heart gave a stiff kick and set a new rhythm he was powerless to regulate. He wrenched his gaze away to peer into the surrounding wall of swaying pasture and willed himself to more mundane thoughts.

Before he could find them, she spoke several words—a polite request, by the tone and upward inflection—but he refused to look at her lest he soften. Who was he fooling? He had softened already. May the spirits strengthen him if he was called upon to silence her.

Old Grandfather's frail voice returned to him. *You were born a man of counsel, a White Stick. Beware of misplaced desires. A warrior's rank will bring you much pain.* Wishing the **Beloved Man** had never spoken the words, Totka tensed, his nostrils flaring. "Nokose! Waiting for the pale faces to arrive? To challenge them to a **stickball** match, perhaps? Hurry up!"

At his shout, the woman emitted a squeak of pain, fright at last enlarging her eyes.

He instantly loosened his pinching grip on her wrists, then growled at his base instincts. At times, he wished himself a ruthless warrior, like Tall Bull. Then, maybe he wouldn't be so conflicted. Of all wishes, he wished Nokose would finish repacking and rid him of this female!

She squirmed, and Totka, eyes averted, tightened his thighs until Nokose came and, gleaming with sweat, stood beside them. Arms folded, he avoided Totka's inquiring gaze, while meeting the woman's from between slitted lids. He cocked his head at her and frowned. Did he recognize her? If so, she gave no indication it was mutual.

After a moment, he loosened his stance and addressed her in English. They exchanged several lines, and she relaxed somewhat, allowing Totka to ease the tension on his aching leg.

When she was done speaking, Nokose turned to Totka, the corner of his mouth twitching. "She claims she was **hunting dreams**. She also chides us for our rude behavior, seeing we are guests on her father's land."

"Does she now?"

A quizzical sneer lifted Tall Bull's lip. "Don't believe her. Why would she sleep in the grass?"

Nokose ignored him. "And she insists she did not see a store of English muskets in our possession."

Totka leveled a flat expression on his brother. "She said nothing of the sort."

Nokose shrugged, the twitch returning. "True. I failed to ask, but how could she see anything with your beautiful face and charming disposition so near?"

"You have chosen the wrong vocation, my noble friend. Perhaps instead of **Great Warrior**, you should aspire to village clown."

Nokose angled away from the woman and grinned. "Bad news though—you must release her."

"I had begun to think you would never give me leave." Totka freed her hands and flipped his leg off her.

Like a startled rabbit, she bounded up and back-stepped, studying his war club and scrubbing at the crusty blood on her face. Indignation elevated her chin, but as he climbed to his feet, he noted the tremble in her hand as she straightened the apron tied about her waist.

She alternately eyed him and scoured the field. For whom? Long Arrow had cleared the area so that only Totka, his cousin, and his brother remained with the woman. This was her land, however, and she knew who may or may not be about. When these people found her, they would be presented with a picture and story to boil their ire and launch them into pursuit.

Wariness constricted the muscles in Totka's back, but Tall Bull looked bored, and Nokose stood placid. Nokose offered her a few slow phrases, mollifying in tenor, and jutted his chin toward the smoke snaking into the westerly sky.

She moved to leave, but Totka halted her with a quick reach of his arm to hers.

Confusion and a hint of anxiety scrolled across her face. Her arm went rigid while he scrambled for correct pronunciation. "Wait. Small wait." The words felt bulky on his tongue, but they worked.

Some of the apprehension eased from her eyes, even as she licked dry lips and rose up on her toes as though considering flight.

Tall Bull edged closer. "You should take that stunning hair and be done with her."

"Hold your tongue and back away," Totka warned lowly.

What had Leaping Waters been thinking to choose Totka's cousin over him?

Without breaking eye contact with the white woman, Totka gestured at Nokose's waist. "Give me your water gourd." Surprisingly, Nokose complied without argument. As he did, Totka tore a length of fabric from the ripped hem of his shirt, wet it with a generous splash of water, and swiped it across his chin in demonstration before passing it to her.

A bob of her head and a tentative touch to the splatter on her neck told Totka she'd understood.

Palm down, he flicked his fingers at her. "Woman, go. Home."

She didn't hesitate to accept the dismissal.

When Nokose made no move to leave but watched her lengthen the distance between them, Totka spoke. "She was expecting someone. We should go."

"I will trail her." Tall Bull set onto her path of broken pasture. "To see that she does not raise an alarm."

Totka whipped his gaze to his brother whose lips were beginning to curl.

"Not you," Nokose said. "Totka, see it done."

Totka adjusted the quiver on his back and did as his brother said.

Ten long strides inside the aromatic forest, Adela McGirth bent and propped herself against her knees, her feet sinking into the carpet of red pine needles. Her mind swirled, unable to land on the moment things had gone wrong.

She'd been asleep. Then, there was a horse—a terrified horse—and a Native. And blood! Using the rag, she scrubbed at her chin and hairline and jerked with a tearless sob.

Indians, out of nowhere. Everywhere. A line of them! Behind, in front, on top.

Lungs heaving, she clutched at her corset. She'd done well to maintain a brisk walk clear to the tree line, but now she dragged in air as though she'd sprinted the distance.

Red Sticks. She panted through an open, cotton-dry mouth. Had to have been Red Sticks.

They wore the garb of traders, but she hadn't been fooled. Every trader along this route knew to waylay at her mother's table for turnip and rabbit stew. No, these were Red Sticks. The secrecy, the slivers of unease in the younger's manner, the red club, the feather bound to a long, thin braid that sprouted from his cropped roach, the little voice inside telling her so—all indicators.

She fingered the scrap of wet cotton and went cold at the reminder of his proximity and her vulnerability.

Without consent, his image—the one emblazoned on the backside of her lids—swept up before her: narrow brows arched above heavy-lidded eyes that subtly yielded to her probing; a crescent moon inked a patch of skin above one ear; a swirl of markings trailed his neck and disappeared beneath the wide, ruffled collar of his pale blue trade shirt; over his sleeves, a thick silver band nestled in the muscles of each upper arm; several arrows, held in a quiver invisible to her, fanned out to one side of his head.

And that feather. Blue-red. The color of fresh blood.

Except for the nick of a scar on his chin, his russet jaw had been so smooth Adela would have thought him a boy but for his breadth and brawn.

Brawn indeed. She flipped her quaking hands before her and probed her wrists. They prickled where he'd held them, but there was not a scratch or bruise to be felt.

Why hadn't she been allowed up? "I know why," she spat as she beat shreds of hay from her gown. They'd been hiding something, and it took little imagination to guess *what*. She would need to tell someone. Her father. And Captain Bailey—he would want to know, as would his younger brother Phillip.

Phillip!

Spinning back around and stretching on tiptoe, she looked out toward the darkening meadow. It was late—well beyond the agreed-upon hour. Had he come and gone? Surely, he would have called, and she would have woken. Then again, she'd been oblivious to a column of Indians until she'd been practically under hoof.

Should she wait or go home as the Native had instructed? Her family would be worrying by now—a well-placed fear. There were Red Sticks lurking about for goodness' sake. And Phillip might be out there, alone. What if he'd come across them, too? What if they hadn't been as merciful to him as they'd been to her?

Her throat constricted, and for the first time that evening, tears threatened. "Oh God, keep him safe."

Endless minutes passed as she waited, her dread growing with each jagged breath. Finally, the sun's sharp beams dissolved, leaving their orange and purple reflection in the sky. Fireflies awoke and sprinkled the forest with their enchanting light.

From beyond the pasture, a wolf raised a long cry to the encroaching night. Another responded. They smelled blood and would get first pickings on the horse. Fright skittered down her backbone.

What was she still doing out there? Had she lost all reason? She lifted her skirt to avoid the prickly blackberry bushes hung heavy with fruit and sought out the slender trail leading home. Phillip would berate her for an imprudent child when he found out she'd waited for him in the dark. With Red Sticks and wolves on the prowl, no less. Her father would never let her leave the house again, and her mother . . . Well, her mother would *not* find out.

"Adela . . . Adela . . . " Phillip's voice rode on the breeze.

Her heart seized and then leapt. Haste sped her back through the underbrush. She burst onto the field at full speed and didn't slow until she'd flattened herself against him. "Phillip! I waited forever. I-I thought—"

Laughing, he enveloped her in his arms and held tight. "Missed me that much did you?"

Face buried in his chest, she drank in the security of his touch.

"You're shaking! Adela, what's wrong?" He unpeeled her from himself, bent to look her in the face, and brushed strands of hair from her eyes and mouth. "Is that blood on your dress? Did you hurt yourself? What happened?"

"I thought you were dead. You took so long!"

"Dead? Why would you think that?" His incredulous laugh gushed warmth over her face. "I was busy. That's all. There's a list of things to do before I can leave in the morning. Even with Dixon's help, I couldn't get away any sooner."

Head shaking, she swallowed to clear the knot in her throat. "There were Red Sticks." The blustery weather compelled her to raise her voice.

"Where? Here?" His hand migrated to the hilt of the long knife in his belt, but his tone indicated he wasn't convinced.

"Right here. In this field. But they're gone now. At least, I hope they are."

"Red Sticks? Are you sure? Have you ever seen one before?"

"Not until tonight."

Lips balling, he studied her a moment. "Were they painted?"

"No war paint. They looked like..." Heaven help her, she sounded unstable in the head. "Like hunters, no—traders. Only they weren't. They were hiding something. Weapons, I think. They might have been muskets. Or maybe rifles."

"You know the difference, Adela. Which was it?" He spoke slowly, softly.

"I don't know, I... They wouldn't let me see what they were doing." She sucked in a quick breath to quell the frustration escalating her pitch. "They—he toppled me and—"

Phillip grasped her shoulder again. "You had contact with them? And here I've been thinking you were watching from the trees! He *who*?"

"The Red Stick! He kept me down so I couldn't see, but I'm telling you—"

"On the ground? He kept you on the ground?" The fingers on her shoulder hardened, along with his voice. "Adela, did he... Did he violate you? If he so much as—"

"No! Thank God, no. He was..." What was he? All things considered, he'd been gentle, except for the burn of his brown eyes, which had explored her mercilessly, unabashedly.

Until near the end when, for whatever reason, he'd become flustered and ignored her as he might a dog at heel. Then, just when she'd figured him for a stone heart, he'd destroyed his shirt so she could clean herself. A strange, generous act.

She squeezed the wadded fabric inside her fist and recalled the rich, swarthy hue of his skin.

"He was what?" Phillip's question snatched away the image.

"He wasn't a bad man. At least, not that I saw. But he *was* a Red Stick. They all were. And any one of them might have killed you had you come across them the way I did." Blast the squeak in her voice! Where had her bravado gone?

"Oh, sweet thing." Phillip pulled her to him. His bear-claw pendant dug into her breastbone, and the skirt of her gown billowed with wind. "I'm perfectly well, and there are *no* Red Sticks. Not for

24

miles and miles. They're too busy killing their own people to care about us. For the time being, anyway." He cupped her cheeks and stroked downward with his thumbs. "And if it makes you feel better, an extra ship passed the British blockade this month. It docked in Mobile last week. So naturally, we'll see an increase in traffic on the trade route."

"Oh?"

"Some traders we won't recognize, but that doesn't mean we should label them Red Sticks." He smiled. "All right?"

No, it wasn't all right, but clearly, it would make no difference if she said so. She gave him the nod he wanted.

"Good. No more stories about lurking Indians, or you'll have the entire settlement up in arms. And you know it doesn't take much to build a fire under some of these hotheaded farmers. They'll sharpen their pitchforks and impale the first Red Man they come across, and before you know it, there really will be a fight on our hands."

He had a point. Unless she was absolutely certain, she shouldn't utter a peep. Was she absolutely certain? Until a few minutes ago, she had been, but now . . . "You're right. I won't say anything else about it."

"That's my sweetheart." The whites of his eyes sparkled in the dusk. "Earning a commission will be tedious with you occupying so much of my mind. How will I last three months?"

She drew a deep breath and took his cue to change the subject to his upcoming commission in the **standing militia**. "What kind of nonsense is that? You'll be in **Milledgeville**. I hardly think you'll be pining for boring, old Tensaw."

His full-mouthed grin charmed and inspired a smile of her own. He was the catch of Tensaw Settlement, and there were no other choices worth having. She was a lucky woman, or so she told herself. If only she could feel it deep down, where it mattered.

"I've waited all day to be with you." He cradled the back of her neck and tipped her chin to meet her mouth. When he'd captured it, he attempted to entwine his fingers with hers but was met with her tight fist. He broke away and took her by the wrist. "What's this?"

She cracked open her hand. "He gave it to me to clean my face."

"You mean the Indian? He gave you this? That's . . . odd." He heaved a sigh. "Red Sticks taking you down, a secret arsenal being transported through an open field in broad daylight, and now this." He pinched a corner of it, whisked it from between the fissure of her fingers, and let the wind have it. It fluttered a few feet before it became hooked on the jagged top of a clump of broomsedge.

She stared after it.

He'd flung it away as readily as he had her terrifying experience. Lips drawn between clamped teeth, she withheld a protest and let the ringing insect chorus of twilight fill her head.

"Are you sure you're all right?"

To hide welling tears, she rubbed her eyes. "I'm worn clean through." Could he hear the thickening of her throat?

"Come here." He tugged her elbow — once, twice — but she refused the invitation. A gap ripped open between them until he loosed a conciliatory sigh. "I'm sorry. I've been an insensitive lout. Let's not part this way. I love you, wild notions and all." The smile in his voice didn't lessen the sting. "Now, tell me you've changed your mind, that you'll come with me to Milledgeville. It's not too late."

"Have you talked to Papa?"

"Well, not yet, but I will once I know you'll say *yes*." He traced a line across her forehead to keep hair from blowing into her eyes. "The minister's back in the area. Staying over at Mims' place, I hear. If we tied the knot first thing in the morning — "

"Tomorrow?" An abrupt laugh burst out of her. "And you say *I* have wild notions. You haven't spoken to Papa about courting me, much less marriage. And there's my sister. Did you forget how much she cares about you?"

Eight years earlier, during the annual social, Phillip had mounted a stool in the middle of the Mims' great room and declared undying love for Elizabeth. She'd had eyes for no other since. Never mind he'd done it on a dare.

"You have to make your own choices. For you, not for your sister."

"You don't know how it is to be at odds with her."

"She'd better get used to the idea, because it's you I want. I want to build a home together, provide for you, give you beautiful things. We belong together, Adela. We always have." Intense and unrelenting, he pressed his case, undaunted by the shake of her head and the inflexible hand she stationed between them.

"Stop. It's too soon. I need time to—"

"Fine, fine. It was a crazy scheme, but worth asking. I can give you time." He took her hand and laid it against his neck. Day-old whiskers stabbed at her fingertips. "But I'll talk to your father in July, the very day I'm back. So you'd best prepare your sister." He removed his pendant and laid the leather thong across her palm. "Wear it. Please."

"Phillip, it was your grandfather's! It's too important to give away."

"I'm not giving it away. You're to be my wife. That means what's mine is yours. I love you, Miss McGirth." His husky voice rang with sincerity, longing.

She wanted to reply in fashion, but it caught in her throat. Instead, she slipped the thong over her head and took his hand. "Walk me home?"

"Always." The smile returned to his voice as he squeezed her hand.

She reciprocated, warming at the feel of his calluses and the reminder that he was a good man, as his father had been, as his four brothers were—able frontiersmen who knew the meaning of hard work, dedication to family, and sacrifice. He was all she needed, and she was a fool to dither. Come end of next month, she would be prepared. She would marry him. In the meantime, she would pray for peace.

A wolf bayed, followed by a chorus of replies. The pack was drawing near.

In response to her shiver, Phillip tightened his clasp on her hand and passed her a reassuring smile, invisible in the dark woods except for the glow of his teeth. He was truly all she needed.

They reached the McGirth yard, quiet now except for the yowl of a cat in the hayloft and her mare's soft nicker. Phillip reached over the paddock rail and greeted Wind Chaser with his usual scratch beneath the forelock and murmur of affection. The mare returned it with her usual head-butt against his chest.

Adela grinned at the two. "I'm not sure which of us you love more."

"I can remedy that." He hopped down, descending on her before she knew what hit her. His mouth collided with hers, easing at her muffled grunt, then regaining momentum, sucking the breath clean out of her.

Her knees weakened, but he was there, slipping an arm up her back and dragging her against him. In the momentary break, she hauled in air. "Phillip, you're — "

"I know. I'm sorry." His mouth landed again, more gently this time. "Just please . . . kiss me . . . "

Arms dangling, she had yet to respond, but her mind was spinning too fast to keep up with him. This was new behavior — startling.

He spoke against her mouth, but it was garbled, and her ears were pounding with a heady rush of blood. Her mind told her to reciprocate, that he expected it and wouldn't relent until she did. Squelching insecurity, she commanded her hands to his shoulders and tried to sync her lips with his and give back.

His response was instantaneous, attentive, accommodating. He transformed from ravenous to doting, and her insides felt their first flutter.

She tightened her hold on him and pressed into the unknown like the frontierswoman she was.

Tamed, he heeded her untried movements and took each one as though she were presenting him a gift, but she had only so much to give, and when she expended her supply and pushed him back, he released her, albeit reluctantly.

"Two months, Adela," he said between puffs of air, "and there will be no stopping." He deposited another kiss, this one sweet. "Two months. Enough time for me to get my commission and for you to keep the blood-lusting savages at bay."

She prickled, not sure which stung more—his blithe jest or his assessment of the Creeks.

"It sickens me to think one of them touched you," he continued.

"He didn't hurt me, and they don't lust for blood. They aren't savages." At least not the ones she had encountered.

"Where's this coming from, Adela? They *are* savages. Every last one of them, and as soon as you forget it, you'll find yourself missing this handsome scalp of yours." He waggled the braid draped down the front of her, and it resonated with a dull *clunk* against her collarbone.

But she *hadn't* lost her scalp.

Her father had spent several years among the Creeks, and later, before Elizabeth came along, he and Mama had taken in a Creek orphan. Sanota left them for his own people when Adela was still quite young, but he and Papa had taught her to respect the Natives and their ways.

Phillip's biased assessment of the Creeks scalded, as did his lack of trust in her judgment. She was no silly female, and the Indians were not mindless beasts thirsting for carnage. A retort came to her tongue, but she bit it back, not willing to send him off on a sour note.

"I'll remember," she said. "Now off you go. Bring home another proud commission for the Bailey men."

"And a ring for my darling girl." With one last tender kiss, he said farewell and left her standing by the barn, flustered in more ways than one; although, why she should take offense for the Creeks, she wasn't exactly sure.

They hadn't deserved his censure. She'd been treated strangely, yes, but with consideration. Didn't the swatch of homespun prove it?

If Phillip hadn't tossed it out, she would hold it up to his retreating back as evidence. An insane compulsion to go after it took hold of her. She could find it if she wanted—because she was smart and capable—even in the blinding darkness.

Her mind zipped to the lantern in the barn and the hatchet by the woodpile. She *would* go. For once in her life, she would be rash and imprudent. She would stand by her convictions, and when it came time to tell Elizabeth she'd lost Phillip, Adela would cling to that bit of fabric and remind herself she was brave.

She'd almost made it back to the glade, lantern lit and swaying before her, when a howl struck her ears like a club.

The wolves. She'd forgotten.

Spiders of fear scurried over her, but she assured herself the wolves were coming for the carcass, not her, and it lay on the opposite side of the meadow. Almost there, she couldn't turn back. She tightened her hold on the hatchet and increased her stride, cutting through a sea of fireflies. Let no man call her a wilting violet.

At the northeastern border of her father's land, she reached the forest's edge and hesitated. The quarter moon presented precious little light, but all seemed still. A gust blew through the longleaf pines. It rustled the needles that towered above, creating a comforting, familiar whistle, then swept over and behind her as though nudging her into the dark, foreboding expanse.

In the meadow, the wind greeted her in its whipping embrace, tangling loose strands of hair about her neck. Despite the weather's ravaging effects on the grass, she found the telltale streak of bent stalks with little effort. Papa would be proud.

Hurrying now, she followed the trail, sweeping the lantern out to the left until its beams illuminated the fabric flapping like a pennon on a lance. Beaming with self-satisfaction, she plucked it off the broomsedge, shoved it inside her bodice, and spun to find a set of glowing red eyes straight ahead.

Just within the outer ring of the lantern's reach, a scraggly, black wolf stared at her, one paw raised, seeming as surprised to see her as she was it. Two new sets of eyes joined the first.

Her heart lurched. Cold fear swept over her. What had she been thinking coming out here? She was going to die for an insignificant snippet of fabric and a heaping portion of pride.

Options for escape raced through her head. Nothing to climb—the nearest trees stood on the other side of the beasts. Running was out of the question. One good bound, and they would be on her. Unmoving, she prayed they would get a scent of that horse and remember what they'd come for.

An explosion of wind caught the lantern and swung it on its hinges. Metal squealed and shuddered.

The foremost animal jolted, crouched, and bared its teeth in a growl. The others mimicked it.

Adela eased the lantern to her feet, praying for all she was worth they would tire of the stand-off, but the alpha had other plans. At its first quick step, she widened her stance, limbered her knees, and double-palmed the hatchet. There would be time enough for one good swing before being taken down. Focusing on the animal's head, she timed her strike to coincide with its leap.

Directing her energy into aim instead of force, she released her coiled muscles. The crack of bone ricocheted up her arms as the wolf flew into her, knocking her over.

A sharp yelp split her ear, but it hadn't come from the creature weighing her down. She climbed out from under the corpse and, hatched raised and ready, scrambled to her feet in time to see a black tail bounding away.

There had been three. The other one. Where was it?

She twisted at the waist, looking for the ominous glow of its eyes, but saw nothing more than a golden ring of illuminated grass. Had it also figured her more of a fight than it was willing to give? *Lord, please, yes.*

Near the outer reaches of light, the grass had been disturbed, flattened. Shaking violently, she collected the lantern and inched her way to a pile of twitching fur and limbs.

Before her lay a second wolf. Dead. A vibrating arrow protruded from its chest.

Dread poured through her veins like molten iron, hardening inside her limbs, solidifying her to the spot.

She wasn't alone.

Had the Creeks come back for her? Stories abounded of white women being captured. Even so, it had been many years since such a taking. There was also the possibility they'd regretted letting her live.

They're savages. Every last one of them. Her scalp tingled at the memory of Phillip's words.

No, no. She shook her head to clear the panic. They weren't savages. She wasn't thinking clearly. They'd killed the wolf. Not her.

And this had been a perfect kill. Straight through the heart. Very little blood. How close would a bowman have to be to make such a shot in this wind? Twenty feet? Thirty? As far as the trees? He could be anywhere outside of her perfect ring of light. Watching.

Protecting. Yes, protecting. Relief overpowered her fear and reignited her heart.

Gulping through a dry throat, she neared the lantern to the arrow's dyed fletching, four narrow black stripes on brilliant red. Brain whirring, she tried to reconcile the fletching with what her father had taught her about their Indian neighbors. Each warrior used distinct markings for his arrows, and these markings, she recognized.

She'd had plenty of time to study them from her position beneath their owner.

He was near. Not in the trees but close. She felt the scorch of his eye. If she swung the lantern in a circle about her, she might catch a gleam of his armbands or those silver ornaments dangling from his ear lobes.

The man's voice rang through her mind—musical, rhythmic, pleasing to the ear. As placid as he'd been, she had no desire for another encounter.

Why he would still be there in the meadow, and why he would

protect her, she could only guess. But did it matter? He *was* there, and he'd saved her from an awful mauling and certain death. An answer to prayer if ever there was one.

Fresh howls carried past on the wind, reminding her she had no business in that glade. She hurried past the wolf, brushing the soft fletching with her fingertips. Then, she stopped. The man would come for his arrow. On impulse, she withdrew the embedded shaft and wiped it on the animal's fur to clean it of gore.

Leaving it, she set her face toward home and didn't look back.

Chapter 2

Adela climbed the ladder to the loft, careful not to wake her sisters. Phillip's bear claw thudded against her, reminding her of its presence. In a panic, she clutched it through her gown. Had she hidden it from Mama? She must have. Otherwise, Mama would have questioned her about it.

She abandoned the pendant to reach timid fingers into her pocket. Loose fibers reached back; she withdrew as though burned, wondering at herself for having retrieved the scrap.

Bravery? Foolishness? Either way, she was alive. Her dress might be ruined, but she was alive to scrub it clean. She hung it on a peg, turning the bloody front into the wall, and slipped into her nightgown.

The bed ropes squeaked as Adela climbed in, and Lillian sat up. "Where have you been?" she whispered, her anger unconcealed. "I've been worried sick."

"Shh! You'll wake Beth." But their oldest sister's breathing remained deep and even.

"I heard the whole conversation with Mama, but I want the truth."

The whole conversation included Adela falling asleep in the meadow, going back for something she'd dropped, being confronted by wolves, and surviving.

The terror in Mama's eyes, the way she'd clung to Adela when she'd walked through the door, the questions, the insistence, the resignation—all brought the bitter taste of guilt fresh to Adela's tongue, and she couldn't swallow.

Phillip's warning to not propagate needless fear was just as fresh, and Mama couldn't afford another attack of the lungs. Adela would speak to Papa first. He was due home tomorrow.

"Well?" Lillian demanded.

"I was . . . "—all but trampled, nearly scalped, roughly kissed, not quite wed, almost mauled, saved in the nick of time by a strange Native— "stupid."

"That goes without saying, but that's all? You're not going to tell me anything else?" She waited for an answer; she waited in vain. "I can't believe Mama didn't have a breathing attack."

"I know." Adela had walked in a blood-smeared mess but calm and unperturbed. It had worked. "Contrary to what you insinuated, I didn't lie to her."

Lillian practically snorted. "No, silence would be more your style." She thumped Adela on the shoulder. "Am I not getting any more details, like where you got that-that whatever-it-is hanging around your neck?"

Adela grasped the pendant. "You saw it?"

"When you got undressed, I did, and if you don't want anyone else to find out, you should be more careful. So, out with it. What have you got there?"

"It's nothing. A trinket."

"Nothing? I saw the way you were holding it," she rasped.

"Shh! That's not what I—" Would Lillian understand? "It's . . . from a man."

"Well, it's about time. I'm tired of having to say I have a twenty-one-year-old unwed sister. Give me all the details. Who is he?" Lillian had always sworn she would be married before her eighteenth birthday. She had less than two years to make it happen.

"If I tell you, you have to promise to keep it to yourself. For a while, at any rate. Promise?"

"Fine. I promise."

Adela took a deep breath and said his name on less than a whisper.

"What? No! It's not as if he has no reason to care about you, but *you*? I never imagined you to be so audacious as to set your bonnet for Beth's man!"

"See why it's a secret? No one would understand." The effort of withholding tears set her jaw to quaking. "Besides, he's not Beth's man. And I'm not even sure I feel anything for him."

"You've got to be half mad. You do realize she'll all but disown you?"

Adela inhaled sharply. "Do you think so?" The tears won out and spilled out the sides of her eyes and into her hair.

"Come on. Don't cry. It won't be so bad. She'll forgive you eventually. She's never really had a claim to him and will see it in time. But you must tell her. You can't keep it from her forever, and if she finds out from someone else, it'll be worse."

"I've tried a dozen times, but I just can't."

Adela moaned and Lillian put a comforting hand on her shoulder.

"It'll humiliate her, if it doesn't kill her first," Adela said. "He's going to ask for my hand the day he gets back, but Lilly, I'm not even sure I love him even though I have every reason to. He's so . . . "

"Handsome? Daring? Everything a woman could want in a man?"

Adela sighed and rolled the leather strap between her fingers. Soft snoring from the other side of the room confirmed Beth still slept. "Yes, he's all that, but there's something missing, or maybe it's what he has too much of. A bit too brash, maybe? Arrogant? He's rather . . . demanding." The memory of his kiss spawned a rush of heat. "And I don't see much of the Lord in his life."

"Is that what's bothering you? Do yourself a favor and stop focusing on his faults. We all have them." Lillian propped herself up on an elbow.

Moonlight from the small window washed her face in its glow. Their Mama's full Spanish blood displayed most in Lillian. The dim light couldn't veil her beauty: small, rounded nose, delicate jaw, narrow mouth yet full. Everything about her was petite, except for her eyes. Doe eyes, Papa called them.

"It's simple," Lillian continued. "You tell Beth. She's hurt. When Phillip proposes, you accept, and in time, Beth recovers." She tugged the pendant from Adela's grasp. "This was his grandfather's. I take it he loves you very much."

"He claims he does."

"And you saw him tonight to tell him goodbye?"

Adela bobbed her head as it filled with the daunting images of the warriors — erect, robust, wild and formidable in their feathers and tattoos. Blood whooshed in her ears. She should be dead.

"Your secret is safe with me, but my advice is, sooner is always better than later." The comment brought the subject of Phillip back into focus.

"I know, I know. When it comes to Beth, I'm such a coward."

"Hardly." Lillian patted her hand.

It felt awkward to be the one consoled. The tables were usually turned.

"I didn't plan for it to happen, and now, I'm risking Beth disowning me for a man."

Lillian snickered. "I might have been exaggerating a little about the disowning. Why don't you get some sleep, and tomorrow, we'll talk about how to handle it. Sounds like there'll be a wedding when he returns, and you can't prepare for a home of your own and keep it a secret. We'll think of something."

"Thanks, Lilly. Love you." She deposited a peck on her sister's cheek. Much later, her mind exhausted, she followed Lillian in sleep and dreamt of a red feather and a war drum.

Kossati Village, **Upper Creek Towns**

Totka pulled back the deer-hide flap covering the doorway of his sister's lodge. The moonlight went ahead of him. Its soft glow spilled across the dirt floor and illuminated two of Singing Grass' little ones piled like **broken days** on their raised, split-cane **couch**. Arms and legs sprawled in every direction.

Speaks Sweetly, his youngest niece, stirred flipped to her back, and wiped drool from her pudgy cheek.

Noiseless, Totka entered and inhaled the bittersweet scent of his sister's *sofkee* kept in a gourd hanging on the wall by the door. He took the ladle from its center and downed a few mouthfuls of the sour corn soup. It was good to be home.

While removing his quiver, he skirted the small trestle table, then propped his bow, quiver, and club beside the couch extending from the wall opposite his sister's. Times as they were, he kept his sheathed blade strapped to his waist.

Singing Grass' couch squeaked as she flipped to face him. "Totka Lawe, you are home early." Her whisper was a shout in the stillness.

Running the gauntlet of little appendages, Totka stole across the room, ducked under the bunk where his nephew slept, and lowered himself to sit beside her. "Sorry to break your sleep."

"Where is Nokose? Did he send you home to see that I'm not dead?"

Totka rubbed the scar on his aching leg and decided to let her believe the lie. "You know your husband well."

She laid a warm hand on his knee. "I also know my **brother** and the pain he suffers. White Stone has fretted day and night."

Totka angled away, and her hand dropped. "White Stone would fret about whether the sun will set, if she was not already worried about whether it will rise again." Their eldest sister made worry a pastime. "So then, are you dead?"

"Quite alive and hungry as a spring bear." Her voice went tender. "I regret you needed to come home early."

"It's no matter. They had little use for so many men. Not this far north. Tomorrow, the muskets will be in Red Eagle's hands, and Nokose will turn toward home. We are better served by my hunting. I leave at dawn." He tamped down frustration at being forced to hunt during the summer. Their winter excursions had yielded far too little.

It was a good thing they'd battled to win back the hunting lands overtaken by the Long Hairs. Without that land . . .

"Surely, you do not wish to hunt alone."

"I would rather hunt alone than listen to ceaseless talk of war, death, and starv—" He cut short his disparagement.

"Why do you try to hide the truth from me, Brother? I'm with child, not blind and deaf. I know what happens around me."

"We will cope just fine."

"My husband has taken up the talk of that crazed **knower** Francis and has done the bidding of his red club. You call this coping well?"

"Give credit where it is due. He hasn't moved his family to live on the Holy Ground, has he?" Knower Josiah Francis, or Crazy Medicine, had established a new town to which Red Sticks were flocking by the hundreds.

He'd drawn a sacred circle around it in the earth and claimed no white man could cross it and live. "It is one thing to join the Red Stick cause. Another to blindly follow the visions of a knower with a split tongue. Your husband might rendezvous with the English to collect arms, but he is no heedless fool. He'll not uproot us, and he'll not kill without just cause."

A White Stick at heart, like their father, Singing Grass was reluctant to approve of killings of any nature. She was for diplomacy, peace.

Civil war had raged in the **Creek Confederacy** since the **1811 Grand Council,** after which Josiah Francis had shared his visions of a pure nation, one free of whites and their influence. Not everyone agreed with his methods of eradication. For over a year, Nokose and Totka had remained neutral, along with Red Eagle, a *micco* — or chief — of the Coosaudas.

The time to choose sides had long since passed. Not a warrior of piddling rank, Totka faced the same pressure as Nokose. He'd chosen to lift the club alongside his sister's husband and would bear whatever fate befell him.

"If we do not stop the **Long Guns'** expansion," he said, his tone flat, "the Muscogee people will be led to starvation or, as the Blacks, forced into slavery."

"Bah! Six **sleeps** under Francis' influence and you spout his words. Tomorrow, you will be executing anyone displaying American sympathies. Will you start with me? I spin my own cotton, cook in an iron kettle."

"Be droll if you like, but think of the shortage of food."

"Yes, they encroach on our land, but can you truly justify fighting them? They have been our good neighbors these many winters, and they are powerful. Look to the east, to the north, and you will see no end of them! They come and come; like locusts, they come. We will never stop them."

Totka had no defense against such blatant truth, but unless he fought the Red Stick cause, they would find themselves rotting in a shallow grave. It was the more immediate threat.

"I have taken up the red club, and I will swing it with loyalty and passion until war's end without another word or thought against it. I am a Red Stick. This will not change."

Singing Grass shook her head, despair warping her voice. "They will die in vain. Must my husband? Must you?"

"Your words are those of our sister. Do not let White Stone's plague of fears become your own. I am a man of twenty-five winters living under his sister's roof, and I have done far too little of late to contribute to the People." Provided not one child to build their numbers. "Would you deny me the desire to make that right?"

41

His personal sacrifice during the Beaver Lake battle, coupled with his achievements on the ball field, had propelled him through the ranks, but the resulting wound had laid him flat for well over two winters. The year following had seen him on a slow path to recovery. As a result, his position in the **Warriors' House** had grown stagnant.

"Of course not, but you can barely . . . Your leg, it is . . . " Her voice trailed off on an irritated huff.

With all the tenacity of a newborn colt finding its footing, he'd overcome a gunshot wound and a killing fever. Then, he'd fought his way off a cripple's mat. Last summer, he'd been found fit enough to rejoin the war party. Was that not proof of what he was capable? Her lack of faith in him stabbed. Only she could say such a thing and not earn his resentment.

Except for his nephew's heavy breathing from the bunk above, silence surrounded them. Totka bit back offense and sought levity as a distraction. "Fear not, Sister. The **knowers**, our wise prophets, claim no harm will come to us. Josiah Francis says the Long Guns' bullets will bounce off our chests like pebbles. The great comet and the shaking of the earth prove it."

"The knowers have gone insane! You, of all people, should hate their — "

A soft chuckle left him, and she poked his arm. "You tease! But you cannot deny madness has overcome our people. They are being led to the slaughter." Singing Grass' voice filled with grief. "We shame ourselves, Brother, and our children will pay."

"Red Eagle has joined Francis. If he — as influential and powerful as he is — has been forced at the threat of his family's life to join the Red Sticks, we have no chance of dodging the same tomahawk."

She sat up. Her single braid slipped from her shoulder and landed on the mat with a soft thud, and his mind instantly transported to another thick braid, albeit a wholly different color, warm in the light of an evening sun.

"I care not what Red Eagle does." Singing Grass brought him back to Kossati. "You should go to Big Warrior. Join his White Stick ranks in Tuckabatchee. I hear all who desire peace with the pale faces are flocking to his protection."

"Lower your voice." Totka gestured upward to his nephew and namesake, Totka Hayeta — Fire Maker. "Do you want the boy to hear and repeat your words?"

"If not Big Warrior, then Pushmatahaw," she continued, unheeding. "He is a wise micco to the Long Hairs."

"The Long Hairs," he spat out the name. "You speak of the madness of the Red Sticks, yet you suggest raising arms with our ancient enemy!" The same who'd stolen their lands and killed their mother, their grandmother. The same who'd almost succeeded in rendering him a useless cripple.

"Forgive me." She released a weary breath.

He cradled his head in his palms and massaged his scalp. "Soon, Tuckabatchee will be under siege, and Big Warrior will be forced to surrender. There is no escape. For them, for us."

She clutched at his hand and pressed it to her cool, damp cheek. "I need you here, little brother, to protect the children."

Heart squeezing, Totka's eyes wandered to their shadowy forms. It was cruel of her to use their **lineage** against him.

Being the children's maternal uncle, their *pawa*, he was responsible for their upbringing, far more so than Nokose, their father. Since Totka's own pawa had taken the journey to the spirit world, the heavy burden of rearing Singing Grass' children had fallen to him. He loved them as though they'd come from his own body, but who would provide for them if both he and Nokose went away? If they were killed? So many of their **clansmen** were already tied up in the war . . .

He shook his head and retrieved his hand. "Since we have embraced the Red Stick cause, there is no need to protect the children. Red Eagle is the faction war chief now, and he is a shrewd warrior. He will lead us well." If not to victory, then to honorable death.

Singing Grass flicked the back of her hand across her cheek. "And you will fight?"

He stood and stretched his leg, still stiff and painful four winters beyond having been shot. "I am a Red Stick who must protect his People. I go where I am called."

Singing Grass grabbed his fingers and squeezed. "Wipe the worry from your face, Brother." Resolve strengthened her voice. "As you said, all will be well. Do what you must." She eased herself to the couch and pulled the blanket across her legs.

Totka smiled into the dark. "Rest well. Morning comes soon." Two steps away, her voice came at him again.

"Totka? Did you find the English? Any trouble?"

"We found them. No trouble" — his mouth went aslant — "unless a dead horse and a bewildering redhead asleep in a field counts as trouble."

"You found a woman . . . in a field?"

A weighty pause followed as his fingers went to the ragged edge of his long-shirt. "I did not mention a woman."

Singing Grass' slow, deep laugh grated his pride. "A man does not use such words as *bewildering* except for a woman."

Why had he even spoken of it? "You think yourself clever, do you?"

"I do, and to prove that I am, I will —"

Fire Maker mumbled in his sleep, and Singing Grass waited until he'd settled before she picked back up. "To prove it, I will tell you one more thing you may or may not have admitted to yourself."

Amused, he wedged a shoulder against the wall in casual repose. "Let me hear it, oh wise elder."

"You have thought of this woman often. Often enough for her to be your first thought when questioned about your travels."

Arms tossed in the air, Totka feigned exasperation. "We have no need of the knowers with one such as you in our midst. But you're wrong. I have not thought of her often." The little copper-haired woman came to his mind only periodically.

"There *is* a woman." She was too quick for him.

He gave up. "A woman, a woman. Yes, a woman! A *white*

44

woman."

"With copper hair."

"And white skin. Do not forget her skin. The color of our enemies."

A white woman with a Red Stick spirit, a warrior's spirit.

He'd been branded with the image of her girded by a circle of light and facing down three wolves, his own totem animal. They'd been scrawny, hungry, and surely had smelled the woman's fear and vulnerability.

He'd growled lowly, but they'd not fled as they should have when alerted to the presence of member of Wolf Clan. Not until the end, and then, only one had listened. The others had stood their ground, forcing him to choose between the woman and his beloved spirit helper.

When her plight became certain, his arrow had been in the air before he'd registered that he'd made a choice. The white woman had been more valuable to him than the totem animal he'd been born to protect.

Tall Bull, in Totka's place, would have let the wolves have their way. An easy fix for an unfortunate situation. He would not have defied the **Order of Things** as Totka had done.

When Wind Spirit had challenged his skills and sent his first arrow off course, he'd been certain he would be patching her up before the night was through. But she'd eliminated the animal with a single, skillful swing, and *that* image still left him a little breathless.

He'd seen how shaken she'd been. But fear and the control of it were separate creatures, and she'd slain both. He wouldn't swear to it, but he suspected she'd recognized his arrows. While under his hand, she'd eyed them plenty enough for it. That she'd removed and cleaned it was . . . a message? A small show of gratitude? If so, it had worked.

But it had not removed the nagging guilt he'd carried with him since that night. Shame had taken him straight to Old Grandfather's lodge upon arrival in Kossati. The ancient one had guided him through rites of purification that had carried his body to the limits of endurance, but he'd emerged forgiven, pitied by the spirits for his sacrifice.

It had been a test, he'd been told. The first of many. Again and again he would be forced to choose between the pale faces and the code of blood laws. He feared he would rarely emerge a victor, but through all the guilt and reparations, he could not bring himself to regret saving the woman's life.

No, no regrets. She was too lovely, too brave, a worthy match for the wolves.

"Tell me about her." Singing Grass broke the image of the copper-haired woman aglow in lantern light.

With a few succinct lines, he complied, skipping the wolves and ending with, "I saw her with a man later that night."

"You saw them *together*?"

"Not in that way, although clearly not for his lack of desire. She refused him."

She gave a contented grunt. "It makes me happy that another woman caught your eye. It is past time, and it is good."

He couldn't disagree. It was long overdue that his mind made room for a woman other than Leaping Waters, even if no more came of it than fleeting admiration.

Singing Grass continued. "It's a trifling matter that she's white. If the woman pleases you, consider pursuing her. If she refused the other man, she is available."

"What fabled world do you live in, Sister? It does matter. Now more than ever. And don't forget that chastity is a virtue held dear by whites. They do not couple freely before marriage as we do."

"Well then, teach her our ways. Invite her to share our fire. We will feed her the meat you bring home to show her what an able provider you are." She giggled, and Totka rolled his eyes toward the gourds and herbs hanging above him.

"Whatever pleases you. I will extend the invitation next time I'm in Tensaw."

Her giggling petered out. They both knew what sort of invitation would be extended at his next visit to the settlements.

A vision of that copper hair dangling from the council square **slave pole** curdled in his stomach. But if his faction had its way, hers along with many others would do just that.

Singing Grass cleared her throat, all childishness gone. "Find a wife. You were not made to be alone." Not affording him a chance to reply, she left her couch and wrapped her arms around his neck for a hasty embrace. "Goodnight, Brother."

He returned to his pallet, her words heavy upon him. There was no denying the copper woman had left her mark on him, but when it came time to take up the tomahawk and club, her memory must not interfere with his purpose. He must put her out of his mind and brace for whatever duty required of him.

Chapter 3

*O*n the far side of the McGirth's spacious kitchen, Adela and Elizabeth stood across from each other, a stretch of fabric laid out on the table between them.

"I'm telling you," Elizabeth said, "if we cut it on the bias, there'll still be plenty of fabric to trim your bonnet." She slapped the yardstick on the tabletop with a *crack*. "Stop being a ninny and trust me on this one. Who has more experience with this anyway? I do, of course. Now, pull the fabric straight and hold it still for me."

Adela cast a beseeching glance across the way at Zachariah, her father, who'd entered moments before.

For a man nearing a half century, his russet hair remained free of age. His skin, on the other hand, had the leathery texture of every rancher and farmer in the sunbaked South. Permanent crinkles around his eyes divulged his tendency to smile.

He came to them, smelling of toil, damp earth, and tobacco, kissed Elizabeth on the temple and moved to Adela. "How's my girl?" he murmured, tugging her sideways against him.

It had been two days since she'd gone to him rattled and tremulous, despite having spent a day in complete control of her emotions. At the sight of him, her strong tower, she'd allowed way to bottled anxiety, and she'd kept no detail back.

He'd held her and stroked her hair and listened without interruption or skepticism. After she'd stormed him with questions, he'd put her mind at ease, saying the explanation Phillip had given was logical and judicious. No mention had been made of the fact she shouldn't have been meeting Phillip in the first place, alone and at night.

No outrage, no condemnation, and she loved her papa the more for it.

The little smile and nod she passed him now said she'd understood his deeper meaning. "I'm perfectly well, except for this spat over how to cut the fabric."

Elizabeth's lips twisted. "She thinks I'm going to ruin it."

Hands lifted, palms up, Papa shook his head and backed away. "Don't look to me for advice. I know my limits."

As broad as the kitchen door, he could wrangle and best any creature except his eldest daughter. But then, who could? Their mother, Galena, had pled abstinence from the argument a good half hour before. She now rocked in her chair, fanning herself and chatting with Hester who prepared their noon meal.

Adela was on her own. "Maybe we should measure again."

"Again? Whatever for? Just go over there and do as I said."

Although only one year Elizabeth's junior, Adela felt much the child in her sister's presence. Always had. This time, however, she wouldn't be bullied. Not with a gown at stake, not with the social drawing so near, and not with her possible engagement pending announcement. Adela would have to find her backbone eventually.

If she could defy a trio of wolves, she could defy her sister. "There isn't enough fabric for all those pleats *and* bonnet trimming. This is my gown, Elizabeth. I will not allow you to cut it unless it's done my way."

As though she were deaf, her sister bent over the fabric's edge, shears in hand. They yawned, primed to snip.

Indignant heat flushed Adela's body. "Take those shears to it, and I'll hogtie you and leave you for the birds!" Her voice rang out above the kitchen din, startling everyone as well as herself.

Gaping up at Adela, Elizabeth paused mid-cut. All racket ceased until the stew bubbling over the hearth could be heard.

Hester wiped her hands against her broad, aproned stomach. "Was that Adela I just heard screechin'?"

Mama's grin brightened her sallow features, not quite obscuring the illness that plagued her. "No, it could not be." She wheezed. "An angry cat must have snuck in when we were not looking." Her Spanish tongue entangled itself around her words.

"Sorry, Mama," Adela's pulse still raced. "I didn't mean to yell."

"Don't go stoppin' now, girl." Hester laughed. "You just got started. What else you got in that pretty head?"

The smile Adela offered was weak, but she felt her back straighten ever so slightly.

Elizabeth jabbed her hips with her fists. "Why in heaven's name are you encouraging her? Do you *want* her to hogtie me?"

The question brought on more laughter, including that of their father.

"Ay, *mi hija*," Mama said, gasping for breath. "Learn to laugh a little, eh? And let your sister do what she wants with her gown."

Elizabeth released a low rumble that grew into a full-fledged growl. "Fine!" She clunked the shears onto the table. "She can do it her way. Alone. And when she ruins her gown, she can go to the social in a potato sack. Also alone because no man will dance with a potato sack!"

Hester redoubled her laughter, coaxing Adela to join in, even though she was sure as sunrise that there was at least one man who would dance with a potato sack so long as Adela was in it.

The sight of Elizabeth charging out the door, coupled with the thought of Phillip's proposal, sobered Adela rather quickly. It was one thing to stand up to Elizabeth over a length of cotton. Quite another to do so over a man.

In sore need of some quiet, Adela shooed the other women out of the kitchen and into the house, insisting she be allowed to finish the dishes alone. She dampened the fire in the hearth but left enough glowing coals to survive the night. After gathering the last of the scattered cooking utensils, she plunged her hands into the water and scooped up a wooden spoon. Steam drew perspiration, and she wiped it from her neck with her sleeve.

Phillip had been gone two weeks, and still she tortured herself with qualms regarding their relationship.

He wasn't the first man to seek court. Since her sixteenth birthday, there had been a goodly line of them—some, young but ignorant; most, old or foul.

In spite of herself, Adela snickered at the memory of one in particular.

"If I had known washing up was so much fun, I would have joined you sooner."

As Adela spun, she slung dish water across the floor.

Mama stood in the doorway, her dress hanging from her gaunt frame. "What were you thinking about?"

"The Tennessean who stopped by last fall on his way north."

"The one who spit tobacco on my porch?" Nose crinkling, Mama took up a towel and began drying dishes.

"That's the one."

Mama nodded. "Oy, sí. You have definitely had better offers," she said with a laugh. "The rich *caballero* from New Orleans?"

The accent had been enchanting, but his flattery hadn't impressed Adela. The stoic Indian she'd chanced upon had had finer qualities than the Frenchman.

"But he could not reach your heart, either," Mama continued. "I wonder . . . What is mi hija waiting for?"

Adela handed her a plate, feeling drawn to confide in her about Phillip.

Mama bumped shoulders with her. "Or has someone already caught your eye? Eh?" The congestion in her lungs was stronger than usual tonight.

"You should rest, Mama." Adela took the towel from her and patted the back of a chair. "If you sit, I'll tell."

Mama accepted the chair. "I always love a good story."

"I don't know how good it is. You can be the judge of that." With increased vigor, Adela resumed her washing. "Phillip has shown interest in me. An interest beyond friendship."

"The Bailey boy? The one Beth—? Ah."

The way Mama said it, as if the truth were too awful to voice, made Adela feel like the traitor she was.

"Do you love him?"

"He treats me like a princess, and he'd be a good provider."

"That is not what I asked."

A puff of air from between tense lips sent a lock of hair flying from Adela's face. "He shared his feelings with me only a few weeks before he left. It's too early to talk about love."

"But not too early to meet in secret?" Mama's body might be failing her, but her mind was as sharp as ever.

Memories of being with Phillip under the gaze of her father's longleaf pines brought on an apologetic smile. But it was her subsequent thought that hurtled her full force into meadow, heart spluttering. She shivered and purged the unflinching Muscogee with an abrupt exhale.

Mama stood and wrapped her arms around Adela. "You respect the Bailey boy, but you question it, no? You question whether he is the one God has chosen for you. Whether there is another."

"But who else would there be? No one."

If her primary motivation was fear that she might never receive a better offer of marriage, was it fair to him to follow through with the suit? Then again, Phillip was one of her oldest friends, and didn't Papa always say, "In marriage, best of friends first and foremost"?

The bear claw under her blouse pricked her skin, a reminder that the clock was ticking.

"When he returns from Savannah, he intends to ask Papa for

permission to marry me. Should Papa approve, I plan to accept."

Mama turned Adela so that she faced her and rested a cool palm against her cheek. "I do not need to tell you to seek God in the matter. I am sure you already have. When the time comes, when you must give Phillip an answer, God will give you peace one way or the other. If you cannot find peace, wait. Spend more time with Phillip. Get to know him better. These decisions should not be made in haste."

Adela nodded. "You're right. No reason to rush." She coerced her lips into a smile. "Think Papa'll be back in time for the social?"

It had been bizarre of Papa a few mornings back to suddenly pack a bag and head out to visit Sam Mason in Tuckabatchee, the capitol of the Creek Confederacy. She felt uneasy in his absence. Although he'd assured her she had no reason to be concerned, rumors of unrest among the Creeks had spread like a virulent disease, rumors such as the Red Sticks going to Pensacola to obtain weapons from the Spanish — a story eerily like her own.

Chills ran rampant across her scalp.

Mama toyed with the knot in her apron. "Only the Lord knows."

Not one to pry, Adela hoped Mama would offer more information. She didn't. "I'm sure he'll finish his business and get home to us as soon as he can." Adela swept her hands along the bottom of the wash bucket. "All done. I'll dump the water and be over to the house in a minute." She pecked her mama on the cheek and opened the door for her.

She tossed the dirty water into the yard and filled it with fresh from the well. A scan of the small room assured her it was tucked in for the night. Leaning against the open door, she peered into the twilight and inhaled the scent of approaching rain.

Lord, help me see clearly. Through your eyes.

She listened for His soft voice in her heart, but the only thing she heard was the patter of rain against dirt.

Chapter 4

Little Harvest Month (July)

From his couch, Totka stared at the underside of the slanted, gabled roof and listened to Nokose's disturbed breathing.

Sounds of thrashing carried across the lodge. Totka wondered how Singing Grass slept through it. In the eight winters Nokose had lived with them, Totka had never grown accustomed to the man's nightmares. What caused them, Totka could only guess. Perhaps Nokose was tormented by the ghosts, the same chilling **Shadows** that occasionally visited Totka. Hovering, pecking, evil things they were.

The increased mutterings told Totka if he didn't wake the man soon, it would probably culminate in a shriek that would frighten the children. At Nokose's side, he did the one thing that ever worked. He placed a firm palm over his brother's mouth and braced himself for the fist that swung through the air.

Totka ducked. "Calm yourself. It is me," he whispered.

Nokose went limp, and when Totka released him, he dragged in air and let it out on a shudder. "*Maddo*. Thank you."

Totka patted his brother's damp shoulder and left him, but before he could reach his pallet, a soft rapping broke the stillness. In a flash, Totka's knife was unsheathed, his back pressed against the wall adjacent the door.

Nokose leapt to his feet and grabbed his tomahawk.

Singing Grass sighed and flipped over, not waking.

Tomahawk cocked, Nokose primed himself as Totka spoke through the door's flap. "Who is there?"

"I am Gray Hawk, Totka." His father whispered from the darkness.

Nokose lowered his weapon but kept it at the ready. As they stepped into the thick night, Totka scanned the area. The sliver of new moon did little to illuminate the three buildings completing their **compound**. The rectangular courtyard consisted of winter lodge on the eastern edge, open-sided cook house directly ahead, and storehouse outlining the west.

Their shadows were deep. If someone wanted to eavesdrop on his conversation with a senior warrior from the white faction, it wouldn't be difficult. The night, though, seemed right and good: a dog barked from direction of the ceremonial grounds, a warm breeze rustled the hickory towering above, a toad croaked to the chorus of a dozen crickets, the river rushed faint in his ears, and above it all, White Stone's snores rattled the shingles of the winter lodge.

Gray Hawk laid a hand on Totka's shoulder. "We are alone."

Totka sheathed his weapon. "Father, what brings you here when the **owls** are on the wing?"

"Word has come from Big Warrior in Tuckabatchee that Bird Creek Fekseko, Kossati's own peace micco, is sought after by the Red Sticks. The knowers have declared him a **witch** and will execute him should he be caught. He leaves before dawn with a band of faithful men to join Big Warrior. I go with him." It was impossible to read his father's features in the dark, but his tone portrayed urgency. "Will you reconsider? Will you give the White Stick miccos your bow and your loyalty?"

Totka grimaced.

It had been less than two moons since he had publicly renounced all attachment to the pale faces and vowed his loyalty to the warring party. All, including the man now standing before him, had congratulated him on his decision. But his father had always planned to join the White Sticks when it became imperative. Too soon, it had.

Totka walked a few paces from him. Hands on hips, he gazed down the blackened alleys in the direction of Kossati's council square. He could scarcely remember the days when peace and sanity ruled, when grief and hardship had not consumed Totka's family, when he'd been carefree with no more responsibility than to learn the ways of manhood and contribute to the stores of winter meat.

Theirs had once been an affluent family, well-respected. Totka had been the **Upper Towns'** most skilled stickball player. Every brave within a four days' walk had aspired to his skill and fame. A Long Hair's musket ball put an end to the sport. Two summers later, swamp fever took White Stone's husband and only child. Shortly after, a spark carried from the fire pit to the thatched storehouse, sending it up in a blaze.

Fortunately, Singing Grass' household had been spared the bad **medicine**. Still, many said that their family had somehow defied the Order of Things, that one of the **four** law-giving elements — Fire, Wind, Water, Earth — had been thrown out of harmony.

There was no denying the spirits had been angry. The three days he'd lain delirious with fever from the wound, he'd been visited by Shadows, ghosts of unavenged ancestors or spirits of those improperly buried. Their evil had been palpable and terrifying, their greed for his soul, undeniable.

For many moons after, the talwa had raged with gossip and suspicion until another, more urgent matter had driven the topic from their tongues — civil war.

Above him now, a multitude of stars glittered serenely, unaffected by the turmoil within him and the folly strangling his people.

Nokose joined him. "I will understand if you wish to follow your father."

"Perhaps. But my sister's children will not." Totka returned to Gray Hawk. "How many men go with you?"

"Over one hundred."

"A substantial number," Totka said. "More than I thought might remain loyal to Bird Creek Fekseko. But it's not enough. Your men will increase Big Warrior's band to six hundred, yet against almost five thousand Red Sticks, they will be defeated. No, Father. I cannot go with you."

"You are certain? Peace has always been your way, and the Red Sticks pursue violence. Old Grandfather advised you against such a course. Will you discard his counsel?"

"My heart wishes no man harm, white or red, yet if I must, to protect my sister and her children, I swear to you I will raise the war club alongside the Red Sticks and slice down every Long Gun and **Bluecoat** on our warpath!" The vehemence in his vow surprised him, as did the effortlessness with which he made it. There had never been a time Totka wouldn't lay down his life for that of his sister or any other member of Wolf Clan, but he'd never been one to boast of bloodlust.

Gray Hawk allowed for a respectful pause, then gave a slow, deliberate nod. "So be it, but take care you do not allow yourself to be guided by dread of what may or may not be, but by truth and justice."

A noble enough statement, but whose truth? Whose justice? These days every man laid claim to a different version. Out of deference to his elder, he gave thanks for the guidance. "Maddo, Father."

The bushes rustled. Nokose swiveled, tomahawk raised. A rabbit emerged but darted off at the sight of them.

"Behold, the deadly hare." Gray Hawk rumbled with contained amusement. "Do not come up behind this one in battle, Totka. You might find an arrow through your eye."

Nokose feigned a swipe at his father-by-marriage, then seized him for a brisk embrace. "May the spirits guide your steps."

Totka grasped arms with his father. "Go, before you're discovered. Singing Grass will understand that war waits for no man. I will give her your love."

Before Gray Hawk released Totka, he beat a fist against his own chest in a vow. "Your club may be red, but your blood flows in my heart. I pray we'll not meet on the battlefield, my son."

"Dance, Adela!" Lillian shouted over the sound of music and stomping feet as she swept past. Her dress hung low on her breast, and Adela discreetly signaled to her to pull it up.

Lillian shrugged and took over the dance moves, leading her willing partner to the other side of the dance floor.

Adela checked to make certain the drawstring of her own scoop-necked bodice still held. The peach and burgundy floral fabric brought on a sigh of contentment. No potato sack for her. The satin ribbon Mama had pulled from her sewing basket had matched perfectly with the blue highlights in the flowers.

Adela reached behind her and patted the neatly formed bow holding her empire waistline in place, then chose a seat along the wall and admired Lillian from a distance. Large, brown eyes batted full lashes with expertise. Her complexion was clear and smooth and a shade lighter than their mother's olive. Since she refused to pin up her hair, the black tresses hung thick and wavy; a ribbon kept them from her eyes. She moved her narrow hips with grace and skill, drawing masculine eyes toward her with little effort. She was stunning, and she knew it.

Wilting against the back of her chair, Adela beat her mother's fan, whooshing hot, stuffy air against her face. With her handkerchief, she dabbed at perspiration beading on the back of her neck and thought of Mama at home.

For years, she'd retained a tenuous hold on her health. However, the past two winters she had been tormented with severe chest congestion, further weakening her lungs and heart. When spring arrived this year, the illness had hung on.

Papa had been expected home days ago. He would be heartbroken to find their mother looking so pale and drawn.

As stiff as a dried sock on the line, Elizabeth presided over the far corner. Contrary to what her inflexible demeanor conveyed, she longed to dance, but unless she softened her features and attempted a smile, she would get no offers. Except from Lucy Mims, perhaps, who would dance with a mule if it meant keeping off the wall.

She jabbered at Elizabeth now. Gossiping, most likely.

The Mims' home was the only one in the settlements large enough to host a gathering such as this, and situated on the shores of Tensaw Lake it was also a centralized, convenient location.

The **Acadian** fiddlers hired from Mobile struck up a lively tune, their volume chasing Adela from her perch adjacent to them.

As she neared the girls, snippets of their conversation reached her, but she didn't need to hear it all to know Lucy was overstepping the bounds of propriety again. Elizabeth's bulging eyes said it all.

"Have you heard from him yet?" Lucy was asking when Adela arrived at Elizabeth's side. "Surely, he's told *someone* when he'll be back. He's been gone so long already. I bet he's been assigned to his new post by now."

They were talking about Phillip? Adela should have stayed where she was.

Lucy continued, oblivious — purposefully or otherwise — to Elizabeth's agitation. "He'll be so dashing in his new uniform. Shiny brass buttons all in a row, just begging to be touched." She giggled.

Elizabeth's pinched face reddened.

"Lieutenant Bailey. Has a nice ring to it, but then, it's not the first time we've used it. Of the brothers, he's certainly the most handsome." Lucy redirected her barrage to Adela. "I told Beth she should hold out for Phillip. He'll come to his senses soon enough. I think the two would make an excellent couple. Don't you agree?" This time, Lucy pointedly stopped and waited for a reply. A sly smirk raised one corner of her lips.

Adela's mouth went dry. The room suddenly became warmer, the music obnoxious. "Well, I, um . . . I . . . " She searched for an adequate reply but came up blank. She'd never been good at wording her way out of tricky situations. That was Lillian's forte.

"Come to think of it," Lucy continued, "maybe Adela is better suited for Phillip." She blinked innocently then shrugged. "At least that's what I hear."

"Lucy Mims, are you pestering my sisters again?" Lillian moved between them and curled her fingers around her friend's arm. "Come here. There's someone I want you to meet." Lillian whisked Lucy away.

Adela had never been more grateful to see Lucy's backside as it sashayed toward the opposite side of the room. She fastened her sight to Lillian and prayed Beth hadn't caught what Lucy had been insinuating.

Beth huffed — a sound Adela well knew.

An apologetic look already glued to her face, Adela lifted her gaze, dreading what she was sure to see.

Arms crossed over a thin chest, Beth tightened her lips into a line. "What was Lucy referring to? You wouldn't go behind my back and let Phillip court you." Every clipped word held an edge of disbelief. Her piercing eyes dared Adela to lie.

"Phillip and I have . . . We were meeting a short time before he left."

Beth's eyes became flint. "You compromised yourself?"

"It's not like that! We never —"

"Of course, you didn't, but you may as well have!" Her voice rose an octave.

Adela glanced around. "Please, lower your voice. I have nothing to be ashamed of." The words themselves were bold, but they lacked conviction. What was it about Beth that always made Adela feel like a reprimanded child?

"Except for your deception and betrayal," she spat. "For you to be so devious is shocking enough. But toward your own sister . . . I'm quite disappointed in you, Adela."

She spoke the last sentence with just the right amount of anguished offense. Beth was, indeed, a master at lathering on the guilt.

"I never meant to hurt you, Beth." She lifted her chin, stilled her nervous hands, and conjured as confident a tone as she could muster. "You know as well as I you have no claim on Phillip. I should never have hidden it from you, and for that, I apologize. What I will not apologize for is considering his offered courtship and possible marriage. In fact, there's a good chance I'll take him up on it, and you can either accept it or be miserable. It's completely up to you."

Beth's jaw hung like a plumb line.

With a defiant tip of her chin and swish of her skirt, Adela left before Elizabeth could find her voice.

She'd not gone far when the front door of the Mims' home flew open, slamming against the wall. Davy Tate, a local farmer, launched himself into the house.

The fiddles squeaked to a stop, and the floor cleared around him.

"It's true!" Davy panted, red-faced and bedraggled. "The Red Sticks are rising. They've gone to Pensacola. I followed them myself."

A buzz of chatter whirled through the room. Beth reached for Adela's hand.

Lucy's father, Samuel Mims, raised his voice. "Quiet! Let Davy finish!"

Davy shook his head as if unable to believe it himself. "I followed them straight into the city to Governor Manique. Appears they've got friends in high places." The Spaniards were aiding the Red Sticks. And that, in opposition to their neutrality agreement with the United States. "I got myself back here lickety-split when I saw a train of packhorses being loaded with more than enough ammunition to do the job."

Packhorses? Adela flinched and touched her forehead almost expecting her fingers to come away with blood.

Loaded with ammunition. It was true. The Creeks intended to war against them, and she'd been in their clutches. She went lightheaded

62

and clung to Beth's arm.

The very warrior who'd held her to the ground—the one whose gentleness she'd valued, whose offering she'd kept tucked away—might well slit her throat if given another chance.

She touched her hair, recalling how he'd examined it. Had he wanted it for himself? Her eyes slid shut as horror stole over her. No, if he'd wanted her scalp, he would have taken it. Right after he let the wolves have her.

Mr. Mims spoke up. "They've been warring against each other for over a year. How do we know the weapons they're collecting aren't meant for their own cause?"

George Gaines, liaison to the Choctaws, stepped to the front. "Their civil war has fizzled out. The Red Sticks have wiped out or scared off the peace faction. Since they have the people eating from their hands now, they'll focus on their main objective."

Like cannon balls, questions exploded around the room.

Captain Dixon Bailey, Phillip's eldest brother, stood on a chair and raised his hands to settle the noise. "We'll get nowhere like this, and there's no call to stand around and question whether we'll be attacked. We should be prepared no matter what, and this is what we'll do." Eager silence greeted his pause. "Starting tomorrow, we'll fort up, gather at designated locations and build stockades as fast as we can swing a hammer. Bring whatever food you can carry. We'll open kitchens and have communal meals. Bring only what's necessary for survival. Spread the word to your neighbors and get them into stockades."

This was no hastily drawn-together plan, and Adela, for one, was relieved he had a solid grasp on what needed to be done. Leave it to a Bailey to take charge.

"We can use my place, Bailey," Mr. Mims offered.

"Good. Everyone within a ten-mile radius will come here. Those of you living farther out will need to decide for yourselves whose property would be the best defensive location."

A voice shot out of the corner. "What's all this talk about defense?

How about we attack *them*?" Harry Cornells cut a path to the center of the room, and masculine voices rumbled in agreement.

"I hardly think it wise." Captain Bailey raised his voice to be heard. "Remember, we only have speculation to go on. Sure the Creeks are stocking up on weapons, but we still don't know why."

"Well, I dare say it's not for target practice!" Mr. Cornells said. "I don't intend to sit around and wait for them to attack. I say we meet 'em on the road back from Pensacola. Surprise would be on our side. We should get the ammunition before it's handed out to every bloody warrior in Creek country. Stop 'em in their tracks!" The burning hatred in Cornells' eyes transferred to the men around him.

As if on cue, Adela and Lillian locked gazes from across the room. Lillian, eyes large with fright, abandoned Lucy and shoved her way through the crowd toward Adela.

"Listen to me! Be reasonable!" Captain Bailey said. "If we attack them unprovoked, we give them reason to war against us. Harry, are you prepared for war against the entire Creek Confederacy?"

Cornells shut his mouth. The Tensaw settlers were outnumbered a hundred to one and practically defenseless. An organized attack from any front would mean their end.

"I didn't think so. None of us are. Everyone feels betrayed and threatened. We want to lash out, but we must not let our emotions rule the day." The power and authority in Captain Bailey's argument made way through the sea of passion, quieting the crowd. "Confiscating the weapons would be a wise move, but we should first petition General Flourney for troops. We'll need the protection of the military to back us when we return."

Nods of approval encouraged Captain Bailey in his plea. "We'll send a rider with the request within the hour."

Mobile would hear of their need before dawn, and if General Flourney didn't come to their aid, then General Jackson in Nashville would. Those two frontier-hardened soldiers would not abandon them.

Chapter 5

$\mathcal{P}$eering sideways at the sun, Totka noted its midday position. A hot wind berated his bare chest, adding to the sweltering heat. He adjusted his leggings and massaged a sore muscle in his calf. His horse walked with an awkward gait. Although Totka could relate, he grumbled about the uncomfortable ride.

The thin road leading to Pensacola wound behind him like a basking snake. Burnt Corn Creek bordered the field in which their party stopped to rest. Its hypnotic gurgling coaxed Totka to stretch out on the grass. Stomach sated, he let his eyes droop to the burping and belching of frogs in the nearby canebrake. Laughter and banter surrounded him as the warriors relaxed, content from their productive trip to Spanish country.

It was no secret Nokose had been chosen for this task to prove his loyalty to the Red Stick cause, but Totka's coming had been his choice alone. When he had announced he would join Nokose, Singing Grass had packed him food and wished him well. What could she say? It was a trip south for supplies. Nothing more.

The tread of Nokose's light foot sounded beside Totka's head. His brother grunted as he lowered himself to the ground. "Singing Grass will be rounding up the little ones for their afternoon rest."

The thought pinched Totka's heart like a taut bowstring between his fingers. The trip to Pensacola had been longer than most expected, the Spaniards having suddenly regretted their offer of assistance. "It is good to be back on Muscogee soil." Grandmother Sun shone bright behind his closed lids.

"Twelve sleeps is too long without a wife's comforts."

Totka's marriage had ended before it had officially begun, and he didn't appreciate being reminded. His fingers located a rock in the grass. He tossed it in the direction of Nokose's voice and listened for the satisfying *thwack* as it connected with flesh. Those stickball shooting skills still came in handy.

Totka discreetly braced himself for the return assault. When a rock thudded against the ground by his head, he cracked an eye and looked sideways at Nokose. "Fire Maker might give you throwing lessons if you ask kindly."

"Insult me if you like, but you could have any woman you choose, and you know it."

"I don't want *any* woman."

"Then you should not have let her go."

"It was her choice. Not mine." He snapped out the words. Why were they having this conversation again? What good did it do? There was no going back, and the reminder of Leaping Waters and the unhappiness she suffered with Tall Bull was a rancid stench. But she'd made her choice.

"I wonder if we speak of the same woman."

Totka rose up on an elbow. "There has only ever been the one. Your niece."

Nokose shrugged and gnawed at a piece of dried venison.

"Who else would there be?"

The jerky gave way, and Nokose manipulated the bulk in his mouth. "A certain copper-haired daughter of the pale faces? Singing Grass tells me—"

"Singing Grass!" Totka flopped back down. "Your wife has a colorful imagination and a singular purpose in life—to see me wed. Why do you not close your ears to her?"

A slow grin spread Nokose's full cheeks. "We'll return to Tensaw, remember, and this time, there will be no secrecy. She seemed partial to you. We can find her, you know, and—"

"Invite her to sit at our fire. Yes, it has been suggested to me before, but I feel she might not be keen to—"

A single shot whistled over Totka's head. He snapped to attention, and his breath caught at the sight before him. Like a herd of angry buffalo, a flood of white men stampeded from the pine-covered hills rising steeply to the northeast.

How had the war party been so unaware as to walk into a trap?

In moments, the settlers were within range and firing as one.

A handful of warriors fell.

Blue-gray smoke filled the air and hovered above the knot of assailants as they charged across the field.

The pale faces reloaded on the run, bringing with them the certainty of their victory. Mere seconds had passed, but already he could distinguish the features on their faces.

"Totka! To battle!" Nokose's command recovered Totka's senses.

He snatched his musket and released a jolting round.

The Long Guns pressed on like a pack of wolves narrowing in on their prey.

Nokose poured powder down the barrel of his musket. "There are too many. We'll not slow them."

"To the cane!" The cry flew across the glen.

Totka rushed toward the dense forest of river cane growing in the shallows of Burnt Corn Creek. Each step shot pain through his hip and up his back, but the thunder of feet coming from their rear infused speed into his flight.

Nokose passed him, but Totka managed to stay a few strides behind.

The reeds, taller than a man, snapped and cracked as Totka crashed into them. Several yards deep, he swiveled to face the enemy and dropped to his knees in the muck. A few rods distant, Nokose did the same.

Spreading a clump of reeds, Totka glimpsed the field. He steadied his musket arm against his raised knee, squinted down the barrel, and spied a suitable target.

Unexpectedly, a large number of the whites ceased pursuit, changing course for the hobbled packhorses. Their hoots of self-congratulation sifted through the Muscogees' sporadic fire. They slapped each other on the back and tossed their hats into the air.

Totka gritted his teeth. "You will not so easily make fools of us." The words came out on a hiss punctuated by the blast of his musket.

The discharge jerked his shoulder, but his target continued unscathed toward the horses.

Totka threw down the useless Spanish weapon and strung his bow. The reassuring feel of its slick body against his palm propelled him to his feet.

Nokose leapt up to join him, but Totka gripped his brother's arm before he could emerge onto the field.

The hoops piercing Nokose's ears beat against his neck as he spun back. True to his Bear Clan roots, he growled, lip curling. "They take our weapons!"

Totka retained his hold on Nokose's forearm. "Wait for others to join us."

Nokose yanked his arm free but stayed put, rocking on his toes.

Several others appeared at their sides, tomahawks and clubs in hand. Totka coiled himself like a stalking panther and waited until Chief Peter McQueen's birdcall signaled the attack.

A hundred war whoops split the air, raising gooseflesh on Totka's neck and propelling him from the cane. Warriors gushed from the creek like water through a sieve. Tomahawks raised and war clubs brandished, they advanced, angry and vengeful.

Rushing the field, Totka focused on the distant line of trees, musket barrels jutting from them like teeth from an alligator. Dust from the pale faces' retreat hung in the air and coated his throat, but not every settler had fled because the trees rained lead.

Nokose loped along at his flank, keeping time with Totka's stride.

Although protesting, Totka's weak leg held firm. Emboldened, he pushed harder. His hair whipped back from his face as the wind he created dried the sweat on his skin. The anticipation of battle urged him on. His feet hit a pocket of water, splashing cool liquid to his chin. He slid in the loose gravel but kept his footing. With a lunge, he reached solid ground.

A war cry peeled from his throat as he charged toward the pine thicket. Around him rose the familiar sounds of war as he narrowed the gap. Without warning, his thigh seized; his knee locked. In the next instant, the world flipped upside down as he tumbled headlong to the dirt and came to a sliding stop.

Totka spat fodder from his mouth and brushed dirt from his arms. His screaming, traitorous leg would get no acknowledgement from him. His cheek smarted where his face had made contact with the ground, but it was nothing compared to the sting of his humiliation.

The bulk of the warriors charged past, their bodies now brown spots against the backdrop of the hill. Except for the wounded, Totka alone remained behind—a common occurrence, yet it never grew easier to handle.

A nearby moan drew his attention. He struggled to his feet and followed the sound.

A warrior lay on his side, fist pressed against his stomach. Blood drained from a yawning wound. In the man's eyes, Totka detected calm acceptance. He lowered himself and laid a hand on the man's quivering shoulder.

"I am Muscogee," the man said through his teeth. "Not afraid to die."

Grandmother Sun slid across the sky, beating down without mercy, but from beyond the thick rushes, Burnt Corn Creek burbled happily. A beautiful sound to accompany a warrior onto his **four-day journey**.

At last, the trembling eased, then stopped. The man's fist dropped to the ground as he yielded to the **Master of Breath**, Wind Spirit, the one who gave and took life.

"I know his micco." Nokose stood a short distance away. Had they run the whites off so quickly?

Totka nodded. "He died bravely."

"I'll tell his wife that her husband did not die alone. It is a brave man who stays by another's side as he takes the journey."

Totka couldn't conceive of leaving a man while he breathed his last. Pulling his thoughts from death, he stood and took in the sight of his sister's husband. Blood dripped from a laceration on his upper arm.

"You are wounded."

Nokose shrugged. "As are you."

Totka's eyes flashed to where Nokose gestured. Blood oozed from a gash in his thigh and trailed the length of his leg. How did he not feel the pain? Feel it? His entire leg throbbed with it, but that was nothing new.

Nokose punched Totka's arm. "Welcome to the war. Next battle, bring home hair. We will make Big Warrior of you yet."

Peter McQueen, their expedition's half-Scot head micco, neared to examine the warrior at Totka's feet. "How many dead?"

"Only the one that I know of. Will we pursue the pale faces?" Nokose asked.

"Let the whipped dogs run home to their mothers. We'll kill them another day."

"They took the powder."

Eyes going dark, McQueen pivoted and hurled his tomahawk into the trunk of a tree ten paces distant.

Totka understood the man's anger. They'd labored long and hard to supply the red faction with arms.

McQueen plucked a stray arrow from the ground, loosened dirt from around the head, and pulverized it between his fingers. "Our great chief, Josiah Francis, will lead us to retribution. The whites will crumble before us like earth in our hands." Satisfaction smoothed his features. "They will be an easy foe to conquer, but we cannot defeat them with bows and arrows alone. We'll return to **the Floridas** to ask for more muskets."

Totka was not as certain as McQueen of the Long Guns' weakness. The few settlers who had showed to fight might have been distracted and unorganized, but they were also untrained. The regular army, the Bluecoats, would be another matter altogether.

Adela massaged a tender shoulder and ducked out from under the flap of the McGirth tent. It had been a couple of weeks since she'd slept in a bed, and weariness had become a permanent part of life.

Lillian sat cross-legged in their tent's shade, stabbing one of Papa's shirts with a mending needle.

Their tent was one of many arranged in neat rows throughout the newly erected stockade. The ring of hammers carried from two corners where cabins were under construction. No one expected to leave soon; they may as well make themselves more comfortable.

Several hundred settlers buzzed about, tending children, washing laundry, whetting knives, casting lead bullets. Like the sulfurous stench of the nearby marsh, foreboding permeated the air. Tension lay in a thick layer of impatience: husbands scolded wives, bedraggled mothers snapped at children, officers lectured recruits, babies screamed protests at their fetid life.

"It's Papa! He's back!" Lillian bounced to her feet, trampled the shirt, and ran to meet him. She threw her arms around his neck. "We heard all about it, but we knew right off you weren't one of the ones running."

Details of the battle had trickled in along with the men who'd straggled back in various groupings. The attack had been flawless, but instead of pursuing the Red Sticks and ensuring defeat, a large portion had become distracted by the loaded packhorses and broken off to steal them. The Creeks had rallied then, emerging from the cane like a mama bear from her cave. Colonel Caller's order to retreat to higher ground had been interpreted as absolute retreat. Most had fled the knoll entirely, leaving a few faithful men to repel the wave of warriors.

Although the militia had left with a great portion of the weapons, the success of the venture was debatable. To Adela's way of thinking, they'd succeeded only in riling their enemy and justifying an answering attack. She prayed she was wrong.

"You didn't run like a greedy coward, did you, Papa?" Lillian persisted. "You didn't retreat."

Papa laughed. "Why do you even ask?" He hugged her until she squeaked a giggle, and then, he made room in his ample arm span for Adela. He was damp and dusty and handsome, and she drank him in. Above all, he was alive. Not every woman in the fort could say the same of her loved one.

Elizabeth hung back until he shook off Adela and Lillian and reached to kiss her brow. "Welcome back, Papa. We missed you." Her smile was subdued but genuine.

Mama stood, hands folded in front of her, waiting her turn. She seemed to have put on a pound or two. There was color in her cheeks and vivacity in her eyes. She'd pulled her gray-black hair into a loose bun, and wispy strands floated on the breeze, softening her angular features. "Hail the conquering hero." A mischievous smile played around the corners of her mouth. She pulled him down and wrapped her arms around his neck. He lifted her off her feet and held her tight, burying his face in her hair.

"I am so proud of you," she said, voice cracking.

Papa set her down. "You're probably the only one."

"Never mind what others say," Elizabeth broke in. "We know you fought bravely."

Mama huffed. "Foolish of them! Leaving with the weapons, and you still fighting. Wretched lot they are. Should be whipped, every last one!" Her accent was always heaviest when upset.

When Papa smiled at her vehemence, Mama responded in kind. "But you are here and alive with not a scratch. We must thank the good Lord you are home."

Adela swept her arm toward the tent. "If you can call this *home*."

"Anywhere with my four girls is home. I've been away too long. There's much to tell." He paused and cocked his head at Mama. "You look good."

"I feel good." Mama fingered the silver cross hanging from a slim chain about her neck. "But I think I will visit *Doctór* Holmes today. It has been a while since he's seen me. Adela is going with me."

"Good idea. Let me know what—"

They all turned at the clatter raised by a large procession of men entering the stockade.

"Finally!" Elizabeth threw up her arms. "It's about time General Flourney sent protection."

"Is that tub of lard the commanding officer?" Lillian whispered in Adela's ear.

The march was led by an officer of the United States Militia, who marched with military precision and an air of superiority. Notwithstanding his thinning, blond hair, he couldn't have been any older than thirty. His blue-eyed gaze darted about the compound, and his nub of a chin disappeared into a flabby neck that jiggled with each crisp step. His gut pressed against the front of his uniform and strained his buttons.

"Appearances can be deceiving. He must be competent, or they wouldn't have sent him," Adela said.

Lillian gave her a dubious, half-cocked smile.

The men, anything but trained solders, were dressed in every sort of frontier attire.

The officer led the lumbering crew to the center of the fort and stopped just short of the Mims' house. "Halt!"

The men came to a gradual stop, some dropping to their backsides to rest.

"You there." The officer waved his hand toward a few. "On your feet!"

The men dithered before dragging themselves up in a halfhearted attempt at obedience.

Papa approached the officer and extended his hand. "Name's Zachariah McGirth."

The man eyed Papa before accepting. "Major Daniel Beasley. I've been assigned this fort per General Claiborne's orders. Quite small, if you ask me. No stables." His lips curled. "Our horses are outside the walls at the mercy of the thieving red man. But we'll remedy that soon enough."

Major Beasley gestured behind him with a flap of his hand. "These here are the Mississippi Volunteers. All pitiful one hundred and twenty of them." He lifted his voice to carry across the lot. "If they don't look like much, it's because they're not. No doubt a few weeks of hard work and rigid training will shine them up like proper militiamen. That's the hope anyway."

Papa cleared his throat and addressed the weary men. "Any man with a gun to add to our firepower is much appreciated, military training or not."

Adela couldn't agree more.

Several hours later, she studied the improvised curtain drawn across a corner of the Mims' front room—the same room she'd danced in so recently. From behind it came Dr. Homes' indecipherable murmur and her mother's soft reply.

The line of sick needing the old doctor's care was long today. It curled around the cabin's main room and out the front door. Incessant coughing filled the room and several babies whined inconsolably.

The number of bodies in such a small space intensified the heat and added to the misery. If not for the blazing sun and the lack of shade, the patients would be outside where at least a warm breeze might brush their skin.

Adela fanned herself with a limp handkerchief. Sweat trickled from her scalp and down the side of her face. She followed its track with her finger and wiped the moisture onto her dress.

"When's this awful heat gonna let up?" The elderly woman to

Adela's right, Mrs. Whitfield, cradled a small girl.

Adela gave the woman an acknowledging smile but had no answer. It was almost August, after all. Except during sporadic thunderstorms, the heat *never* let up, but the sweltering temperature bothered Adela little compared to Elizabeth's silence. In the weeks since the Mims' social, her sister had hardly spoken a word to her.

However, it wasn't an angry silence, but one of reflection. Elizabeth, in her black-and-white world, rarely took more than two minutes to ponder a matter, but that was exactly what she seemed to be doing. Adela might even go so far as to say she'd been morose, walking about as if lost and in search of her former confidence. It disconcerted Adela to see her in such a state, but she decided to give her sister a bit more time before broaching the subject.

A whimper dragged her back to the clinic. The child next to her squirmed and displayed fever-red cheeks and pale lips. Another unfortunate victim of malaria? Heart tugging, Adela ran a hand across the girl's damp brow. "Doctor Holmes will give you something to make you feel better. You'll see."

The girl rewarded her with a weak smile. "Why are you here? You don't look sick."

"My Mama's with the doctor now. I'm here for her, just like your grandma's here for you."

Almost imperceptibly, she nodded her blond head as her eyes drifted shut to Mrs. Whitfield's humming and rocking.

Adela sighed and stretched her legs. The room was stifling, but at least she had a moment with her thoughts. If there was one benefit to her spat with Elizabeth, it was the solidifying of her courtship with Phillip. Unless her father disapproved, there was no turning back now. Every home in Tensaw twittered with talk of a Bailey-McGirth marriage.

As to whether she truly loved him, she'd concluded that love meant next to nothing in the swamps of Mississippi Territory, a land of disease and asperity, vipers and gators, want and back-breaking toil. Finding a desirable mate was difficult enough. Finding one with love attached was tantamount to stumbling across Ponce de Leon's fountain of youth. Tensaw had no place for romantics.

According to the Red Sticks, Tensaw held no place for any of them. The Mims and Tates, Mrs. Whitfield and her darling granddaughter, the Baileys, Adela's own family—all must go. Wondering what would become of them, she scanned the room until her gaze came to rest on her lap and the fragment of tattered blue homespun pinched between her fingers.

Her forehead tightened. How long had she been holding it? She shoved it back into her pocket lest she be questioned about something she would refuse to explain. But if she *could* tell, she would say holding that stained bit of nothing gave her a sense of hope. She would say she'd been thrust into the Red Sticks' power, and they'd shown themselves reasonable and kind. Here was proof, and she couldn't bring herself to discard it.

At last, Dr. Holmes pushed aside the curtain, allowed her mother to exit, and graced Adela with a dimpled smile. In his early sixties, Dr. Holmes was still of a fine frame. Robust and full of life, he could keep pace with any man twenty years his junior. "I'd like to see you again in two weeks' time, Mrs. McGirth. Remember to take it easy."

An odd trepidation bathed her mother's face. "Yes, Doctor. I will."

Once outside, Adela grabbed her mother by the elbow to slow her pace. "Are you going to tell me what's going on, or do I have to guess?"

Mama stopped short and took in the crowded camp. Was there ever a moment of privacy?

"Never mind them," Adela coaxed. "Are your lungs stronger? Did he give you a tonic to help your breathing?"

"Actually, he told me to try lobelia. I know just were it grows, too. Maybe your father will let us go look for it, eh? We will ask." Mama tucked Adela's hand into her own and resumed walking.

"Oh, no you don't! I'm not brainless. There's more, and don't you deny it." Adela laughed and her mother joined in.

"*Muy bien*, but it stays between us for now. *Prométeme*."

"Of course, I promise."

"Well . . . the doctor confirmed something I had already suspected." A cautious smile spread across her face. "You are going to be a big sister again."

"You . . . you're expecting?" She studied her mother's abdomen. "That explains the extra paunch. And that smile." She threw her arms around her mother for a snug embrace. When a portent of doom coursed through her, she pulled back. "This could be bad, right? I mean . . . you're not strong. You've lost babies before. What if . . ." She couldn't finish the thought. Tears pooled as the possible outcomes scrolled across her mind.

"Now, now. No crying allowed. No *what ifs* either. God has the baby in His care, not ours," her mother gently chided, holding Adela's hands in both of hers.

"It's not the baby I'm worried about."

Mama cleared her throat. When their eyes met, Adela saw a peace in Mama's she'd never experienced herself. It was a peace born of suffering, hardship, loss. The kind the Lord gave to those who had special need of it.

"No need to worry about tomorrow, Adela. God controls that. I am ready to meet Him should He decide it is time." She caressed Adela's cheek with her thumb. "My only regret would be leaving you and your sisters. Your papa, now, he might be better off without me." She laughed, but it did little to lighten the moment.

Adela's tight throat kept a lock on her words.

"Why speak of death, mi hija? *Mírame.* Look at me. I'm well." She gave Adela's hand a tight squeeze. "By early spring, we will have another baby to love. Doctor Holmes says there's no reason to worry. All right?"

Adela nodded.

Voices carried across the yard. Major Beasley and Captain Bailey exited the main house alongside General Claiborne.

The general had made an appearance that morning to give the

stockade a once-over. At the risk of his own life, he'd traveled the breadth of Tensaw inspecting the twenty-one fortifications that had been erected in the last several weeks.

"Mama," Lillian called as Adela and their mother neared the tent. "Look who came to visit, all the way from across the compound." Grinning, she handed their mother a cup. "You look like you could use some water."

"*Gracias, querida.*" Mama accepted the cup and turned a gracious smile on Verna Bailey. "Verna, the sight of you always brightens my day. What brings you?"

Captain Bailey's wife laughed sweetly. "Well, I simply needed some feminine company." Her husband and three grown sons tended to dominate all conversation in the Bailey home. Adela could understand a woman's need for some time away.

"Take your fill. In a week, Zachariah will want to visit your husband's tent. Four women in a small space is a little more than he can handle sometimes."

Mrs. Bailey's laughter redoubled. "I can only imagine."

"Any idea what General Claiborne's opinion of the stockade is? Will it hold against attack?"

Mrs. Bailey let out a quick breath and wiped her hanky across the back of her neck. "Dixon told me this afternoon the general's ordered the picketing on the east side extended sixty feet. Major Beasley's volunteers and Dixon's militiamen will move their tents into the new enclosure."

"*Que bien.* A second wall of defense. Good advice."

"Yes, well . . . " Mrs. Bailey hesitated. "He's put Major Beasley in command of the fort."

"What is the general thinking?" Lillian interjected. "Anyone with a brain can see he's vain, inexperienced, overly confident. Shall I go on?"

"No, you will not." Mama shot her a purse-lipped reprimand and turned back to Mrs. Bailey. "How are all the Baileys? Anyone ill?"

"Just little Emma, poor thing," Mrs. Bailey said. "She's burning up with fever but seems to be doing a little better today."

Emma, the youngest of Mrs. Bailey's twelve nieces and nephews, belonged to Daniel and Myra Bailey, Daniel being the second eldest of the four Bailey brothers. Theirs was the largest family in the area. The Bailey men were known for their high standing in the community as well as their rugged good looks. Only Phillip remained unmarried.

Through the tent flap, Adela glimpsed Elizabeth, a flush to her normally pallid cheeks, hurrying toward them. Elizabeth ducked her head into the tent. "Papa said our cabin should be done by tomorrow. The Wilsons and Thompsons just finished theirs, so they're helping Papa with ours." Her eyes glowed.

It had been a while since Adela had seen Elizabeth so enthusiastic about anything. It was refreshing, but the stilted look Adela received from her wasn't lost on any of them.

Adela feigned busyness by folding clean linens. Elizabeth excused herself and left as suddenly as she'd arrived.

An awkward pause followed until Mama spoke. "It will be wonderful to be in a house with walls and a door."

Since Papa had been a part of fort life for only a week before the battle at Burnt Corn Creek, the McGirths were among the last to finish their cabin. They would share it with several other families who'd recently moved into the fort.

Throughout the last weeks, family groups had joined efforts to build temporary board shelters, cramming anywhere from thirty to fifty people in each. Others had chosen to remain in tents, but overall, most of the three hundred settlers were lodged in some sort of stable dwelling.

Adela folded the last of the linen undergarments and set them in the pile with a little pat. What a consolation it was to have her family together again tucked safely within the walls of the fort.

Chapter 6

"Adela, can I have a word with you outside?" Verna Bailey whispered from the doorway of the McGirth cabin.

Adela glanced at her napping mother before quietly stepping into the late July sun. "You look a bit flushed, Mrs. Bailey. Is everything well at your place?"

"One of our slaves returned from tending the cattle and claimed to have seen a large band of Red Sticks moving in this direction."

Adela's hand flew to her mouth.

"Major Beasley sent some men to verify, but they found no Indians. Now, the major is accusing Willy of lying."

Did they expect the Red Sticks to hang around, to leave breadcrumb trails? "Is it a habit of Willy's to lie?"

Mrs. Bailey shook her head. "The man's always been forthcoming. That's why Dixon refused to have him whipped, but the major said if we don't, we'll be out of the fort on our backsides by morning."

Adela gasped. "He wouldn't! No man in his right mind would—"

"It's not our place to judge him, Adela. I'm sure the major has the best interest of the fort in mind. At any rate, Willy is scheduled to be whipped tomorrow at noon. It breaks my heart, but it must be done. For the good of our family."

"Of course. I understand." But she wasn't sure she did. In fact, she was more certain than ever that Major Beasley was incompetent.

"I didn't come to worry you. I'm actually on a mission today, and I hope you won't think me too forward." Mrs. Bailey dropped her voice to a whisper. "Phillip sent me."

Adela felt her cheeks grow pink and hoped her expression remained neutral. "Oh? You've heard from him?"

Mrs. Bailey bobbed her head and lost the fight to keep down a grin.

"Is he well? When is he due back?" Adela asked.

He'd been gone longer than expected, and Adela had wondered more than once if the tension in the region kept him from making his way to her. There was no telling what might happen to a white man outside these walls. The endless months of silence and emotional seesaw suddenly overwhelmed her, sparking moisture in her eyes.

"It's true," Verna said. "You *do* love him."

"What did he tell you about us?"

"I received a letter just today. With things as they are, it took some time getting here. He mailed it three weeks ago from Fort Pierce—that's his new post. He said he was coming to get you."

"To get me? When?" And why hadn't he written to her himself?

"His letter said he would arrive the evening of the thirtieth. That's tomorrow!" She pulled a weather-beaten letter from her apron pocket and pressed it into Adela's hand. "Let me be the first to welcome you into the family. Dixon and I are so happy for you both. Phillip couldn't have chosen a better bride." Mrs. Bailey drew her into a sisterly embrace.

"Thank you, Mrs. Bailey. I know Philip is dear to you." She pulled back to retrieve her handkerchief and dab at her nose.

"Like my own flesh and blood. I expect Fort Mims will have its first wedding this week?"

"This week?"

"It'll have be the day after tomorrow. You'll find it in the letter. He says he only has three days of leave. So it's either now or . . . well, with war around the bend, who knows when?"

"I see. It's sudden." Far too sudden.

"Are you having second thoughts, dear? It's normal, you know."

"Elizabeth will be heartbroken."

Mrs. Bailey patted her hand. "How can you be certain? Go find her. Share the news as gently as you can. Whatever her reaction is, you must love her anyway, and above all, you must not let it ruin your wedding day." Mrs. Bailey gave her another quick squeeze. "I'll leave you to Phillip's letter. Imagine! A wedding in the midst of this madness. We'll all be grateful for a reason to celebrate."

Adela plopped herself onto the nearest stump and watched her future sister-in-law walk away. Dust swirled in her wake but was swept away by the searing wind. How lovely it would be to fly away with it, to be carried over those splintery pickets. Molding a smile to her lips, she opened the letter.

My dearest love, it began. By the end, it confirmed what Mrs. Bailey had explained.

"Wish me luck, Phillip." Muttering, she added the letter to her pocket and plodded toward the kitchen and the inevitable clash with Elizabeth.

She found her sister sitting in a line of six women, white in one group, black in another. Each held a potato and a knife. As they peeled, they chatted, sharing the latest bit of fort gossip.

"Beth, do you mind taking a break? There's something rather urgent I need to talk to you about."

All conversation stopped. Who would want to miss the confrontation of the month? Certainly, every woman in the area had her opinion on how the situation between the sisters would end.

Elizabeth wore an indecipherable expression. "I suppose not. Do you ladies mind?"

"Not at all." The matriarch of the group shooed her off. "Just don't be too long. We're already running a little late with dinner."

Elizabeth abandoned her bowl of potatoes, wiped her hands on her apron, and followed Adela to a quiet place under the shade of one of the few trees in Fort Mims. "Is this so important you need to pull me from kitchen duty?"

Adela rubbed her palms together and tried to net the butterflies in her tummy. "Yes, it is," she said, attempting to regain the edge of authority she'd managed at the social.

She forced her hands to still and folded them in front of her. For the first time in her life, she was stepping out from her sister's shadow, making a decision without her consent. It should be a momentous occasion, yet Adela felt ill.

Wanting it over, she dove in. "I've just learned from Mrs. Bailey that Phillip will be here tomorrow. He plans to marry me the following day and take me back to Fort Pierce with him. Assuming Papa approves."

Elizabeth opened her mouth to speak, but Adela barreled ahead. "Let me finish." Her sister complied, throwing Adela off track. "I-I wanted to say I don't need your approval to marry, but I would certainly cherish it. You and I have been at odds for too long and . . . and . . . "

Eyes unreadable, Elizabeth waited.

"I'm weary of it, Beth."

A long pause followed as Elizabeth shuffled dirt around with the toe of her boot. She finally looked up with a mixture of emotion in her eyes. "I'm proud of you, Adela."

"Proud of me?"

"I thought you had no backbone, but look at you. I don't think I could have been more audacious myself. You were right when you said I had no claim on Phillip. I never did." The admission had to sting, but Elizabeth spoke with dignity, her voice steady. "He could never love me. We're both far too brash, but you . . . You're perfect for him."

"I am?" Wasn't that what she'd been asking herself for two long months?

Elizabeth nodded emphatically. "I've had these weeks to think on it, and I believe you are. I've grown accustomed to the thought of the two of you together, and I'm a little surprised to find that giving you my blessing isn't as hard as I imagined it would be."

Adela planted an abrupt kiss on her cheek. "Thank you. I would have been miserable knowing you were still angry."

Elizabeth cocked her head. "How could any woman be miserable married to Phillip?" She grinned, easing the last of Adela's worries. "It takes me a while to cool off, but I could never stay mad at you, Adela. You're too dear. Lilly, though, she's another story."

They shared a laugh, and Adela breathed easy for the first time in weeks.

Elizabeth sobered. "I will, of course, stand beside you during the ceremony."

"There's no one else I'd rather have."

"Hester, I'm so glad you've come."

The sound of Mama's voice woke Adela from her nap on the blanket she'd spread over the dirt. Mama sat beside her in the shade of the communal kitchen, mending a shirt.

Looking over the sack she carried, Hester caught sight of Mama and beamed. Adela had known it wouldn't take long for word to reach Hester that Mama was expecting. They had all figured she would find a reason to make a prompt visit.

"I done brought supplies, ma'am." She dropped the sack and spread her arms to embrace Mama who stood to greet her.

"Seeing you makes my heart happy." Mama's grin was contagious.

Hester gave Adela a cursory inspection. "You lookin' too scrawny, missy."

"Why, thank you, Hester." Adela's lips squirmed to the side. "How are the children?"

"Oh, they's fine. Growing bigger by the minute."

"As they should. And the plantation? Is it holding up?"

"Stop your worryin'. It be better than ever. Nineteen calves born since June and not one loss. Nineteen! The Lord be blessin' the McGirth home for sure."

"This is wonderful news," Mama exclaimed.

"You go on and sit yourself back down. I heard about that baby you's carrying. We got to take extra good care of you." She spent the next few minutes fussing over Mama.

"I am fine, Hester. Where is Caesar?"

"He found your husband workin' on the pickets. They be here shortly."

"Any sign of Indians out near our place?"

Passing Adela a judicious glance, Hester busied herself untying the sack. "Don't you go bothering your head over that, ma'am."

"The truth will not break me into pieces, you know."

Hester dropped the sack's ties and, at Adela's slight nod, took a deep breath. "Caesar told me a war party been through Murrell's place. Just talk to the slaves and be on their way is all."

"No harm done?"

"No, ma'am. They come and gone peaceful-like. Here be our men. Hoowee, they's sweaty!"

Carrying an ax over his shoulder, Papa strode toward Mama and kissed her on the cheek. His face was ruddy, his clothes rumpled. "How's the prettiest lady in Fort Mims this morning?"

"When I see her, I will ask."

Adela laughed, pleased to see the two holding up so well.

"I see you're doing good, Hester. Thanks for the food."

"You're mighty welcome, suh. Nothing was going to keep me away from Miz Galena, once I heard. I had to see with my own two eyes she was being cared for proper."

"Are you satisfied?"

"Hmm. I reckon I ain't got no choice but to be satisfied."

Caesar bellowed a laugh. "What you talking about, woman? You ain't never satisfied."

Hester swatted at her husband. "You go on, now! Hush your

86

mouth."

"Hester, would you mind staying the night?" Papa asked. "I plan to go back with Caesar within the hour. I'd like to look things over at home. I'll be back first thing in the morning."

"Zachariah, must you go?" A pout protruded Mama's lips.

Adela didn't blame her. "Don't go, Papa. This is no time to be traipsing the countryside by yourself."

"I'll be back before dinner tomorrow. Just one night."

"*Bueno.* Just one, but please be careful."

"Always am." Swinging the ax off his shoulder, he leaned it against the kitchen wall. "Hester, can you take this back to the cabin when you go?"

"Yes, suh."

"Are you leaving now?" Adela asked.

"As soon as I say goodbye to Elizabeth and Lillian. Any idea where they are this morning?"

"Around the corner. They have kitchen duty."

Papa bent and placed a tender hand on Mama's abdomen, then whispered something in her ear that brought a twinkle to her eye. He turned and enveloped Adela in a hug. "Take care of your mother."

"Always. Be careful."

The sight of Phillip making his way through the compound sent Adela's heart into spasms and turned her knees into jelly. He was early by half a day.

He strode toward her with a self-assured smile on his sun-darkened face. Not a smudge marred his gray trousers, and the seams of his caped, thigh-length jacket were so newly sewn they had yet to fray. The red officer's sash knotted about his waist competed with the brilliance in his eyes. His well-loved butcher's knife was stationed at his belt, and a musket hung over one shoulder, a broad hand holding it in place. He was the essence of a militiaman with his hair shaggy about his ears and his high-topped shoes dusty with red soil, but there was no missing the childhood playmate who still lurked behind the cavalier facade.

He turned every feminine head the length of his approach, but his line of sight didn't so much as flicker their direction. What woman wouldn't promise her life to a man who looked at her the way Phillip looked at Adela now?

Reaching her, he swung the weapon off his arm, removed his floppy felt hat, reached for her hand, and bowed deeply. "Miss McGirth," he whispered against the back of her hand before brushing it with lips.

She wedged a smile in place. "Well, Lieutenant Bailey, don't you look the part with your fine red sash and genteel manners."

Straightening, he stuck a finger behind the collar of his white hunting shirt and tugged. "It isn't made for this heat, but I'm getting used to it."

"No one is made for this heat." She pulled out her handkerchief and dabbed at her face. "I wasn't expecting you until this evening. I must look frightful." Work gown soiled, hair in kinks, bare toes poking out from her dusty hem. There was probably an oily gleam on her forehead too.

"You would look elegant in a potato sack." He grinned, and Adela laughed away some of the tension cramping her back.

"I suppose with four sisters-in-law, a man can't help but learn how to smooth-talk a lady." But hadn't she known he would take her in a potato sack?

"I've picked up a thing or two, such as which women aren't worth the time of day and which I'd be a fool not to spend the rest of my life with." He held up his pinky. A gold band hugged it above the middle knuckle. "I told you I'd be back for you, and there's nothing to stop us from marrying."

"Only a thousand skulking Indians." The words came out on a titter. Why was she avoiding the commitment? If she wasn't careful,

88

he would think she was being coy.

He *tsk*ed and donned a frown. "So easily spooked?"

"Have you looked around? The fort isn't exactly impregnable."

The humor tumbled from his tone, and his eyes took on a razor's edge. "I have, and I know." His voice deepened with purpose. "Which is precisely why I want you out of here. Today."

Her gaze vaulted, locking on his eyes. He was serious. "Today?"

"This very afternoon. On the ride over, everything seemed quiet, but I don't trust it. And this place is laughable. Have you seen the gates? There's a foot of sand blocking them. Aren't they closed at dusk?"

Her brows tugged downward. "I thought they were. Yes, surely they are."

"Either way, I won't risk leaving you here another night. We'll marry after lunch and be well on our way before sundown."

"I-I was hoping we could talk for a while, get reacquainted. You know, make sure we're doing the right thing."

"Do you mean your father? I've already asked his permission."

"How? He's not here."

"I stopped by your place first."

"Oh." He'd been busy. "But I can't marry without Papa being here."

"He'll be back early. Said he'd be sure to be back an hour or so after the noon meal."

"So he gave his go-ahead? What did he say?"

"Do you think I'd be standing here offering you a ring on my finger if he'd said no?" He laughed and grasped her chin between his knuckles.

She breathed easier, appreciating this version of him more than the one from moments ago. "I'm not sure, Phillip. It's so sudden. Mrs. Bailey told me just *yesterday* you were coming. There's a war on, and—"

"Your father had no objections, but he told me you might need persuading." He sank to one knee. "Why wait longer when we can be together tonight?"

Her heartbeat quickened with the insinuation. What would it be like to be loved by this man? She could find out tonight, if she wanted. But did she? Did she want him? All of him, until death? She could learn to.

At the softening of her face, his intonation grew hopeful, his speech more rapid. "We'll leave immediately after for Fort Pierce. The road's clear. Not a trace of Indians. If we marry right after noon, we can be there before dark. Several of the officers have promised to empty out their cabin for the night. After that, I'm afraid we'll have to share a cabin with two other families. But we'll be together."

"You've got it all planned." Awe filled her at his thoughtfulness.

Genuine perplexity slanted his brows. "Isn't that what a husband does? I said I'd take care of you, and I promise I will. Starting today, if you'll let me." He stood and buried his face in her neck, lifting her until her toes scraped the dirt, clutching her to himself so fiercely, so possessively, he left no room for doubt—he would protect her. He would be enough.

"I will. I'll let you." Every muscle in her body relaxed as she surrendered to his hold.

A long sigh left him. He nuzzled the hollow of her jaw and trailed a finger around her neck where it hooked onto the leather strap. He pulled until the pendant met sunlight.

"No more hiding," he said against her ear.

Tingles gripped her stomach and ran the length of her spine. She wriggled free and, noting the audience they'd drawn, felt her cheeks bruise with discomfiture. She straightened her apron. "We wouldn't have had a choice anyway. After that compromising display, Papa would whip you if you *didn't* marry me before sunset."

"Exactly what I was counting on." He laughed and claimed her lips.

"Phillip! People are staring," she said when she caught her breath.

"Let them watch. We'll be the best news within miles." He directed his next statement at the onlookers. "There's going to be a wedding after lunch. You're all invited!"

Chapter 7

*L*adle in hand, Adela stood before a table bearing a steaming cauldron. Two other tables stood end to end with hers, each with a woman behind it ready to serve.

Adela shooed flies away and glanced at the dinner bell hanging motionless from the kitchen doorpost. The sooner it rang, the sooner the job would be done, the sooner she would be out from under the broiling sun. And the sooner the marriage would be carried out.

But where was Papa?

Looking to the east gates, her gaze rested on Willy, Mr. Bailey's slave. Tied to the lashing post, the man awaited his whipping. It disgusted her that Major Beasley would refuse to take a Bailey at his word, that poor Willy would be feel the lash.

Lillian exited the cookhouse carrying a tin platter heaped with sliced fresh bread. "Doesn't it smell wonderful?" She tore off a corner and shoved it into her mouth before Adela could stop her. "Where are your shoes?" she asked around the lump in her mouth.

"It's too hot for shoes."

"Who cares about the heat? You're getting married! Are you ready?"

"Yes and no."

"What do you mean *no*? How could you possibly not be ready?"

"I reek of sweat and onions. That's how."

"Do you?" Lillian leaned in for a deep whiff. "I hardly noticed over my own stench. Think they'll let us go down to the lake and take a quick dip after lunch? It *is* a special occasion."

"Major Beasley would let us, but Mama wouldn't." Elizabeth joined them. She whisked vagrant hair off the back of her neck and begin re-pinning it. "I'd give my lunch for half an hour at the lake and a course towel to scrub with."

"We'll have to settle for a bucket of well water. I'll wash your hair, if you'll wash mine," Adela suggested, letting her gaze roam the compound, hoping for a glimpse of Phillip.

Outside one cabin, an intense game of cards continued uninterrupted. Nearby, a group of girls danced a jig, giggling and squealing. An old man accompanied them on a harmonica. Where had Phillip gotten himself to?

"What about me?" Lillian said. "Who will wash—?"

The dinner bell drowned her out. The piercing sound cut the air, and the fort became alive with movement. Cabin doors opened and families stepped out, utensils in hand.

From the new enclosure, hungry troops bustled toward the tables. Some remained behind, as usual, waiting for the line to shrink. A few stragglers from the fields and surrounding outbuildings trickled through the open gates.

"I'm coming to your wedding, Miss Adela."

Adela's first customer stood before her—a little girl with pale brown ringlets poking out from under a yellow bonnet. When she grinned, she revealed two missing front teeth. "When I grow up, I'm going to marry a man just like Lieutenant Bailey."

"Smart girl." Adela winked at her, and they giggled together.

"Can I have some lunch, please?"

Adela tapped the girl's freckled nose. "Since you asked so politely." She poured a ladleful of split pea soup into the girl's bowl. "Don't forget to get a piece of bread."

An eagle's screech drew Adela's gaze to the sky. Again, the bird announced its presence, but this time, she noted an unnatural, human quality to it. Just inside the main gates, Willy kicked and flailed, hollering something lost in the clamor of the noon meal.

Painful fear tightened her stomach.

There came a flash of gray in her periphery. Phillip. When their eyes connected, his smile vanished. He was nearer to Willy; could he understand the man's cries? If so, it mustn't disturb him because he had yet to look Willy's direction.

"Miss? My food? I'm kinda hungry here."

Adela ignored the troop. "What's Willy yelling about?"

"How about you serve me up some of what you got there?"

But the slave in the distance had paralyzed her. He screamed, his gaze riveted to the gates, or . . . Was it beyond?

Adela squinted. Like a disturbed ant bed, the field between the fort and the ravine was alive with movement.

The sight pierced her with fear. It weakened her so that her legs threatened to buckle. The ladle clattered to the tabletop.

Hundreds of war whoops sliced the air and roiled her stomach. The shrieks came from all sides of the fort and drew closer by the second. Ahead, scores of painted bodies streaked toward the open gates.

"Indians! Indians!" Major Beasley rushed heedless toward the gates, toward the bellowing Natives.

"Adela, behind the firewood, quick!" Elizabeth said.

Unable to peel her eyes from Major Beasley, Adela stood rooted to the ground. The officer threw his weight into the heavy gate, but it didn't budge. With his hands, he dug into the ground at the gate's base. Sand flew out behind him.

Why wasn't anyone helping him!

The Indians were now within a tomahawk's throw. The fort was wild, wriggling with panic.

Her eyes flashed back to Phillip, but he was gone, lost in the soup of scrambling humanity.

Someone slammed into Adela, sending her sprawling. A man stumbled over her. "Camellia!" he shouted as continued moving away from Adela.

Adela crawled under one of the lunch tables, then pulled to her feet on the other side. She scoured the crowd for a glimpse of Phillip. The compound began to clear, and she gasped.

Willy hung limp at the post, his head dangling, a feathered shaft protruding from his side. Major Beasley, a tomahawk in his back, dragged himself along the ground. A dark river of blood stained the earth behind him.

Like welcoming arms, the gates hung wide.

Oh God, save us!

Clubs raised, Creek warriors poured in. The sky released a shower of arrows. They shrilled through the air. *Fwump, fwump.* Two landed at her foot.

Adela scampered back under the table, and pulled her knees to her chin.

The pickets trembled with the force of Indians' arrival. They thrust their firearms through the portholes, and the air reverberated with the intermittent explosions.

Benumbed, Adela cowered under the table. What had gone wrong? How had this happened? The portholes had been cut for the Americans to shoot from — five hundred at one time, if need be. But in less time than it took to form the lunch line, warriors had reached the walls uninhibited. Did even a single porthole remain free of an enemy musket?

She clamped her hands over her ears. The whooping was maddening. They screamed for blood. White blood.

Her blood. And she knew without a doubt they would drain her of it, first chance they got.

Someone grabbed her arm, and she screamed.

Phillip crouched beside her. "What are you doing? Come on!"

Sprinting, he half led, half dragged her to the side of the cookhouse and shoved her unceremoniously behind the stack of firewood piled high next to it. She crashed on top of Mama and Elizabeth.

In the confined space, she fumbled to right herself. Phillip flipped her roughly around, his face inches from hers, his eyes ablaze with a shade of alarm she'd never seen before. What did it mean? Were they doomed?

Terror punched her heart.

He took painful hold of her jaw and shouted, "Live. Do you hear me, Adela? Live!" Whatever reply she might have given was consumed in a severe, terse kiss.

He'd been gone but seconds when a musket bullet thudded into the kitchen wall just above their heads. Adela sank lower and peered around Elizabeth to Mama.

"Where's Lilly?" She craned her neck, but saw little from where she sat.

"She's still out there!" Mama cried.

Without hesitation, Elizabeth leapt from their shelter. Long minutes later, she crashed down on them dragging a dazed Lillian behind her.

Mama wiped dirt from Lillian's cheek and smoothed the hair back from her face.

Lillian lay motionless, tangled with Elizabeth, who pushed away from her. "Are you crazy making me go out there after you?" Noticing Lillian's pale face and trembling lips, she changed her tone. "Are you hurt?"

She adjusted Lillian so she could check her back. "There's no blood."

Lillian blinked several times before tears surfaced and skidded down her cheeks. "Major Beasley . . . he, he's dead. The gates are wide open, and the fort is full of heathens. Full of them! We're all going to die!" A sob shook her chest.

"Get a hold of yourself, Lilly," Elizabeth shouted above the musket blasts. "We're not dead yet, and I'll fight tooth and nail before they lay a hand on you. Beasley's dead and so are others, but you're *not*, and neither are we. No more tears. Mama needs us."

Lillian wiped a dusty hand across her cheek and sniffed. She straightened and lifted her chin. "All right, Beth. I can help Mama. Tooth and nail, huh? Me, too."

"That's my tough girl." Mama pulled Lillian in for a kiss on the head. "They will not have us without a fight."

"Where's Hester?" Adela asked.

"She went for our dishes right before the attack," Mama said.

Poking her head above the stack of wood, Adela took in the condition of the fort. While she scanned the scene, an unfathomable sense of doom overwhelmed her.

"How does it look?" Mama yelled.

As far as Adela could see, not a single white man occupied a porthole. Instead, enemy weapons rained a continuous shower of lead on the stockade's interior. Fish in a barrel, they were. Easy pickings.

Adela ducked back behind their shelter.

"Tell us," Mama said.

"Our men are holding them at the inner wall."

Barely. The Mississippi Volunteers were staying their position, felling line upon line of advancing Creeks. But with every Native down, two more took his place.

Elizabeth touched her hand. "Did you see Phillip?"

Adela clutched the claw hanging outside her bodice. "No. No, I didn't. The powder haze is too thick."

The fringed uniforms brought a sense of comfort, but they were too few, too late.

The Lord is good, a stronghold in the day of trouble. The Lord is good, a stronghold, a stronghold, a —

"How long?" Mama spoke in her ear.

Adela grimaced. "At this rate? Two hours. Maybe three. But what do I know? Surely, they can hold long enough for reinforcements to arrive."

The horror on Mama's face was unbearable. She slid a hand across her belly and with the other stroked Lillian's cheek. In the next moment, her demeanor transformed from dread to resolve. "Listen careful, yes?" Her face was a sea of calm, but the slight quake in her voice told the real tale. "We cannot stay here. The Mims' house is safer. We will go around the back of the kitchen, under the covered walkway and through the back door." She spoke as if they were planning a morning stroll along the lake.

"Elizabeth, your papa left his ax against the kitchen. I want you to get it, and bring it into the house with you. Do you understand?"

"Yes, Mama."

"Are you ready?" Mama pulled her legs up under her and gathered her skirt in her arms. "The ax, Elizabeth. *No te olvides.*"

"I won't forget." Elizabeth smiled. Always confident and in control.

Adela wished she felt half as secure as her sister appeared to be.

"Run fast and look straight ahead. Ready? Go!"

All four sprang to their feet. Mama first, followed by Lillian and Adela. Elizabeth trailed them.

Bullets pelted the ground at their feet, kicking up dust.

Hoots and wails from outside the walls pushed Adela harder toward the covered walkway. When she reached it, a bullet grazed a nearby beam, spraying splinters into her face. With a cry, she lurched toward the back door.

Elizabeth darted to the side in search of the ax.

Just ahead, Mama reached the Mims' and slumped against the wall, panting heavily.

Having passed her, Lillian was already pounding on the door. It gave way, and Lillian shoved Mama through. Stumbling over each other, the three fell in a pile just inside.

Unseen hands dragged them away from the threshold and slammed the door shut.

"Beth!" Adela sprang to her feet. "She's still out there!" When her hand reached the latch, a man—a stranger—slapped it away and pinned her to the door.

"You're not opening that door again! We risked enough letting you in here."

"Risked? What are you talking about? Beth was right behind us!"

At her back, the door rattled its hinges, and Elizabeth's voice carried through. "Open the door! Someone open the door!"

Adela strained against the immobilizing hand on her shoulder. "It's her! Someone get him off me!"

A muffled cry sounded against the wood behind her.

"I said, no! Those heathens'll get—" He jolted, and his eyes rolled back into his head.

He slid to the ground, revealing Lillian standing just behind, a pressing iron in her hands.

She dropped it to tug on the fellow's legs. "Help me!"

Springing into action, several women had him moved aside in a moment.

When Adela released the latch, the door fell open, and Elizabeth tumbled against her. She wrapped her arms around her sister to hold her up, and warmth oozed from her back and through Adela's fingers.

"I found it." Elizabeth slipped from Adela's grasp and sagged to the floor. She lay lethargic, her fingers clamped around the ax handle. A widening stain of red on the back of Beth's dress glared at Adela.

"Elizabeth! No, no, no! Oh God, don't take her!"

With a cry, Mama crawled to Elizabeth and pressed her hand against the hole in her back. "Don't worry, mi hija. We'll get Doctor Holmes. Someone get the doctor!"

Elizabeth closed her eyes and shook her head.

"Do not give up. Let me see that fighting spirit!"

Elizabeth's paling lips lifted in a half smile, but when she opened her mouth to speak she released only blood.

Mama sobbed, her body convulsing with unrestrained grief. "I am sorry. *Perdoname!* I should never have sent you for the ax."

Adela saw her arms embracing her mother, heard herself utter soothing sounds, but she seemed strangely detached from this nightmare.

Elizabeth lay limp in Mama's arms, her gaze searching. "Lilly," she said on the cusp of a strangled cough.

"I'm here!" Lillian leaned over their sister's face, tears plopping on Elizabeth's cheeks.

"Tooth . . . and . . . nail," she rasped.

Lillian laid her head on her sister's breast and wept. "They won't have me without a fight. I promise, Beth. I promise."

Adela took one of Elizabeth's hands and with the skirt of her dress, wiped her mouth clean of blood only to have it blossom again with red.

Elizabeth shifted her eyes to Mama, and her head fell limp, the last of the air leaving her punctured lungs.

Mouth agape with a voiceless cry, Mama pulled her eldest to her chest and rocked.

Outside, the battle raged on.

Chapter 8

Totka readjusted his awkward position behind his makeshift barricade and wiped sweat from the handle of his war club. The race from the ravine to the gate had been easier than any had expected, and now that he'd had a chance to rest, he wanted to move from this confining spot, from Nokose's churning temper. From the Shadows.

They were near. Beside him, before him. He felt their presence in the hairs standing upright on the back of his neck, coating his spirit with black dread.

His knee jerked from inactivity and the itch to battle.

Soon. Soon, it would begin in earnest, bnd the victors had already been determined. The whites were outnumbered three to one. It was an issue of when, not if . . . and how many would die in the process. By the end, though, the Red Sticks *would* take this place and every settler in it.

Time was all they needed. Time to drive the pale faces back, barricade by barricade. Time to weaken their numbers. With each white man lost, those remaining would fight as men doomed whose last chance at life lay in the death of yet another Red Stick. Their motivation gave them strength, but time was more powerful.

The woman Red Eagle loved, Lucy Cornells, was rumored to have fortified here. How would he maintain focus with the thought of her under a warrior's scalping knife?

As far as Totka knew, his own father was still with Big Warrior's band far from here, but the Muscogees had experienced decades of friendly relations and intermarriages with the Tensaw settlers, so it was likely Totka was acquainted with a number of those trapped inside these pickets, many of whom had Creek blood.

The copper-haired beauty from the meadow came to mind, but he shut himself to the thought. This was war. Casualties abounded.

For the last two hours, no more than a handful of warriors had made it past the inner wall. Those who succeeded hadn't lasted long enough to do much damage to the soldiers holding Red Eagle's warriors at bay. The soldiers were well entrenched behind barricades and inside buildings and were giving their lives at a precious cost to Red Stick ranks.

Totka rubbed his thigh and flexed his knee to keep blood flowing. The **medicine bundle** hanging from a strap of rawhide swung out and thudded back against his chest. The **medicine maker** had sung a war song over it, but it was Totka's prayers to the Master of Breath that he trusted would see him through battle.

Studious and sedate, Nokose squatted beside him, his musket resting on his knees. Like red and black sunbeams, paint streaked from beneath his eyes. The man's mood had changed since the attack began. It was almost as if his mind were not in the battle but in some distant place Totka was not allowed to follow.

"Fight by my side. Do not wander," Nokose said for the second time since they'd become fixed behind the cart.

Did his brother have no faith in him at all? Annoyed, Totka ignored the command and let his eyes travel.

The dead, white and red alike, blanketed the ground. Among them were the prophets who had rushed into the fort at the front of the assailing body. Allegedly immune to white man's lead, they had charged, screaming and taunting; they had been the first to fall.

"Our warriors attack from all sides of the fort, yet most of our enemy fights at this gate." With his lips, Nokose swiftly smoothed the **cock fletch** of an arrow. "If we choose this place to rush in many of ours will die, but there is another way." He pointed to Red Eagle. "Our chief thinks as I do."

A stone's throw away, Red Eagle directed one of the warriors. His words were almost inaudible through the noise of battle. "Gather twenty warriors and lead them to the wall facing the lake. Break your way through." The warrior nodded and disappeared.

Totka re-primed his weapon. "It will not be long now." He looked down the barrel and took aim at a blue coat. The trigger gave way beneath his squeezing forefinger. Smoke filled the air for a moment before the wind shifted and opened a window in the haze.

The soldier had disappeared behind his shelter.

Punctuated at intervals by his flintlock, time ticked past until at last the whites sent a substantial number of men from the front gate — the Muscogee warriors had made quick work of penetrating the pickets on the opposite side of the compound.

Red Eagle sprang to his feet and swung his war club in an arc above his head. "Through the gate! Take their lives that they surely know the wrath of our people! Let the ground flow with their blood and make it ours again!" He bolted forward.

A rush of exhilaration zinged through Totka as he and Nokose followed. All around, hundreds of feet drummed the earth in rhythm with the war cry.

Just ahead, three pale faces appeared from behind a stack of logs as high as Totka's chest. All three reloaded their weapons.

Nokose raced toward them, launching himself into the air. As he sailed over the barricade, he knocked one senseless with his club.

Totka rounded the logs to join him, but Nokose had disappeared. Whipping about, Totka spotted him running a jagged line through the fort. With a growl of frustration, Totka turned to follow but was met with a sword slashing toward his chest.

He arched back and felt a sharp blade of wind cool the sweat on his naked chest. Without missing a beat, he swung his club low, connecting with his opponent's thigh.

The soldier toppled, but before he hit the ground, Totka seized him by the hair. A quick slit and a firm yank lifted the scalp. Hair in hand, he dropped a crushing blow to the Bluecoat, then braced himself to tangle with another streaking in.

The man came at him with an ax raised over his head. A fraction of a second before it came down, Totka sidestepped.

The force of the man's failed swing caused him to teeter. As he brushed past, Totka whisked the knife from its sheath at his waist, spun, and drove it into his opponent's flank. Before the man collapsed, Totka ripped out his blade, collected another scalp, and continued his search for Nokose.

He was compelled to slice through lines of oncoming soldiers. Some fought with skill, but most had little chance of survival when confronted with Totka's keen blade. He fought on, hacking and weaving, moving deeper and deeper in.

The corpses were thicker here. Bodies on bodies. The frenzy was abating and Totka, pulse throbbing and senses on high alert, slowed to a walk. He stepped over and around the dead, keeping his eyes level with the horizon. He would not look at them. He would not feel pity or remorse. He would not shy from his duty to his people.

Before him squatted a cabin with doors closed and windows shuttered; beyond, in the far corner, a stockade. The last stronghold. And still, Nokose was nowhere to be seen.

Flaming torch in hand, a warrior wrapped an arrow with grease-drenched cloth.

The end was near.

Weapons, weapons . . . What else could Adela use?

Remembering its effect on the belligerent farmer shortly before, Adela snatched up the iron and tossed it onto the growing pile in the center of the main room.

Mama sat on the floor stroking Elizabeth's hair. Her free hand clutched Papa's ax.

Lillian crouched next to her, her eyes glazed.

Shortly before, Jesse and Daniel, the two middle Bailey brothers, had pounded on the door, giving them all a start. Before disappearing to the loft, Daniel relayed an ominous update from their brother, Dixon. The fort was all but lost.

They were to hold out here as long as possible, fighting with whatever tools they found at hand. Should they be overrun, there was still a chance at the bastion, which for the moment, remained in American hands. Their message had given Adela purpose and put her unsteady hands to good use.

As she rummaged through a trunk, she did her best to block out the sounds around her: babies wailed in terror, the wounded begged for water, women cried in hopelessness, some knelt praying, others tended to manageable wounds. Dr. Holmes, who'd joined them not long ago, made continuous rounds, but there was little he could do.

Lucy Mims huddled in a corner, feet tucked close, arms wrapped around her knees. A blank expression filled her face as she stared at the arrows protruding from her mother's chest.

Adela understood her grief. The urge to lie down next to Elizabeth and never get up about overpowered her. The one thing keeping her moving was the need to protect Mama and Lillian.

And Papa. He had to be alive out there somewhere. Did he even know they were under attack? Or had he been overcome on the way back to the fort? He could be lying out there scalped, bleeding, dead.

No! She wouldn't think of it, and she wouldn't think of Phillip who shouldn't even be here, except for his love her.

She stepped over the bleeding bodies strewn across the floor and, refusing to glance at the stack of corpses in the far corner, moved toward the back of the house and the Mims' bedroom.

Verna Bailey lay halfway under the high four-poster bed. Her son, three-year-old Micah, stood by her feet, moist locks of hair plastered to his forehead and a chubby hand filled with his momma's skirt.

Adela wondered if the fear she felt was as apparent to others as Micah's was to her.

A few dusty items lay about—a hat box, an empty tin, a pair of boots, nothing with which to defend oneself.

A musket lay on the bed. "Is this your musket, Mrs. Bailey? Have you gone through the chest of drawers?"

"The one on the bed is mine. Oh! Look what I just found." Hair askew, she re-emerged brandishing a rusted Revolutionary sword.

"Well done. I'll add it to the pile."

Mrs. Bailey handed it over, then opened the wardrobe doors and jumped back with a squeal.

"What is it?" Adela opened the door farther. From beneath a row of dresses extended a pair of boots attached to two trembling legs.

Mrs. Bailey parted the clothes and revealed an ashen face, that of the man who'd impeded Elizabeth's entry. "Mr. Murrell! Of all the cowardly things!"

"The savages'll cut us to pieces!" He fumbled to readjust the dresses around himself. "Close the doors. Go find your own place to hide. There's no room for you."

Launching himself halfway out, he grabbed for the doors.

Mrs. Bailey stumbled backward, knocking Micah to the ground.

Adela reached for the boy who recoiled with a shriek. At the sound of a scuffle from the wardrobe, she threw her body over the child and pressed his head against her chest.

The moment she glanced over her shoulder, she wished she hadn't.

Face contorted, Mr. Murrell clung to the muzzle of Mrs. Bailey's musket. From the back of his shoulder protruded the bloody tip of the bayonet.

"Coward! Get out and fight," Mrs. Bailey shouted over his yelps of pain. "This very minute my husband is risking his life for yours, and here you sit, shaking like a leaf." With a grunt, she withdrew the blade and brandished it before his chest. "Get out, or I'll run you through the heart and save the Indians the effort!"

Mr. Murrell hauled himself from the closet and staggered down the hall, looking behind as he went.

Micah bolted toward his momma and almost disappeared in the folds of her skirt.

"I never would have guessed you to be capable."

Mrs. Bailey's smile wobbled. "Me neither."

An acrid scent wafted into the room.

"Is that smoke?" Mrs. Bailey sniffed.

A scream echoed down the hall. "Fire! Fire on the roof!"

Mrs. Bailey snatched Micah into her arms and flew from the room, Adela following.

Within minutes, Adela's eyes burned and Mama's breathing became more labored. Lillian dunked her handkerchief in a bucket of water and slapped it over Mama's nose and mouth.

Flames consumed the loft and traveled the walls devouring everything it touched like a ravenous beast. To stay much longer was to burn alive.

Above her, in the loft, the Baileys' muskets had grown silent. Longer than Adela thought possible, the men had stayed faithful to their post, taken at last by the flames. Many from the cabin had already made a run for the bastion, but the Red Sticks continued to cut them down mere yards beyond the door.

Death was certain. It was a matter of choosing which form—fire or tomahawk.

The wounded and helpless had the matter decided for them. Others lingered, tolerating the roasting heat a little longer. Anything to delay an encounter with the Red Sticks.

Nearby a mother wept, begging God for mercy on the little ones under her skirt. Adela forced her mind away from the terror-stricken children.

God, spare Papa. Keep him safe.

Her throat screamed for water. The planked floor scorched the soles of her feet. She gagged on the smoke and knew their air was almost spent. "We've got to—" Adela doubled over coughing and thought she might never regain her breath. "It's . . . time, Mama." The roar of the fire almost drowned out her voice.

"I know." Mama kissed Elizabeth, then crawled toward the door, which was almost impossible to see through the heavy black smoke.

Lillian led the escape, dragging Papa's ax. She ducked as cinders fell from the roof.

The beams above creaked and groaned, and Adela prayed it would hold a minute longer.

The latch of the door lay within Lillian's reach, but she paused.

Adela followed her gaze to Lucy. The girl lay just steps away, her arms locked around her mother's neck.

Lillian shoved the ax into Adela's hands and grabbed Lucy by the shoulder. "You've got to come. Your mother's dead!"

Lucy didn't budge.

"Lucy! The building . . . is coming . . . down," she said between coughs.

Lucy shook her head; Lillian pulled harder.

Adela grabbed her sister under the arms and tugged. "Let her . . . die her own way. Leave her!"

"I can't!" Lillian flung her arm wide and snagged the leather cord around Adela's neck.

The bear claw flew into the smoke and disappeared. For three breaths, Adela stared into the blackness where it had vanished. *Phillip . . .*

"Help me!"

Seeing no other choice, Adela joined Lillian and forced Lucy toward the door. When Mama opened it, the fire sucked air into the building. A living monster, the flames spiraled.

"Out! Get out!"

Others left with them. Coughing and sputtering, they staggered aimlessly. The screech of myriad war cries filled their ears. The clang of weapons joined the bellow of the flames.

Her eyes burned and wept, obscuring her view. She wiped and squinted and tried to collect her thoughts.

Vicious hand-to-hand combat surrounded them. Everywhere Adela spun someone lay dying. The few Americans remaining fought two and three Red Sticks at once.

For the moment, no one seemed to notice the women, but the bastion was too far to reach without a man to protect them on the way, and every structure was a raging inferno. Even the pickets wore crowns of flame.

In the opposite direction, the gate hung open. What were their chances of making it through? If there were as many Indians outside as in, they were already dead.

"*Agua.*" Mama pleaded for water. Between coughs, she wheezed, her lips turning blue, her eyes wide.

Lillian pointed toward the well, some yards distant.

Ax still in hand, Adela skirted a fight. The others followed. Reaching the wooden well, Lillian propped Mama against the side. Adela grabbed the rope.

"Adela! Behind you!"

A warrior sprinted toward them.

Abandoning the rope, she drew the ax to her chest. She swung to the side, aiming for his bare chest, but before she could bring it forward, the long-handled ax's weight set her off balance.

While she regained her footing, the warrior closed the gap, and grabbing both of her hands with his, forced the ax from her grip. It plunged into the well.

Unexpectedly, he freed her hands. She managed one half-step away before he backhanded her across the face. The earth spun, and she hit the ground before she realized she was falling. The taste of iron swathed her tongue. Patches of deep blue sky winked at her from between billows of black smoke. Three arrows sailed across her vision.

Vague awareness of the warrior stepping over her tugged at her stunned mind. It was the glint of a knife that brought her senses back full force.

She gasped, her eyes opening wide. In the same instant, Lillian flung herself onto the warrior's back and dug her fingers into his eyes.

He screeched and, dropping the knife, scratched at her hands.

Lucy lunged for the knife and pressed it into Adela's hand. "I can't!"

As Adela reached her feet, the warrior threw his weight and tossed Lillian over his head and onto her back.

Bent at the waist and hands over his eyes, he didn't notice Adela double-fisting the knife's handle, lurching, raising the blade high above her head. It ground against his ribs on its journey through him.

He released an *oomph* of surprise before his knees gave way.

The effort to extract it was more than Adela had anticipated, and while she wrenched, a young warrior came at her from a wall of smoke. He leered, revealing a blackened front tooth.

She braced herself, knife at the ready.

Another moved in from the side, but by the time she saw him it was too late to react.

Red-painted arms encircled her and lifted her off the ground. A scream stuck in her smoke-tortured throat.

He plucked the knife from her hand, and she bit hard into his forearm.

He released her, and she hit the dirt with a jarring thud. On all fours, she obtained a clear view of the black-toothed warrior leaning over a bloodied Lucy.

Yanked to her feet by the back of her dress, Adela readied herself for the killing blow.

Instead, the Indian clamped the crook of his arm around her neck. He lugged her a few yards, but his attention was now elsewhere. Speaking rapidly in Muskogee, he jostled her about as if he'd forgotten she dangled from his arm.

Her toes grazed the ground; her air supply was cut short. Life was reduced to a fight for each new breath. As her sight blurred and she began to wilt, she sucked at the air but only managed a hacking cough.

He freed her, and the ground leapt up. When she lifted her head, she found Lucy lying within easy reach, her beautiful blue eyes, lifeless.

Mama! Where was she?

Adela blinked and tried to focus, but she couldn't make herself move or look beyond the red-armed warrior who stepped away to speak to Black Tooth. Waving in Adela's direction, he spoke as if giving orders.

Almost faster than she could register, the younger twisted and struck.

Red arms bobbed, then rammed the butt of his club into the other's gut, doubling him.

Lifting a hand in resignation, Black Tooth moved on.

The victor set his black-eyed sights on Adela. She retained just enough presence of mind to crawl the opposite direction, a last ditch effort at survival. But it was useless. He dragged her to the well and deposited her next to Mama and Lillian.

They pulled her into their huddle, and still, she couldn't find her voice. With her back pressed to the well and the warrior standing over them facing away, Adela marveled she was alive. For the moment, it was all that mattered.

Mama's head rested on Lillian's shoulder, her breath coming a bit easier.

A **breechcloth** dangling between his thighs, the Red Stick stood so close his moccasin pressed against Adela's hip. His fingers fumbled with something at the sash tied about his waist.

Adela chanced a look at his profile. The long, black hair of his roach was tangled and matted. Tattooed geometric patterns segmented his neck.

She knew those markings, but from where?

Hoops pierced his ears, and feathers stuck out from his head like a one-sided crown. The blood smatterings on his painted face bespoke his success in battle and obscured his identity. Naked but for moccasins, breechcloth, and belts supporting weapons, he was everything she'd ever imagined a Red Stick to be.

His eyes never settled but darted from place to place, as if looking to avoid someone, or . . . Was he looking *for* someone?

He turned, bent, and grabbed Adela's hands, then bound them with the strips of leather he had produced from his waistband. He shot a glance over his shoulder, first one direction then the other. "Where is your father?"

Adela stared at him, confused, certain now about that sense of familiarity in his features. But the paint, the blood . . . She couldn't place him.

"Speak! Your father, is he dead?" He tightened the strap, and Adela bit back a cry.

"N-no. He's not here."

He moved on to Lillian. She whimpered and scooted away from him, so he took a fistful of her hair and wrenched her back into position, after which she offered him her wrists. His eyes flicked back Adela's direction, but he had yet to look her in the eye. "Are there others?" His voice, his English—she'd heard it before. "Are there others!"

Others? Other what? Adela balked, afraid to anger him with the wrong answer. "Family? Not anymore."

He moved on to Mama. "You are slaves. Obey me, and you might see another sun." At last, he locked eyes with Adela, and she knew him for who he was. Her galloping heart took a frightening leap. He had come for her? "You-you're the one—"

"Make your mother well." His dark eyes shifted to whatever drama unfolded beyond the well. "A sick slave is useless to me."

As the full reality of his statement sank in, prayers began to stutter through her mind.

His finger under Mama's chin forced her pallid face upward, but she kept her eyes averted.

"Look at me."

Startled, Mama obeyed, but her fleeting look converted into a brow-wrinkling study. "Sanota?"

He laid a finger over her lips and gave a brief shake of the head.

Sanota? He couldn't be. Adela would have recognized the Creek orphan that day in the glen. Wouldn't she have? On second thought, she hadn't seen him since he'd been a scrawny brave, marching from their home with a full head of hair, a face soft with youth, and the dream of earning chiefdom.

This fearsome, flinty eyed warrior couldn't be their sweet Sanota! Mama must be mistaken. The discreet affection in his eyes, however, told her otherwise.

So, he hadn't come for Adela. He'd come for Mama. Did he even recognize Adela as the one who'd cost him a packhorse? If she looked anything like Lillian—eyes puffy and red, hair thick with ash, soot blackening her face—there was a good chance he didn't. They hadn't spent but a triplet of minutes in each other's presence.

With several firm tugs on the well rope, he had a sloshing bucket of water set next to them.

"This boy you speak of—Sanota—he is now a man with a warrior's rank." He beat a fist against his blood-spattered chest. "I am that warrior. I am Nokose Fixico."

Chapter 9

Totka's chest heaved, and his arms pulsated with fatigue. For the first time since the barricade, he noticed the nagging pain in his leg. Pushing it aside, he stopped to scan the area. He hadn't seen Nokose since the beginning of the second assault, and he began to wonder if his brother might be among the dead.

From the right, amid a curtain of black smoke, Totka caught a flash of yellow. A woman's skirt.

The smoke shifted and blocked his view. He squinted to make out movement beyond the well, but it was futile. Just as he lost interest, Nokose emerged from the smoke, and Totka lifted an arm to arrest his attention.

Blood stained every part of Nokose's body, but judging by his sure stride, little of it was his own.

As they grasped arms, Nokose looked everywhere but at Totka. "Where is Red Eagle?"

"I saw him leave the fort a short time ago, but you will find Francis outside the blockhouse."

Nokose nodded and stowed his club. "Our work here is done, but I must speak with Red Eagle." He peered over his shoulder in the direction he'd come. "I've taken captives. You will find them on the other side of the well, bound. Take them and meet me outside the west picket."

Totka snatched Nokose's arm in a freezing hold. "Is that the cause of your restlessness? A slaving raid?"

"Some men value scalps, and others, slaves." He indicated Totka's belt where scalps dangled from a length of twine. "What is it to you which I prefer?" He jerked his arm free.

"Singing Grass will reject them, not pleased by more mouths to feed." *He* was not pleased to have more mouths to feed. And where would they sleep? Not on Totka's pallet.

Nokose jabbed at his chest with a blood-stained thumb. "I am her husband. Do you think we have not spoken on the matter already, that I do not know her mind? She's eager for the extra hands in the garden."

Totka hedged, then thought of the assistance a slave might be to her as she grew heavier with child. He gave a reluctant nod. "I'll take them to where you ask, but when you return from this business with Red Eagle, I will have nothing more to do with them."

Totka didn't give Nokose time to reply. Lips pressed and eyes narrowed, he stalked toward the well. Slaves slowed a man down, depleted his provisions, and if the pale faces learned some of their own were being held against their will, there would be no end of trouble, as if leveling the stockade were not trouble enough.

Weapons still at the ready, Totka entered the choking smoke. Heat from the nearby inferno singed his back and added length to his stride. Coming out on the other side, he found an ashen huddle tucked against the well's side.

One of the slaves caught sight of him and screamed.

Irritation mounted. There would be no easy way to do this, and before the next sleep, Nokose and he would have words.

The fort would fall soon, and the unlovely task of burying their dead would begin. It must be finished with time left to start the trail home. White reinforcements might be on their way, and the Red Sticks could not spare sunlight wrangling with captives.

Sweat and smoke stung his eyes as he stood over the wretched cluster. Gray-black clouds passed over them, obscuring the view, torturing Totka's lungs, and making his eyes water. He squinted down at them, mentally untangling the monotone limbs, torsos, and skirts. How many were there?

Two it seemed. One of them whimpered and hid her face in the singed clothes of the one with the yellow skirt whose arms banded them together. She lifted her ash-coated head. He felt her dauntless scrutiny, but his gaze was focused on a third woman in the middle.

Not two, but three. Three!

What household needed three slaves? And Totka was to herd them out of the fort? Which meant he would have to pollute himself by touching them.

Touching a woman before battle was strictly forbidden. Their sex was strong medicine and would pollute a warrior and rob him of his prowess. Risky business in time of war, but at least for Totka, the battle was over.

Thoroughly angered, he squatted and used the club as a prop as he determined how best to get them on their feet without sending them into fits of hysteria.

Over the howl of **Fire Spirit**, a wheeze reached his ear. Which one was struggling? He swatted aside the hair of the one in the middle.

Her breath came in ragged gasps through lips as white as death. Leaned against the quiet one, she seemed unable to keep herself upright, much less carry herself out of the fort.

Was she wounded? He saw no blood, but it was a near certainty that she would not last the arduous journey to Kossati.

Her lids drooped as she gazed at him in a near stupor. This woman suffered from more than smoke in her lungs. Had Nokose been too preoccupied to notice? Surely, he hadn't intended to take a sick captive.

Should Totka leave her where she sat?

Pity stabbed at him. She would be killed if he abandoned her here. She would probably die anyway, but if he took her out and left her hidden in the cane, she had a small chance.

He took her wrists and flipped them to inspect the knot of her binding—a token effort, considering her condition. The haze got the better of him, and he coughed, feeling the squeeze of his lungs. He released the woman's hands, and they dropped to her lap like a stone in a pond.

The other two seemed well enough—one silent and studious, the other a shameful, sniveling mess. It was a toss-up which of the two would give him more trouble. The serious one broke away and fumbled with bound hands over a bucket stationed beside her.

Its contents awakened Totka's thirst, but when she lifted green eyes up at him, unruffled, as if she knew his weakness—that he could never harm her—his mind bolted back to the month of the blackberry moon and the wind-swept glade.

A contusion on her cheekbone and another on her lip distorted her once-lovely features, which were now a medley of dust, soot, and caked blood. A hint of copper, however, gleamed from beneath those layers of ash.

On her knees, she lifted the overflowing dipper with hands discolored by stagnant blood. It wavered and sloshed, but she held it aloft.

She offered him water? She was supposed to fight him, spit on him, hate him. This generosity of spirit did not sit well with him. It weaseled through his defenses and rubbed raw a well-guarded place in his gut.

He retreated a step, eager to put distance between himself and the perplexing woman, but his evasive action and the accompanying scowl didn't deter her.

Leery of admiring her courage, he reached for aggravation and snatched the dipper from her hand. As he poured the sweet liquid down his throat, he kept surveillance from the bottom of his eye. In her place, he would use the distraction to blindside his captor, but she responded with nothing more than a shadow of a smile that nudged one corner of her mouth.

Dipper empty, he lowered it and wiped his mouth with the back of his hand as her sight slid downward to the scalps hanging from his waist.

Her throat convulsed before she met and held his steady gaze, held it with more courage than he'd seen in many of the men he'd killed that day. There was no mistaking this woman. She was the same from the meadow who'd held him captive as assuredly as he'd held *her*. "The wolf slayer, the copper woman," he mumbled.

Had Nokose done this intentionally? Had he captured this woman for Totka? He might if Singing Grass had a hand in it. Hadn't he said they'd already discussed the matter? Whether his own idea or his wife's, Nokose had gone too far, but there was nothing Totka could do about it now.

He tore his gaze from the woman and reached for the whimpering one. With a shriek, she bucked and landed the heel of her shoe against his bad leg.

"Foolish girl!" He raised his club in threat.

The other flung herself at his feet, speaking and turning pleading eyes on him. In the clamor he understood none of it, but that didn't diminish its subduing effect.

Totka lowered his weapon and motioned for her to stand.

When she obeyed, her head barely reached his shoulders. Her chest fluttered with rapid, shallow breaths, much the way it had all those moons ago. But as before, her resolve didn't falter. She kept a humble eye on his chest, and he became aware of the blood spattered across it.

In the face of her composure, Totka considered liberating her hands. Being bound gave her a measure of security; it stated she'd been spoken for. However, if she were freed of restraint, she could better help the feeble one. He severed the thong, pointed at the elder with his knife and jerked it upward. "Get her up."

As the copper one complied, Totka fisted his club and picked a path along the burning picket. When they reached the place where the Red Sticks had hacked open an entry, he climbed over hewn pickets and crouched through the hole. The lot beyond was relatively quiet, but his appearance with three women would be the oddity that would draw attention he didn't care to entertain.

Stooping partway back through, he dropped his club into his belt and extended his reach. Not hesitating, the copper woman unhooked the elder's arm from around her neck and deposited her into Totka's care. He brought her through, waited for the others to follow, then flung the older one over his shoulder.

He skirted the younger women and kept moving. They could follow or die. He swung toward the rear of the fort where the action was almost nonexistent. Best avoid the front where hundreds of battle-hungry warriors swarmed.

The pickets lay to their right, the lake to their left, and between the two, bodies littered a wide stretch of open ground. At the fort's corner stood the bastion where the whooping was most intense. But for all the wild battle cries, the shrieks of women and children were louder.

The battle was won. There was no one left worth fighting. Why did it not stop?

The woman over his shoulder panted and coughed, but he didn't slow. He glanced behind him. Eyes firm and level with his, the strong one upheld the dark-eyed girl who teetered on the verge of a faint. If she did, she would die, for he would not go back for her.

Beyond them, the picket splintered open from the inside. One last attempt at escape for those entrapped within the bastion. The hole was small, but two people squeezed through at once, an old man and a black woman.

In moments, the place would be crawling with warriors.

Cursing Nokose, Totka darted into the canebrake and, hugging the edge, slogged through ankle-deep water. He'd not gone but a few strides when one of the captives screamed a shout. Burdened as he was, his backward twist was slow, and he lost his club before he knew Copper Woman was aiming for it.

He unloaded the sick one onto the darker girl, and as they tumbled, he braced for assault, but he wasn't the target.

Dress hiked to her thighs, the captive spun and tore through the narrow curtain of cane—in the direction of the fort. Had she finally cracked? Lost her reason?

His eyes zipped ahead, following her trajectory. There. A white man, pale hair, garb of a Long Gun. He sliced at a Tuskegee warrior who parried the sword with a musket.

She knew that man. And so did Totka.

The dark girl screamed after her, but she gave no heed, and she would pay for it with her life. Foolish, foolish mettle.

He should let her run to her death if that was what she wanted, but he'd not saved her from wolves and a massacre to lose her now. Grunting displeasure, he leaped out of the cane.

Another Red Stick—was that Long Arrow?—stood to the side poised to finish the Long Gun should the Tuskegee be struck down.

"Phillip!" She lost hold of her dress, tripped, regained her stride. Precious moments to Totka's advantage.

All three turned—the soldier, the Tuskegee, and, yes, thank the spirits, Long Arrow. Brows lifted, he tracked the woman who came at him from a confusing direction, hair streaming and club cocked.

"Stop her," Totka shouted.

"Adela, no! Run!" The soldier gave a darting leap toward her but was countered by the Tuskegee with a clip of the musket butt to his chin. He reeled backward but kept his feet.

Long Arrow stowed his weapons and angled to meet the woman, an amused leer bunching his painted cheek.

She was swifter than Totka expected, but propelled by urgency, he ate away at the ground between them. And still, she was just out of reach.

At the last instant, she veered from Long Arrow and directed her rage at the Tuskegee, coming at him from behind. But Totka was upon her now—just there, within reach. He swiped at her back, catching nothing but hair, which tipped her head but didn't slow her.

Mere strides from the skirmish, he'd used his one chance to nab her before she sank his club into the Tuskegee's brain. Firming his hold on her hair, he dug in his heels and lurched to a stop.

Her head snapped back; her arms and legs flew out before her, but the club kept going, spiraling ball over handle.

When her momentum reversed, he loosed her hair, hopped to the side, and let the ground incapacitate her. Eyes round and confused and watering, mouth gaping, fingers clawing at her chest, breaths coming in pathetic little gasps, she rolled to her side in an attempt to get up.

Not in a mood to deal with her yet, Totka toed her shoulder, popping her back down. "Stay!"

The white man shouted, enraged, but he was spent and helpless to do more than stave off the Tuskegee's next swing, and the next.

"There are easier ways to get a scalp," Long Arrow grinned and lobbed Totka his club. "Such as using a blade."

Totka caught it and directed the handle back into its loop. "I've been told her scalp isn't for the taking."

"Then you had better put her in strings."

A gurgle and grunt pulled them around. A forearm's length of steel protruded from the Tuskegee's back. The soldier gave a cry, extracted the sword, and landed his heel in the Tuskegee's chest, toppling him. Dripping sweat and grappling for breath, he turned on Totka and Long Arrow.

In the next heartbeat, Long Arrow armed himself. "This one refuses to die."

"He has saved his hair for you." Totka hooked the woman in the pit of her arm and hauled her up.

No sooner had he locked an arm around her ribcage did an arrow pierce the pale face's shoulder. The impact whirled him, exposing his side to a second shaft that took him to his knees.

The shooter stood some twenty rods distant, looking smug. Long Arrow stalked toward him, his barrage of insults drowned out by the strangulated scream leaving the woman's throat.

Arms outstretched, she released a flurry of English, her tone pleading, beseeching, but Totka shut his ears to it. Better the man die fighting than be taken captive. The archer, ignoring Long Arrow, already strode toward the downed Long Gun, blade drawn.

Totka spun, flinging her legs out and around, away from the inevitable scalping. She slumped then, letting him take her weight, all fight gone out of her, and Totka wasn't sure whether to be relieved or disappointed.

"Go. Go!" he said in English, then set her away from him and shook her until her knees locked. He lapsed back into his own tongue. "You will run, and you will not look back." She might not know his words, but she wouldn't misinterpret his flinty battle tone.

Sensing her body had all but given out, he recaptured her arm and set out for the rushes, diving in at the nearest point. They'd just entered when her legs buckled, but he'd anticipated it and held her aloft, not yielding his pace.

"Stand," he barked in English, toting her weight, needing her to overcome this, to push past this wall. "Stand!" If she couldn't, and if Totka could not convince Nokose to abandon his objective, it would be a mercy to slit her throat now. She could not leave this cane until she'd found the woman who could slay a wolf or charge a set of armed warriors.

Clinging to him, she dug her nails into his arm and bit out a heated retort. A good sign, but still her legs were useless. They dragged behind her, bumping and snapping the cane.

"You will be pecked to pieces by a dozen warriors," he snapped in Muskogee, not sparing her his wrath. "Is that what you want? Find your strength, Copper Woman, or they will have you for supper." He certainly did not intend to be there to fend them off.

This was Nokose's doing. Nokose's problem. Totka had done enough for the captive.

As her legs churned, she locked her green eyes on his, conveying a multitude of sentiments: fatigue, grief, fury. But above all, determination. To obey. To stand. To live. It seemed her warrior spirit had yet to be crushed.

His lips curved upward.

Eyes sparking, she let go his arm, yanked her dress out of the mire, tripped several steps, then stood upright and stumbled forward.

No sooner had she matched his speed than he released her. If she ran again, she was on her own. He tromped ahead, beating back the cane as he went and wishing it were Nokose.

When they reached the others, he was pleased to find the sick one sitting upright, face semi-washed, and drawing deeper, cleaner breaths. Even so, he had little hope for her survival. He got them on their feet and prodded them onward, leaving the cane and slipping into the thick forest.

The cries of the women coming from inside the fort had diminished to a sad few. The last stronghold had fallen. He cast a quick eye at the sun. It had taken five hands of time to bring the stockade down. Only five. The burying would begin soon, but first, he and Nokose would speak of this thing he had done.

When they arrived at the designated point, Nokose was already there. He directed the women to rest behind a cluster of palmettos and passed his water gourd to the one with sunset hair.

"I would speak with you." Totka moved farther into the woods, and when they'd reached a discrete distance, he rounded on his brother. "Why did you capture that woman? Do you find it amusing to play with people's lives? To arrange mine as you see fit? Do you truly believe she will have me now, after all this?" He flung his arms wide, indicating himself, the flaming fort, the dead and dying, the blood-soaked ground.

"Which woman? What are you —?"

"Which do you think? The one from the glade!"

Nokose stared at him, lips flat, eyes flatter. Slowly, he directed his attention to the women. Something turned behind his eyes, and when they came back to Totka, they were lit with indignation. Lip curling in typical fashion, he spoke with unquestioned authority. "I do not explain myself to you."

"You will, seeing I help sustain your household! We don't need slaves." Totka watched Copper Woman put the bag to the elder's lips, and he steeled his resolve. "Leave the women here."

Nokose pierced him with an eagle-sharp glare. "No."

"Do you intend to trade one or two of them?" In time of war, purchasing a concubine was the last thing on a warrior's mind, but if that were Nokose's plan, Totka might support it. "We could use a horse or a reliable musket." Preferably both.

"Forget the horse. Have you not seen what has been done beyond those walls? Besides a few slaves, they are *all* dead. Every last one. These here would be destroyed same as the others. You wish that on them?" Incredulity escalated Nokose's pitch.

Totka wrenched his gaze from the copper woman. No, he wouldn't. But he had a responsibility to his sister. "It's not a pleasant choice, but what of your children? I am their pawa and will stop at nothing to keep meat in their bellies, but I cannot conjure the deer. If the conflict reaches Kossati and if our crops are destroyed and our stores are burned again, what then? Singing Grass, the children, they will all suffer hunger. All the more with three extra stomachs to fill!"

"Do not speak to me of my children as though I have not given them full consideration." Nokose's low voice lacked no amount of fury. "I am their *father*. And what of your own father? Have you so soon forgotten his counsel?"

Do not allow yourself to be guided by the dread of what may or may not be but by truth and justice. Gray Hawk's last bit of guidance struck Totka across the heart.

"I do seek justice! For our people. Not for our foes, as you would have me do. Until this war is through, these women, as well as my father, are foe. Let me hide the captives deep in the cane. They will not—"

"I have already spoken to Francis. It is done." Nokose pivoted and began beating a path back to the fort. "The women travel north with us."

Arms trembling, jaw burning, Totka followed, biting his cheek until he'd wrangled the boiling oil in his gut. "In that case, we say you changed your mind and ridded yourself of them."

"And when I have no scalps to prove it, they will scour the cane and uncover the women along with any others who might have sought refuge in it. Is that what you want? To sully our good names? To send more pale-face women to the darkening land?"

Hand to Nokose's arm, Totka spun his brother to face him. "Let me tell you who will take the journey. Your unborn child! When my sister shrivels from hunger."

Nokose smacked Totka's hand off him and gave full measure to the disappointment sagging his lips. "You will not dissuade me. I vow to make a difference in the lives of these three. I will show the pale faces that I am no savage, while you"—he flicked a finger at the scalps Totka had collected—"waste your efforts to disprove an old man's prophecy. A prophecy clearly false, for you are a heartless, cold-blooded warrior through and through."

Nokose's head was snapping to the side, spittle flinging, before Totka registered that his fist had taken flight.

"You want the women?" Totka ground out, feeding off the pain in his joints and the fire in Nokose's eye. "Very well. They are all yours, including the one from the meadow. I am through with this madness."

Chapter 10

Totka sank into the cool, pushing waters of the **long snake** Alabama. The **Water Spirit** filled his ears and drowned the euphoric banter of those on shore. An earlier dip in the lake called Tensaw had relieved him of battle gore. He bathed now, some four hands of sun later, as ritual prescribed—to cleanse himself of pollution from the enemy, to scrub away the remnants of war paint, to rid his hair of embedded ash, to purge his mind of bloodshed. And to peel away the madman who'd entered Fort Mims. And left it.

A vortex wrapped him in its watery grasp, coaxing him to follow. It was tempting, but duty wedged his feet against underlying stones. When he'd wearied and his chest burned for want of air, he reemerged calmer, more focused. With fistfuls of sand he buffed his neck, torso, and face, then submerged once more to complete the required four dunks.

As he trudged up the steep bank, the river poured off him, and his buckskin breechcloth slapped heavily against his thighs.

Nokose, his expression grim, stood two paces from the long snake's lapping edge. The crack on his swollen lip complimented the various other bruises and scrapes he'd acquired that day.

Totka smirked. "Why so glum? Have your slaves run off?"

One obviously hadn't—the strong one. What had the white soldier called her? Adela? Totka didn't care for the name. It ill-suited her.

Set against an eerie backdrop of cypress and dangling moss, she faced the water seven long strides downstream of him; pale eyes looked out from a blackened face. Her torn dress hung on her lopsided, one shoulder exposed and in stark white contrast to her sooty neck. Her hands, again in strings, were limp before her, but her straight back retained her dignity. What must she be thinking standing so brazenly among those who would as soon kill her as they had her loved ones?

"Their provisions are lost." Nokose shifted his weight, revealing the other captives who sat some distance behind him on a grassy patch of sand. They were slight of frame, but to keep up the rigorous pace, they would require almost a man's portion of food. That Nokose had brought food other than what he could carry on his person proved he'd left Kossati with captives in mind. Unthinkable.

Totka wrung out his hair, and water splattered his toes. "Are you claiming there is a thief afoot?"

"I suspect the sack was loose and fell off when the horse bolted."

Ah yes, the squealing girl and the bolting horse. Totka had almost managed to forget that fine, disgraceful start to their journey. After that, the girl with the bitter eyes had been relegated to walking, and Totka had taken a position in the line eleven horses back. He was, after all, a man of his word.

"I have what little I carry on me," Nokose continued, "but there are three sleeps between here and Kossati. The hominy in my wallet will feed one, and we are four."

Totka cocked a brow and waited for the inevitable request.

"My own strength will hold, as will that of the daughters, but a fast will kill their mother."

Sisters? Two females could not look more different. "The sick one will die either way. You should have left her in the fort or ended her suffering yourself." The instant Totka gave life to the thought, he wished it dead. He continued to prove Nokose correct—he had been too long among Francis' men.

Anger distended Nokose's nostrils. "Better to cut out that tongue of yours than to let it flap with arrogance! Whom are you trying to impress? None of Francis' chiefs are within hearing! You know as well as I that war should be waged against men, not babes and helpless women." In the privacy of their home, he'd said the same for as long as Totka could recall, and somewhere along the way, he'd convinced Totka it was true.

Guilt nipped at Totka's conscience, but he wouldn't lower his eyes. "Take care, Brother, lest your white talk be heard and it be your own tongue that is severed."

As a weighty, tempering silence settled between them, Nokose glanced about at the warriors—strangers and clan alike—preparing for the night. At last, he spoke, his tone firm yet shaded by a hint of imploring. "Take one of the women under your care, and I will be in your debt."

Totka might pity Nokose, except that he'd been warned and warned again. "The women are your prize. Your responsibility. If you cannot control or care for them, you should let them go."

"You would leave them to lose their way and be devoured by the swamp? I think not." After a meaningful pause, he waved an arm in the direction of the copper-haired one. "Pick one, or I will pick for you."

"You are not my chief, and they are not clan—mine or yours! Why are you doing this? Why are you forcing my hand?"

"This is not about you! It is about *them*." Nokose's fiery statement drew the attention of Copper Woman as well as that of several men lounging nearby.

Tall Bull emerged from cleansing in the long snake and passed within touching distance, but his intense eye was not on the argument—it was on the woman. Whether mere curiosity or something more, Totka couldn't be certain.

Apprehension tensed Totka's fighting arm until his cousin's saunter led him elsewhere. How could he even glance at other women with Leaping Waters at home waiting for him? She was woman enough for any man. Except Tall Bull. It was common knowledge he'd not asked her to his couch for a number of moons.

Nokose's lowered voice brought Totka back to the matter at hand. "You will do this thing because we are brothers and because I ask it of you."

Put in such a way, how could Totka refuse without spitting in the face of all that Nokose had been to him? And yet, he must. "When the Long Guns learn we have their women, when they hunt us down, who will pay for this breach? Their ropes are eager to squeeze our necks. Would you **widow** Singing Grass for a few slaves?"

Nokose's iron glare unexpectedly mellowed. "Singing Grass will understand."

Totka stepped back and angled his head at Nokose, perplexed. "I have presented you many reasons to free the whites, and that is all you have to say?"

Lips pursed, Nokose nodded. "Plenty enough has been said between us."

A laugh, curt and humorless, left Totka.

What was he to do? Abandon his brother with the hope he would come to his senses? Join him in this foolhardiness and do whatever necessary to counterbalance the adverse effects it would have on their family? Taking slaves during battle was not uncommon, but taking three — three *white* captives — was lunacy.

Giving his back to Nokose, he rubbed his chin and observed the woman downstream. Another option was to release her himself. He had a responsibility to his family that went beyond the need for Nokose's approval.

Of the three, this woman would be the most physically able, but was she savvy enough to elude the bands of Red Sticks patrolling the area? And if so, would she be able to guide the others back to their people, or would she die in the wilderness as Nokose believed?

They were one day's march from the settlements. If she followed the Alabama south, she would eventually stumble across help. Assuming the wolves didn't get her first. What a shame it would be if, in the attempt to help, and after all the effort he'd already expended on her, he condemned the noble creature to death.

As though hearing the direction of his thoughts, she turned her eyes and struck him with a silent, unsettling plea.

His feet begged to shift, his gaze to dart elsewhere, but he held the link until she broke it off, descended the bank, and sloshed into the water.

He cast a nervous glance downstream. To maintain balance and purity, men and women must bathe separately. Satisfied the area was clear, he folded his arms over his chest and chided himself for having taken even fleeting responsibility for her actions.

"When her eye meets yours, it does not waver," Nokose spoke from behind, admiration warming his tone.

"The woman doesn't fear me as she should." She hadn't from the beginning. But why *should* she fear him? Hadn't those rich eyes seen into his soul, seen that—for all his bravado—he could never raise his hand against her? He'd convinced Nokose he was a heartless warrior, and he'd almost convinced himself, but she seemed privy to the truth. The nagging question was, did valuing the lives of innocents make him a warrior worthy of praise, or did it make him a traitor to the ways of his people?

The water lapped her belly; her gait ebbed and became unsteady. The current berated her, and still, she moved deeper.

"She does not fear Water Spirit as she should either," Totka said.

"Mmm." Nokose went around Totka at a slow, observant pace.

Her breasts vanished beneath the green gloom. Three steps farther and she would be over her head. Did the vortex extend to where she was? If so, she would be swept away. Was that her intent? Escape? But her hands were bound and her garments were heavy. She wouldn't survive.

She went under, and Totka's heart stilled.

Nokose leapt into action, but Tall Bull, much closer than they, dove in first.

When ten strokes remained for him to reach her, she broke the surface. In full control, she regained her footing and used a sleeve to scrub at her smudged face. She was bathing, only bathing.

Totka's pulse resumed, but she was not out of danger. One misstep could carry her beyond help.

Oblivious to Tall Bull's approach, she sank to her chin and tipped her head back into the water. It splashed over her nose and mouth, and she spluttered.

From behind, Tall Bull pulled her flat against him.

Startled, she fought for a moment before ceding to his will and allowing herself to be dragged through the water.

Nokose returned, giving Totka an uncompromising look. "Since you will not choose, I put that one in your care. Either feed her or — since you approve of killing defenseless women — kill her." The challenge dripped with sarcasm. "Either way, from here on, she is your charge."

Not removing his eyes from Tall Bull, Totka firmed his stance. "And if I refuse?"

"Why would you? You have favored her since long before today." When Totka refused to respond, Nokose shrugged and began toward the horses. "Tall Bull has been unhappy with Leaping Waters of late. He might be willing to take the copper-haired daughter as a concubine."

Totka's gaze hurtled to Nokose's receding back, then to Tall Bull who lugged her, feet dragging, up the beach. She called out, her tone pleading, her feet fumbling inside her knotted gown.

Tall Bull was doing the very thing Totka had done that afternoon, but where Totka had pushed her to heightened stamina, Tall Bull was careless, unthinking. As he was with Leaping Waters. It fermented in Totka's stomach like a nauseating herb.

Dishing out a growl and naming Nokose a fool, and himself the same, Totka squared his shoulders and set out. "Cousin," he called. "Let her go!"

When the man looked his direction, the woman's knee found his groin. As he would a beast's carcass, he dropped her in a heap and doubled, unable to disguise his pain. "That's the thanks I get for polluting myself to save her?" He gave Totka a heated look of warning. "Long Arrow told you to keep a better eye on the little viper. Lose track of her again, and you might not get her back."

Moments later, Totka and the woman were alone—he with fists clenched, jaw hardened, pride pricked for having been so weak as to abandon his decision to remain uninvolved; she, matching the determined set of his jaw, fumbling uselessly to stand with hands bound, flailing in her sodden skirt, revealing every curve through her wet clothes—and he found that the prospect of his new task was more agreeable than it should be.

Put out at the revelation, he reminded himself he'd been given license to do with her as he deemed best. And often what was best was not the most pleasant option.

Lying on the hard ground, Adela shivered inside her wet clothes, but the damp had little to do with the tremors wracking her. Mama snuggled against her, and Lillian lay on the other side of Mama. The rhythmic sounds of their sleep comforted her, even while her own breathing was quick and irregular.

They'd traveled about four hours from the fort before stopping. She'd been ready to drop with exhaustion when Nokose pulled her from the horse, but now, she couldn't close her eyes for fear some Red Stick hadn't gotten his fill of blood.

Stomach grumbling, Adela studied the stars and focused on the river's constant rush, but neither could overpower the screams and visions of carnage filling her head. Her last image of Phillip—body pierced, eyes hot and determined, willing her to live—flashed intermittently before her. It was one of many memories that made her chest hurt and her throat constrict.

An abrupt rustling emanated from the adjacent woods, and Adela twitched and propped herself on an elbow for a better view of her surroundings. She would not be taken unawares, and she would not die easy.

Her eyes fought the shadows. Where *was* Nokose Fixico? Wherever he'd bedded down, it wasn't close enough. Right that moment, she would take his somber companion, too, but she hadn't seen the younger warrior since he'd left her floundering on the bank like a landed fish.

The form of a man, silvered by the three-quarters moon, stole across the far end of the camp. He moved her direction.

Heart lurching, Adela flopped back down and told herself he wasn't after their scalps. She forced her thoughts into the following day. To Mama. What was to be done about her?

Until Nokose had lifted Mama onto the horse, Adela and Lillian had supported her weight. There was no telling what might happen if someone complained that Nokose had taken a sick woman as slave. If she slowed them, they would finish her.

Adela lifted her head to discreetly check the progress of the skulking warrior—his path persisted in her direction. She hurled a prayer heavenward and shuddered at the memory of being hauled across the sand, of watching Nokose walk away, of her absolute helplessness.

Adela sniffed and wiped her drippy nose with her sleeve. Her wrists burned, and her fingers were stiff and cold despite the sultry night. Was it necessary to keep her bound so tightly? Nokose must know she would go nowhere without her mother, and Mama was in no condition to run.

She shouldn't disparage him so—not even to herself. That she drew breath at all was by his grace and that of the fellow with the crescent moon and the black-striped arrows.

The warrior entered her vision and stopped a horseshoe toss from where she lay; he angled his body toward her, arms relaxed at his sides.

Willing herself to stay calm—and willing him to move on—she

remained motionless, but he equaled her fictitious composure and refused to leave.

Could he feel her gaze resting on him? Except for the river's loud scurrying, he would most certainly hear the up-tempo of her breathing.

He stepped closer, and Adela recognized the man by his gait, silent and fluid except for the slight offbeat.

She released a pent-up breath and a measure of fear. Would he stand watch? Oh, that he would.

When he crossed his arms as though settling in, every muscle in her body relaxed, and for the first time since she'd lain down, her eyes grew heavy.

Three times now, the enigmatic warrior had intervened on her behalf, and each new image of him was a stark contrast to one before — from leggings and loose-fitting hunting shirt, to red and black war paint awash in blood, to nothing but sleek skin and a distracting breechcloth. And the scalps he'd worn . . . Did he wear them now?

Chills ran the length of her spine. He was as fearsome as the rest, but this warrior's touch, though bloody, had been gentle — as it had been the first time. He was an intriguing contradiction.

Tall for a Creek, and taller than most whites by a good five inches, he was sinewy and built for war. His silhouette blurred as she became drowsier. Her lids drooped, and in her memory, his body glistened, first with blood and sweat, then with water, which had sprinkled her when he'd whirled away, leaving her to struggle on the beach. But he was here now, as he'd been before. Watching, guarding . . .

A cougar's scream snatched her from the lull of semi-sleep. She jolted and scooted closer to Mama.

As though waiting for such a signal, the warrior padded to her side and descended to one knee.

Fully awake now, Adela did her best to appear collateral, despite her erratic heart.

He laid a warm hand on her damp sleeve, then slid it down to the leather thong digging into her flesh. From nowhere, cold iron wedged itself between the strap and her skin. A sharp wrench preceded a *pop*, and she was free.

Quickly, he unwound the remaining thong then massaged her lifeless fingers — one hand in each of his.

Feeling returned, bringing with it needle points of pain. She sucked in a sharp breath and pulled away.

He tugged back, insistent, and continued to knead. Biting her lip to keep from crying out, she allowed him to minister to her. Such a simple act of kindness, yet it confirmed her long-held hope that not all Red Sticks were bloodthirsty, mindless killers. She'd known from the first his was a good soul; she had the proof in her pocket.

The pain began to ease, and her fingers began to move on command. When she sensed him releasing her, she squeezed one hand to detain him and with the other, withdrew her little scrap of hope and pressed it into his palm.

Without acknowledging the offering, he backed away. When he did, Adela was startled to find another man standing a few yards off. The arrangement of feathers matched that of Nokose.

Nothing passed between the men as the younger crossed the elder's path.

Nokose lay down were he stood, and Adela watched the other until he faded into the night.

Several deep breaths unwound a knot in her neck. Perhaps she would sleep. Vying for illusive comfort, she wiggled off a pesky stone and onto a stick. Where had it come from? She dug it out from under her hip and winced at the prick of a finger against cold, sharp metal.

Not a stick. A knife.

Totka made his way back to his patch of earth and worked the tattered fabric between his fingers while telling himself it wasn't what he thought it was.

It couldn't be. There was no way the copper-haired woman had kept the dirty remnant of his shirt. Why would she? And if she had, why would she give it back to him? It was laughable to think she meant for him to patch up his already mended shirt.

Was it in gratitude for the use of her hands? No, it would be too strange; although, it wouldn't be the first time she'd acted strangely. The cleaned arrow came to mind.

None of it made no sense. He flicked the fragment aside and scouted out the flattened patch of grass that marked the spot he'd chosen for the night.

A gust of wind left his mouth when he dropped to his back. He stretched out, feeling every sore muscle and strained joint. The night was half gone, but he couldn't still his thoughts long enough to catch sleep. The woman's curious gift plagued him, but what did it matter?

He'd accepted the task to care for her, and he had chosen to free her. If luck was on his side, she and the others would be gone before Grandmother Sun announced the day, but when day arrived and she was still there, he found himself retracing his steps.

The piece of cloth remained where it had fallen. Pale blue, it stood out against the grass. There was no more denying where it had come from. He flattened it smooth against his palm. Except for a faint, red stain it was clean.

"Adela will not run." From behind, Nokose tapped his shoulder with the flat side of Totka's own knife.

He took it, crumpled the bit of old shirt inside his fist, and feared Nokose might be right.

Chapter 11

Adela rode behind her mother as they trekked the northern bank of the Alabama River. After three days of rough travel and even rougher nights, she fought a hunger-induced weakness she couldn't beat, and she feared that soon, she wouldn't have the strength to support herself, much less her mother.

Papa had once told her that while on the warpath Creek warriors fasted before battle and ate little to nothing after. All correct. Captives, it would appear, were expected to abide the same strict regime. Only twice over the course of their travels had Totka dipped into his small pouch and poured a meager handful of cornmeal into her cupped palms. A little water made it into a palatable paste that had done little to ease the gnawing in her stomach.

The war party had been jovial that morning, reapplying paint. Within the span of an hour, the red and black colors robbed them of their humane appearance and morphed them back into the demons who'd plundered the souls of her loved ones.

Lillian had trembled like a whipped dog until Adela had reassured her they painted themselves, not to war again, but to enter their village with fanfare. She prayed her assumption proved true.

Through a constant drip of tears, Lillian kept up a brisk pace next to their Indian horse. Blue ribbons dangled precariously from her disheveled braid, which swung across her back like a church bell tolling for the dead. Still tied, her hands were leashed to their saddle. She'd walked the entire way from the ruins of Fort Mims, her feet dragging by day's end.

Ferocious travel had buried the war party deep into northern Creek country. Along the way, bands of warriors had detached from the main party and taken separate trails. Earlier in the afternoon, along with thirty other warriors, Nokose had split off and guided them across the river at a wide, shallow point.

An hour ago, a final dozen had pulled off onto a trail that led to a village a short way off. Long after Nokose's party had left the village behind, the sounds of keening had traveled on the wind. Adela couldn't help but grieve with them, for their losses and for her own. War was merciless, destroying every home it touched, regardless of tribe.

She felt almost widowed herself. Why was it Phillip had to die before she fully appreciated him? Discouragement and the ravages of hunger had pursued her throughout the day so that, now, a sob rose in her throat. She leaned into her mother's shoulder to squelch it.

Mama tilted her head and rested her cheek against Adela's hair. "God will see us through. He did not save us from the fort to have us die under Nokose's care." Air wheezed through her chest. She made a valiant effort to appear strong, but Adela wasn't fooled.

"Best you not speak, Mama," she whispered.

Yesterday, she'd asked Nokose for the younger warrior's name— Totka Lawe. Nokose told her it meant *Hungry Fire* because his passions had always burned hot. She believed it.

Without looking, Adela knew at every moment where Totka rode—usually at the end of the line. This morning, he'd not made his usual appearance, and she suspected he'd split off with some of the others. She hadn't considered Totka might live in a village separate from Nokose. What she *had* wondered was whether Nokose had given her to him as a gift or prize. Apart from the fear of being separated from Mama and Lillian, the notion wasn't abhorrent. He would feed her and, should her life or wellbeing be threatened, he would protect her, as he had already proven. But what might he expect in return for those services?

At least for the moment, her fears were moot because Totka was gone, but who would stand in for her should the need arise? Nokose didn't seem as willing as she'd like him to be. Fortunately, so far, they'd been ignored by all except for the two. Even Totka, when not doling out the far-too-occasional bite of nourishment, pretended they didn't exist. An annoyance at their very presence most likely. Despite being diligent in his duty, he was none too pleased at having it.

Elizabeth would probably have given the dour man a piece of her mind. The hollow chasm in Adela's heart deepened as her thoughts shifted toward her sister. The last three days had been so fast-paced there had been no time to mourn her. Poor Beth. Her body was probably ash, left for the wind to carry wherever it took a liking. Adela couldn't imagine how life would proceed without her. Beth had been a hard one to love . . . until now.

Nokose caught her eye, stripes of red bedecking his own. "Kossati ahead." It was the first time he'd spoken to them that day.

As their string of horses emerged from the mixed forest of oak, pine, and hickory, Kossati came into view below them. It was neatly laid out with lanes and lodges arranged in straight, parallel lines. Just beyond at the base of the valley, the Coosa River ran its course, sparkling in the setting sun.

If she followed it, where would it lead? West, then south. Back to Papa. He was alive and grieving for them. She was sure of it. If not for their mother, she would take Lillian by the hand and stop at nothing to prove it. She would find the Wolf Path, that well-known trail through Creek country, and she would follow it home. Better yet, the **Federal Road**.

For today, the picturesque village before her would house them. A group of children played in a field waving with tall bromegrass. Beside an arbor heavy with grapes, several women stretched hides in the sun. On the outskirts, an elderly man sat on a stool near a fire, children squatting before him. His gnarled hands moved with the rhythm of a tale, and the little ones laughed and clapped.

A boy digging in a small garden plot caught sight of the returning war party and ran through the village shouting. The warriors broke into their cries and sent Adela straight back to the fort. She gripped Mama with her arms and the horse's sides with her thighs.

Lillian shrieked and clung to Adela's leg but was shoved aside by their horse who sidestepped away from several warriors galloping past, devouring the field between the trees and Kossati's outlying buildings. Most, including Nokose, took their time, approaching at a dignified yet prancing pace, drawing out the triumphal return to its fullest.

The dirt roads overflowed with women and children, young boys and elderly, each searching for a father, husband, or son. There was worry on each face, then joy as a loved one was spotted. The chilling whoops droned on, seeming never to end.

Farther down the road, a young woman stopped a horse to speak to its rider. When he shook his head, she backed away, her face contorting. With a wail, she collected handfuls of dirt and smeared it on her face and down her neck. As their horse passed the widow, she smacked Lillian across the cheek, leaving a dirty handprint.

Lillian cried out, backing into Adela's horse. The animal jibbed sideways, and Adela swayed in the saddle. Her legs strengthened their grip.

The assault continued, growing more feverish with each strike, and no one moved to stop it. Others joined the widow, releasing their frustration and rage. Jeers evolved into fists and stones.

Adela shielded her mother. "Hold on, Mama!"

Before the last word left her mouth, she received a stunning blow to the temple. The horse's legs appeared briefly before her as she tumbled headfirst from its back.

Her forehead connected with the ground, concussing her spine. The world spun. A patch of hard-packed dirt stared up at her. At the border of her narrowing vision, a set of moccasins drew near.

Nokose. He would save her . . . Wouldn't he?

Pain lanced her head, and she closed her eyes tight against it. Battling the bile rising in her throat, she barely noticed being turned onto her back.

Her feet dangled. Was she being carried? The myriad angry voices muffled and then vanished just before blackness consumed her.

Totka'd been given one small task. One. Initial reluctance aside, the fact remained he'd accepted the duty. And failed.

"Singing Grass!" he called as he strode into their courtyard.

Copper Woman's dead weight, carried from the main thoroughfare two lanes over, taxed every muscle, including the one pumping furiously beneath the strain of indignation. Rivulets of blood coursed down his bare chest and slicked his thighs. The memory of her awkwardly crumpled form made him fear the worst.

Of the three captives, this one should not die. She deserved to live until the gray years, to tell her white grandchildren how she'd been spared the Red Sticks' wrath. How, with fortitude and grace, she'd earned a warrior's respect.

Wind blew at Totka's back and sent the dust he'd raised galloping before him. He bypassed the quiet winter lodge. Although a widow, White Stone would be with the other women in the lanes shouting a welcome, but the frenzy of returning warriors had never appealed to Singing Grass. She would be here, waiting. "Sister! Where are you?"

Nokose's brown- and white-speckled dog bounded from behind the potato house. Barking, it navigated tight circles around Totka's legs.

"Hush, dog!" Singing Grass' shout emerged from the dim summer lodge before she filled its entryway. "Totka, you are—!" Her joy vanished. "Where is Nokose?"

"This woman was knocked from a horse. Tell me where to put

her." He panted, not slowing, compelling Singing Grass back into the airy lodge. He angled his body to avoid hitting the woman's feet on the doorpost and ducked into the cool interior. "Clear the table."

Singing Grass took one sweeping look at the situation and jumped to perform. With a whisk of her arm, she dispensed with several hollowed gourds. They careened across the room. She snatched up a bowl of soaking beans an instant before he deposited Copper Woman on the table. Water from the bowl sloshed over Singing Grass' sleeve and onto her son, Fire Maker, as he skipped by her.

"Pawa!" Fire Maker slapped his naked body flush against Totka's leg, unconcerned with the blood wetting it. "You did not die in battle!"

Singing Grass hurried to her mending basket.

Totka clamped a hand over the gushing head wound and found a light-hearted chuckle buried beneath his alarm. "I did not die, but this woman might if I do not tend to her. Where are your sisters?" Blood welled up between his fingers, and his worry intensified. Why would the bleeding not slow?

At Mims' place he'd shed blood without a thought, but the sight of this woman's draining into his hand struck him deep, and he cared for it not one bit.

"They are in the storehouse with the puppies. Dog had five puppies yesterday, but one died." Fire Maker peeked over the edge of the table. "She's very pale. Is that why she is dying? Will the Master of Breath take her? Like he did the puppy? I cut Speaks Sweetly's finger with my knife. I didn't mean to, but she — "

"You must go to the puppies," Totka said, glancing impatiently at Singing Grass. "Go now. I'll meet you there soon."

"But I want to see if the pale woman dies or if — "

Totka whipped his head about to put his face in his nephew's and administered his most withering glare.

Eyes bulging, Fire Maker scrambled out.

Singing Grass ripped an old shirt for bandages, wadded a

portion, and wedged it under Totka's hand. "Press harder," she instructed before turning to fetch water into a bowl from the large clay vessel by the door. "My husband. Where is he?" The question trembled on her tongue.

"Coming behind me." It had been callous of Totka not to say right off. "Delayed by the other two captives."

Her head shot up and the water from the dipping gourd missed the bowl by a hand's width. She ignored the splatter and bent for another scoop. "Is he well?"

"In body, although I cannot account for his sanity. *Three* captives, Singing Grass. Tell me you did not ask for slaves. Tell me you'll trade for them."

"Why would you have me lie to you?" Hurrying to the table, she bent over Copper Woman and rifled through her unkempt hair. "So much blood! Is there only the one wound? Ah." She located an angry, red lump protruding from just inside the hairline on the opposite side of the main lesion. "What of this?"

Ire scorched the length of Totka's throat. This captive had displayed endurance equal to any Muscogee's. She didn't deserve such treatment.

Each day of the journey, he'd expected her to give in to tears or collapse from exhaustion or hunger. Each evening he had been surprised when she hadn't. By the last day, Totka feared she might tumble from the pony, but she'd held firm. It had taken a blow to bring her down.

"A stone, I believe," Totka finally managed. "I didn't see who threw it, but with such an aim it could none other than Amadayh. And when I find the woman, I will—"

"You will do *nothing*." Her eyes flashed at him before flitting to the silhouette filling the doorway.

White Stone's plump frame blocked their only source of light. Her cropped, unattended hair stuck out in disarray. Widowhood did not become her. "What is this?"

Singing Grass' stern look twitched the dots of ink tattooing a curved line beneath her eye. "Nokose has brought home captives, and Totka threatens to seek out Amadayh and exact revenge for this one here."

With a sharp click of her tongue, White Stone crossed over to him and poked at him with a brittle scowl, not affording the captive a solitary glance. "I did not raise you to behave in such a way! Our mother's spirit will rise up in protest if you bring shame on Wolf Clan. The woman is but a slave. Did you expect a welcome of a different sort? A feast laid out in her honor? Our women have a right to grieve as they see fit. To deny them this is to stir up trouble."

Uneasy silence filled the space between them. His sisters were right. The women's introduction to the talwa had been mild compared to a captive's typical welcome. What had taken possession of him? Whatever it was, it was not good.

"What do you need of me?" White Stone asked Singing Grass.

With the sleeve of her blouse, Singing Grass wiped sweat from her neck. "Keep the children out for a while. And prepare two pallets in the winter lodge. This one will stay here with me until her fate is determined."

"Very well." On her way out, White Stone cast Totka one last stern look. "Mind yourself, little brother."

Singing Grass resumed toiling over the smaller of the two wounds, and he blinked some sense into himself. Or attempted to. "She will need a **healing song**."

Singing Grass' doctoring paused mid-stroke. She thrust the weight of her scrutiny upon him, but he ignored her and focused instead on the unsteady flutter of Copper Woman's pulse beneath his fingers.

After some moments, she slipped light fingers over his own. "We can sing over her, but she is badly injured. Prepare yourself. It may be she is taking the journey."

He shook his head. "You must make her live." His sister would not understand the burden he'd undertaken.

"I can promise you nothing. You understand as well as I the

148

damage a blow to the skull can cause."

And Copper Woman had received not one, but two. Totka winced. "Nokose gave her over to my care, trusted me." Remorse scratched his voice.

He should have been there. No. That was hardly true. He'd been tending to his first duty—providing for his family.

"At dawn, I split off to follow a buck and was late catching up to the party."

Otherwise, he would have had this woman riding with him as they entered Kossati, as he'd planned. The Wind Spirit had been contrary, and Totka had been forced to tack and come in from the north, causing undue delay. The **Sacred North** was associated with trouble and defeat. He might have known it was an ill wind.

"What of the buck?" She combed Copper Woman's hair to cover the lump.

"I left it with Old Grandfather. It slowed me down."

When the riot began, Totka had almost caught up to her. From three horses away and through the throng, he'd felt her fear and heard the *crack* when she hit the hard dirt. Looking back to how that sound had gutted him, he knew he'd done the unthinkable—he'd allowed his emotions to become chief to his mind. He'd let his admiration obscure the fact she was the enemy and a slave.

"And what of the battle? Were you successful?"

"Mmm." Although to speak of that now in the woman's presence—even unconscious—seemed somehow vulgar. Her lips were white, the breath issuing from them, shallow. He stroked her forehead with a forefinger and willed her to fight a little harder.

"You did well, Brother."

Uncounted heartbeats elapsed before he noticed his sister had stopped moving. She beamed at him, a motherly smile softening her mouth—the same smile she'd bestowed on Fire Maker when he'd completed his little set of darts for his blowgun. But Totka was not a boy in need of petting.

"Is there nothing else you can do for her?" he asked.

Her expression turned quizzical, and he envisioned the pulley of her mind straining to draw a conclusion. The bounce of her gaze divided itself evenly between Totka and Copper Woman, and the sudden sly tilt of her lips set him on the defensive.

"Whatever you're thinking, you are wrong."

"Am I?" She gestured to his hand. "Has the bleeding slowed?"

He peeled back the sodden bundle. "A little. Give me another cloth. This one has taken all it will hold."

She handed him a fresh wad in exchange for the old. "We'll allow another moment before cleaning the wound. In the meantime, what will we find under all this dirt?" She squeezed out a fresh rag and applied it to the bridge of Copper Woman's nose, unveiling a faint string of chestnut freckles. "I wager," Singing Grass said, not looking up, "she has hair the color of these charming spots. And it occurs to me that this is the Tensaw woman you met during the blackberry moon. When I told you to invite her to share our fire, I never expected you to take the challenge. Clearly, I underestimated you."

"She is not here of my own doing, and well you know it. Do not pretend that you and Nokose had no hand in this. You've been scheming since the night I returned from Tensaw."

"How could I have anything to do with bringing her here?" Laughter shook her rounded belly. "The least you can do is claim your own clever handiwork."

"Bah! If not you, then your husband. It is his doing, not mine."

"My husband is not crafty enough to devise such an elaborate scheme. In the name of war, yes. In the name of love? I think not."

"Love has no place in this talk." Neither love nor friendship and especially not forgiveness. He would get none of those things from this captive.

Bent over her patient, Singing Grass flashed a cheeky grin up at him. "Scalps, a buck, *and* a woman. Not bad for one campaign."

Was she not listening? Even if he were interested, and assuming the woman survived, she would never have him, the man who'd had a hand in destroying her life. "Enough of this. Open your ears, woman. I refuse to repeat myself."

"I hear what your mouth tells me, but I'm not deceived. The only person you are skilled at lying to, Totka, is yourself."

He huffed and glared at the exit. As soon as Nokose's shadow fell across it, Totka was done. If only he could bring himself to walk away now. Moments later, when Nokose did arrive, it was only to drop off the other captives, collect a hasty kiss from Singing Grass, and rush out again for the council square, leaving Totka with Copper Woman's head still bracketed by his flattened hands.

Singing Grass, eyes round with consternation, ushered the mother straight into a chair at the table near her daughter's head, snagged a bowl from a shelf, and tramped to the courtyard fire.

The mother took Copper Woman's palm and held it to her sallow cheek until Singing Grass pushed a serving of thin soup beneath her nose. When she resisted—eyes trained on her daughter—Singing Grass, in her sternest mother-voice, made perfectly clear who was mistress of the lodge.

As though treading through a snake-infested swamp, the dark-eyed sister found her way to the stool in the corner. A bruise was forming on her forehead, and blood from a scratch mixed with the mud and dampness on her cheeks—she possessed a vexatious reservoir of tears.

Singing Grass arrived with a second bowl for the girl.

His own riotous stomach would have to wait.

Copper Woman stirred—the fingers of her right hand flexed, her lips moved, soundless.

Totka's lungs stuttered.

The women exclaimed and clucked and coaxed, but he was oblivious to all save the strengthening pulse against his fingers and the tentative movements inside his grasp. Looking down on her from behind, he listened with a wide heart for proof she retained her faculties.

Her lashes rose, dipped, and rose again. "Mama?"

Singing Grass grinned, and Totka exhaled a stout breath.

He kept his station as several lines were exchanged between daughter and mother.

"What do they say?" Singing Grass looked up from threading a stitching needle.

Totka shrugged. "She is being quizzed, I believe. Something about blood and lying still, and something more about your husband."

"Ah. Whatever it is, she gives correct answers. Otherwise, the older one would not look so pleased. It might be early to speak so boldly, but it appears the spirits have been kind to you. Your *bewildering* woman will live." She bit the thread and grinned at him through the *click* of its breaking. "But you cannot have her for many weeks yet. She will need complete rest."

There was no sense replying. Singing Grass had sketched out in her mind another version of reality and — he knew from experience — would not be convinced otherwise.

While the wound was scrubbed and stitched, he restrained Copper Woman who, unflinching, shed silent tears at each prick of the needle. After she demonstrated clear possession of her bearings, he left her so he might wash up at the larger water vessel, but he'd made it only short distance when the whisper of his name halted him.

"Totka?" Copper Woman's voice came again, more robust this time.

Half turning, he marveled that she knew his name. The sound of it on her lips was strange and strangely beautiful.

Through a slanted smile, she asked him a question, and his lips curved south. Why had he not followed Leaping Waters' urging and schooled himself in English?

Her lids hung heavy with pain, but she studied him regardless. It was an intense gaze — one he didn't understand, one a little more complicated than a casual glance should be. He told himself to look away, but curiosity held him captive.

What would it be like to do as Singing Grass said and take this woman as his own? She presented a rugged picture, but he'd known her before hunger and fatigue, before the ravages of the fort and its flames had left their marks on her—and the memory made the image forming in his mind an enticing one.

With that thought, he begrudgingly admitted to himself that his sister had never been more right—he was skilled at lying to himself. The copper-haired woman had indeed gotten into him. Armed with nothing more than stoicism, bravery, and a fragment of unraveling homespun, she'd cracked his chest and burrowed into places he'd thought long dead.

But was she worth pursuing? Could he make her want him? After all he'd done? Drawn by the invisible thread of longing, he faced her full on.

In the span of time it took for her eyes to rake his body—painted in her blood and the colors of war—her face transformed to one of shock, followed by fear. She squeezed her eyes shut and jerked her head to the side, then held her temples and groaned.

He didn't need a knower to tell him she'd left the room, that she trembled again before the battled-crazed warrior with trophy scalps. Nor did he need confirmation he'd been a cursed idiot to entertain for even a moment the notion of pursuing her.

As her mother soothed her, Totka went limp, unable to do more than stare at the distress the mere sight of him had caused.

"Move. You upset her. Get out." Singing Grass spun him around and nudged him across the lodge and into the courtyard. "To the river. Don't come back until you have washed."

Until he'd washed? He didn't plan to come back at all.

The room spun; Adela's ears rang. The eagle's cry filled her mind along with a hundred hair-raising war cries.

It's over. It's over. You're safe. It's over.

"Adela. Adela!" Mama's voice penetrated the ringing.

Adela drew a shaggy breath and commanded her eyes to open.

Totka had left. She'd sent him away. Remorse dueled with relief.

"I'm sorry, Mama. I was . . . dazed for a moment." Her entire head throbbed.

"Give yourself time. You might be confused for a while."

Mama looked as though she should be the one in bed. She'd recovered her breathing, but her sunken eyes said she was not at all well.

"Lillian, let me see you," Adela said.

Her sister moved into the light, and Adela gasped. "Oh, Lilly, you're bleeding." And her hair looked as if it had been pulled in ten different directions.

Lillian touched her cheekbone. "It's but a scratch."

"Do you hurt badly?"

"Shouldn't I be asking you that?" Her forced cheeriness fell short of the target.

Adela chuckled then cringed. "I guess so, but you sound, I don't know. I guess you sound . . . scared." Adela had wanted to say *angry* but decided against it.

"Shouldn't we be?"

"Not anymore. How did you get away from the crowd?"

"Nokose stepped in."

"See? He'll make sure nothing happens to us. God put him in our path for a reason."

Lillian huffed. "Like he protected you just now? You could've been killed."

"But she was not killed," Mama said thoughtfully, evenly.

Without reply, Lillian returned to her place in the corner, and Mama dabbed at the blood on Adela's dress. "We will have to ask if there is something else for you to wear."

A shadow fell across them as Nokose stepped into the cabin. He came to where Adela lay. "You are well?"

"Don't worry. I'll be as good as new in a couple of days, ready to be your humble slave." She feared her smile was more a grimace.

Nokose stopped the Indian woman on her way out the door, a bowl of water in her grasp. She wore a yellow blouse with billowing, cuffed sleeves. It was tucked into a vibrant blue skirt that reached to the tops of moccasins ornately beaded with bright blue and red flowers. Her black hair was swept up into a knot and tied atop her head with a blue ribbon. And, were those tattoo markings along her cheekbone?

"She is Singing Grass, my woman," he said. "Our children are with White Stone, their aunt and the sister of Singing Grass. She is childless and a widow. You will lodge with her." He lowered his voice to a discrete level, and Adela's droopy mind couldn't maintain his pace. "Bury the past. Singing Grass alone knows of my white mother. It is best."

His gaze paused at each of them until he'd received confirmation they understood, then he continued in a curt voice. "You will work for food and shelter. You will serve Singing Grass in her lodge and garden. You will learn our language and respect our ways. If you escape and are caught, you will be maimed."

Adela's lids drifted shut. The room hummed with unintelligible mummers until the word *Totka* yanked her from stupor.

Nokose hooked his thumb at the door. "He is the brother of Singing Grass. Our harmony is broken. He quits our lodge for distant clan, but he leaves his buffalo skins. These you will share in the winter lodge where White Stone sleeps."

She'd figured as much—the wallop Totka had given him outside the defeated fort had said it all. It pained her to know she was the cause, almost as much as the thought that he had once lived in this lodge but now would not.

Chapter 12

Big Summer Month (August)

The big summer moon was half gone before Totka believed himself strong enough to enter Singing Grass' courtyard without losing his judgment over Copper Woman.

He'd spent the last thirteen sleeps with distant Wolf Clan, alternately resting, raiding, burning white farms, and purging the woman from his system. When her image threatened to dominate his thoughts, he took to the woods and let his arrows fly. He visualized the packed-hay target as a blue coat, a white chest, a Jackson-loving Long Hair—anything to remind himself she was the enemy.

But with each nocked arrow, Old Grandfather's prophecy stung his ear. *A warrior's rank will bring you much pain.* And it had. Wasn't his leg proof?

Because he'd taken the prophecy to heart, from a child he'd disciplined himself through ritual **scratching** to endure any amount of pain in silence, but he'd not accounted for torment of the mind. How many winters had his heart bled for Leaping Waters? He had lost himself in the agony of yearning for a woman no longer his. Somehow, about the time he'd begun to heal from the loss of her, his moccasins had found a similar snare-strewn path to tread.

Never again, he vowed to himself. Never again.

And so, each morning during his routine dip in the long snake, he submerged until his need for air superseded his desire for Copper Woman, and when he surfaced and his mind colored in the memory of her—water lapping at her distended, bound hands—he dunked again.

All that only to round Singing Grass' winter house, spot the copper-haired daughter shucking maize and dressed as an eligible Muscogee—loose, white blouse tucked into a boldly colored skirt, hair unfettered—and lose himself. His mouth went slack, and he knew his stringent quarantine had been for nothing.

This was not the startled settler's daughter with plaited hair he'd pinned in the grasses, nor the bedraggled captive he'd left bleeding on his sister's table. This vision affirmed what he'd been denying—that she could become one of them, if she chose.

A hasty comparison with the bitter-eyed one beside her confirmed his assessment: the younger matched the diligent rhythm of Copper Woman's labor but lacked her confidence, ease of manner, and ability to scramble Totka's common sense.

Copper Woman uttered a small laugh at Fire Maker's antics, and her creamy skin glowed with life. The color of a maple leaf in autumn, her long wavy hair, held from her face by a blue sash, undulated in the soft breeze. Even through the pain that narrowed her eyes and drove her lower lip between her teeth, she radiated joy and contentment, and he wanted it for himself.

Like flint locking into place above a flash pan, ready to strike, a solid *click* reverberated in his mind—he wanted *her*. But wanting and having were not the same.

"I see the sunset hair still catches your eye."

Totka jerked at the sound of his sister's voice spoken from just behind. If she had been a Bluecoat, he would have a bayonet protruding from his ribs.

Singing Grass carried a basket of corn on her hip clear of her swollen abdomen. A teasing smile quirked her lips. "She's close to recovered. If you are humble, Nokose might forgive you for abandoning us. He might even trade her for a bargain, considering you are brothers in all but clan."

"If the meat I provide is considered abandonment, I will—"

At the sound of his voice, Copper Woman clipped her laughter short, her attention deserting Fire Maker for Totka. Her pleasure at noticing his presence was unmistakable: forthcoming yet prim, bold yet lacking guile—all lured him more powerfully than seductive poise.

"I will . . . " Totka continued, vaguely aware Singing Grass waited for the completion of his thought. "I will happily keep it . . . for myself."

A stiff forefinger speared him in the side. "I commend you, Brother, for finding your tongue and for growing a clever eye for a good woman. This one is gentle of speech but strong of spirit and worthy of my brother. No more hiding in the past. No more hiding at all." She clucked her tongue and waddled away.

He caught up to her, took the basket, and walked with her in direction of the corncrib where Copper Woman worked, more subdued than before.

"Stay upwind of the youngest." Singing Grass passed him a warning look. "The girl was not understanding about confinement to the **moon lodge** during her flow. I released her this morning on her word she'd completed her cycle, but there is a seed of doubt within me. I would not have you harmed." She kept a direct route, but Totka, to avoid polluting his war medicine, crossed the girl's path on the opposite side.

Singing Grass entered the crib's musty interior. "Speak to the elder sister. Befriend her. You must start somewhere."

"Should I start with an apology for allowing her lover to be scalped, or should I offer compensation for burning her home?"

"You jest." She held the corn sack while Totka poured. The grains hissed as they tumbled over top each other in the transfer. Floating dust tickled his nose and rode beams of sunlight that streamed between the slats in the wall.

"Only in part. I know nothing of her home, but we saw the man killed, she and I, and I did nothing to save him. I barely managed to shield her eyes from his scalping."

He let his gaze wander out the open door to where she worked, lip still clamped between her teeth, eyes squinted as though resisting pain. "Why have you put her to work so soon? She shouldn't be up."

"Gone thirteen sleeps with hardly a word for us, yet you know what is best for the woman five minutes beyond your return?"

"Who said I've returned?"

"That drunken look on your face speaks a thousand words." Singing Grass' droll expression extracted a snort of laughter from him that drew the captives' curiosity.

Ignoring the Bitter Eyes, Totka directed his good humor at Copper Woman who responded with a hint of a smile that released her lip and strung a thin cord across the gap that yawned between them.

"Could you have saved the man?" Singing Grass asked, severing the connection.

"Her lover? Maybe. Probably not."

"And if you could have?"

He met and returned Singing Grass' acute eye. "I would have left him to his fate." What did that say about him? *You are a heartless, cold-blooded warrior through and through.*

"As well you should. The man was your enemy. She will understand that."

"I am *her* enemy. She will understand nothing."

"The soldier she will forget. He is dead, and you are not."

True, although there was a good chance she would rather the situation immediately reversed. The younger sister certainly did. She told him so in every heated glance. How Singing Grass endured the girl's sullen nature was beyond him. "You do not mind having them here?" A firm shake of the sack settled the contents and allowed room for the remaining measures of grain.

"The women? We can hardly speak a word to each other, and

still, they are fine company. The Copper Woman is diligent to learn all she can of us. She is bright, and the mother smiles on her daughter's eagerness to speak our tongue. A most unusual thing to be so at ease. But good. Yes, good." Singing Grass paused while knotting the twine at the sack's mouth. "The youngest suffers, but the other two seem only grateful to be alive. There was another sister who did not survive the attack."

"And the father?"

"No one knows. He was not at the fort."

"So, there is a chance he lives."

"I suppose."

Totka absorbed the information with dismay. How much simpler the situation would be if they knew for certain the man was dead, that there was no one for Copper Woman to return to. "Until the women know otherwise, they will seek him. Try to run."

"They wouldn't leave their mother."

Totka studied the eldest, the strong one, how she watched her sister with what resembled a mother's care. "No, but Copper Woman would go alone. If she succeeds and finds their father, he will come at us with an army and a well-earned vengeance. If I survived his wrath, he would do the right thing and keep her away from me. The dark-eyed girl is too weak-minded to run, but we must watch the eldest. I would be grieved to put her in slave cords, or worse yet, maim her, but we cannot have her bringing the Long Guns to our doorstep." Was it a mere sixteen sleeps past he had slipped her his knife in the hopes she would do that very thing? At that point, she hadn't known from what village her captors hailed. It made all the difference.

"Consider this, Totka. She will likely not run, and he'll likely not take her back . . . if she is already yours."

He narrowed his lids at her. "What are you suggesting?"

A slow arch of her back protruded her belly and brought on a grimace. "Only that you need a wife, and the moment she is willing, you should not delay." She was right, of course.

Wed nor not, once Copper Woman had lain with him, the whites would consider her spoiled, and she would be left to him. "When did you become so crafty?" So audacious.

"When I saw my brother sinking again into his old, familiar mire." She landed two stinging smacks on his chest. "Will you come back to us? The children miss you."

Totka considered her request and cast a sidelong glance at the white sisters — the elder, alluring and untouchable; the younger, bitter and wary — and he knew coming back would bring trouble.

"Nokose was chosen to attend the Long Hairs' Council undercover and to report back," Singing Grass said.

Totka's brow wrinkled at her sudden shift in subject. "I know. He asked I go with him." An attempt at reconciliation, no doubt.

"And I ask that you do not. The women will need watching while Nokose is away. And protection. The chiefs and clan mothers were far too reluctant to let them live. Nokose dared not ask Beaver to adopt them. As it is, my husband has been warned that any wrongdoing on their part will fall on his own head. The People are not the least receptive to having whites among us." My, how times had changed.

To stay because of the captives would be to concede Totka's side of the argument, but had he not already done so by returning? Their strained relationship had long grown wearisome. Totka missed his brother. Wouldn't the most direct path to reconciliation be to take on the responsibility Nokose had requested of him at the start?

"Prepare bedding. I will stay."

He went out the door ahead of Singing Grass, passing so close to Copper Woman he could rake his fingers through her fiery hair if he took a notion. He didn't. "I do not want her working yet," he called behind him. "Send her back to my bearskins."

"Who are you to concern yourself?" Singing Grass replied, her playful tone absorbing the heat in her words. "The woman is not yours."

Totka flipped around and walked backwards several steps, his eye connecting with his sister's before settling on the captive in question.

Copper Woman, the fearless settler's daughter once again, gazed back at him in that unsettling way of hers that told him she knew what he said, what he thought, how she stirred him.

"Not mine *yet*, Sister."

Adela woke to a quiet courtyard save for Mama's humming, the squeak of reeds bending beneath her hand, and the irregular rhythm of Lillian beating a bearskin beyond Singing Grass' airy, wattle and daub lodge. Only her sister's billowing skirt was visible past Nokose's form leaning against the frame of the flapless door. He stared into the yard, pensive. A whisper of movement behind Adela betrayed Totka's presence.

Rather unusual for both to be around at this time of the day. Creek men and women, she'd noticed, kept to their separate roles and tasks quite stringently, not mingling during their day-to-day lives. Even so, she, Lillian, and Mama were rarely allowed out of sight of one or the other of these men.

No doubt Totka remained as he'd been before she'd laid down for a nap: on the opposite side of the cabin, straddling a bench at the rough-hewn trestle table, working a bone awl through a piece of hide. Since returning from parts unknown two days previous, the man had become a bur—albeit a bur lacking prickles. Toward her and her mother, he was neither prickly nor pleasant. He simply was. Lillian, he ignored. Avoided, even.

With the children, he came alive, but they weren't here, so he was quiet and studious. Dare she say . . . of her? It often seemed so; although, she rarely caught him in the act. Since she'd woken, she had yet to look his direction, but his eye was heavy on her.

Had he nothing to do outdoors? Was there no roof in need of

gabling? No pipe to smoke or beast to gut? Something, anything to free her of his uncomfortable scrutiny.

The afternoon shadows had lengthened considerably. How long had she slept? She breathed deeply, dreading the moment she must move and wake the monster gnawing at her brain. "Where is everyone?"

Mama's hand stilled over her basket making. "Singing Grass and White Stone took the children to play at the river." She graced Adela with a closed-mouth smile. "*Dormiste bien?*"

"I slept too well. The day's escaped me." On Totka's couch, Adela stretched her legs and gasped as the pain struck. When would it abate? Over the last two weeks, the dizziness had all but gone, but the lance in her temple persisted.

"Nonsense. You need your rest."

Nokose looked back at Mama. "Your youngest beats the bearskin as if to kill it again."

Mama chuckled. "Lillian is a passionate girl. She takes her work seriously."

"She imagines she beats a Red Stick." Nokose's statement lacked humor.

Adela guessed he wasn't too far off the mark, but it had been a short time since the attack, and Lillian was young—sixteen in September. She needed time to grieve and heal.

With care, Adela pushed herself into a sitting position.

Totka swung a leg over the bench as though to rise, but when she gentled her head against the wall behind her, he stayed where he was. The bench wobbled as he rested his elbows against his knees and resumed threading the hide, the lengthy rope of sinew dragging the dirt floor.

Nokose pulled a stool up next to Mama and lowered himself onto it, then cast an eye across the room before speaking. "Your song. I remember it from when I was a brave at your knee."

Did he not believe Totka would understand? Adela followed the trail Nokose's eye had taken, intending to make it a mere glance, but

Totka commandeered it, as he did every time she became absentminded with the direction of her gaze. This time, though, she didn't fight it but let it linger, curious to see his reaction to Mama's answer.

A wheeze whispered through each of Mama's exhales. "And still, *mi hijo,* you do not understand its meaning." The rebuke fell softly. "I have sung it to all my children—even Esperanza, sweet baby."

It wasn't often Mama spoke of Adela's half-sister, the one from Papa's first marriage. Mama had cared for the mestizo child until she'd died in the first year of life. Mention of the baby still brought her mother waves of sadness, but it did nothing for Totka.

His intense stare conveyed only that some part of Adela intrigued him—a meddlesome discovery. Satisfied he hadn't understood enough to grasp their connection to his brother-in-law, she peeled away from him.

"You are not still angry for losing the child?" Nokose asked.

Mama looked long and deep into Adela's eyes and shook her head. "Ah, no. How could I live with anger so long? No, no. It is no good for the health or the spirit. One must forgive."

Nokose harrumphed.

Adela changed the subject. "How did you convince the chief to let you keep us?"

"You are young and strong and will make good trade items. The both of you together might bring me a horse. A hog for sure." His boyish grin was charming but melted away too quickly. "When I leave for battle, your help will be welcome. I told them White Stone, who has no children, will have your mother's."

Mama dropped her reed. "You will give my baby to another woman?"

"So I told them," Nokose said. "But the war will end before the spring maize breaks the sod."

Adela rubbed her temple. "How can you know?"

"We are a brave and determined people, but we will fall to the pale faces and their weapons." His muted tone was heartrending.

165

"You will keep your baby."

As he spoke, Adela wondered whether the child Mama carried would live long enough for the issue to play out.

"The baby is . . . well?" Nokose's thoughts followed the same line.

Mama rested a hand on her belly. "I feel him move every day. He grows stronger, and I know he will live."

"He?"

"I asked my God for a boy," Mama said with a shrug, "and I want to believe He has finally given me one."

"Ah, yes. The God who watches the sparrow but hides while women and children are scalped."

"The One who has brought me to you to remind you He loves you still," Mama said just above a whisper.

"Ha! You are wrong, my white mother. He did not bring you to me. You live not by God's hand but by *mine*."

His vehemence and mockery stunned Adela. "It's the same, because it was His plan that you find us."

But Nokose had words only for her mother. "As it was His plan to have your eldest killed? As it was His plan to have my parents murdered before me? In exchange for a stack of pelts?"

Adela knew his story and the suffering he'd endured. Even through all these years, he'd held tight to his anger.

Adela grieved for him. And feared for Lillian.

Mama covered his hand with her own, tears trailing her cheeks. "We cannot understand God's ways, but if your parents had never died, if you had never wandered the forests, I would never have found you. You would never have found me and my daughters at the fort. And you might never have heard of the God of forgiveness and love. The God you still deny. The God who saved your life that day."

He withdrew his hand and stalked back to the door. Children's laughter, though distant, wafted through the opening and contrasted with the tension in the room.

Nokose let out a slow breath. "Forgive me. My heart still cries for blood."

After a long pause, Mama rose, went to him, and placed her hand on his back. "Do you still have nightmares about the trader?"

Nokose nodded.

"And you look for him still? To carry out **blood vengeance**?" Without it, the Creeks believed the souls of their loved ones would not reach their spirit world.

"With each new face I see."

Lips pressed into a grim line, Mama returned to her basket making. The squeak of reed against reed filled the room until Totka interrupted it with a question for Nokose. As Nokose answered, Adela picked up on several words, "Master of Breath" among them.

Totka listened and nodded, setting his red feather on a hypnotic oscillating path. Nokose's Muskogee was its usual lyrical self and contained none of the bite from moments before, but the slow downturn of Totka's lips said he didn't approve of what he heard.

Adela's mouth replicated his. If she stayed in Kossati long enough to learn the language, she would give Totka a scriptural version of God in place of whatever it was Nokose portrayed to him. In the meantime, she would strive for her life to give testimony of Him.

When Nokose finished, he moved to the table, rummaged through a basket of seasonal fruit, and selected an apple. "My white mother must eat. She is too thin." He fashioned a grim smile, placed the fruit in Mama's hand, and left them.

Wanting to stretch her legs, Adela considered asking her sister to accompany her on a short walk. She'd ventured out several times, but Lillian had yet to leave Singing Grass' property. Adela sympathized with her. Fear was a powerful force.

She rose and went to the door, swaying a little when the room tilted. She caught herself against the post and stepped into sunlight diluted by an ocean of fleecy white clouds.

Dust no longer puffed from the bearskin rug, yet Lillian continued to beat it with *thwack* upon vicious *thwack*. Sweat dampened her hair, and tears streaked her dirty face.

Adela would walk alone today. She missed Lillian as if she'd died alongside Elizabeth.

Elizabeth . . .

She swallowed tears, and wanting to be free of it all — the fear for Mama's life, the worry for Lillian's stability, the trepidation over her own future — she wandered past her sister and into the courtyard.

Three of Singing Grass' children, naked as shorn sheep and still glistening with river water, rounded the winter house at full speed, squealing and chattering and tumbling over each other in their haste to reach the puppies that rested in the shade of the hickory presiding over the yard. Fire Maker, a lad of six or seven and the eldest, tripped over Rain Child, a cherub-faced sister, and skidded chin-first across dirt.

Adela uttered a small cry of alarm, and Lillian stopped beating to stare.

Fire Maker, war contorting his little features, bounced to his feet and wielded his miniature blowgun like a tomahawk. He felled it across Rain Child's head. The girl's shriek rivaled Fire Maker's war whoop.

Instinct drove Adela toward the fray until Totka passed her. She halted while he continued several steps farther and planted his feet wide. "Totka Hayeta!"

The boy shot to attention, the blowgun falling from his fingers as rapidly as the guilt expanding his eyes. If Adela figured the child should wilt confronted with such a formidable vision as his uncle — arms crossed and silver bands straining at the swell of his muscles — she'd figured wrong.

Fire Maker cocked his bloody chin, stalked to Totka, and deposited the blowgun into the man's open palm.

Dress wet and face flushed with heat, Singing Grass waddled into the courtyard, shifting her youngest around her pregnant belly to the other hip. White Stone skirted her sister and called to Rain Child who ran to her, wailing, arms outstretched.

While the women clucked over the minor wound, Totka handed the blowgun right back with an abrupt command.

Backbone a ramrod, Fire Maker arranged his face into a picture of rebellion.

Adela wouldn't have thought it possible that in the span of a blink a man could become so coolly inflexible, so toweringly frightful. He repeated the order twice more, each time sterner and more near the boy.

Lillian gaped. "What is he saying to that poor child?"

"I have no idea," Adela said from beneath the hand that covered her mouth.

Setting his jaw, Fire Maker raised his knee and brought the reed down hard upon it.

At the dull *thump*, Adela blinked and jerked.

The effort flung the weapon out of the boy's hand, but Totka pointed a stiff arm at where it landed and dished out another order. The boy retrieved and tried again. Then again.

Adela's face scrunched into a wince as, lips twitching and squirming, Fire Maker beat his own leg red in an effort to break the blowgun. But he labored diligently and in silence like the unshrinking warrior he'd feigned to be. At last, it relented and broke in two with an awful *crack*.

It tumbled from his grasp and lay at his feet, its ends jagged and ugly. As broken as the instrument, he panted and slumped and offered his uncle a short, submissive line.

Totka collected the pieces, then dumped them into Fire Maker's trembling arms. After he said a few curt words, he ruffled the boy's hair, smiled grimly, and sent him on his way.

"Odious man. Smiling at his handiwork." Lillian yanked at the bearskin to remove it from the line, glaring at Totka who'd carried on to join his sisters.

"No, I think . . . he was proud of the way Fire Maker took the discipline."

"You *would* look for the good in it." Lillian bundled the skin and made for the lodge, tossing her words behind her. "But if you ask me, that right there is explanation enough for why they grow up to be savages."

Rain Child's tears became giggles as Totka tossed her into the air and swooped to catch her just before she hit the ground. The women gasped and scolded him, and Adela slid past them all, eager to reach the lane and put the unpleasant episode behind her. But some minutes later, not bothering with subtlety, Totka left Singing Grass' property and set out on Adela's path.

What could he want this time? There were no battling Red Sticks to fend off. Only swarms of gnats. She swatted at them. She was safe walking the lanes, wasn't she?

The scar forming on her forehead proved that at least one in Kossati resented her presence. Totka must be privy to something she was not.

The man loped to catch up—an easy feat considering her turtle pace and his lengthy stride, a stride that had pursued her once before.

Her scalp tingled at the recollection. He'd saved her life with his swift actions outside the fort, but that knowledge didn't prevent tension from scaling her spine in anticipation of his touch.

He didn't touch her, though, nor did he come alongside her. Several yards back, he slowed and maintained his distance. It had been his order that had sent her back to her pallet two days ago, so she fully expected him to curtail her exercise. Instead, he held back, lengthening the span between them, and she breathed easier.

His intention soon became clear: he would shadow her outside the lodge as well as in. Would she never again have a moment's privacy?

A slow, ten-minute walk from Singing Grass' lodge, they reached the junction where his quiet lane met with the road that had carried them into the village from the warpath. Up till now, this intersection had been her self-imposed boundary, but emboldened by Totka lagging three steps behind, she set upon the main thoroughfare, choosing to delve deeper into the town as opposed to retracing her steps out of it.

Foot traffic increased, and Totka closed in, but the villagers, while curious, didn't seem to mind her bold foray. How much that had to do with her oversized shadow she could only guess.

Her bare feet hissed along the stinging-hot, dusty lane until the crooked road broadened into an expansive clearing. It housed several fields as well as the council square, which sat nearest her on a mound, its fire crackling hot and its four rectangular sheds opening to the center. Their benches were dotted with men whose laughter ebbed when they noticed her. Her gait faltered at their dark expressions, then stopped altogether at the sight of the crimson pole at the square's far end. Too late, she turned her head from the scalps adorning it.

Her stomach turned, and the ground tilted, and of their own accord, her legs went into reverse until her back collided with a palisade. When hands grasped her shoulders, her head cleared enough to realize it was Totka she'd backed into.

He spun her around him and nudged her in the direction she'd come.

Futilely blinking away the gore that flashed before her mind's eye and staving off a savage ache in her head, she floundered at obedience. The road stretched out before her long and steep. She hadn't noticed the incline on her way down.

The sun emerged with stinging strength, and suddenly, the heat became unbearable, the walk exhausting, the environment alarming. But she wouldn't show faintness of spirit, nor would she tremble before this man. Praying for strength, both mental and physical, she placed one foot before the other and vowed to herself that somehow, no matter how long it took, she would get her sister and mother out of this place.

Nokose and Singing Grass had done well by them. More than well.

But they couldn't stay here. If Lillian laid eyes on that pole, all their efforts to bring her to a place of healing would be undone.

A glimmer to her left drew her gaze down a narrow side path that ended at a tree-studded field overlooking the river.

171

Totka went around her and entered the blue shadows outlining the first lodge of the lane. He stopped and looked back at her, expectant. The idea of willfully following him nettled her conscious. Why should she go with this Red Stick anywhere unless constrained to do so? On second thought, why *shouldn't* she?

The man had saved her life, not once but twice. He'd rescued her from a mob, carried her to sanctuary, and stood by her until she'd woken.

He flicked his fingers toward himself once before proceeding down the lane.

Lips quirked to the side, she muttered, "Rather confident of yourself, aren't you, Red Stick?" But with a sigh, she accepted his invitation.

The lane broke on a gentle slope carpeted by clumps of blue-green love grass, their graceful heads bending and rippling in the wind that swept up from the valley below. She waded through it and joined Totka who stood on the brink of a bluff that fell sharply to the Coosa River. It twinkled red and orange in the gloaming.

Below, several women collected stiff clothes that had been drying on boulders ensconced along the sandy shore very near a row of beached dugout vessels.

Skirt and hair snapping in the wind, she peered at the river longingly, envious of its freedom, envious that the water rushing before her now would soon pass within an hour's walk of her home, of Papa. If their lives hadn't been upended, what would he be doing now?

Coming in for dinner. Heading to the well to wash away the day's labor. Lillian would fling herself at him, hording his embrace; Elizabeth would point out his dirty fingernails, then forgive him the transgression; Adela would wait her turn to kiss his whiskered cheek. Then, Papa would pluck an apple from his pocket, toss it her way, and ask her to fill a basket with him after dinner.

And she would say yes. She always said yes. A smile warmed her insides and tugged at her cheeks.

She considered the dugouts and the western horizon where the Coosa eventually emptied into the Alabama. How many days would it take to paddle the distance? And how many hours' head start would she need to avoid a maiming? Far more than this warrior would ever give her.

He shifted beside her, tapped her arm.

She collected her whipping hair into her fist to clear her view of him.

His height, more pronounced with his unexpected nearness, compelled her to look up. However, it wasn't his eyes he wished her to see but the red-splotched peach encircled by his hand.

"For me?" She laid a finger against her chest.

Although he made no response, the corners of his lips tipped upward.

Tentatively, she accepted the fruit and, unable to resist, rubbed its velvet against her lips, closed her eyes, and inhaled. Its delicate aroma sweetened the back of her throat and told her that life could be beautiful again.

Ironic that a Red Stick was responsible for the reminder.

Heat scorched her eyes as tears surfaced. Unable to speak, she thanked Totka with a smile, then cupped the fruit in both palms and tucked it under her chin.

It was too precious to eat just yet.

Chapter 13

With a basket shelved on her hip, Adela navigated the muddy ground on her way to the fire pit outside the winter house and, out of habit, skimmed the courtyard for Totka. Her gaze bounced over the cookhouse, lingered at the storehouse and corncrib, bypassed the garden plot, and came to rest on the gap between the winter house and the adjoining courtyard, which exposed the lane leading to the town's center. He must not have returned yet from the river and his ritual cleansing.

They all **went to water** — the entire village — together in the early morning, always at dawn and always before breaking their fast: to cleanse themselves in their Earth Mother's lifeblood, the water. Adela was discovering that much of Creek ceremony revolved around ridding oneself of pollution of the mind and spirit. It was a continual effort.

At break of day, she had accompanied Singing Grass and White Stone to the Coosa for the first time. Stripped to her skin she'd plunged and prayed to her own God, then settled onto a boulder to watch crimson waves of sunlight lap at the piney hills.

God had given her yet another day of life — twenty-one more than she'd thought she would have when she fled, choking, from the Mims' burning home. Despite the sometimes confusing and fearsome practices of this people, and her grief for all she'd lost, Adela would never stop thanking God for directing Nokose across their path and sparing their lives.

Nokose had left several days ago—for where, she didn't care to know. It was the second time he'd donned weapons and sobriety, then taken his leave before dawn. He'd left instructions for them to go to Totka with any problems. No such issues had arisen, but if one did, she wouldn't have far to go.

Totka slept in Singing Grass' lodge, and when he wasn't hunting or fishing or at the council square, he was nearby. His demeanor toward her remained as rigid and expressionless as ever, his perusal equally thorough and constant. She felt exposed under it and wished he would speak to her instead of trail her or stare from a distance, thinking only God knew what.

And yet, though the man set her nerves on edge, his presence had become a stabilizing element she sorely needed. Was it his self-assured poise? His carriage was that of a man who knew what he wanted and didn't intend to let anyone or anything get in his way.

Perhaps it was the loyalty he exuded toward those under his care. The children perceived it, so that around him they were more relaxed, more carefree, less affected by the apprehension that tended to percolate in their parents.

Either way, constant proximity had led to a startling desire to speak his language so she might unlock the mystery that he was. What prompted a Red Stick to sheath his scalping knife in favor of saving a dying enemy . . . then offer her a peach?

She rested her basket next to the fire on which sat an oversized clay pot filled with simmering water. Lillian joined her, and together, they scooped handfuls of hickory nuts from the basket and pounded them into large pieces on a stone. When the basket was empty, they whisked the nuts into the pot. Adela brushed off her hands and sat on a stool to wait for oil to rise. Her mouth watered in anticipation of the delicate flavor this hickory milk would add to White Stone's corn pones and venison stew.

Inhaling the crisp air, Adela closed her eyes and let the earth's clean fragrance saturate her senses. Soaked earth, decaying leaves, and a hint of hickory smoke—there was nothing like it.

The small family garden had become a playground for Fire Maker as he cackled and chased squawking chickens, his long black hair all a riot. From the sidelines, Rain Child, hands on hips, took him to task while Speaks Sweetly, the littlest, cuddled a fuzzy chick, oblivious to her siblings' antics.

"Aren't they precious?" Adela asked.

Lillian squinted across the way. "Creek children do have an endearing quality, but pups soon grow into wolves."

Adela took her sister's hand and gave it a squeeze, but Lillian distanced herself.

"Nokose saved us, and I'm thankful," Lillian said, eyes misting. "I really am, but I can hardly think straight for wondering what he's doing this very minute." Her doe-eyes darted toward the road he'd taken, as though envisioning the scene. "Which settler's farm will he raid? Do we know them? Or is he battling our soldiers? Whose scalp will he bring back?"

Singing Grass poked her head out the door and called to the children. Fire Maker plucked Speaks Sweetly out of the dirt, and they all scampered indoors, leaving the yard empty and quiet and giving Adela a moment to search for an answer.

The truth was, she had none. It was impossible to reconcile her own feelings of gratitude toward Nokose and Totka with the horrors that originated, in part, by their hand.

Adela let her arms fall limp to her sides. "They're just desperate, Lilly. Desperate to retain their land and their traditions. It's become harder and harder for them to provide for their families. If they don't defend what's theirs it *will* be taken from them."

"Are you excusing them?" Her voice squeaked with disbelief. "Are you telling me you aren't bothered by the thought of where Nokose goes and what he does when he gets there?"

"Of course not! Never. And yes, it does bother me a great deal. I meant only that they do what they think is best for their own survival, Nokose included. How could they not?"

In the span of a breath, water filled Lillian's eyes and cascaded over her delicate cheekbones. "So, Lucy's death and Mrs. Bailey's and little Micah's and Beth's" — her voice cracked — "and the hundreds of others, their deaths were all essential to the survival of Creek traditions?"

Adela sighed and moved the paddle through the simmering water. "No. I don't pretend to know their ways, but I do know that the Creeks have different views on war and how it should be carried out." To the Creeks, every enemy regardless of age or gender must die. It was their way. It had always been their way. Nokose was one of the few exceptions. "But every Anglo who's ever cut his plow through Creek soil has been aware of that. They've known the risks. *We* knew the risk of living on their land."

Head tilted in horrified wonder, Lillian sniffled and backed away. "I can't speak of this with you."

"Please, don't say that." Adela reached out, but Lillian raised her hands to ward off the approach and kept moving backward.

"Stay," Adela said. "Talk to me. We'll get through this. Together. I know I'm clumsy, and I don't always say the right thing, but—"

"You went with them this morning, didn't you?" Quiet accusation filled her sister's question. "To the river."

She felt betrayed?

"I—I want to understand them, to know what drives them to do what they do. Think of the opportunity, Lillian. If we can come to grasp their belief system, we might be able to lead them to an understanding of Christ."

As she spoke, Lillian's eyes hardened into bone-tipped spears. "I don't plan to stay around long enough to lead them *anywhere*." She spun and, arms swinging, marched to the house.

Adela's breath caught. If anyone heard Lillian and understood . . . A glance of her surroundings erased her anxiety. The yard was barren. But she would have to warn to her sister to guard her tongue. Adela wouldn't put it past Totka to tie either of them to the slave post in the council square if it meant preventing their escape while Nokose was away.

He'd proven his loyalty to their survival, but he was a man with an iron will and a heightened sense of honor. Besides, no Creek in his right mind would allow a captured enemy to escape in time of war.

No, Lillian mustn't speak of escape so blithely, so carelessly. But Adela understood the draw. She'd nurtured the idea of waking on a moonless night and slipping a dugout into the Coosa's swift waters.

Adela murmured a prayer for wisdom. "Lord, preserve Lillian. Preserve us all." Especially Papa. If he still lived, he would be on a warpath of his own making.

The wind stirred, blowing the first of autumn's fallen leaves into mini whirlwinds about her feet. It swept into the trees, brushing water off the leaves and onto her face.

Kossati had just been drenched, but the mass of storm clouds heading south was still heavy with rain. It would reach Tensaw before noon.

Tensaw. Home . . .

She released another sigh, stretched her legs, and wiggled her toes to free them of the mud they'd collected. Only minutes had passed when fingers of awareness tickled the back of her neck.

Forging confidence, she twisted smoothly, deliberately and looked behind her.

Totka leaned against Singing Grass' lodge, shoulder against the split-cypress clapboard. His hair, black and glossy, hung wet about his neck, and the wind flattened his loose blue shirt so that it appeared pasted to his damp chest. The sleeves were rolled to above his elbows, and those ever-present silver bands hugged his bronze forearms.

She knew those arms, the feel of their smooth, muscled surface. Although why she should recall that detail as this moment eluded her.

Something was off. He'd arrived at his post later than expected, and the bold, unhurried manner in which he studied her was new.

Usually, he combined a discrete watch with a task that kept his hands busy—dying fletching for his arrows, sewing moccasins for Mama, and most recently, fashioning thistledown darts for the replacement blowgun he and Fire Maker were crafting.

Not so this morning.

He studied her without qualm—much the way he had in the meadow. This time, at least, distance lessened the burn of his blatant scrutiny.

Adela had confirmed that she belonged to Nokose. It seemed logical, then, that she fall under his guardianship, but when Totka behaved as he did now, she sensed he included her, along with his sisters and her children, under the umbrella of his safekeeping. She told herself it was the residual effects of his provision during the journey to Kossati that made her feel it, but in an obscure corner of her heart—a stubborn place that refused to be destroyed—she suspected that her earlier deduction was more on target. Nokose, to alleviate his own burden, had either consigned her to his brother-in-law's care or had given her to him outright.

It made no sense for Nokose to promise her future to another man, but the evidence continued to prove otherwise, for the men's interaction with her was not equal to that of her mother and sister: Nokose overlooked her, while Totka focused on little else.

Every day she chose again to trust that Nokose's deep fondness for his white mother would lead him wisely regarding her daughters. But if Adela trusted Nokose, why did her chest tighten with anxiety? She pressed the heel of her hand against her breastbone and released a slow breath to ease the tension. She pitched Totka a tremulous smile, aiming for the perfect balance of subservience and cordiality, and went back to stirring the pot.

After some minutes, she cast a subtle glance back to where he stood, but he was gone. She sucked in a breath, relieved the awkward moment had passed, while oddly disturbed it hadn't developed into something more. They couldn't continue in this vein for long. Either he would address her and make his position in her life known, or she would come undone.

Behind her, the animal skin covering the cabin's entryway slapped against the doorposts. The whisper of footsteps soon followed and sent her pulse into a frantic rhythm: there was no mistaking that uneven tread.

Determined to put on a brave front, she stood, faced him, and—steeling herself against those trenchant eyes and their unnerving effect—dropped into a neat curtsy.

The man came to a stop before her, sieve in one hand, clay vessel in the other. Had he taken them from Lillian? Where *was* her sister?

Adela leaned to the side to see around him, but the yard was still deserted.

Face a mask, he extended the sieve, and she took it.

"Maddo," she said, purposeful in her use of his language to thank him. "*Likas?*" Motioning to the stool behind her, she invited him to sit. If he joined her, she would use the opportunity to practice her newly acquired Muskogee.

His brows arched gently, stretching the thin, nearly invisible scar that slanted across his cheekbone, but he didn't accept her offer. Had she chosen the wrong word? Or maybe she'd broken a social rule?

He spoke slow and deliberate, enunciating each word, his eyes migrating to her forehead.

Adela sorted out one term she understood and forked fingers through the hair at her temple. "*Eka?*" Was there something wrong with her hair? Wind-blown debris caught in it?

A brisk wag of his head said she'd misunderstood, but instead of repeating the statement, he drew to within an arm's reach and continued his scrutiny. Whatever he was looking for, she wished he would find it.

Flustered, yet fearful of insulting him again by reacting poorly, she focused on the red feather quivering against his hair, and endured. But when she felt the touch of his hand against her hair, she flinched, her entire body careening backward, her foot becoming entangled in the stool. The horizon went askew, and she tipped toward the boiling kettle.

Totka fisted the blouse at her waist and yanked her upright, overcorrecting her posture, and flinging her against him. The sieve clattered to the ground, and hickory milk from the vessel in his hand sloshed over the top and showered them both.

Stunned, she gazed up at him, mouth agape. Nut oil seeped into the crack of her lips, and she licked it away.

It spotted his shirt sleeve and skidded down his cheek. He blinked it from his lashes and said something she didn't understand. His tone was even, but for all she knew, he could be cursing her.

"I'm sorry. I didn't intend—" She began in English, distracted by his nearness, by the hand still clutching her blouse. "I mean, you startled me and—" Where was that Muskogee she'd been rehearsing? At a loss, she heaved a breath and settled on the one word she was sure of. "Maddo."

She funneled indebtedness into her eyes, lifted them to his, and repeated her thanks. "Maddo." Thank you—for catching her, for staunching the flow of her blood, for shielding her from the heat of the Red Sticks' wrath.

The taut fabric at her side loosened as he released her.

In an instinctive, self-protective measure, she put a cushion of space between them, though she may as well have stayed put because he canceled it out with a reciprocating step. When he lifted his hand, he sought permission to touch her by pausing and offering a questioning look.

He'd had many opportunities to harm her yet hadn't, so she gave him license to do as he pleased by dropping her gaze and maintaining her position.

He returned his hand to where it had been moments ago—at the side of her face—and with the back of it, he brushed her hair away in a motion so tender it gave her heart a jolt and contradicted every apprehension she clung to.

Just when she felt he would never make another move, he tipped her head to the side, ran a light finger over the zigzag of tender flesh at her hairline, and gave an abrupt nod.

That was what he'd wanted? To inspect the progress of her healing?

He tapped the side of her head, one corner of his mouth lifting. "Eka."

"Ah. Eka is *head*. Not hair." She knew that. If she hadn't been so addled . . .

Taking a strand of her hair, he ran it between his fingers, and the Muskogee word for *hair* popped to her tongue. "*Ekaesse.*" They spoke at the same instant.

She gave a nervous, airy laugh, and he broke into the first true smile she'd seen him wear. His smooth skin folded into shallow grooves at each corner of his mouth, molding the angular contours of his face into a mesmerizing blend of beauty and savagery; the feather that fluttered against the tattoo scrolling up his neck added the touch of ferocity.

"*Apeleta,*" she tried for more.

He chuckled, and the sound was a cool dip in the Coosa on a hot summer's day. A doubtful look crossed his face. "Smile?"

Delighted by his use of English, Adela surprised herself by laughing again. "Smile. Yes, that's right."

But the pleasurable moment passed when his gaze drifted from her eyes. With it, he caressed her mouth, then moved to her throat and back to her mouth.

Her chest rose sharply and held. Ill-timed, hickory oil dribbled from her hair onto the bridge of her nose where it made a trail to the tip.

As bold as brewed chicory, Totka caught the droplet on his knuckle, then sucked it off the joint, that familiar aura returning — the one that stated he knew what he wanted and he intended to get it.

With that look, she became frightfully certain of two things: his days of watching from a distance were over, and her wound wasn't the only part of her he wished to inspect.

"Woman. Beautiful." He deposited the words on her like a man notching a tree for harvesting, and she felt the etching clear to her bones.

Heat rushed her. Before he could make the declaration a triad and tack *mine* onto the end, she whirled back to the kettle, fumbled for the wooden paddle, and whipped it through the simmering liquid.

Oil coated the water's bubbling surface. She needed the sieve from the ground behind her, but she would affix roots to the earth before voluntarily facing him again. Surely, he would perceive he'd crossed a line and leave soon. She could wait him out.

But the man wasn't to be sloughed off. He edged up next to her, the utensil in his grasp. Instead of passing it to her, he laid a hand on her shoulder and nudged her around.

At his touch, her shoulders bunched and her cheeks flamed. She kept her eyes downcast and prayed he would think the heat of the fire was the cause.

Muskogee poured from him.

She shook her head, not having recognized any of it.

He repeated, slower this time, and she understood one key word.

"Friend?" she whispered.

"Friend." He rapped his breastbone. The remark was simple enough, but the implications read in the undercurrents of those sable eyes said he wanted more. A noble goal for a man with the power to take what he wanted. An ambitious goal for a man with his reputation.

He'd had equal share in the slaughter at Fort Mims. She'd looked long and hard at the scalps he'd lifted. They'd hung just there at eye level, at his hipbone, right where the knot of his sash now rested.

Her mind screamed for retreat, but when her foot slid backward, he captured her hand, and flattened it against his breast—the same that had been spattered with gore.

Adela jerked, but he held on.

"Friend," he repeated, pressing harder.

The fire crackled. The wind shifted, and the stench of smoke filled her senses. Her eyes flicked to his face, and for the span of a breath it was streaked with paint and blood. She crammed her lids shut and focused on the thrum of each of his heartbeats.

He was a man. Same as any other. Except that he was supposed to be the enemy. Not a friend. But hadn't she befriended Nokose? And he'd taken lives, same as Totka.

A frown bent her lips. Nokose's friendship didn't have strings attached; his sights weren't set on . . . whatever it was Totka had in mind.

Adela had heard of white women forced to marry their Indian captors. If she denied Totka his attempt at an amicable relationship, would it turn out less graciously for her in the end? Would it be better to avoid his displeasure and accept his friendship?

She wanted to, but she dared not. Not now that she suspected his end goal. Even if she felt strangely drawn to the man, despite her aversion to what he'd done, he didn't hold her spiritual beliefs. And as fastidiously as he held to his faith, she held to hers, and she'd pledged not marry outside it. Besides, Nokose had assured them the war would be over before Mama delivered. At which point, Adela would be home where she belonged, cultivating friendships with her own people.

With that thought, she wrestled her hand free and, though some strange part of her yearned to know this warrior better, she backed up a step.

For an instant, injury filled his eyes.

Adela lamented it, but she wasn't prepared to apologize. She couldn't. Not anymore. Not after that desirous look he'd given her.

"Go wash." Dignity regained, he brandished a finger at her hair and clothing, then gave her his back and ran the sieve over the water's surface.

When Adela complied, she did so with a satisfied sigh—he had spoken in Muskogee, and she had understood.

Movement from the cabin drew her attention. Lillian stood in the doorway. How much had she seen?

As Adela drew near the house, she whisked her oily hair out of her face and straightened her twisted skirt.

Shadows hid Lillian's face, but there was no hiding the tension in her voice. "We'd all benefit more if you'd occupy your mind devising a way for us to escape instead of befriending the savages."

"I'm trying, Lilly, but we would need many hours' advantage, and I don't know when we'll find that. Maybe next time Nokose and the war party leave, *he* will go too," she spoke softly and tipped her head Totka's direction. "Until they're both gone, we can't risk it."

As if a shade lifted, Lillian stepped into the sunlight and smiled. "Come inside. I'll help you out of your clothes."

Chapter 14

Little Chestnut Month (September)

The sigh of bare feet against dirt yanked Totka from sleep. His eyes popped open in time to see Fire Maker's backside disappearing through the doorway into the night.

The boy let the hide smack against the post. His stealth lacked training.

Freeing the handle of his blade, Totka relaxed back onto his couch. After a long while, when Fire Maker had not returned, Totka kicked off his blanket. His nephew was either ill or up to no good, and since Nokose was due to set out on the warpath in the morning and had spent the last four nights in fasting and dance at the Warriors' House, Totka went in search of his son.

After a hasty scan of the privy, courtyard, and cookhouse, Totka set his eyes upon the winter lodge. Fire Maker had become fond of Copper Woman, dogging her heels almost as faithfully at Totka—an exasperating yet endearing practice. Although, what business he might have in the winter lodge in the black of night eluded Totka.

Still, he must check.

On the way, he tracked the rumble of White Stone's snoring. How Copper Woman got any sleep, he didn't know. Regardless, she always looked well rested and—he smiled—beautiful.

But then, from the first, there had never been a day she had *not* been beautiful to him, even when bloody and battered. Perhaps during that time, it had been her warrior's spirit that had caught his eye and tied slave cords about his heart.

He hesitated outside the larger cylindrical dwelling, fully aware that tomorrow he would have to maintain decorum while juggling her nearness and the image of her asleep on his bearskin. After a fortifying breath, he pushed aside the animal skin covering the doorway and stepped inside. The three-quarters moon did fine work illuminating the meager interior. Against the western curve was White Stone's narrow couch, occupied by her expansive figure. No room for even a boy. From the east wall, Totka's bearskins extended out along the ground. Three forms rested atop them.

And curled against one, another smaller shadow.

Fire Maker. The little weasel.

If Totka had to hazard a bet, he would lay next season's buckskins on Copper Woman being the one his nephew had chosen to sleep beside. What male wouldn't if given the liberty? Even Fire Maker, as young as he was, knew a fine woman when he saw one.

Soundlessly, Totka came alongside the pair.

The pale hair blanketing the woman's bare arm identified her. Copper Woman reclined on her side, chest to Fire Maker's back, knees and arm curled around him.

Fire Maker's snuffled breathing indicated he was already hunting dreams, and Totka couldn't decide if he should be moved by the scene or violently envious.

Copper Woman's face pointed at Totka—though whether she slept or gazed at him in wide-eyed shock was impossible to decipher. The not knowing unnerved him enough to drop him into a crouched position to note whether her head tracked his descent.

It did.

A pang of want shot through his chest, consuming him so instantly and completely that he took no notice of his hand until the cool of her arm penetrated the calluses on his fingers.

She lay as still as before, unperturbed, her flesh relaxed beneath his hand, as if she'd anticipated his move and found it fitting. But why should she not? The moon had completed a full cycle and a half since that morning by the fire pit when she'd cringed at his touch and fled. That had been the day it had dawned on him there would be no winning her from a distance. He'd spent every idle moment with her since, resolved to earn her trust.

In all that time, he'd kept his hands to himself.

But tonight, he indulged and traced the length of her arm. Was the gooseflesh due to the cold or in response to him? The answer lay in her frigid fingers. He caged them inside his warmer palm. Why did she have no cover? Little chestnut moon nights called for it. Had White Stone provided none? He glanced around, but his search was cut short by the reciprocating squeeze of Copper Woman's grip.

It was a sign, his heart told him, that she returned his affection.

It is nothing, he admonished his misguided thoughts. Only a friendly response same as either of his sisters would give. The aching throb in his chest, however, didn't correspond to that of a sibling's affection, nor did the crazed notion to cull Fire Maker from the picture and fill the gap with himself.

Totka clenched his jaw. He shouldn't be in this place. His will was weakening.

Fire Maker loosed a jagged sigh, and Totka loosed the woman. He would remove the boy, then fetch them a blanket and —

Copper Woman reached for him, and when he retook possession of her hand, she pulled him closer to whisper, "There is no harm done. Leave him. Please."

Totka filled his senses with the poignant scene and cursed his feeble will.

He should yank the boy to his feet and chide him all the way to his pallet. But he wouldn't. He would leave and not look back. He wouldn't even return with a blanket. Morning would come soon enough, and she had the little weasel to keep her warm.

Totka stood and told himself to return to his couch and study the art of sleep. So he did.

Except morning did *not* come soon enough, and when it did, he rose in a foul mood and was a poor example of a brother as he sent Nokose off to battle. Totka himself would go if not for tomorrow's ceremony in which he would receive honors. Nokose would miss the event, but war was a fickle woman, ordering man about on a whim.

By the time Totka had gone to water and broken his fast, the sun's lowermost edge was leaving the horizon.

Singing Grass left for the communal garden with Copper Woman and the children, creating an unnatural hush in the summerhouse. He was pulling out his tools to finish the season's last pair of moccasins when Fire Maker trotted in, hair amok and eyes perky. Was he just now waking? He'd missed going to water with the women.

Totka tossed his awl onto the table and dispensed a wry smile. "Did you rest well, Nephew?"

"I did not." He climbed onto the bench and before his backside settled was using the awl to bore a hole into the tabletop.

Totka plucked it from him and tapped his skull with the handle. "I cannot imagine why."

"I dreamed that the horned **tie-snake** ensnared me about the foot when I went to water," Fire Maker said, rubbing his head and seeming not the least bit perturbed that he'd missed the ritual that very dawn. "It dragged me down to the bottom where it was dark and cold. When I woke, I was afr—" He hedged, seeking a way around the shameful word *afraid*. "Sleep would not return."

"And in whose pallet did you seek comfort?"

Fire Maker gaped at him, a beady-eyed rabbit stunned into inaction.

"You think I do not know when you come and go and where your naughty feet take you?"

"I only went to Copper Woman."

"And why would you not go to your mother?"

"Because the baby makes her fat and steals her rest, and I would not add to her weariness and wake her."

Moments such as these, when the boy showed insight and wisdom and generosity, gave Totka hope he wasn't completely failing his nephew.

White Stone bustled into the lodge, followed by Bitter Eyes whose arms were laden with blankets.

Adequate use of the distraction was not lost on Fire Maker. He stroked the soft buckskin of the completed moccasin. "We are almost done. Copper Woman will be pleased." If he thought to use the woman's name to distract Totka from his misdeed, he succeeded.

Totka began the final stitching of the other moccasin and let his mind wander to several days ago, to the long snake and Copper Woman in that flimsy under-dress, holding Singing Grass' hand and splashing, both of them giggling like girls in braids. His skin had crackled with heat. As it did now.

It had been the first time he'd accompanied them to the river for an afternoon swim, and it would be the last. A man deprived had better uses of his time than torment.

Such as teaching the woman to communicate. And he had. Under his tutelage, her understanding of the Muskogee language flourished, and alongside it an inevitable friendship, despite her initial repulsion.

In their lessons, they'd covered many topics, from the creation of Earth Mother to the sacred number four; from those who shared a fragment of the creative force *Ibofanga* — plants, animals, man — to the necessity of hardening a boy to pain in preparation for war and possible torture.

At the close of each day, she was more Muscogee than the evening before. More his. But it was slow progress, understandably slow, aggravatingly slow.

Singing Grass had urged Totka to pursue Copper Woman, but she hadn't warned him how difficult it would be.

From time to time, fear surged in the woman's eyes, and he watched, helpless, as she relived whatever episodes haunted her. The flashbacks had yet to conquer her, but their existence was enough to keep her just beyond his reach. That, and the fact he'd had a hand in creating them.

And so, sleep after sleep, as time slipped past at an alarming rate, he watched fear and trust wrestle within her. But trust was winning out — last night was proof.

Trust and forgiveness. The two quagmires she must traverse.

A muted *thump* sounded as Bitter Eyes opened her arms over Singing Grass' couch.

"Pawa, *Pawa*." Fire Maker nudged him hard. "May I tie the knots? I have been practicing."

Totka blinked at his nephew who waggled a strand of knotted sinew before his nose.

"Look how I have tied this knot," the boy said.

"It's a fine knot. Now, tell me why you would go to Copper Woman in the night."

White Stone's head whipped around to gawk at them, and Fire Maker's thin shoulders jerked with a shrug as though sleeping with the woman were an everyday affair. "Copper Woman listens. I told her the dream meant I would die, but she said it did not. She whispered to her Creator called Jesus, and then she blessed me, and then my fear left." His eyes bulged with the admittance of his fear. He hurried on. "I slept and did not wake until Aunt stopped snoring."

White Stone grunted, and Totka withheld a grin. "He hides well beneath a blanket," she said. "I never saw him."

"And where did you find a blanket?" Totka asked the boy. He better not have taken it from the white mother.

"The Bitter Eyes woke and gave me hers."

Totka eyed the girl as she stepped outdoors, her face tight with subdued hostility. So, she had a tender place after all. Not that it would induce him to trust her.

"Can you put a knot here?" Totka passed the moccasin to the boy and half-watched the child's clumsy efforts. His mind was still hooked on the idea of Copper Woman petitioning the spirits on behalf of his nephew. They had spoken of her god-man, and Totka had witnessed her in prayer — both silent and voiced.

She was a woman with great sensitivity to the spirit world, and it pleased him, but her Creator was that of the whites and did not belong under a Muscogee roof. Her invocations, however, had soothed his nephew, and Totka could find no fault in that. He would not forbid her.

"They are beautifully made," Fire Maker said when he had tied the last knot. "Copper Woman will like them."

"We've done good work, and because you helped, you may give them to her."

"But not today." White Stone's shrill voice gave the boy a start. "Not until the first frost. She will have no need of them until then. Unless she plans to make a long journey south." She bestowed Totka a pointed, brow-arching look.

White Stone, for all her misguided fears, had struck dead center this time. Unshod, Copper Woman would be an easy catch should she run. Providing protection for her feet was equivalent to handing her keys to her shackles. Thinking of her in such a way was a bitter herb on his tongue, but friendship aside, she was still a captive who oftentimes looked upon the Coosa with longing. And he was still a warrior with the responsibility to keep his people safe.

White Stone screwed her lips. "Except for the harm it would bring to Nokose, I would encourage that trek."

"But Copper Woman is not going on a journey, Aunt."

"It is for your pawa to decide." White Stone brushed her dangling, unkempt hair out of her eyes and knelt to roll up the children's sleeping mat. As a widow, she wouldn't go to water for another two autumn harvests.

"Give the moccasins to me." Totka held out his hand. He would do nothing to aid the woman in foolish notions of escape.

The boy hugged them to himself. "But she is kind to me, and I have nothing to give her. Today, Pawa. *Today.*"

"When the frost comes and not one moment sooner. Put them in my hand and go to water."

With a pout, Fire Maker relinquished the moccasins. "Of all Father's captives, I favor her most. Same as you, is that not so?"

Totka felt his sister's inquisitive gaze. He shrugged. "Everyone favors the copper-haired daughter."

"But you favor her as Father favors Mother." The boy was too perceptive. He would be prattling to the woman herself before long, if he hadn't already.

Totka busied himself storing his tools, then slipped the moccasins into the darkness beneath his couch. "You are but a boy. What a man thinks of a woman is not your concern."

"She will need a lodge."

"The woman needs nothing," he snapped and plucked his sharpening stone from where it soaked in a small vessel of water. "Did I not tell you to go to water?" He plunked down on the bench, rattling it and jostling his nephew.

Fire Maker huffed. "Do you not want her because she's a captive?" Did the hinge of the boy's jaw never lock?

White Stone shoved the rolled mats against the wall and spun on the boy. "Enough, Fire Maker! When he is ready, your pawa will bind himself to a good Muscogee girl, not a weak-minded slave who can bring nothing but trouble."

Totka withdrew his hunting knife from the sheath at his side and with a fierce swipe ground the stone against its edge. "She is not weak-minded, and I will bind myself to whomever I please." He glared first at White Stone, then at Fire Maker and directed the tip of his blade at the door. "Go."

The only parts of Fire Maker that moved were his lowering brow and his firming lips. "Tall Bull does not mind that she's a captive, but his face is set in anger, and he already has a wife who is always sad, and Copper Woman would be sad as well, and I will not let him take her from us!" He thumped his fist on the table.

Totka's heart halted mid-pump; his knife, mid-grind; his gaze jumped to White Stone whose round-eyed surprise must rival his own.

A tiny shake of her head confirmed her ignorance of the matter.

It couldn't be true. His cousin would not dare take yet another woman from him, even a slave. But it would be very much like the man to desire, above all else, the thing he couldn't have—such as their pawa's favor, which had rested fully on Totka's shoulders.

Pawa Cetto Imala had been their mothers' brother. He had made the soul's journey some time ago, but Tall Bull's envy would never die, nor would his accusation that Totka had been the cause.

Totka rounded on Fire Maker with more heat than he could contain. "What do you know of Tall Bull?"

Tears brightened Fire Maker's eyes so that he looked away. "Only that he wishes to trade his speckled mare for her." He swiveled back, emotions properly controlled. "I am strong now. Nearly grown. I can help you build a lodge."

Totka had heard nothing of Tall Bull's interest in Copper Woman. Matters of slaves were handled by households—Nokose in this instance—and marriage, by clan mothers. Regardless, any discussion pertaining to Copper Woman's future would have reached Totka's ears right off. Singing Grass would have seen to it.

This thing Fire Maker claimed must be a fabrication. Although, the moisture in his eyes was no lie. That alone set Totka's pulse on an unholy rhythm.

"Will you not let me help you, Pawa?"

Totka forced steadiness into his voice. "When the time comes to build a lodge for my intended, I will be glad for your strong arm. Now, go fetch your mother to me. Quickly!"

Seeming relieved that Totka had at last taken him seriously, Fire Maker leapt to obey.

"Surely, you're aware," White Stone said, "that Nokose captured the young women to trade for goods that will get us through this war. He brought their sick mother with them to hobble them in our compound until a profitable enough bid is put to us. Prepare yourself, Totka. You will not outbid our cousin."

White Stone continued, but Totka barely heard for the tramp of his feet as he paced the lodge.

Minutes later, Singing Grass crossed the threshold. "What riles you, Brother?"

"What do you know of Tall Bull's interest?" Totka asked, impatient.

"His interest in what?"

"Not in what. In whom."

Singing Grass propped a fist on her hip. "Totka, straighten your thoughts and lay them before me neatly."

White Stone injected herself between them. "Fire Maker told our brother that Tall Bull wishes to trade his speckled mare for your captive, the eldest daughter. Is it true?"

"Bah!" Singing Grass batted the air. "Fire Maker is at his tricks again. If Tall Bull spoke of the matter, it could only have been in passing, for Nokose has said nothing to me of it."

"The boy was earnest." Totka was sure of it. "How would he know to create such story? I fear there is some element of truth in what he says."

"You? Afraid?" White Stone shook her head as though ashamed. "The white woman has bewitched you."

"No woman bewitches me!"

Singing Grass quirked her lips to the side, and White Stone laughed.

He had no time for their childishness. "If Nokose has said nothing to you, then Fire Maker is crafting tales." He shrugged, but the flippant gesture didn't soothe his mounting rage at even the insinuation that Tall Bull might take another woman from him.

An insane urge to lay eyes on Copper Woman overtook him. How much longer would she be gone? He looked to the entryway, hopeful.

On her way back out, Singing Grass gave his shoulder a sympathetic pat. "You'll find her at the garden with the children."

"I know," he bit out. Should he seek her there? What if his cousin already had?

With a shot of alarm, he recalled Tall Bull filling his eye with the sight of her, clutching her about the ribs, dragging her along the sand as if he owned her.

Totka must know she was safe.

But there was no time. He was due at the council square to receive instruction on tomorrow's ceremony. The headmen would frown upon his tardiness.

Totka would send Fire Maker to her. The boy made a fine guard and would be honored with the task. Totka owed him, after all.

Behind the winter lodge where the morning sun was most generous, Adela sat knees together, legs tucked beneath her, skirt encircling her like a green calico moat.

Fire Maker, wearing nothing but his russet skin and a hemp breechcloth, perched sideways on her thighs.

She stroked his back, now firm where hours earlier it had quivered with fear from a nightmare. God had come through for His children yet again, providing peace. For as long as Fire Maker lived, he doubtless would never forget their midnight prayer. Nor would she.

While he ensnared her unbound hair in one hand, he dragged the finger of another across the ground in a mirror movement to hers as they wrote the English version of his name.

"It must be straight." Adela traced the sticks of his wobbly letter *k* with confidence, then wiped the character away. "Again."

The second attempt proved more accurate, and she praised him with a laugh and a squeeze. "You make beautiful letters."

"And what of the moccasins? Do you like them?"

She wiggled her toes inside the soft buckskin tucked beneath her and orchestrated a Muskogee reply in her mind before opening her mouth. "Very much. Your hands are skilled. With moccasins and with letters." It sounded right to her. It always did. But her rudimentary speech couldn't possibly be accurate or pretty. Fire Maker's frequent giggles and corrections affirmed it.

Regardless, she made herself understood.

The sun was high in the sky before Totka strode onto the property, a dark cloud on his brow.

Over the many weeks, despite her best efforts to resist him, Totka Lawe had become a friend, a man to be respected, trusted, admired. Her respect, he'd earned at the start. She dared any woman not to stand in awe at such a warrior.

Trust, though, had many facets. She trusted Totka with her life, her safety, her basic needs; but that which he seemed most bent on obtaining, she couldn't give. Her heart wouldn't be so easily won. And certainly not by a Red Stick.

The admiring, however, came maddeningly easier every day.

He cut a fine figure. Even while storming across the lot. Finer than Nokose. Finer than any other Creek man she'd encountered while out and about with him, and they had been about plenty. So much so that the few times she went out alone, she'd been asked if Totka was ailing.

She'd come to appreciate the man's presence for the security it afforded and because it was agreeable, but being paired off with him in the villagers' minds, if even casually, was disconcerting.

Was there no Creek woman in another courtyard languishing over him? Why had he not taken a bride? It couldn't be because none found him attractive or noble or skilled in battle.

Every man had his flaws, but she'd not seen any in this one that should earn him bachelorhood at such an age. Unless it was his flinty will that kept women at bay or that he was prone to periods of distemper, such as now.

A frown set up on her lips. After their extended time together, she'd learned to interpret the nuances of his mood, and the one propelling him across the lot was not difficult to read.

Fire Maker caught sight of his pawa and huddled against her, entrenching his fingers in her hair as though to anchor himself. "Pawa is on the warpath."

Indeed, he was.

Was it that Nokose had left for battle, and Totka couldn't? He had been testy last time Nokose left, too.

Or was the man still upset over her request to allow Fire Maker to stay with her the previous night? At the time, he'd seemed compliant, accommodating, tender . . . She harked back to the sight of him filling their doorway, every firm contour of his shirtless chest standing in sharp contrast to the bright moonbeams silhouetting it.

He'd been a remarkable sight, heaven help her.

And his touch . . . Warm and transparent. Needy.

At the recollection, her stomach wobbled like an upended turtle — until she gave her mind a stern shaking and replaced the night's image with the one beating a trail toward them. It was an effective exercise.

"And whom does Pawa seek to scalp?" she asked Fire Maker, and when he mumbled a sheepish response, she surmised he was the cause. She leaned back to dole out a tight-lipped reprimand. "What have you done?"

"No, it is said, 'what have you *done*?'"

"I did not say this?" She would've sworn her Muskogee sounded identical to his.

He didn't have time to answer before Totka reached them, the cords of his neck on prime display. This was no passing squall. "Nephew, is this the task I gave you? To sit on the woman's lap? Should I fetch you a cradleboard? Remove yourself."

"But, Pawa, we were —"

"Obey." Adela bumped the boy off, and when she raised her face to Totka, she found him drilling into her with disturbing intensity. Any number of things could have triggered his roiling mood — unfavorable news at the council house, a failed raid, the corn ravished by deer — but whatever it was, it involved her. "What disturbs you?"

The lines of his face mellowed, but he shrugged off the question with a shake of his head.

Fire Maker squatted and pointed at the letters in the soil. "Do you see what she's done? Copper Woman has put words in the earth. She is clever, Pawa. Is she not?"

Hands on hips, Totka jetted a heavy breath from his nose, then another. He wasn't fully present, but he pushed aside whatever unwieldy matter occupied his mind and formulated a smile believable enough for Fire Maker. He fisted a handful of the hair at the boy's crown and gave it a gentle shake. "She and my nephew have much in common. Show me these markings." He peered at the word from the topside down, tilting his head. "What do they mean?"

"Come." Adela waved him around to look at the name from the correct angle. When he stood beside her, the fringe of his buckskin legging too close for comfort, she tapped the ground beneath each word. "Fire Maker."

He lowered himself, brow furrowing. "The first is *totka*?"

Following his train of thought, she wrote two more words on a clean patch, and spoke them aloud. "Hungry Fire."

Totka nodded absentmindedly, shade drawn again, eyes distant.

But Fire Maker clapped. "Write another, Copper Woman. Write another!" He yanked on her arm until she laughed and asked which word he would like next.

"Your name."

She wrote *Adela* and pointed at the letters, sounding out each in turn.

Fire Maker interrupted. "I do not know that word. Can you not make the symbols of your name?"

Ah. He wanted the name that Totka referred to her by. "This" — she underlined the word — "is my name. I have no other."

Fire Maker tipped his head back and chortled. "You're playing a game with us."

This was no game.

The child erased the markings with an energetic swipe of his little hand. Dust clouded the air, and she used it to stall by coughing while she drafted a polite response.

Her mother and father had given her a name she cherished, and three months among the Creeks — as kind as they'd been — didn't justify setting it aside, even briefly.

"Copper Woman, look at me." Totka spoke over the boy's giggles, drawing her questioning eye. Amusement tweaked one side of his mouth until it curved upward in a cocky half-smile that tripped her pulse and made the turtle renew his thrashing.

"Yes?" She blinked and tried to recall what had upset her moments ago.

He shrugged and examined a fingernail. "A woman does not respond to a name unless it belongs to her."

And she'd responded to *Copper Woman*. Lips pursing, she fought ascending heat, the heady ripple in her tummy quite gone. For a moment, Muskogee failed her, but she scrambled through her meager vocabulary to find words resembling the thoughts storming her head. "Responding and accepting are different."

His smile hardened, and his eyes lit with challenge. "Put your name in the dirt."

"I will." She swept her hair over one shoulder and, flicking him a narrow-eyed, mulish look, made long, firm strokes until she had reformed the word *Adela*.

Fire Maker bubbled with laughter and went to erase it again, but she stopped him with a tone more barbed than intended. "Leave it, Fire Maker." The child peered at her, his black lashes fluttering in confusion, but she didn't waver.

"You are one of us now." Totka nudged her elbow. "Do as I said."

Obstinacy flared. To test Totka's patience while his temper was raw was foolhardy, but she couldn't relent. To replace her name was to cross enemy lines, white flag held aloft. "Do your eyes fail you? It is written already." She dusted her hands on her skirt and made to rise, but he stopped her with an impregnable grip on her wrist.

Her sharp inhale didn't lessen his purchase on her nor on his resolve.

His jaw shifted; his lips stretched into a flat line. The Red Stick, armed and painted, took up residence behind his eyes.

Fire Maker wisely distanced himself, but she held her ground. The man didn't intimidate her.

She knew compassion welled beneath that stormy exterior. Aiming for it, she lessened her hold on anger and whispered, "I should not have taunted you before the boy but, Totka . . . " Moisture stung her eyes. "Do not make me do this. I cannot."

His shoulders eased, and the warrior retreated, stored his bow. Huffing, he removed his hand but bound her in place with his inescapable scrutiny. "Why do you try me so?"

"Family honor."

"And is honor the reason you teach my nephew English marks instead of Muskogee?"

"She cannot write our language," Fire Maker supplied, his cheery disposition rebounding. "But I do not mind since she told me there are no writings in Muskogee. Copper Woman has promised to teach me her language until my tongue is as skilled as hers. And then, Pawa, I will read English." He trumpeted the declaration, and Totka shot a leery glance at White Stone in the cookhouse.

Did he believe his elder sister would betray their innocent lessons to Kossati's Big Warrior?

Totka stood and kicked dust over the words. "English is the tongue of our enemy. There will be no more of this."

She should thank the man for reminding her she was the enemy and a slave, that she had no business letting her insides giggle at the sight of him. Assuming the role, she clamped her lip between her teeth and said nothing, but Fire Maker leapt to his feet and confronted his pawa, his little fists trembling at his sides.

"Copper Woman is not our enemy!"

Totka's dour features slackened. He stared at Fire Maker, then Adela. Was that fear shadowing him? Insecurity? She'd never seen him wear either, and the sight filled her stomach like too much sour corn soup.

"I know the face of my enemy, and it is not hers." Totka's tone softened, and the flame in Fire Maker's eye dimmed in proportion to it. "Did I not already say she is one of us?"

The boy gave an abrupt nod.

"By protecting the woman's honor you show yourself a noble brave. Even so, there will be no more English. You will mind me in this." He cocked a brow and waited.

The boy unwound his fists and lowered his chin, but when he looked at Totka through the tops of his eyes, he was far from subdued. "Yes, Pawa."

"Are you not bird chaser at the maize field this afternoon?"

"Yes, Pawa." Fire Maker bent and kissed Adela's cheek before stalking off to fulfill his duty. For all his willfulness, he was a good boy.

When he'd disappeared around the winter house, and Adela could no longer bear Totka's study of her, she rose and hoped against hope he'd let her go. Alone.

"Stay with me a moment longer. Please." The contrition in his voice stalled her escape. He bent and began drawing figures in the red earth. Soon, the second word of his name, *Fire*, glared up at her. He'd replicated it almost perfectly.

"Is it good?" He straightened and smiled, pleased with himself.

He was the only one.

The headstrong Fire Maker would have met his match with the defiance she meted out through the tops of her eyes. "And now, you seek praise for writing enemy symbols?"

"Symbols," he corrected her enunciation, but she was in no mood for a lesson. He shrugged. "A boy with a loose tongue should see his pawa as unyielding to the ways of the pale faces. Much trouble could come for us if it is believed otherwise."

The flame in her gut petered out. When it came to Fire Maker, discretion was essential. She should have trusted Totka to have proper motivation for his actions.

She sighed and added a dot to the *i*. "It is good." Was there nothing this man could do to make her hate him? Life among the Creeks would be a trifle less complicated if she did. "So, you are *not* unyielding?"

"I am the stoutest of oaks." Totka's roguish smile spawned a laugh within her, but when she let it free, instead of joining her, he sobered. "However, a little breeze has come to live in the oak's courtyard." He brushed hair off her shoulder and watched it run through his fingers. "If the oak does not strengthen his roots, the breeze will become a gale that bends the oak with little effort."

Tingles of pleasure scaled the back of Adela's neck, and she chastened herself for it. It wasn't the first time he had exhibited attraction to her, but until last night, she'd never responded to it in any way other than dismay. Now, she was paying for it, both in his increased boldness and in her increased pleasure.

It was startling and frightful and called for swift execution. There was no place in a white captive's life for girlish sentiment regarding a doting Red Stick. Two reverse steps rectified the improper advance, but they failed to calm her thundering heart.

He allowed her retreat and frowned. "Show your feet."

Confused, she lifted the hem of her skirt to reveal the folded toes of her new moccasins. How could she have forgotten? "They are beautiful. Maddo. Fire Maker said he helped."

The frown deepened. "Fire Maker says and does many things he should not."

Including, perhaps, giving moccasins to her that belonged to another. Totka had made a new pair for Singing Grass and another for White Stone, followed by two tiny sets for his nieces. When Fire Maker had presented these, Adela hadn't thought it strange, seeing how Totka provided for her in equal measure to his sisters.

Provision, however, was the only way in which they were treated equally. She was the sole beneficiary of his constant company and his often-ardent gazes. Because of those looks, it had made sense that Fire Maker be the one to give the moccasins since to accept such a beautiful gift from a man might also mean acceptance of his pursuit.

Evidently, she'd been wrong to assume. Of a sudden, the moccasins felt hot and stifling, and she wished them off. "Are they . . . for another?"

He waved a stiff, dismissing hand. "They are yours, but Fire Maker was instructed not to give them to you until first frost. You have no need of them until then."

"I . . . understand." But she didn't. The others had received theirs in the full blaze of summer. He was hiding something, but far be it from her to pry and open a door she couldn't close. She presented a smile, little though it was. "Do not go hard on him. His spirit is a good one."

"His spirit is too strong for one his height." He set out toward the lane, brow wrinkled and voice burdened with doubt.

As was their habit, she came alongside him. "You are a fine pawa and will see him well to manhood."

He rubbed the back of his neck, cocking an eye half open. Many minutes passed before he spoke again. "Three winters past, during a raid on the Long Hairs, my pawa, the head of our household, took the journey. The following summer, swamp sickness claimed many lives, including that of my grandfather. White Stone's husband as well. I, alone, am left to bear the burden of family headman. My kinsmen were wise and experienced, and I am not their equal."

Adela had wondered how a man Totka's age had inherited the position. Tensaw, blessedly, had been spared the plague he spoke of, but its wrath had dented the Creek Confederacy. Its hand was still visible in White Stone's blunt, cropped hair; in her unattractive, unwashed clothing; in Totka's burden-weary eyes.

Adela grieved the loss of his mentors, for the role thrust upon him prematurely, but she had no doubt he was equal to the task.

He led them down several quiet alleys, through a neighbor's courtyard, and down an overgrown slope. He went before her, gliding through the thicket with little effort, but her sleeves and hair caught on shrubs, and she tripped over unseen roots and sticks that snagged at her feet, which would have been shredded if not for the moccasins. A briar bush scratched her cheek, and she halted to liberate her hem from its thorny grip.

A few minutes into the brushwood, she scowled. Why had he brought her this way? She couldn't ask because he was too far ahead and increasing the distance. Shoulders above the thickets, he was easily tracked but it would be some time before she caught up to him. At last, she broke out at the river's edge, panting and sweating and grumbling, but he wasn't near enough to appreciate her irritation. He'd taken up a meandering trail, picking his way along the rocks and around grassy outcrops.

In no hurry to reach him, she followed at her own pace, choosing her route with necessary care. This was not a well-used segment of riverbank, nor should it be with its slippery stones and crumbling bank.

At last, she reached him, but only because he'd stopped. He looked fresh and unaffected by the jaunt, not a bead of perspiration to be seen. Framed by low-hanging nets of Spanish moss, he stared into the placid water. "You speak truth; the boy's spirit desires what is right."

Still catching her breath, Adela lifted the hair off the back of her neck to allow the mild breeze to dry the moisture. She had spent the last half hour trying to stay upright, but he'd used it to ponder their earlier conversation. And it appeared he seemed no less burdened than when he set out.

Licking dry lips, she cleared her mind to allow room for his concerns.

"His motives are pure," he continued, "but he does what he believes best without regard to authority or instruction. Such a boy will make a troubled man and a poor husband." By his urgency and the hush in his voice, she sensed he shared a long-held, unspoken burden.

She nabbed a droplet sliding down her temple and ushered up a prayer for wisdom, for words that might guide him. "He is young. In time—"

The broad wag of his head silenced her and sent his ear bobs on a wild arcing swing. "He has age enough to know which of us is chief. The child does not consider the weight of his actions, and others suffer for it, as you have, believing yourself in error for accepting a gift. There will come a day when my small stores of wisdom will fail me. And him." The wind stirred, and he batted swaying moss from his face, then ran an agitated hand over the indigo moon cresting his ear. "Before the end of each day, Fire Maker bears out his name by starting a fire I must put out, and sometimes, when we are alone, Singing Grass tells me his spirit will break under my discipline."

"Hmm." The child was bullheaded, but he didn't shy from rebuke, nor did he carry bitterness, but who was she to contradict his mother?

"You do not agree with my sister?" He twisted and took in the sight of her with a sweep of his eye. Just as swiftly, he directed his gaze to a chaotic flock of red-winged blackbirds spreading out in a line across the sky.

While the birds dipped and chattered, she held her tongue until she had crafted a delicate reply. "As you said, his spirit is strong." She closed her eyes to the sun. Its tepid September rays seeped into her skin and contrasted with the breeze cooling her neck. "You may not see it, but you are the sun to him, Totka. He worships you. Continue to love the child as you do, and see if he does not break." When her cheeks began to sting, she opened her eyes to Totka's, but his blunt appraisal no longer took her by surprise. In fact, she would've been surprised to open them to anything less.

Balancing politeness with the need to put distance between them, she dropped her hair, bent her lips into a soft curve, and led the way along the bank in the direction of the village shoreline.

He came apace with her and guided them over a ridge to a hard-packed trail. "You are wrong, Copper Woman. I am no sun. I am like the pale-face cowman who prods and whips and sends the willful, little calf from one place to another. *You* are his sun."

The prattle of birds and the increasing sounds of village life filled the air between them as she mentally floundered for a way to divert the conversation from herself. "Like the puppies, I am new and different. He'll weary of me."

Totka smirked. "Do not tell him, or he will take it as a challenge, and I'll be forced to fetch him from your side every night."

Adela chuckled, but there was truth in what he said, and it spurred a fresh line of thought. "Wait." She touched his arm to stop him as an idea took hold. "Fire Maker needs a new challenge, a new name." At his blank look, she rushed on. "There is power in a name. You honor Fire Spirit, but your nephew's name is one that rings of the trouble unattended fire can cause. You said so yourself. He needs a name that tells him he is a good boy. We become what we are called. Do you see?"

Understanding lit, and within moments, he caught her flame of discovery. "And what name would you have me give him?"

"A noble name. One that speaks of his helpful spirit or his protective ways. One that makes him desire honor, strength, and goodness, anything but trouble." Changing a boy's name wasn't done on a whim. They would first need an event to inspire it, but they could be on the lookout.

"Yes, honor and strength . . . " The length of his stride shortened as he lost himself in thought. Before long, their feet touched down on the broad sandy bank of the village's shoreline, and he broke into a grin. "If we become what we are called, you will soon become Copper Woman."

The roll of her eyes didn't mask her restrained smile. "And who *is* Copper Woman?"

"She is . . . " His eyes grew intense, hot, and she held her breath, fearful his answer would require more of her than she was prepared to give. But laughter a stone's throw downriver drew his attention to a group of women who beat clothes against the washing stone; another harvested a fish trap basket alone. It was she who'd snagged Totka's eye and tongue.

208

The woman was beautiful. Small yet round in all the right places. Her glossy black hair wound about her head in the fashion of married women, exposing a lovely brown neck and ink that scrolled up it and around the back of her ear.

Creek women often embedded pitch pine soot into their skin, creating decorative patterns, but *this* pattern Adela knew well. She saw it every day on Totka's own neck. Could they be clan markings? Was there such a thing? If so, Adela had no knowledge of it. No, this pattern must be unique to the two of them, and she wondered what it meant.

Silver hoops threaded the woman's ear lobes and tapped her jawbone as she worked, but they stilled when she straightened and noticed Totka and Adela.

Adela had mere seconds to read the woman's expression before Totka stopped and angled toward Adela, intentionally, or otherwise, blocking her view. It took only those seconds to see surprise, pleasure, and the hastened masking of it flash across her eyes. And lastly, pain — the instant Totka gave the woman his back.

"Copper Woman is my friend, a white woman who is fast becoming Creek," he continued as though he didn't recognize the woman ten paces from him, as though she hadn't drilled his markings into her skin.

"And who is Adela McGirth? Your enemy?" To lighten the accusation, Adela tossed in a playful smile, but he wasn't diverted.

His crisp answer came quick. "Adela is the captive I pursued at the fort, but Copper Woman is Indian. She smokes squash and harvests tobacco and goes to water with my sister. Copper Woman comforts my nephew when his dreams disturb him, and she smiles upon my return from the council square."

"Can I not be both? Adela and Copper Woman?"

The press of his mouth said *no*, but after a moment's consideration, he shrugged. "That is a question only you can answer. Adela pines for the mouth of the Coosa. She might shod her feet, fill a pouch with hominy, and run to her father." There it was, the reason he'd groused about the moccasins. "Can you be both Adela and Copper Woman and put escape out of your mind?"

Most certainly, not. If he and Nokose would give her but a single day free of their presence, she'd abscond with the first dugout she came across. Unabashedly, she fixed her gaze on the dugouts and let her tight-jawed silence be her answer.

He stepped between her and the line of vessels, and although she wouldn't meet his gaze, she knew by the rigidity of his neck that it scorched. "Woman, put it out of your mind! My words are sure like the stars that never set—only bad can come from this thing you would do."

Again, she made no response but matched the stubborn set of his lips.

"Will you not clear the smoke of folly from your eyes? Vow to me you will not run, Copper Woman." His voice blazed with intensity. "Vow it!"

She would do no such thing. "I will not lie."

"Then you will go. Now." He nabbed her elbow and marched her to the nearest dugout. "I cannot continue in this way, always watching, always wondering when you will force me to hunt you down. Go!" He pushed her forward. "Take it."

Mouth open, tongue and throat drying from her hastened breath, Adela stared at him, then glanced at the women who'd ceased their work to watch the exchange. The lovely one dropped the basket. A fish escaped her grasp and splashed back to the water.

Adela swung her gaze to him, expecting to find that cocky, teasing smirk. She didn't. "I cannot go—"

"You can and you will." He took a paddle from another dugout and tossed it with a clatter into the bottom of the one she stood beside. "Put the dugout into the water."

He couldn't be serious. And she couldn't up and leave without so much as a grain of corn, without a word to her mother. "Totka, I—"

"Do it!"

Startled, she leapt to obey and threw her weight into the vessel. It didn't budge. She dug in her heels and tried again with little more to show for her efforts than a few inches of progress. It was far heavier than she'd imagined. Even with Lillian's help, she might never manage to move it. How could she have ever thought she would simply slip into the night and disappear over the horizon?

Moisture sprang from her hairline — from exertion, anger, humiliation. She swiped at it, but he moved in close to her ear.

"Do not stop now. You are almost there."

In fact, she was several yards from the water and making no progress. She elbowed his chest, and biting her lip to contain the string of ugly names he deserved, she gathered her strength and gave the hollowed cypress another shove. It went nowhere, but she went down. Her knees hit the cushioning sand, but her chin cracked against the bow of the dugout. Pain shot through her head, reminiscent of her tumble from the pony. She gritted her teeth to keep from crying out.

When he touched her, she flipped away from him and got to her feet, albeit unsteadily. "You have made yourself understood." She would never make it into the river, much less down it, and she would never outmaneuver him on foot — their jaunt through the thickets had proven that. "But know this, Totka Lawe. My mother cannot last the winter, and my mind cannot rest for want of bringing my father to her."

"Foolish talk!" Even as the words left him, his eyes softened alongside his voice. He neared and spoke in a hush meant for her alone. "You would risk his life and your own, for what? A final embrace?" He brushed sand from her smarting chin, and when she tried to elude him by bowing her head, he wiped the scratch traversing her cheek. "Do not think my heart a stone, Copper Woman, but no last words between a man and his woman are worth your life, for if you bring the Long Guns to Kossati's borders, you will *not* be forgiven."

It was understandable that he feared what might happen should the Kossatis become a target, and they would if word got out they had taken captives from Fort Mims. Never mind that Nokose had saved them from certain death. The details would be lost in the drive for vengeance.

But she planned to tell only her father where Mama and Lillian were being kept. They could come back together, pay a ransom, and leave quietly. If nothing else, he would know they were alive. And if she found him dead—

No, she wouldn't think it, and she would *not* abandon the hope of escape.

"Kossati is your home; Nokose, your **elder brother**. And when he is not enough"—Totka thumped a fist to his chest—"I will be. But if you run, Copper Woman, I *will* find you." He gave a superior lift to his blunt brow and paused long enough to let the certitude of his statement sink in.

She believed him.

"Come. We'll speak of this no more." He held out a hand as if in offer of assistance, but she needed none.

What did he plan to do? Walk hand in hand with her? Surely not. What message would that send the women?

From the corner of her eye, she felt them watching, waiting for her response. Was that what he intended? To make a statement? A claim?

He waited, hand outstretched, face an unmarked slate, honey-brown eyes unblinking.

In a stroke of desperation, she slid out of the moccasins and placed them in his palm. For all the women knew, he'd demanded them of her. "There. You need no longer concern yourself now that I am unshod."

He stared at the crumpled mound of tanned hide until his lips tugged enough to show he fought a smile. "Fire Maker spoke well. You are clever."

"Clever enough to know you will still watch me even though my feet are bare." But not clever enough to consider how much a Creek dugout might weigh.

212

"You may call me Hawk Eye." Totka released his grin and began toward home. "Watching you is a beastly chore"—he jerked a shoulder—"but I'm willing to bear it."

She laughed aloud. "Killing a wolf in the dark is a chore? Then you are not the skilled warrior I believed you to be."

The humor dropped from Totka's face, leaving sobriety accompanied by a stiffened gait and . . . was that pallor entering his lips? What had she said? She'd never known him to not recognize a tease, to take such injury at one. Her mouth opened for an apology, but he spoke first, his timbre subdued and tight. "Today's chore is keeping men at bay." A neat change of subject.

"But you must not," she said through another small laugh, an attempt to reestablish their banter, "for Fire Maker has won my heart, and I will wait for him."

"Wait. The word is said *wait*." The smile did not reemerge, and his tone deepened. "And Fire Maker is not the only male in Kossati who wishes to share your pallet."

Her feet stuttered. "What? Who?" She could think of no one. No men had interacted with her apart from Totka and Nokose.

Totka didn't slow and didn't reply until he'd turned onto their lane. He glanced at her from the corner of his narrowed eye. "Unless I am at your side, you will not journey beyond the compound, not until I share words with Nokose. Tell me you understand and will do as I say."

Understand? Vaguely. But enough to know the man was not himself, and the one he referred to, didn't meet his approval. "Yes, Totka. I do."

Chapter 15

Frost Month (November)

Adela pulled her woven grass blanket around her shoulders and stepped from the toasty winter lodge into the chilly air. Tomorrow night, she would surely see her breath.

The sound of Totka's voice stopped her outside the dwelling, and she looked back.

In the banked firelight, his face glowed dark orange. He bounced one niece in each arm and spoke around the little fingers tugging at his nose. "Tomorrow's ceremony will go long. These two will not last and would be happier here with you."

"And I would be happy to tend them." Happier here than there.

For all her interest in Creek customs, tomorrow's rites filled her with dread. There would have been no avoiding that mind-scarring red pole, and from what little she understood, honors were to be given. Honors for feats of courage and skill. Feats attained in battle, such as the slaughter at Fort Mims.

Singing Grass had told her that any other year the town would be nearly deserted now as families left for the great winter hunt. The war kept them close to home and conducting ceremonies that honored the slaying of her people. Their storehouses were depleting while their red pole accrued trophies. A shivering fact.

The following afternoon, Adela stirred the sofkee bubbling over the courtyard fire, taming it to a simmer.

"That smells good." Lillian looked up from weaving a yellow ribbon through Rain Child's braid and smiled. A beautiful sight that—Lillian, deep, golden skin burnished in the slanted afternoon rays, black locks sailing the air, eyes crinkling with contentment. Rain Child sat statuesque at Lillian's knee, wearing the simple frock Mama had stitched, snuggling a cornhusk doll bound to a tiny cradleboard, and awaiting the results of Lillian's handiwork.

"Want some?" Adela offered. "I can fetch you a bowl."

"It'll wait. Finish what you're doing."

Adela stroked Lillian's hair on the way to the summer lodge where she unhooked the gourd from its spot by the door. She paused inside and let her eyes rove the silent, dim interior: Two couches, one on each side. A small trestle table off-center lined with a rough-hewn bench. A stash of weapons in one corner, sleeping pallets in another. Herbs, baskets of drying fruit, and tobacco leaves, hanging from the ceiling poles. No fire pit—the family would join them in the winter lodge soon—no windows, and no Totka.

The place was almost lifeless without him, but this was one afternoon she was happy to spend alone. She heard plenty from where she stood; the wind carried the drumbeats and ceremonial songs far too eagerly.

Gourd in hand, she returned to the fire and ladled sofkee into the container until it was full. When she'd replaced the gourd and its spoon, she moved on to the winter lodge to do the same.

White Stone's snoring was raucous enough to wake the spirit of the dead husband buried beneath her couch, but Mama and Speaks Sweetly miraculously slept through it. Afternoon naps had become a regular occurrence for these three. Speaks Sweetly, because she was but a wee thing; Mama, because she weakened by the day; and White Stone, because she swore it helped her rheumatism.

In one of the lulls between White Stone's rumbled wheezes, hoof beats sounded in the courtyard. Adela hooked the newly filled gourd on its tack and stepped into the doorway.

216

A man reined to a stop by the main lodge but didn't dismount. He was Creek — there was no mistaking the red feather — but his head was unshaven. He wore it long and straight with the upper portion collected in the back. It was a rare sight and, she admitted, an attractive one.

His skin was unblemished by tattoos, but he needed nothing more than his cutting eye to give full-bodied appreciation of his fierceness. With it he skimmed the quiet yard and settled on Adela.

Foreboding tightened the base of her spine as Totka's warning came back to her. Before she could act, Lillian rose, drawing the man's attention, which snagged on her and held fast.

While stepping protectively in front of Rain Child, Lillian returned his frank appraisal with more nerve than was prudent. She was far too lovely standing as she was: back straight, figure accentuated, skin fresh, lips flushed, and in her eyes, a challenge any warrior would feel shamed not to meet.

Adela doubted those details were escaping the man. His keen interest was written in the way his eye came alive, his mouth curved, and his body tensed.

His horse wandered three steps before he yanked it by the bit, stopping it short. The animal snorted and stamped a protest, instigating a nervous prance from a second horse tethered by the man's hand. In her attention to the rider, she'd failed to notice he led another animal.

Adela left the shadows of the lodge and strode to greet him. "Welcome. I am called Copper Woman. This lodge belongs to Singing Grass of Wolf." No need to tell him her status. Her skin spoke loudly enough.

He took his time abandoning his perusal of Lillian, and when he finally brought it to Adela, it was altogether different. Cold. Concentrated. Calculating. "I am Tall Bull. Totka Lawe's mother was sister to my own." His narrow smile didn't move beyond his lips, but it stirred up wraiths of memory that wouldn't take form.

Tall Bull. Also Wolf. Totka's cousin.

Had she heard of him? Not that she recalled. The face was familiar but elusive. That struck her as odd because his features were becoming and not those a woman soon forgot.

"Totka is away, but come to your home," she said, extending the expected greeting to clan members.

Half his mouth arced into a lazy smile. "My cousin is away? How terribly unfortunate."

The tightness in her back convulsed. "Are you hungry? Will you . . . join us at the fire while you wait for your cousin?"

"I will speak with White Stone."

"She is resting."

"Then wake her," he replied smoothly.

Casting a reassuring glance at Lillian, Adela turned to do as the man bid, but White Stone was already hobbling across the yard, a grimace deepening the folds of her neck, sleep lines furrowing her cheek.

"What have you brought us, my ever-ambitious cousin?"

"The speckled mare, as arranged." He guided the animal into better view.

Threads of memory wove themselves together in Adela's mind. The meadow. This man had been part of Nokose's packhorse train, but her eyes had been full of Totka, and Tall Bull had made no impression on her other than his presence.

Today, he made up for it.

White Stone snapped her gaze to Adela and back to Tall Bull. "You made no promise to me."

"Nokose Fixico and I have an arrangement. I am here only to settle it."

"He and my brother are gone." Her eye squinted. "But you know this."

Tall Bull's shoulder shot upward. "Did he not leave his property in your care? Your household is in greater need of a horse than three slaves, but Nokose drives a steep bargain. The animal alone did not please him, so I've brought this." He removed a wrapped item from a saddlebag, handed it down to White Stone, and lifted a resolute eye to Adela.

The air thinned.

No, they couldn't. They wouldn't. Not with Totka and Singing Grass a ten-minute walk down the lane. Singing Grass wouldn't approve. Adela was certain of it. And Totka . . . Adela had no doubt his reaction would fall on the wrong side of pleasant. Did these two think they could get away with this?

But what did Adela know of these things? Didn't Nokose own Adela? Singing Grass owned the rest of the property, but White Stone was the family matriarch. How much power did that give the woman? Did it override Nokose? Surely, it did not.

Despite her self-assurance, her heart pattered like a rabbit's.

A blinding light flashed her.

White Stone examined a silver hand mirror and traced a floral pattern embossed on its back. She flipped it over and scowled at her reflection. After raking fingers through her natty hair to little effect, she thrust it back up. "And what makes you think I want to look at myself?"

His hand remained draped over his thigh. "Give it to Singing Grass then, and keep this for yourself." He untied a bundle of deerskins from back of his saddle and let it fall. Enough skins to keep them all in leggings and moccasins through the winter and beyond. Next, he dropped a small leather pouch down to White Stone.

The woman unwound its thong, peered inside, and smiled. "I suspect Leaping Waters will appreciate the extra help."

"Leaping Waters will appreciate both the help and the companionship."

White Stone nodded. "We need the horse more than the slave, and feeding the pale faces drains our storehouse. You may have her. My sister's husband intended to trade them both eventually. These items will please him, I am certain. Besides, better you take the woman before Totka puts it in his mind to have a white woman as wife."

As smug as a rat in a stocked corncrib, Tall Bull passed White Stone the mare's lead rope and cocked a brow at Adela.

She glanced at the summer lodge and judged the distance. Was she swift enough to reach it and Fire Maker's bow? It was small but effective. If she could wield it.

"She is no mule, Cousin." White Stone began toward the horse pen. "Mind how you handle her, or my brother will have more than words with you."

He would regardless! Did she know her brother so little? Adela's legs tensed, ready to flee.

Tall Bull ignored White Stone and nudged his horse to block Adela's path to the lodge. Too late. Perhaps the cookhouse? White Stone kept her knives on the shelf beside the table.

"Adela, what's going on?" Fear warbled Lillian's question. "What does he want?"

Me. But Adela's throat had closed, and she had no reply.

Running would frighten her sister, and Tall Bull would take Adela no matter what.

But Totka would take her back. Before sunset, she would be home.

The man didn't stop his horse's plodding gait until he looked directly down on her. "It would seem your value is equal to that of a brood mare, a few skins, and five strings of trade beads."

"You've forgotten the tarnished looking glass." She fisted her hands and told him with a look she would not budge.

"Your sister is quite beautiful. Her coloring is more to my liking, and I perceived just now that she and I are two leaves from the same stalk. Given time, we would come to understand each other well. Shall I go to White Stone about it?" At Adela's marked inhale, he smirked and extended his arm, palm up.

"Lillian, be a dear and tell Mama I'll be gone a spell."

"Where are you going?" Lillian called, having come no closer.

"I'm not sure, but don't worry. I'll be back." She took hold of his upper arm, gripped the stirrup with her toes, and timed her jump to coincide with his skin-burning yank.

He seated her in front of him, reined the horse around, and heeled it into a canter that threw her against him. His steel lock on her ribs more than kept her in place, but she didn't fight him. Totka would do that for her soon enough.

"Your cousin will come for me."

The muscles of his arm hardened. "Let him come."

With a practiced hand, Adela plucked a tobacco stalk clean of its long, yellowing leaves, then laid them in the basket behind her and moved to the next plant.

Reserved yet cordial, Leaping Waters worked beside her, passing off a meek smile whenever their eyes met. The sun had made a full cycle since the woman's husband had ridden onto Singing Grass' property, and in that time, she had been gracious, Tall Bull had been aloof, and Totka had been scarce.

Yesterday, before the sun had spilled the last of its light, Totka had arrived with two other men — one about her father's age, another so bent with age he was brought in a cart behind which trotted the spotted mare.

Not an hour later, from between the wide slats of her storehouse prison, she'd watched with mounting anxiety as they exited Leaping Waters' lodge, mounted up, and left. The last she'd seen of the party was the mare's swishing hind end.

Night had fallen swiftly after that, and it had stretched long and sleepless as she'd waited for either Tall Bull or Totka to come for her. She'd been resolute in her belief that Totka would slip back in under cover of dark, that he would go to whatever lengths necessary to set this injustice to rights. He hadn't, and that fact still stung her eyes and made her nose drip.

He hadn't come for her. Neither man had.

And all she had to show for her vigil was a pain inside her skull and an ever-increasing desire to curl up somewhere warm and sleep away her fears.

She rubbed the underside of her nose with her sleeve to catch the moisture and avoid a revealing sniff. Shameful, these tears. If Totka saw, a *V* would form between his eyebrows as he told her to put a rod in her backbone.

But Totka wasn't here. Without a word of explanation, he'd taken the horse and left her to Tall Bull's devices. All she could do was trust he had good reason.

Leaping Waters emptied her arms into the basket, then crossed to the row in front and resumed harvesting. She was a beautiful woman, with her dimpled smile, sun-kissed skin, and plentiful curves, every one of them outlined by her traditional buckskin dress.

It hugged her body much the way Adela imagined her own did. Doing away with Singing Grass' cotton frock had been the first command Tall Bull had issued.

He'd not touched her since he'd nudged her off the horse, but she wasn't so innocent to the ways of men that she believed herself safe from him. Part of her believed him wise enough to keep himself in check, but the other part told her the man had more in mind than providing an extra set of hands for his pretty wife.

How could any man have Leaping Waters and wish for more? That being said, it seemed Totka had once had her yet now did not. The why of it itched Adela's curiosity, but she wasn't insensitive enough to scratch it. She sneaked a glance at the serpentine ink on Leaping Waters' neck and wished she hadn't. It only brought Totka to mind. What must it do to Tall Bull?

"My husband comes," Leaping Waters said in English, "and he wears purpose on his face."

Adela grabbed a stripped tobacco stalk to keep from swiveling for a look. She would see the Red Stick soon enough.

"You should leave. Tonight."

Adela gave a disbelieving chuckle. "Do you mean escape?"

Leaping Waters nodded, eyes pasted to the lane that curved up from the river and carried her husband toward them. She rushed on. "Old Grandfather told my husband he is not to have you, but I fear his resentment will blind him to good sense. As soon as he sleeps, you must go. I will help you."

"Totka will come for me."

"No, he has left Kossati." Totka had left? Like a boulder to a clod of dirt, Leaping Waters' statement crushed Adela's hope. "You must try to run." She snapped a leaf from its anchor with such force the stalk broke.

"I can't! I'm too clumsy in the woods. Your husband will hunt me down." Once caught, there would be little expectation of mercy. In her short exposure to Tall Bull's character, she'd learned he was no Totka. He was cunning and meticulous and the staunchest of Red Sticks. Whatever punishment a slave typically received for attempted escape, he would doubtless see it meted out to the fullest.

No, she couldn't run. She would trust God to preserve her, and if He chose not to use Totka, He would use another way.

But . . . what if He didn't? What if He chose to put her through yet another fire?

Surely not. Hadn't she been refined enough for one season? Her faith was too thin to take another beating. Like a gutted doe, she would be split, spilling her spirit all over Creek soil.

"Oh Lord, what should I do?"

"Yes" — Leaping Waters gripped her arm — "seek Creator and consider that his answer might lie with me." She hammered her chest with her knuckles. "My husband has not called me to his couch in ten moons. He is lonely and determined to wound me." She fingered the markings on her throat. "As well as his cousin. This is an ugly, long-awaited retribution, and I sense it is getting the better of him. Do you understand why he does this, why he chose *you*?"

The man sauntered across the grassy expanse between the courtyard and the garden. His handsome features conveyed a disturbing mixture of determination and resentment, and it wasn't directed at his wife.

"Y-yes. I understand."

"He knows Totka will return, and he has set his mind to display his power first. And he will. Soon. Think on what I have said." Her fingers clamped down, then released as Tall Bull arrived.

He towered above Adela, almost as tall as Totka, but that was where the similarities stopped.

He jutted his chin at Leaping Waters. "Leave us."

Without a word or even a fleeting glance at Adela, Leaping Waters deposited her leaves in the basket and made for the lodge.

He watched her with softening eyes until the building's shadows swallowed her, stared at the space she'd last occupied, and let what could only be longing tighten his eyes. Did Leaping Waters know his feelings for her ran so deep? "How is it possible, Copper Woman, for love to ache in such a way?" he said at last, sadly, in a hushed confession that rendered her mute. "She's been unfaithful to me."

Adela flinched. Leaping Waters? Unfaithful? It hardly seemed plausible, but why else would Tall Bull wish to use Adela to punish her? And Totka.

Their identical tattoos swirled through her head, and her stomach roiled.

She wouldn't believe it, couldn't fathom Totka bedding another man's wife. "If that is true, why do you not divorce her?" Before marriage, liberal intimacy was encouraged. After, it was met with divorce and mutilation.

If Leaping Waters truly had been unfaithful, then Adela had misjudged the man—for having spared his wife that horror, he was quite merciful.

"No." His answer came swiftly. "I love her. Nothing will change that. I'll keep her for as long as she'll put up with me. She is a good wife. In all ways but one." This last statement brought his attention from the lodge back to Adela where, as a man puts on a mask, he slipped into callousness. She was sorry for it because his scrutiny was full and powerful and terrifying, and it encompassed every part of her.

Tendrils of fear crept about her, but she cocked her chin through it. "Find another to violate. You will not touch me. Totka will return for—"

He seized her by the back of the neck and squeezed. She clutched his arm for support, causing that lazy smile of his to reappear. "I will touch you if I please. And do not speak of my cousin's return again. Totka Hadjo has no claim on you. This, he knows."

"Totka . . . Hadjo?" Who was Mad Fire?

"Has my insolent slave not heard? My cousin has attained senior stature in the house of warriors. The rank of Big Warrior. The clan mothers have given him a new name. These things he earned through great skill in battle." He skidded the backs of his fingers over the side of her face.

She dug her nails into the flesh of his arm, but he continued, unaffected. "During the ceremony, he thanked your people for the chance to prove himself."

White hot fury leapt within her. How easy it would be to spit on this man! Instead, she pulled against his hold. Her neck screamed, but she spoke past it. "You would have me hate him, but I refuse. Unlike yourself, he's an honorable man, and he *will* return for me."

The leer twisting his mouth warned her to guard her tongue. "Ignorance darkens your words, but I am happy to make you see light." He let her drop to her heels, but before she could draw a breath of relief, he marched her by the arm toward the storehouse.

"Totka Hadjo was sent away because my trade with White Stone was deemed lawful by our Beloved Man. Nokose put you under Totka's care on that first day, but it's widely known he abandoned the task and left angry from his sister's lodge."

Adela's legs churned to keep up with his furious stride, her brain with his tale and the possibility that he thought to use the storehouse as cover for his evil.

"Since then my *honorable* cousin has provided for you, but no legitimate trade has been made. White Stone has confirmed it. So, Old

Grandfather has told my cousin he has no power here."

It wasn't true! Tall Bull was lying to strip her of hope, to weaken her for his own purposes.

He flung her up the storehouse ladder ahead of him and shoved her inside.

She stumbled and knocked into a stack of fishing baskets, scratching her bare arm against the pointed edges. She regained her balance and spun to face Tall Bull, vile fear making her chest rise and crash.

Had it been just yesterday Totka had taken her hand and promised a leisurely row upriver after the ceremony? How had life gone so horribly awry?

Tall Bull stalked to her, sent her scrambling backward into the far wall. "Why do you think he's left to join the war party? Because you are *mine*." He hedged her in. "Do not look so troubled, Copper Woman. There is honor in being desired by a Creek warrior. At White Stone's insistence, you will be treated well. As a slave, however, you will do as I wish." After a long moment of deliberate study, his distended nostrils eased, his breathing regulated, and he reached for her.

Was this how it was for a snared rabbit? An inescapable sense of helplessness? Heart a chaotic variety of rhythms?

The Lord is a stronghold in trouble, the Lord is a stronghold. In trouble, trouble, trouble, always trouble!

She cringed in anticipation of his touch, but this time, when his fingers cupped the back of her neck, they didn't crush but stroked.

Head locked in his grasp, she beat back a whimper and went cradleboard rigid, hands flat against him, a pathetic shield.

With ease, he broke through it, pinning her arms between them. Contrary to expectation, he didn't roll in like a hot summer storm, but crept up like a mist, deceptive and cool. He nibbled the edges of her sealed mouth while boring his thumbs into the tender spots beneath her ears. The discomfort grew until it became unbearable, and in the instant she drew a sharp inhale, he invaded her open mouth. He tasted of restrained power and theft, but he lingered only a little while.

When he withdrew, her taut muscles deflated, and her unpinned arms collapsed to her sides.

Would he not force her? Or was he toying with her? Would he give her a few hours yet to-to . . . to what? There was no escape unless she rendered the man unconscious here and now. Such a thought was laughable.

Between bursts of trembling and unorganized prayer, an idea lodged in her mind — the thing a Creek warrior feared above all was the destruction of his medicine.

"You see now that I am no monster." He caressed her jaw with all the tenderness of a lover, but his tone was cast in iron. "Only a man who knows how to get what he wants, and what I want is for my cousin to know I had you between my hands, if even for a little while."

She put confusion into her eyes. "I was told Muscogees believe that to touch a woman during her flow is to defile oneself. Is this not true?"

He blanched, first bewilderment then fury washing his features. He lurched away, careening over a fishing basket. "You've broken your **lunar retreat**?" he shouted.

Adela took her first true breath since she spotted him crossing the yard. "Is it so serious?"

His eyes narrowed. "Do not play the ignorant white woman with me. White Stone would have informed you. And she never would have allowed me near a woman during her moon time."

"The blame does not fall to White Stone." She bent her lips into what she hoped conveyed disgust. "Seclusion is a heartless Muscogee practice. I delayed telling her and subjecting myself to it."

The black entering his eyes told her she'd been convincing enough to keep him at bay a while longer. He spat to the side and scrubbed his mouth with his sleeve. "You are a spiteful woman for harming me this way, and you will pay for your crime!"

Crime?

"If you think *I* mistreat you, we shall see what you think of the slave pole!" He kicked the basket out of his way and rummaged through several shelves until he produced a length of twine.

Adela scrambled for the door, but he caught the back of her skirt and forced her to her stomach. The twine went on burning and tight, and she bit her lip to keep from crying out. Having finished tying her to an inner post, he stepped over her and stormed out.

Backbone a gelatinous goo, she slumped. Was polluting a man such a serious offense? But better to lie about her monthly courses than lose her virtue. Of course, there was still a good chance he would send Leaping Waters in to learn whether Adela was telling the truth.

He did, but Leaping Waters had no interest in the truth. She stayed only a minute and left with assurances she would return.

As best Adela could, she curled up on the slat floor and lay immobile until the shadows lengthened and disappeared. In those hours, she thought of the newly titled warrior.

Big Warrior Totka Hadjo.

It suited him. Beyond question, he'd earned it in full.

Her knowledge of Creek rank was limited, but she did know that a warrior didn't achieve such status from one battle alone, but from a lifetime of worthy accomplishments. Most of Totka's would have been achieved before Fort Mims became a target.

At the realization she was proud of him, Adela gave a wry, disbelieving little laugh. The council knew he was trustworthy and good, and he'd proven it to her as well. By all accounts, he should not have given up on her situation so readily. More than good, Totka was obstinate, a man not to be easily put off a scent, and there was little doubt in her mind, she was the scent he was after.

But he *had* been put off—hadn't Leaping Waters confirmed it?— and instead was making good use of his new rank. The two times Nokose had left for battle, Totka had been restless and irritable. It was clear he longed to join the war party. Well, now he had.

Leaping Waters was right. If he came for her, it would be too late. Adela was on her own, but praise almighty God there was someone willing to help her.

Sleep was beginning to muddle her thoughts when the ladder squeaked. Heart thundering, Adela shot into a sitting position. The doorless entryway revealed Leaping Waters' minute form.

She rushed to Adela and enveloped her in a hug. "He's gone to purify himself, but he will be back soon." She severed Adela's bonds and shoved a sack into her arms, making escape a simple choice.

Leaping Waters pulled her down the ladder and through the courtyard at a near run. "Follow the lane until it curves sharply to the right, then take the path to the river's edge. There, you will find a small wooden canoe moored to a large broken cypress. Follow the current until dawn, hide the vessel in the cane on the western shore, and travel south along the Alabama until you reach Tensaw. Do not slow until nightfall and rest only a short while. If you are caught, the slave pole will be the least of your worries."

She stopped and planted a kiss on Adela's cheek. "Pity it has come to this. I had such hopes. He would have loved you well. Be swift and careful. I will beseech the Master of Breath on your behalf until I know you are free of this place."

After another brief embrace, she left Adela to find her way. The instructions were easy to follow and within minutes, Adela climbed into the little craft.

By dawn, her arms and back burned from paddling, and she was eager to tuck the canoe into the cane. But there was no path through the woods, and the sun hid behind a haze of clouds, making it difficult to determine direction. For endless, foot-tearing hours, she cut a course through the thickets and vines, upbraiding herself for not keeping the moccasins and wishing she possessed even an ounce of Totka's woodland sense.

He would be angry when he learned she'd run, but there was no help for it. If she was quick enough, she wouldn't be around to watch his displeasure play out. The thought wasn't as comforting as she would've liked.

A chill set up in the air, and the haze of clouds overhead grew darker despite the noon hour. The temperature began to drop, but her steady pace kept her warm.

Reciting a ceaseless prayer for deliverance, she kept a careful watch behind her, so careful, in fact, she didn't see the men in the shrubs ahead and to her left until they stepped into her path a few yards distant. Her feet melded to the dirt, and her breath exploded from her in a puff of vapor.

There were two — hunters, from the boar slung over the shoulders of the one with the blue turban. The other, a young man with a nose ring, carried their bows and muskets. She recognized them from Kossati, but didn't know their names, their clan, or whether they could be reasoned with.

The man let his boar thump to the ground and rubbed his neck, perplexity wrinkling his nose. "You are Totka's woman." He scanned the vicinity as though looking for him.

She almost laughed. "Some would not agree with you."

His eyes narrowed as he drew in. "Why are you alone and so far from his sister's lodge?" He studied her pouch and grazed the rest of her with a critical, knowing glance. Smudged clothing, mussed hair, bruised feet — there was no use lying or running.

Defeat coursed through her thick and grisly.

She'd been so certain God had given her the words to rebuke Tall Bull's advance, that He'd blinded the man's eyes to her deception and set Leaping Waters in her path. And hadn't He guided her ignorant feet thus far?

It seemed she'd been mistaken. She'd only dug her pit deeper and now would pay for her recklessness.

He crossed thick arms over his chest. "Will you come willingly, or must I put you in slave cords?"

Go back to Tall Bull willingly? Not a chance. She held out her wrists. The hunter turned her around and bound them behind her back.

Before the day was done, Blue Turban ushered her into Kossati's square where, without ceremony, he tethered her by the neck to the hideous red pole. The lanyard gave her leeway to walk a tight ring around it and allowed her to sit but not lay down.

For hours, she dodged insults and stones, feared Tall Bull's arrival, and longed for Mama. Or Lillian or Singing Grass, or even Fire Maker. No one came, and she was given no food or water, blanket, or explanation.

At last, Singing Grass arrived with a small bowl of water. "Drink slowly. It's all you are allowed." She held it to Adela's mouth.

A sip soothed her parched throat. "No blanket?"

Eyes downcast, Singing Grass shook her head. "Thinking it would help, I revealed your deception to the miccos." Several days earlier, she'd been present during Adela's cleansing, a practice required for her to re-enter society. "But Old Grandfather would not give in. You will remain as you are."

No surprise there. She had escaped, after all. "How long?"

"This night plus one other."

Before Singing Grass left, Adela asked she not allow Mama and Lillian to come — it was best for them that way.

As the moon rose, the temperature plummeted, her anxiety increased, and loneliness hounded her. Why had she asked that Mama not come? Lillian would have fallen to pieces, but Mama would have braved it. Even a glimpse of her across the way would have buoyed Adela's spirits. But Singing Grass abided by her wishes, so that all through the long, freezing night, Adela had only her fruitless prayers and frosty breath for company.

Sunrise brought precious little heat, and Adela, exhausted from three sleepless nights and a frantic escape, could no longer pace for warmth. Hungry beyond reason, she sank to her backside and spent the day huddled and shivering beneath the scalps flapping in the blustery weather.

The tether chafed her neck and made sleep difficult. As soon as she dozed, her body slackened, charging the tether with her weight, restricting her breathing, and jolting her awake.

"The Lord is a . . . trouble, trouble . . . " The scripture left her, prayers languished on her tongue, and hope dimmed.

By nightfall, she opened sluggish lids to a moonless, weeping sky and a world tilted at an unnatural angle. Sleep had won at last. Air skidded through her throat in sips, but her lethargic pulse demanded little.

Then Tall Bull was there, speaking at her, wrapping a blanket about her shoulders. Was it her addled brain or was that chagrin thickening his tone? What was he saying? "To scare you, nothing more . . . craftier than I gave you credit for. Why did you run? *Why?*" Warmth seeped into her cheeks. Was he touching her?

She should shrink from him, but she hadn't the strength.

"Let me . . . free."

"You've taken this out of my hands! Only the spirits can help you now. I will pray their mercy on you."

He left and sleet needled. Blessedly, she'd lost feeling in her hands, but pain shot through muscles stretched beyond capacity. She groaned and sought strength to straighten herself but found none. However, in the attempt, the blanket slipped and exposed her to the full wrath of the elements.

A sense of utter desolation consumed her, and she knew she would die, either by freezing or hanging. Either way, she would be alone. Even God seemed to be hiding behind His mass of cruel storm clouds.

She next woke to someone tugging at her body. "Copper Woman!" The voice was urgent. "Mother says you cannot sleep or you will die. Wake up. Wake up!"

"Fire M-Maker?" Was she dreaming or had the child truly come?

He gave her face several firm smacks, and she knew he was real. A convulsive sob shook her, even as her brain slipped back into the fog.

"No sleeping. You must wake."

"I will . . . try." For all her efforts, she couldn't keep her eyes from rolling closed. "Stay. Please."

He molded his warm hands to her cheeks and spoke in her ear. "Pray to Creator and do not despair." With that, he was gone.

"Do n-not leave me." She'd intended to shout, but her tongue was stiff, her throat swollen. Her own ears barely heard the plea.

In his absence, she determined to stay awake and pray, but her mind wandered a confusing trail, ending on Totka and his warning at the dugout.

Clear the smoke of folly from your eyes, Copper Woman . . . only bad can come from this thing you would do . . . only bad . . .

Chapter 16

The ground, black with night, passed by in a blur beneath Totka and the speckled mare. To ride at such a speed, much less with no moon, was reckless at best. But Totka knew this path well, and it seemed, so did Tall Bull's horse.

The mare's lather flung up and spattered Totka's leggings, adding to the damp caused by sleet and his own sweat. It streamed his back and penetrated both layers of clothing. **Wind Clan** had not predicted this sudden onset of winter. Totka was unprepared. The freezing air they cut through had numbed his nose, cheeks, and fingers but kept his labor to a tolerable level.

The horse's chest heaved, but he couldn't rest her.

For Copper Woman, two and a half sleeps in Tall Bull's lodge were two and a half too many.

The thought of what she might have endured drove his heel into the mare's spotted hide. The animal flinched but did not increase her speed. Could not.

Nokose rode immediately behind, his horse's chuffing and increasingly irregular tread clearly audible. Totka had found his brother-by-marriage near Tuckabatchee, having been routed from Georgia soil by the half-breed William McIntosh and his pale-face-loving warriors from Coweta. It had been disturbing to come across the war party so close to home.

The conflict was nearing, and it didn't bode well for Kossati.

Nokose's proximity and his willingness to return had been the one silver coin in the sack of stones Tall Bull had flung at Totka. That, and the traded mare, which had made it possible for Totka to retrieve Nokose in the first place.

Nokose pulled alongside him on the narrow path, and their legs collided. "A dead horse cannot be traded," he shouted through the hair strung across his mouth.

Without the horse to trade, Copper Woman might be as good as gone. Totka reined in to a canter, and spent the rest of the journey praying down on Tall Bull curses of eternal pestilence and hunger. If the Master of Breath chose to sweep in and take the man's life, Totka wouldn't object.

Old Grandfather had forbidden Tall Bull from touching her because Nokose had yet to scratch his mark on the trade, but Tall Bull made it a habit to flaunt authority, and although he'd given assurances of compliance, Totka didn't believe for a moment, he intended to spend one more night alone.

Half the talwa knew Tall Bull had no intention of finding pleasure in his wife—her punishment for an unspecified offense. For Totka's part, he refused to believe Leaping Waters capable of what she was being accused. Selfishness and weakness, yes. Adultery? Never.

As he'd left Tall Bull's lodge, his parting words had been hastily whispered to Leaping Waters alone. *You are her only defense. Do not fail me.* That demand—along with the hope of its fulfillment—had carried Totka from Kossati to Tuckabatchee and back. As well as now, as they passed their own lane and aimed for Old Grandfather's lodge.

The cylindrical *chokofa*, or winter council house, loomed before them, tall on its mound. They circumvented it and entered the rectangular *chunkey* **yard**. Far off, beyond the other end of the yard, in the center of the council square, the **sacred fire**, a symbol of the sun, battled the winter storm. With its eternal crackle, the fire lit two figures entering the square from the opposite side. Old Grandfather? Yes, had to be. And a boy carrying wood.

"Why is Fire Maker out with the owls?" Nokose nudged his horse around to intercept them, and Totka followed, pleased to have come across the ancient one so unexpectedly. Another silver coin.

Near the sacred grounds, they dismounted and continued on foot.

Fire Maker stopped at the square's center, and Old Grandfather chanted and reverently fed the flames.

Nokose backhanded Totka's arm. "Who is there?" He indicated the dark corner of the chunkey yard that housed the slave pole. Some unfortunate person dangled from it either unconscious or dead. "Has anyone returned from the war party? I'd not heard of captives being taken."

Dread clotted Totka's throat. "Not that I am aware, but . . . I've not been here to—" Nourished, the sacred fire came to life and lit up the red pole and the sunset hair of the woman tethered to it.

Totka was running before her name registered in his mind; he'd arrived before it finished pealing from his throat. Shins skidding and fury mounting, he landed beside her and hauled her onto his knees to relieve her airways, then threw a discarded, frozen blanket over her body.

Pellets of ice were embedded in the hair that scourged her face. He swept it aside and flattened his hand against her throat. Slow but strong, blood tapped his fingers.

His lungs resumed their duty. It would not have been the first time someone had died at the pole from heat, cold, or suffocation. But why, in the blessed name of his ancestors' spirits, was she here at all?

Water Spirit, Wind Spirit, and the sacred North were working in harmony, and their fury was undeniable. Had they finally tired of his defiance of the natural order?

Master of Breath, forgive me. Spare her! he prayed but had only completed three of the four repetitions when Nokose arrived and dropped to a knee.

"Does she live?"

"Yes. Cut her down." He frisked his palms together to create heat and pressed them to her throat to warm her blood. "Copper Woman, beloved, wake for me." A few pats to her cheek brought her around.

"Totka?" Her speech slurred, almost inaudible. "Do not l-let me . . . die alone."

"There will be no dying! Nokose is here. He will make this right."

She went limp again. Were her eyes closed? It was too dark, too blasted cold!

He rubbed her bare arms and grimaced. He'd felt warmer corpses. "You must wake. Can you hear?"

"I t-told him you . . . would c-come."

Why would Tall Bull do this? If she had died . . .

Hate flared and scorched Totka's insides. If he opened his mouth the heat of it would warm Copper Woman in an instant.

"She would not have lasted the night." Nokose unwound his turban.

"Why do you delay? Cut her down!"

"We do not know what she's done."

"Tall Bull no longer has authority over her. Whatever she's done, you will forgive it." He went for his own knife.

"Father!" Fire Maker flung himself against Nokose. "She would not wake, so I went to Old Grandfather to—"

"My blanket, Fire Maker," Totka said. "Get it from the horse."

"Yes, Pawa!" The boy darted around the retired peace micco whose shuffling steps had finally reached them.

In deference to the Beloved Man, Totka's blade stilled against the tether. "Why is she here, Old Grandfather?"

The vertical grooves hemming in the man's downturned lips deepened. His buffalo robe slipped off one shoulder, and the wind seized one of his long, gray braids and flailed it like a whip. "The woman fled."

Of course, she had. Totka's knife-arm lowered. Escape—one of the few crimes with a sentencing he couldn't mitigate. Hers was an offense against the entire village.

Her head flopped and snapped upright. She voiced incomprehensible English.

"When?" Nokose asked, wrapping the length of his turban around her shoulders.

"Long Arrow came upon her where the crooked creek meets the Alabama. She has been at the pole a night, a day, and this night."

Half hidden by the mound of blankets he carried, Fire Maker rejoined them. "I brought two."

Totka took one, shook it out and began tucking it around her, becoming aware of his own plummeting body temperature. "Tall Bull must have threatened her. She would not have fled otherwise. We would not be here at all, if he had not stolen her!"

"The ice has dulled Totka Hadjo's memory. Or is it his bitterness over his loss of Leaping Waters that makes him forget?" His myriad wrinkles shifted into a picture of disappointment. "Tall Bull's trade was deemed acceptable until Nokose Fixico said otherwise."

"Nokose, tell him!"

"Tall Bull was born a liar," Nokose spat above Wind Spirit's howl. "I would sooner trade with a witch than him."

"And White Stone?" Old Grandfather asked.

Ah, yes. Totka's thoughts turned more spiteful. That eager sister of his. Eager to rid them of a burden, eager to do away with the white woman Totka adored. All in the name of fear, that monster that oft times robbed her of sanity. Fear of hunger. Fear of change.

"I know not what possessed her to do as she did," Nokose replied, head shaking. "I gave her absolute authority over the slaves, but I never would have approved of the trade, any trade."

"It is as I feared." Old Grandfather's voice rasped with age and weariness. "I spared the autumn hair a maiming, but she lacks another dawn at the pole."

No! Where was the justice in this? "Is it so hard to believe Tall Bull would ignore your instructions and make demands of the woman? She was forced to protect herself by fleeing!" Totka's raised voice caused her to stir, and she began to tremble—a favorable turn. She was warming. He cinched the blanket tighter about her. "Let me cut her down, Old Grandfather. She will die here and for what? Tall

Bull's defiance?"

The tremble became violent, and she moaned, turned her face into Totka. Fire Maker huffed and paced, Nokose stood morose and silent, and Old Grandfather studied the fire for interminable moments before speaking.

"Escape, especially during time of war, cannot be excused. Her punishment must be meted out."

Then Totka would bear it for her.

Before he could lay claim to it, Fire Maker spoke up. "Let me take her shame, Old Grandfather. I'll stay at the pole this night."

Totka and Nokose swapped wide-eyed glances. If anyone took her place, it should be one of them. Nokose, because he'd pledged he would. Totka, because he loved her.

But they couldn't deny Fire Maker this opportunity to ripen. The brave, dressed in leggings, shin-high moccasins, several layers of shirts, a stroud coat, and a turban to match his father's, would weather the night with little damage.

Old Grandfather shifted and hedged, then lifted a gnarled hand. "I will allow it."

As serious as a warrior about his medicine, Fire Maker knelt before Copper Woman and shielded her from the stinging ice with his body.

Totka applied an approving pat to Fire Maker's jaw and lifted tense lips in encouragement.

"Totka Hadjo will take the woman to Singing Grass' lodge," Old Grandfather said. "The horse, he will return to Tall Bull. The mirror and beads, Nokose Fixico will keep as payment for Tall Bull's deceit. The woman is but a slave and will not be the cause of broken harmony in your clan. The question of whether Tall Bull broke trust by attempting to couple with her is to be buried and forgotten."

Totka would bury nothing, much less forget. At Nokose's slight nod, he took his knife in hand.

"No. T-totka, no." She floundered to pull herself erect, but he restrained her and wedged the steel tip into the gap between the thong and her ear. "Do not allow—"

"Be still, or I will cut you."

"I will c-carry . . . my own . . . sh-sh-shame."

"And how do you plan to do so when you cannot carry your own tongue?"

The thong snapped, and Fire Maker caught the swinging end, handed it to his father, and offered up his wrists.

Copper Woman's arms fell, lifeless. "Nokose, he is b-but a boy—"

"Hush, woman." Nokose removed his woolen vest and gave it to Fire Maker. "Do not dishonor my son's sacrifice." When he'd finished lashing the boy's hands, he lifted Copper Woman off Totka and strode with her in arms to the horses.

Totka gripped the boy behind the neck. "Remember what I taught you: chin high, back strong and proud. Dawn comes swiftly."

"Yes, Pawa. I will not forget." Eyes, bold and black, stared back at Totka, unblinking, unafraid. It took all Totka's willpower not to swoop down for a crushing embrace.

Instead, he took the Beloved Man by the elbow. "Maddo, Old Grandfather. Let me guide you to your lodge."

"Ach, I can guide myself. Go now. Be with your woman."

Needing no further encouragement, Totka jogged to his horse, mounted, and accepted Copper Woman from Nokose who handed her up. Her head lulled with sleep.

"I will see to Old Grandfather then come for the horse," Nokose said. "We'll keep it not one night longer."

"Best warn my cousin to seek asylum in a **peace town**." Totka's voice was gravel.

"Best keep your temper in check. Tall Bull is too proud to flee to a peace town. He will stay and fight, and I'll be forced to save your neck." Nokose's grin was audible. "One more thing. She is yours."

"Mine? But I have nothing to trade for—"

"In truth, has the woman ever been mine? No, Brother, she has always been yours. I ask only a two-fold pledge of you."

"Name it."

"At the next blackberry moon, unless she has agreed to bind her life to yours, you must free her. And she mustn't know of the arrangement."

The wind kicked, and Copper Woman started into consciousness and released a whimper.

Nokose gripped Totka's sleeve. "Do you hear me? Not a word of this to anyone. Only Old Grandfather. I will tell him now."

His brother was in earnest with this strange demand.

"Agreed. With thanks." Totka offered his arm to his brother.

Nokose shook it and smacked the mare's rump, urging her into a brisk walk.

Copper Woman burrowed into Totka as though she knew where she belonged, that she was his.

His . . . The reality of it was heady; the responsibility, sobering. But he was game.

Her quaking hollowed him. He kissed the top of her head and secured her seating. "Did he violate you? Tell me true."

"He d-did not."

"But he would have."

"I think so, yes, and the p-pole was the better ch-choice."

He expelled a great, cloudy breath.

"I was . . . afraid, Totka. And I f-fled." The slur was worsening. She would be out again before they reached Singing Grass' courtyard.

"I heard."

"Is your anger v-very hot?"

She feared he was disappointed in her?

"Far from it. You are the pride of my heart." Although this night, Fire Maker ran a close second.

Inside the stifling winter lodge, Copper Woman slept like a wintering bear. Totka held her until her shivering slowed and their shared heat became overbearing. Then, amid White Stone's protests, he eased Copper Woman onto his own couch, tucked his blankets around her—keeping one for himself—and slipped back into the

242

gruesome night.

His eldest sister, he would deal with later.

A series of side lanes led him into the council square opposite Fire Maker who circled the pole, dancing a shuffled rhythm. His faint chant, pitched high with youth, countered the north wind penetrating the blanket about Totka's shoulders.

He smiled.

In a dark edge of the council square in the east-facing shed, Totka found Old Grandfather huddled on a cane bench under his buffalo robe. He should have known the micco would not abandon the brave. Totka joined him.

The sleet came at them from all angles, drumming, burning, demanding their misery. As brazen as ever, the sacred fire blazed on, its ancient red spirit whipping and snapping, bowing to the wind, only to flare again, more determined than before.

For a long while, neither man spoke, only gazed into the fire and glanced occasionally at the boy.

Old Grandfather broke the silence. "Nokose Fixico tells me he has given the woman to you."

"It is so, but if she has not agreed to bind herself to me by the coming blackberry moon, I must set her free to do as she pleases." The only explanation Totka had arrived at was that Nokose would have her choose him for love, not freedom. As would Totka.

Old Grandfather gave a long, slow nod. "Totka Hadjo has flaunted the order of the ancient ways, but the spirits have been forgiving."

This time.

"I am blessed." They both were. His carelessness had almost cost his beloved her life. But even now, he found it a chore to regret one moment they'd spent together.

"The medicine maker has noted your disrespect. Should you fall ill, he might refuse to treat you. Some have heard our knower say that the copper daughter *is* your illness. Be cautious. They are powerful men, and they are watching."

Something akin to fear weaseled itself under Totka's breastbone. That sham of a prophet would dare call Copper Woman bad medicine, evil magic? He rubbed the bubble of a scar beneath his legging. "And what say you, Old Grandfather?" In the end, the ancient one's opinion was the only one that mattered.

"This old man says the Copper Woman is your healing song." His chuckle warmed Totka through, dispelled every doubt and trepidation.

She *was* his healing song. Singing Grass had been the first to point it out.

"My heart tells me that, one day, it will please her to become your wife. Creator fashions a partner for every man, and it makes my heart sing to know Totka Hadjo might have at last found his. In time, her wounds will stitch together, and she will look favorably upon you."

Yes, before long, she would see Totka for who he was — simply an instrument of war, one willing to slice down any who threatened the existence of those he loved. Soon, she would realize that included her.

But the war was drawing closer. The Red Sticks were losing ground to the Long Guns. Upper Creek Talwas had burned; provisions and ammunition had been confiscated. When the battle reached Kossati, if the People were not gone — hidden well inside the nearly impenetrable woods — he would lose her.

Totka sealed off a gap in the blanket where the elements invaded. "The fate of a man's heart is a trifling matter when conflict is so near to striking our innocents."

"You are mistaken. We must carry on loving, marrying, bearing Muscogee children, so that when the war has ended and our men are few, the People may have hope for a future."

Totka scowled, displeased at the micco's uncensored doubt regarding their future. "Surely, Old Grandfather, it will not end so badly."

"Do not deceive yourself," he said in that slow, deliberate tone that heralded a speech.

Totka settled in as Old Grandfather held up his hand to capture sleet. "The Muscogee are like the ice that appears today and tomorrow is water. We are like the wounded doe that hears the approaching footsteps of the hunter. Our bright star of hope, hovering about the horizon, is dimming. The Muscogees' night is coming, and it promises to be dark."

Old Grandfather's wiry eyebrows knit together. "Our warriors must prepare their bodies for battle. They must sharpen their tomahawks to an edge. But know that, for all the warriors' fighting, the trees you played on as a boy will one day be cut down to fence the land which the white intruders dare to call their own. Soon, their broad roads will pass over the graves of our fathers, and their places of rest will be blotted out forever.

"Totka Hadjo must prepare his heart. The time of our great people draws to a close. But first, the Long Guns will drive us into the woods. They will burn our homes and raze our fields. When that day comes, many will string their bows and take to the battlefield. But a few warriors will be needed to carry our sacred fire, to keep it burning, to protect the old and the feeble, the women and the fledgling braves. When the war has burnt itself to the ground, those same few will be needed to guide the helpless ones back to Kossati, to rebuild.

"Totka Hadjo will be among the few," he concluded.

Totka would be kept from battle? Even after Red Eagle had threatened punishment on any man who didn't take up arms against the pale faces? Bitterness was sludge in Totka's mouth, but he managed the drawn out *maddo* that signaled respect for an elder's counsel.

Hardly a breath later, he voiced his truest thought. "You honor me, Old Grandfather, with this great task and with your trust. But if I were to speak my heart fully, I would say you deal me a strong blow by not allowing me to fight for my people."

Years back, Totka had labored to survive his injury, to stand, to walk, then run. All through that journey Old Grandfather had urged him to hold the war club less tightly and to pursue the way of the White Sticks instead.

Where Old Grandfather had feared Totka would fail, Totka had succeeded. The paint on his rank of Big Warrior was so fresh, it had yet to dry in his mind, and still the micco thwarted his calling to stretch a bow in defense of his people.

"There will be no lack of battles to fight," Old Grandfather replied. "Battles of a different nature than that of bone and blood. The battles that come at us now, Totka Hadjo will not fight so that he might live and, one day, give the copper daughter children. These children will walk with one foot on each path — that of the whites and that of the red man.

"Teach them our ancient ways, my boy. Send them into their mother's world to show the White Man that we are not savages but men with souls."

In a rational corner of his mind, the wiser Totka knew he should thank the man for trying to preserve his life, for giving him months spent with the children, with Copper Woman, for entrusting him with a purpose outside of himself — that of being a bridge between men white and red. But that wisdom was cowed by the wolf snarling to be let loose, to join Nokose, to stretch his skills and courage.

It was no use to argue. Once resolved on a matter, the Beloved Man would not be swayed.

"The boy yet dances strong." Old Grandfather grinned through vacant gums. "He has outgrown himself. He is larger than his name. I will speak to the clan mothers of assigning him a new one."

Chapter 17

Big Winter Month (December)

Winter retreated.

Twelve days after the unexpected ice storm, the ground beneath Adela's moccasins was once again tolerably warm, but it was more than the sun's influence that damped her hairline.

The ceremonial grounds teemed with people, many more than could possibly reside in Kossati. A number of the women Adela recognized from the river, the communal garden, the pole. But the men, in their paint and headdresses, blended into a menagerie of disquieting masks.

She stood in their midst, frantically scanning the expansive plot for White Stone. The woman had been there, several strides ahead. Now, she was gone.

She'd led Adela over the embankment surrounding the ceremonial grounds, past a group of men and women laughing and playing the **single-pole ball game**, and toward the opposite side where the council square crowned a gently sloping mound.

White Stone had hustled at a speed uncommon for her, and Adela had become distracted by a tall, athletic figure absorbed in a game of chunkey. She'd veered toward him, but after he threw his stick at the chunkey stone then swung around to cheer his opponent's defeat, she saw he was only a man with a broad nose and a broader ego. In those lost moments, White Stone had slipped away, leaving Adela alone in a sea of ochre skin and black eyes, each one taking turns alighting on her with curiosity, suspicion, anger.

Adela's skin had never gleamed so white, her hair so red. The pulse in her neck hammered relentlessly.

Where *was* that woman? Or Totka? Adela wished she were back in the safety of the lodge with Mama and Lillian, but she hadn't been given a choice about attending the **stomp dance**. The why of it, she couldn't figure.

The gathering's purpose was to allow for negotiating marriages, to replenish the tribe, and to forge alliances that would be instrumental throughout the growing hardships. None of that had anything to do with Adela.

The dancing had begun earlier in the evening with the women leading out with their rhythmic ribbon dance. Following, the men assumed the square ground and displayed themselves majestically, twirling and dipping, singing and stomping to the beat of a drum and a century and more of tradition. Entranced, Adela had watched from a good distance, wondering if one of them might be Totka, but she'd been too timid to draw closer.

When the drum went silent, the rhythm carried on inside her, rising through her soles, as though the earth's heartbeat were tapping at her toes, reminding her she walked on their hallowed ground.

A reprieve had been called, and Adela had lost White Stone in the masses. She rotated, eyes skimming, squinting into the sun, which dipped its rim into the horizon. Totka could be any one of these men. If only she'd seen him before he'd left that afternoon, she would know how he was dressed.

Adela yanked at the constricting cuffs of her full-bodied sleeves and blustered, nettled by Totka's absence. A knot formed beneath her breastbone; it expanded and pressed and demanded the man show himself.

Her shadow had lengthened by no more than a finger's width

when she decided to take herself home. If he wanted her there so badly, he would have to come fetch her.

She'd turned to leave when Leaping Waters emerged from the crowd, sweet eyes full on Adela. The woman flashed a glance behind her and scurried over. Brightly colored ribbons had been appliquéd to her buckskin dress, and they streamed from her upswept hair; her smile — not quite as bright — pleated the corners of her eyes.

Her kindness boggled the brain. She had no reason for it and every reason to hate Adela for having stolen her husband's interest. Leaping Waters clasped hands with her and squeezed. "You look well, my beautiful friend." Her English, slow and meticulously delivered, was colored with a Scottish lilt; her confident smile, with a long inhale of calming lavender. "My prayers were granted, and your breath was preserved."

Leaping Waters likely prayed to the Master of Breath. Adela considered her own God to be the gatekeeper of life and death, and she had yet to determine whether the Master of Breath was the same God or only a similar version. There was still so much about their spiritual beliefs that remained a mystery to her, but what she did know was that they claimed no ownership of Christ.

If they could grasp his sacrificial death — the ultimate blood vengeance — they would no longer fear the consequences of pollution, and reciprocate killing to ensure a loved one's soul completed its journey would no longer be necessary.

Adela returned the woman's eager smile. "Thank you. God was with me. He always is." The remark stumbled against her conscience. If she had such faith, why couldn't she control the fear?

Leaping Waters lifted her gaze to a place above and beyond Adela, then gave a gentle nod by way of greeting. "Totka Hadjo."

"Leaping Waters." The comfortable weight of his fingers settled on Adela's shoulders.

Startled, she half spun, knocking him with her elbow, and looked up.

Except for lips black as char, solid white paint covered him from cheekbones to jaw. A thick strip of yellow masked his eyes, and a ridge of feathers, fanning out like blue fingers, followed the line of his roach and trailed his upper back.

Breath hitching, she spun right back around.

The weight of his hand increased. "You served us well, Leaping Waters, and you have my gratitude." Totka's chest vibrated against Adela's shoulder blades. "But my cousin is a thief, and the next time he sets his mind to oppose me, I will kill him." The matter-of-fact way in which he laid out his terms raised prickles along Adela's neck, but it was strangely consoling.

"Big talk. Far too big," Leaping Water said, with a slow, disbelieving shake of her head. She began detaching a ribbon from her hair. "You would not raise your hand against my husband because you would not wish me a widow."

White Stone and her four years of mandatory grief came to mind. No one would wish that on any woman.

"Divorce the man and be rid of him!" Totka said.

From the square, a **flageolet** trilled a discordant melody.

"Not while there is hope." She expelled the words on a pain-filled whisper.

"I understand what it is you feel," he said without a hint of empathy, "to wait and hope for love that will never come." The statement left him in a rush of bitterness as though it had long perched on the edge of his teeth. "Leave him now, before he ruins you. Find another who will give you children."

Did they even remember Adela stood between them? Uncomfortable with their intimate exchange, she studied her knotted hands.

"It is not children I long for, neither is it love. No, love is quite impossible." Not giving him time to respond, she switched to English. "Take great care with this one, Adela. He does not easily mend, and he does not easily forgive." With a few swift motions, she bound the green frippery to Adela's hair.

Adela slid her fingertips down the silken strip as Leaping Waters hurried away, wiping a tear as she went. A strange premonition filled her, and she saw herself one day doing the same, running from this man and the hurt she would cause him.

The increased pressure of his fingers on her collarbone told her she was likely not far off the mark. *Beloved,* he'd called her. A term of endearment she should adamantly denounce. But she couldn't because it stroked her ears and soothed her ruffled spirit, and she was too much in need of soothing to consider sparing him future disappointment.

She faced him and tried to adjust to the sight of his paint.

The warring Native who'd guided her from the burning fort had been colored with red and black, the tones of blood and death. This one was equally foreign and wild, unpredictable. Would he sit and smoke a pipe, migrate into a medicine dance, take to the warpath?

Red blurred her vision, and she blinked hard. If she wasn't careful, she would see him covered in gore. She focused on the two elements that remained the same: his crescent moon and his arrow-filled quiver. Not a man present was unarmed — a sign of encroaching hostilities.

A cautious smile perked his cheek, creating miniscule wrinkles in his paint. "Your eyes are as round as Rain Child's when she listens to stories of Rabbit and how he brought fire to the People."

"And why should they not be? With feathers growing from your head, you are as strange to me as a tie-snake." She injected levity into her voice, but she was only half joking. "Next, you will sprout scales, drag me into the river, and take my soul to the dark place."

His smile doubled but hung just shy of natural. She wasn't fooling him. "The only place I wish to drag you is the square. They'll gather soon for the round dance, the friendship dances soon after. Join me." He flipped his palm up much as he had done by the dugout.

Pretending not to notice, she nudged a teasing smile into place. "If I must, but does the friendship dance bind me to accepting your friendship?"

Genuine humor touched his eyes. "Is it so unpleasant a thought?"

A dramatic sigh accompanied the plunk of her hand into his. "It is a beastly chore, but I am willing to bear it."

"Ach!" He slammed a fist against his chest as though plunging a knife. "Wound me less and dig out my heart for your supper."

Her hand flew to her mouth. "It is true — Indians *are* cannibals!"

He burst into laughter, and she joined him, a first since the pole.

From somewhere, a lone male voice began what sounded like a recitation, a call of sorts.

Totka led her by the hand toward the square ground. If he felt the pull of her hesitation, it didn't deter him. They climbed the mound to its flat top where, watchful and expectant, hundreds gathered and blocked her view of the proceedings.

He didn't enter the crowd but stopped at the back corner of one of the four arbors. "Stand here. You will see better." With his toe, he tapped the shelter's underpinning, which rose six inches off the ground. An end protruded the width of her foot. She stepped on it and lifted, right leg hanging, then grabbed onto the vertical pole that supported the thatched roof.

With the height advantage, she saw that the people stood in a wide circle many layers deep. They'd left the center free where the council fire burned low but strong. The sun was gone, and in the fire's glare, she couldn't make out the identity of the speaker, but his cadenced voice carried well above the hush.

Eye level now, Totka pulled alongside and placed a bracing arm behind her. He drew close and murmured in her ear. "The round dance will begin. Watch and learn, then we'll join in." His warm breath chilled her neck, and she resisted smoothing away the gooseflesh.

A leader, singing a signal to start, emerged into the center followed by three others. The onlookers relaxed into quiet, casual conversation.

"How many dances will there be?" Adela said.

Mouth open, he crooked his neck and thought a moment.

"Strange. I've never counted. Enough to last till dawn."

"Dawn?"

"The dancing will go on until sunrise when we go to water, but if you are well behaved, I'll let you leave early." His teeth shone bright against his black lips, which stretched broad.

"And if I enjoy it and do not *wish* to leave early?" Her cheek bunched in time with the playful nudge of her shoulder.

"Then my excursion down the long snake will be a lonely one."

"A row? When you're ready to leave, I will be ready as well."

He laughed. "I thought as much."

Good. Something to look forward to, to get her through this night. As curious as she was about the Creeks' stomp dance, she would be glad to be away from the crowd. Even with Totka at her side, the people were liberal in their distrustful glances.

The dancers were forming two parallel rings around the fire, but her attention was drawn to the slave pole's tip barely visible from where she stood. A shudder threatened, but she subdued it.

"Tell me you are not afraid."

Her gaze darted back to the dancers and their counterclockwise shuffling rotation. She licked drying lips and leaned, using him as a bolster. "I am not afraid. How could I be?" The truth was, she had been and she could be again, if she let herself. She *would* be, if he weren't beside her.

His studious eye told her he knew as much, but he let it go. "See how they line up? A singer, then a shell-shaker woman. Woman, man, woman, man." He pointed, but her focus was on the arm he'd hooked about her waist. "The men sing, and the women provide rhythm with their terrapin shells. There will be four rounds of this. Pay attention to their steps. Left, right-right."

"Left, right-right," she muttered, working to note the other nuances: feather fan in the left hand, knees relaxed, body inclined forward.

The *shah-shuh-shuh, shah-shuh-shuh* of the rattles filled her head but couldn't detract from the impression each of his fingers made on her belly. All else dimmed and melded with the throbbing, repetitive phrases of the song.

The crowd blurred into a conglomeration of bodies, feathers and beads and ribbons, and muted conversations. Only the feel of him stood out sharp and clear: the curve of his chest felt through the arm butted against him, the *thrump-thrump* of his heart, the heat of him, the mainstay of his loyalty, the confidence that radiated from him like warmth from sun-bathed brick.

"Are you ready?" He jostled her out of the trance. The next round was beginning, and the people were moving en mass to participate.

"Ready and eager." She hopped down and took up position in front of Totka in one of the outer rings.

The dance was relatively short, the slapped steps simple. By the end of the fourth round, she was as chipper and carefree as the rest of them, and when it came time for a short break, she was disappointed.

The people dispersed with exchanges of *maddo maddo*, and Totka chose a grassy spot on the top of the chunkey yard embankment. She lowered herself next to him, leaned back on her elbows, and watched insects flutter through the light cast by one of the many torches stationed around the yard's perimeter.

Papa had described a chunkey yard to her once. He'd done it perfectly. It was exactly as she'd always pictured. "Did you know my father is Wolf?"

Absently, Totka traced a circular scar on the outer thigh of his weak leg. A gunshot wound if she had to guess. "Your father sticks to my clan? How is that? Surely, he's not Muscogee."

She shook her head. "Scots, but he lived among the Muscogees many years. He holds the Muscogee in high regard." At least he had before Fort Mims . . . "His first wife, Little Bird, was Tuckabatchee. She took the journey while bearing a girl child. Before the year was out, the baby followed in her steps."

Propped on one elbow, Totka fiddled with a stalk of dead grass, running the dried seed head through the valley of his fingers. "The Bitter Eyes reflects your mother's heritage, but you reflect your Scots father and his love of the Muscogee people."

If she centered on him, on the tawny brown of his steady eye, and let the others on the hill blur into cheery background chatter, maybe she could believe he was right. "The stories of his time in Creek country were always happy ones, and I often wished I had lived them with him. Now, I am here, and although he is not, I would like to imagine I am like him — a pale face accepted into the tribe without suspicion, a woman without memories of war to overcome."

He twisted his forefinger around a lock of hair hanging over her arm. "Soon, you will not have to imagine. The People cannot help but accept you soon, and the memories will fade."

"Maybe you are right." Though she doubted it.

"Maybe?" The straw between his lips bobbed with his grin. "I am *always* right."

She snatched the stalk from his mouth and bopped him on the head with its heavy end. "You are also always *overbearing*." While he laughed, she bounced to her feet and brushed wrinkles from her skirt. "The people are returning to the square, and my feet itch to dance. Take me back, Totka."

He looked up at her from the tops of his eyes, a mock scowl contorting his mouth. "You are confused with which of us is the overbearing one."

Laughter burbled from some forgotten place, and she let it free. "The medicine is bitterest for the one drinking it, eh?" When his response was to smirk and lazily pluck another stalk, she left him at a trot with a few words tossed back. "Very well. I will go alone." She let the earth's pull increase her speed and draw her, running, to the bottom of the embankment.

On level ground now, she'd barely begun to slow when strong arms seized her from behind and halted her by swinging her up and around. She squealed, then laughed and grabbed on until their momentum ebbed and her feet touched down again.

"Now, we have danced both Indian and white-man style."

Adela tried to recuperate her breath while holding her stomach through another burst of laughter. "That was no white man's dance! Stop, stop." She stepped in his path, placed her right hand in his, and lifted it level with her eye. "Let me teach you a dance that is new even to me. Put your other arm under mine. Higher. Shoulder height. Yes, good." Her own left arm she draped across his shoulder. "You are too stiff. Relax."

He did. Barely.

She chuckled at his look of concentration. "You're as serious as Fire Maker during a scolding. The dance is painless. I promise. Count in threes and mirror my steps. Ready?"

At his frown and nervous glance around the yard, she patted his shoulder. "Come now, a brave warrior such as yourself should have no trouble finding the courage to follow a woman's steps."

His eyes flashed back to hers and solidified as his lips shoved upward on one side. He jerked her closer, and she stumbled onto his feet. "Like this?"

Breath coming in nervous spurts, she focused on the bone and bead choker about his neck. "How do you expect to follow if you cannot see my feet?"

"Who said I intend to follow? Tell me the steps, and I will lead."

She laughed again, appreciating the feel of it leaving her chest. It had been too long. "See? You are most clearly the overbearing one. Back away." A hard jab of her elbow to his chest set him from her. "Watch my feet as I guide you. Listen to my instruction. Six steps only. Right foot back, one. Left to the side, two. Bring them together, three. Then back on the left, out on the right, and together again. One-two-three, one-two-three. Yes?"

They moved at a tortoise trot, but several minutes in, when their speed increased, he tried to switch to lead. Their legs tangled, and they almost went down in a laughing heap. Straightening, she whisked disorderly hair out of her face and lifted her arms in the waltz pose. "Again. But there can be only one leader, and you are not ready to—"

"I am." He took the stance—more confidently this time, more

closely—and peered down at her, stroking her shoulder blade with his thumb until her heart tripped and she felt blood rising to her cheeks. "This dance of the whites is shameless," he whispered.

"I like it too," she whispered back, looking at him from beneath her lashes.

Heavens. *She* was shameless. Clearing her throat, she looked away, vaguely aware they'd drawn curious spectators.

A chuckle rolled from him as he pressed into the dance, compelling her right foot back. He caught on quickly, and although still awkward in his moves, he made a fine partner.

"Very good." She forced herself back into the role of instructor. "Loosen your legs and listen to the fiddle playing in your head. Can you hear it?" Shubert's waltz hummed in her throat. Last she'd heard it played was at the Mims' social, but she refused to let her mind wander to the past. Instead, she closed her eyes and allowed Totka to lead her where he may.

"Are there any other steps?" he asked.

"A few. Here is one." On the next diagonal stride, she released his shoulder and pivoted a quarter turn on her stationary foot. It swung her away from him and into the path of Tall Bull's spine-clenching, obsidian eyes.

She stumbled and lost Totka's hand.

The man stood a good five yards away, but in the torchlight, each of his finely chiseled features was distinguishable beneath the rows of his blue zigzagged paint. A beautiful man, even in his severity.

He bore into her, scrutinized her from head to heel, and her insides shriveled. Even though she told her legs to stand firm, they went weak. Where had her courage gone? Was it still tied to the red pole, cowering beneath the scalps, waiting to die? Her back rocked with a shudder.

"It would seem Totka's white woman is stronger than most," Tall Bull said. "Stronger than the pole and a trio of angry spirits. My compliments." It sounded almost as if he meant it. Nearing, he shifted his gaze. "Be warned, Cousin. Your white insides are showing."

Several in the ring of onlookers murmured agreement, and Totka's earlier unease and hesitation came back to her in a rush. Her wind cut short. She hadn't considered the repercussions the dance might have on him.

Totka skirted her and stood between them. "Do not doubt that I am red to the marrow. My sport with the woman embitters you because you are still sore that she bested you at your game. Tell me, have you regained yet the power of your medicine?" Mockery swayed his pitch.

"You would not be so flippant if misfortune had befallen the talwa, and your pretty woman had been blamed and killed for the crime." Tall Bull drew in until he stood mere feet from Totka, whose arms had gone as rigid as stickball poles. "One stolen kiss is scant payment for your own theft, but we were once brothers. In honor of that memory, I'll be merciful and consider us even. We will put this ugliness behind us. There is a war to fight, and I'd rather wage it knowing we have buried the hatchet."

Refusal stamped its mark on Totka's face, but Tall Bull didn't allow for a reply. He spun and left them, becoming but a shadow in the gloom beyond the torch's reach.

Totka stared after him, inflexible. "He has buried nothing."

Even Adela's gentle touch didn't soften him. "Forget the man."

The muscle of his jaw twitched. "The moment I forget my cousin's anger is the moment I lose you, my life, both. He'll not rest until he's had full satisfaction for my betrayal."

"Your . . . betrayal?"

He shook his head and found a smile, brittle though it was. "The dance. It has begun."

Back at the square, another man led out, beginning a new set of rounds. Totka and Adela merged with the group and let the night slip by until a new leader announced the friendship dance.

Much of the crowd dissolved to rest, but the remainder joined hands and formed an ever-widening circle. Totka latched onto the end just as the shells took up their rhythm and the lead singer gave an introductory shout. Several women scurried up to join the line, but no sooner had one taken Adela's hand did the far side of the ring break open.

A woman burst into the circle's belly. "Who is this slave who dances her white man's dance and clasps hands with us around our fire?" Unkempt, cropped hair and patched clothing identified her as a widow. The familiar curl of her lip identified her as the one who'd knocked Adela from the horse with a well-placed stone.

The woman to Adela's left pulled free, jerking her arm. The rattles went silent, the chain wobbled, and the amiable chatter fell into a disturbing hush.

"She is our enemy." Malice shot like darts from the woman's eyes as she circled the fire and drew closer. "Will you let her dance as a friend while her people stand at our door with their talking thunder pointed at our lodges and wish us forever gone? Will you?" She shrieked the last, hurling it in an arc as she rotated to spray all who encircled her.

Blood galloping, Adela cupped Totka's forearm. It hardened, but he made no move, seeming content to let the widow have her say.

The crowd responded with doom-ringing silence. Not a soul moved. Even some outside the square had stopped to gawk, not at the crazed widow but at Adela.

Their censure gouged, and as the pole reared up before her mind's eye, her composure began to crack. Clamping her jaw to hold herself together, she leaned into Totka. "Take me home," she whispered, through her teeth.

Unruffled, he looked down at her aslant. "Three wolves cannot make you run, but this woman can?" The crease of his lips hitched upward. He could smile at such a time?

Then he left her, stepped into the circle.

Her palm was damp and lonely, but as she took in the sight of him, elegant in his bearing and fearsome in his attire, her heart steadied. In the man's presence, fear was often silenced.

"Amadayh grieves the loss of her husband who was sent on the journey by the Long Guns." He addressed the far reaches of the circle, slowly turning to face the opposite side so that all might see him. "Grief is good, but it has poisoned Amadayh against one who never lifted a hand against a Muscogee."

"Totka Hadjo has been poisoned by greed for the woman!" Amadayh said. "His lodge rests upon a foundation of weakness toward the whites. Even now, he would dance their dance and defend them."

"I speak not for the great numbers that descend like a flood, but for the *one* who stands among us defenseless." Unlike the woman's, his voice was steady and strong. It lifted above the crackle of the fire and the wail of a baby in the audience.

Papa had often described how it was to witness a chief in the act of speechmaking, and Totka's self-assured bearing and slow, deliberate articulation gave image to Papa's word picture. If ever there were a chief in the making, Big Warrior Totka Hadjo was him.

His warm gaze came to rest on her, and the storm within her abated. "Copper Woman has done us no wrong, but she has seen more death and violence at *our* hand than many of you will see in a lifetime. Yet here she stands, willing to call each of you friend. Who will shame himself by rejecting this gift she extends?" Totka posed the question to the crowd, spreading his hands wide.

The woman was ready with a response. "What is one slave's meager offering compared to the suffering of many Muscogees? The pale-face soldiers lay waste our confederacy. They defile our sacred fires with water and pray they are never again relit. Who will shame himself by dancing around the same fire as our enemy?"

After a period of silence, the crowd began to murmur, but it was parted by an old man, the same Adela had seen at Tall Bull's lodge, the same who had left her there. Back bowed, skin saggy with years, and gray braids swinging with his awkward gait, he shuffled into the middle where he leaned on Totka's arm, settled his footing, and passed his tongue over wrinkled lips.

"The widow of Mad Dog's brother should have been born a male," he said, "for she would have made a noteworthy Red Stick. Her husband's spirit surely smiles upon her brave speech and noble displeasure. But the burn of Amadayh's anger gives off smoke too thick and black for her to discern between clan and enemy."

The old man was coming to Adela's defense? Her mouth drifted open.

"Old Grandfather's eyes are nearly spent with age," he said, "but they see well enough to tell him this white woman would make an agreeable friend. If Totka's captive is still willing, I would dance beside her." He motioned to Totka who escorted him to Adela's side.

Eyes widening, she took his gnarled hand. "More than willing, Old Grandfather. I am honored." Before she'd finished speaking, White Stone was kneeling before her, strapping turtle shell leggings to her lower legs.

A peace offering? Adela accepted it with heartfelt thanks.

White Stone shrugged it off. "No woman should dance next to a Beloved Man without terrapin shells." She gave a final yank of the strap, then grunting, she pushed off the ground and landed several firm pats to Adela's arm. "You may have her, Old Grandfather, now that she is properly clad."

"Thank you, daughter, but I hear no singing. Have we lost our leader? Why are we not moving? An old man could die waiting for the young to act." He flashed a toothless grin.

The crowd responded with amusement, and the drum picked up its previous tempo. The woman to Adela's left resumed her position, an apologetic smile wobbling on her lips. A whoop sent the throbbing melody back into the air. As many of the participants took up the song, the rhythmic tune wound up and around, coming from all sides.

The leader took them single file in a circle around the fire, spiraling ever closer with each pass. Once he'd all but skimmed the fire, he doubled sharply back. While the end of the line continued its completion of the inward spiral, he moved the beginning of it into an outward spiral and retraced his steps along a path parallel to them.

At some point in the flurry of activity, Adela lost track of Totka. Like a buck blending into the underbrush, he dissolved into the crowd, and that fast-becoming-familiar tremble began again in her belly.

When the dance was finished and the line disintegrated, Adela cupped the old man's weathered hand. "Maddo, Old Grandfather. You are weary. Where shall I lead you?"

"The nearest bench will do, but first, bend your ear this way."

Adela obeyed.

He buried her hands inside his own and spoke softly for her alone. "Our hands—red and white—were created to link together in strength and unity." It was blasphemy the old man spoke, blasphemy against the Red Stick cause, and well he knew it. "Tell them, Copper Woman. When the war is ended and the Red Stick spirit is broken, tell your people we must join arms in mutual respect."

Totka led Copper Woman by the hand and wormed a path through the congested ceremonial grounds. They'd stayed long enough.

He'd seen to it that she'd remained for several more dances, even though she participated in only one more. Over the hours, the whisperings had mellowed into uneasy looks then hesitant smiles. Some of the women went as far as to greet her with brief embraces.

By the time Copper Woman and he left the square, he was satisfied she was well on her way to being accepted by the Kossatis, but she still looked warily about her. Her consignment to the pole had done something to her. She seemed to cling to him with every brush of her gaze as though he might leave her.

That she so thoroughly depended on him both satisfied and perturbed. At last, he'd earned her trust—and dare he say affection? — but it brought little satisfaction if it came at the expense of the warrior spirit he cherished.

Time would play a large role in helping her shed her fears, but that was one item his storehouse lacked. Forced exposure was another remedy, and that he could supply. Gambling on her warrior spirit to resurface, he'd tossed the knucklebones and let them fall where they may.

The gauntlet of the friendship dance had not taken him by surprise. In fact, it had developed much the way he'd envisioned and ended better than he'd anticipated with Old Grandfather coming to her aid. The paint on Totka's cheeks crackled with his self-satisfied smile.

The crowd thinned as they entered the stickball field, its goals now forgotten where, a short while before, men had battled to hurl a ball at them, all but taking hair in the effort.

Apart from Leaping Waters, stickball had once been his burning passion, the skill that had won him acclaim across the Upper Creek towns. He, Tall Bull, and their pawa, had been a force to reckon with. A solid wall of offense, playing the field with unparalleled coordination.

Now, he rarely played, and when he did, it was with considerable pain and without his lineage.

Totka fingered the scraped flesh on his stomach. Minor payment for participation in the **little brother of war.** Today's scrimmage had brought Pawa's death and Tall Bull's hatred to the surface like sickness oozing from a wound, but it would be the closest he came to battle for a long time to come.

"How many villages are present?" She broke into his thoughts.

"I have seen Ockchoy, Ecunchate, **Alabama Town**, and even a few from Pauwocte. Pigeon Roost, of course, since it is part of Kossati's township. Tuskegee, as well." And hardly a battle-fit warrior among them. More would be in attendance if not for Red Eagle's threat. "The clan mothers ordered the dance to bring more children into the tribe, but also to bring back balance. Anger, death, mourning—they've struck the People blow after blow, with more to come. Old Grandfather was correct. The People need to dance, to laugh, to remember who we are and what we protect."

"Old Grandfather is often correct, is he not?"

"Beloved Men do not become so by being often *wrong*." Totka gave a grim smile. He should thank the woman for reminding him that the ancient peace micco rarely gave misplaced guidance.

At any rate, the woman beside him would make the task of staying behind a more gratifying one. Especially since Tall Bull would leave with the last of the war party. There were always others who might interfere. Namely, his enemies, one of which was her own sense of obligation to family, as worthy as it was.

The gentle rumble of the long snake filled his ears as they descended the grassy slope leading to its banks. He waded in, and she strolled its edge. It hadn't occurred to him that his paint might disturb their precarious relationship. A mistake.

He scrubbed his face clean, thrust his weight into a dugout, and heaved it into the water. Minding his bad leg, he held the vessel from the current's influence and turned to call Copper Woman to him.

But she was already there, coming around the other side of him to climb aboard. "I thought to help you shove off." She traversed the rocking vessel, chose the far side, and plopped onto her bottom, facing him. "But maybe I am the only one who cannot dislodge a log boat by herself."

Chuckling, he launched it into the flow and leapt aboard. "Did you not notice I chose the smallest? You might have as well, if you'd had your wits about you that day."

"Better to have had a switch to take to your legs!" The bite of rebuke was lost in her laughter. She buried her paddle halfway up its shaft in the water and gave a mighty, albeit crooked, stroke.

He loosed a chortle and pointed to the bow beyond her. "Turn around, oh terrifying one. You face the wrong direction."

"It is well for you I have come along. My knowledge of boating is quite broad, and when we are returned, you will wonder how you ever set foot in a dugout without me." With a hoist of her chin, she swung her legs around to face the front.

He unbridled his smile. "I do not doubt it, but for now you'd best stow your paddle and hold on."

A series of quick, powerful strokes built their forward drive. He then carved an off-side turn, bringing them sharply about to confront the current head-on. Water sprayed over the bow, and as he'd hoped, she ducked and laughed.

After instructing her in paddling technique, they moved into a productive rhythm. A ways into their journey, she cast a glance over her shoulder. "What lies ahead for us?"

"Short Man's Bluff, three **sights** upriver."

"And what will we find there?"

He squinted into the distance. "A bird's view of Upper Creek land."

They said no more until the riverside bluff towered above them. She rested her paddle against her thighs and tipped back to look up at it. "Little Warrior must love this place. Do you often take him out on the water?"

At the sound of his nephew's new name, contentment blossomed. The clan mothers had been generous in assigning him a name that could be carried with pride. "Some. His arms are yet short, but his stroke is sure and his energy unfailing." The dugout's shallow underside scraped bottom, and Totka went around Copper Woman to disembark and drag the vessel onto shore.

"He has taken to his name," she said. Totka had noticed, too. "This morning, he scolded the dog for nipping at Rain Child."

"Did he?" Using white man's manners, he lifted her out. After she politely thanked him, he set onto the almost invisible path that penetrated the thickets and would end at the bluff's edge.

She gathered her skirt and followed. "He did, and he wiped her scratch with his shirt and sent Speaks Sweetly for their mother."

Many times, Totka had told the brave that a good warrior protects his own. Perhaps he was assuming his role?

"I've prayed daily for him."

"And now you will claim we have your invocations to the white man's god to thank for this remarkable deed."

"It is written that he invites his children to go boldly before his throne to receive mercy and grace and help in time of need." She spoke between labored breaths. "So I do."

"And what of the incantation you uttered over Little Warrior in the night?" He severed a branch extending across the meager path.

"It was no incantation, only the desire of a woman's heart spoken aloud to her Great Father. Any power seen was not my own but his. I asked him to replace Little Warrior's fear with peace. If he answered my petition that night, it was not of my choosing, but of his."

"And did you make a petition tonight when Amadayh would have you ousted from the dance?" She had surely needed one.

When she didn't respond right away, he glanced back but saw only the black outline of her figure drudging up the incline.

"There is a promise that says Creator has not given his children a spirit of fear but of power and love."

She hadn't answered his question, but if she believed such a promise, no doubt it had carried her through the stockade and every trial since.

They reached the top, and when he paused to allow her to recover her wind, she pressed on, not stopping until her toes hung over the precipice.

The river and forest stretched below with ridges of tree-studded hills beyond and nothing above but endless indigo sky pricked with stars and the almost perfect orb of the frost moon. To the left, Kossati's fires flickered, but only in his mind. The distance was too far, the moon too full.

He came up behind Copper Woman, rested one hand on her shoulder, and stretched his arm over the other, indicating. "Kossati is south. Just there. And beyond, down the Alabama, lies Pigeon Roost then Ecunchate. Ahead, over that rise, you will find Tuskegee, my father's tribal talwa."

She nodded, hugged herself, and shivered.

The frigid wind had cooled his sweat, and he too was growing cold. He laid his arm across the front of her shoulders and brought her against him, trapping warmth between them.

She didn't resist, and after some minutes, asked, "And what lies north?"

"Alabama Town, Old Tallassee, Wewocau, and many talwas more. And beyond them all, much farther still, the land of the Cherokees and Shawnees. It is good country, all. Fertile soil. Sweet waters. Our mothers tell us that the Muscogees were made from this good, red earth."

"And what do Muscogee mothers say I was made from?"

He brushed her floating hair from his face and clamped the bulk of it inside his fist. "You, my white friend, came from the frothy sea. That is why the Indian is steadfast and the pale faces rove and are fickle."

"I am fickle, am I?" The smile in her voice prompted one of his own.

"Maybe not, but your feet *have* been known to wander."

Her chuckle resonated through him, and consciously or not, she molded her back to his chest and leaned her head so that her temple rested against his chin. "It is beautiful, this land of yours."

"Ours. It is *ours*, Copper Woman." It belonged to him, to her, to the Muscogee. Always.

She let the thought ripen before responding. "You know it is not *truly* ours. It is written that the land belongs only to Jesus, for he created all things, both in the sky and on the earth. All things visible and invisible. Even kings and rulers. All things have been created by him and for him."

"Beautiful words. More so because they are true." They appealed to his ear and spirit, and he couldn't find fault with them. "You speak as though your own eyes have read them."

Her head bobbed. "In the sacred writings. It is ancient and has remained unchanged through many thousands of winters."

"I would like to see this ancient thing for myself."

"One day, you will. Until then, I can tell you some of what it says, if you would like. The book covers many topics about **This World** as well as the spirit world." The cooling wind played chase with their clothes, and a shiver wracked her body. He wouldn't keep her here much longer.

"That would please me. Does it speak of" — he swept an arm out before them — "the long snake?"

"It does. In many places. My favorite would be, let me think . . . the passage that speaks of the river in the Upper World, where Creator dwells. The river flows from his throne, and the water is clear as crystal."

He'd expected a more mundane answer. "And which prophet has seen the Upper World and returned to This World to write about it?"

"A man named John had a vision and was instructed to write what he saw, so all may know of what is to come."

The tale reminded Totka of the visions of their own prophets. Once, the knower Josiah Francis had declared himself blinded by a vision of the Under World and had allowed himself to be led by the hand for ten days until his sight was restored. Because the man was reputed to be a fraud, Totka hadn't believed the story of Francis' vision, and even though Copper Woman's had a more pleasant ring to it, he wasn't sure he believed hers either. However, she had respected his beliefs. He would do the same for hers.

When he made no response, she asked, "What else would you like to hear?"

He looked out over the land stretching south and wondered at the soldiers marching toward them, hacking broad trails through which to haul their talking thunder. "What advice does your book give for defeating an enemy?"

"Hmm. A good question. A warrior's question. The sacred writings has many stories of kings and wars and of battles fought by Creator himself. Those who trusted in his power and strength overcame their enemies, but Creator's son spoke further on the subject. He added that even as we fight our enemies, we are to love them."

Totka failed to catch his guffaw. "It does not say that." It could not. Every tribe in every nation knew better than to love his enemy, for the moment he did, he would find an arrow between his shoulder blades.

She twisted her neck to peer up at him. "It does. And although it's not easy, I try to do it." Her tone was quiet and sincere, and it checked his laughter.

Was that what was different about her? That she tried to love her enemy?

Then again, wasn't that exactly what he'd done? With her? Yes, but Copper Woman was . . . well, different. And she'd never truly been his enemy.

If the Long Guns had massacred the Kossatis and he alone had survived, he would have let his blood come to a full rolling boil, and he wouldn't have tempered it until blood vengeance had been exacted on every soul lost.

She looked back over the river, and her shoulders sagged. Had he offended her?

He smoothed the hair back from her temple and rested his lips on the mound of a scar inflicted by the very woman who had hurled insults at her a short time ago. "You do try, beloved," he murmured. Would he be holding her now if she weren't trying? But to succeed she must forgive, and that, she had *not* done.

Her shoulders hitched back up, stiff and aloof, confirming his theory. She turned her head away from him, and he exhaled heavily.

"Totka, look!" She lurched away and gestured at the riverbank.

There, drinking at the water's edge, stood a white-tailed deer, the Muscogees' elder brother. How fortunate that the wind and the river's churning racket were in Totka's favor.

He went instinctively for the bow he'd laid on the ground, then stopped and looked to Copper Woman.

"Go! I'll wait here and watch. Only, do not forget me." She gave a stammering laugh and encircled herself with her arms.

He shimmied out of his outer shirt and pressed the wad of it into her arms. "Never."

The downward trail passed beneath his feet in a blur as he took an arcing path to come up on the animal's broadside. Within minutes, he crept silently through the woods, walking only on the balls of his feet and his toes, coming in at the perfect angle. The doe picked her way along the bank, nearing and making Totka's task that much simpler.

Bow strung and arrow nocked, he stepped out from behind a tree at the edge of the woods, caught a glimpse of the bluff and Copper Woman's silhouette, drew the arrow back, and took aim. His muscles bunched; his eye aligned the arrow's tip with the curve of the animal's spine, and he whispered his usual prayer. "Swiftly, the reed stills your heart. *Swiftly.*"

A breath before the arrow's release, the doe's tail flashed white and she took flight, directing her frantic steps straight toward him.

Totka stayed his shot, sparing his arrow, and spun for shelter behind the tree just as she raced past.

What had set her off? He waited for the snap and crash of her hasty exit to abate before tuning his ears to the woods.

The water was too loud to hear much beyond the soughing of wind in the longleaf pines and the shriek of a dreaded owl—an unlucky omen.

Then came voices. Men's voices. A number of them, coming through the trees from the east—no, the west. No, from both directions.

Totka crouched behind shrubs and watched their forms materialize from the darkness, heard their casual laughter, and gritted his teeth at their English.

Long Guns.

Here? So deep into Upper Creek territory?

It couldn't be. They were traders. Nothing more. The distinctive, frayed edges of their caped uniforms contradicted his assessment.

Grateful the dugout was on the opposite side of the bluff, he checked his quiver. Three arrows. Too few. Why hadn't he thought to bring more?

The men filtered through the trees on all sides, passed within spitting distance, and proceeded to the water to fill their canteens.

Copper Woman!

Totka jumped to his feet, exposing himself to the Long Gun's backs.

She stood as he'd last seen her, a black figure, small but for the skirt and hair whipping about her. Why did she not hide herself? Surely, she saw the men! As surely as they would see her if they but looked up.

His heart spasmed.

Was that her intent? To be seen? Rescued?

If she were rescued and he were killed — as he would be in the attempt to retrieve her — there would be no one to warn his people.

Or he could let her go . . .

His stomach revolted. He bore his gaze into her, commanding her not to betray their presence. Could she see him? Hear him willing her with every rapid beat of his heart to back out of sight?

The wind fluctuated, enveloped him in a frosty embrace, swept downriver, and collided with the bluff. As though it had carried his wishes to her, Copper Woman stepped back until she'd disappeared.

Totka's bad leg shook. He swiveled back into his hiding place just before the knee buckled. His back slid down the trunk in a bumpy, skin-tearing trek. Sweat moistened his upper lip and trailed his chest. He wiped its sting from his stickball wound and rebuked himself long and hard for his lack of awareness.

But he shouldn't have had to worry. He was on the northwest side of the river, and the Long Guns were marching up from the —

A thought struck him like a war club to the brain.

These were not the same whites who marched from the Mississippi or from Georgia. These had come from the north, from the Nashville region. These had to be Old Sharp Knife's soldiers.

If there was one white chief the Red Sticks were in awe of, it was the one named Jackson. The man was ruthless, even with his own men, but he rarely lost a fight. And he could be at Kossati's council square by high sun tomorrow.

At last, the white men finished, leaving a careless trail through the brush. All the better for Totka. He followed them to their camp, and while he counted their numbers, he nearly lost the contents of his stomach.

Hundreds. Three? Four? *Too many, too many.*

He tore back through the woods, suddenly realizing he'd been gone an extended time. Copper Woman would be worried. He scaled the bluff where he found her huddled against a boulder, knees tucked to her chin, arms clasped around her legs.

He strode toward her, and when she became aware of him, she sprang from her cubby and threw herself at him, forcing him two steps backwards and adhering to his neck so firmly that when he straightened, her feet left the ground.

Her fingers dug into his shoulder and neck. His arms about her were a mere token; she held her own weight. Had she been so terribly frightened to be alone? It was unlike her.

Her breath puffed hot in his ear. "You were gone so long, I believed you to be captured or worse."

This desperation was not for herself, but for him? He'd hardly feared discovery, much less death. Yet she had spent the last while mourning him. English and Muskogee fused on her tongue, a muddle of incomprehensible phrases, until she shook her head and began anew. "I made up my mind that soon I would look for you. If you had been captured, who better than myself to speak on your behalf? But if I had found your body . . . "

Tears gushed from her as though having been horded in a keg these last many moons. Uncorked at last, they were an unstoppable tide. Had she ever cried in his presence, grieved her losses at all? Not that he could recall, although he *had* abandoned her those many days. A selfish, unthinkable act.

Making soothing noises, he stroked her hair until her tears abated. Finally, she wilted, letting him take her weight. "I've lost so many. If you leave me, if you die . . . I-I cannot . . . I could not have . . . "

"Shhh . . . I am here, beloved, and I am very much alive. When the warriors leave for battle, I will stay with the talwa. Do you hear? I will stay with you."

She gave up a long sigh, and his heart echoed it as he bit back the urge to tell her that she was his already. That if she wanted, she could be his in every way until their spirits left This World.

He buried his face in the curve of her shoulder, breathed in her heat, and pressed his mouth to the delicate skin beneath her ear.

Beneath them stretched a bed of grass; above, nothing but solitude and stars, the twinkling of ancestor spirits who would surely smile on their coupling.

She was ready. Her strongholds were broken. He'd felt it in the fingers stamping his back, heard it in her tears, saw it in the tilt of her head inviting further exploration. He obliged, trailing her jaw and cursing her hair for obstructing his route.

When he reached the corner of her lips, her head continued to tilt. "No." The heel of her hand dug into his ribs. "I cannot. The soldiers. You must warn the People."

Frustration burst from his lungs. She was right. As was White Stone. Copper Woman had bewitched him.

She hadn't been the only woman to do so. The first had been too weak to hold on to. The second, too strong to let get away. But this was not the time to pursue her.

After one last caress of her cheek, he shook off her spell and led the way back down.

"What will the People do after the warriors have left?" she asked, tracking him through the undergrowth and onto the rocky beach. "What if the soldiers arrive? What will you do?"

"If they arrive, we will not be there. Before dawn, we will be deep in the woods."

"The . . . woods? Now? With the cold coming?"

"There is no surrender, Copper Woman." The Red Sticks would never willingly give up a single plot of land.

"How many sleeps? How long will the People hide?"

"As long as necessary." To war's end. Through the winter and beyond.

"And . . . where will *I* go?"

What? He twisted to face her, and she bumped into him. "Where else would you be but with me?" She was insane if she thought for one moment he would leave her behind. Hadn't she only moments before begged him not to leave her?

"If you go to the woods, I cannot go with you. Mother, she is not strong. The cold will kill her. I must stay in Kossati with her."

He stared down at her. If she stayed in Kossati to be found by the pale faces, there would be no end to his sorrow. That being said, Totka understood the consequences of taking a sick woman into the woods with winter on their heels. "It is for Nokose to decide what becomes of your mother and sister, but *you* will remain with me."

"Even if Nokose allows them to stay, Mother will not separate us. If you force me into the woods, she will come, and she will *die*."

"It is her choice to make!" Hardening his heart and his resolve, Totka resumed his previous pace.

The rustle of her skirt and the crunching of stones assured him that she followed. At the dugout, he reached for her, but she backed away.

What was she doing? "Get in."

"Please, Totka. Do not send my mother into the woods."

"Enough of this. Obey." With a jerk of his arm, he demanded she take it.

A rock clattered as she retreated farther. "You are a heartless brute!"

He told himself she spoke out of desperation, but spasms still pained the hollow beneath his ribs. "Remove the spear from your tongue, and put yourself in the dugout."

"Vow you will not force me to go with you."

A vision taunted him, that of her dancing hand in hand with Old Grandfather, her features aglow with the sacred fire. He had been a child to believe she might choose to be a Kossati if given the choice. This hardly seemed the same woman who had, moments ago, leached herself to him and wept at the thought of separation.

To hide his hurt, he gave a bitter laugh.

It lit her up. "Do not send my mother into the woods to die!" If any of Old Sharp Knife's soldiers lingered, they surely heard. "You have never led me wrong, Totka, so I would follow you anywhere. Unless it leads to my sister's harm or my mother's death!"

Yes, she *was* the same woman from the bluff, except now it was her mother she feared losing, not Totka. How foolish of him to not realize she would move the ground they stood on to shield the woman from suffering.

He lowered his arm and decided to appeal to her protective nature. "Your mother's is not the only life at risk. There are many helpless ones who will flee into the cold. The elderly and infirm, the very young. If Nokose or I show preference to three captives, how will the People respond? Already they accuse me of favoring the pale faces over our ancient ways. Do not forget the war that so recently divided our people. The Red Sticks' scalping knives are still wet with White Stick blood. Bury this defiance, Copper Woman. Bury it deep, so the scavenging dogs of fear cannot unearth it. In your hands, it is a deadly thing."

Slowly, her body deflated.

"Time is short. Will you come?" Or must he bodily remove her?

She did, but when he lifted her over the bow, she was distant and as brittle as frozen grass.

Adela peered inside a hole in a tree trunk, wondering whether she might be so lucky as to find some industrious rodent's winter stash. She pulled out handfuls of decaying leaves and twigs, then shoved her hand back in. Her fingers located a pile of something hard and smooth.

"Sorry, little dear. I hope you make it through the winter," she mumbled. "Actually, if you'll come out, I'll save you the trouble of dying from starvation and eat you for supper." Her stomach gave a cruel twist at the thought of squirrel roasting on a spit.

Endless weeks had passed since Nokose had kissed his children goodbye and left with the better portion of Kossati's warriors, weeks since she'd seen civilization of any sort, weeks since the last time her stomach had been satisfied and her feet warm.

Rumor had it every Upper Creek Red Stick town had run deep into the forests with nothing more than their sacred fires and what they could carry in their arms to sustain them throughout the coming winter.

Scouring the woods for edibles was an endless task and few escaped it. The old men and young boys were either too feeble or too inexperienced to hunt with much accuracy. Totka and the few other able-bodied warriors who'd stayed behind did what they could, but they dared not risk leaving the camp unguarded for long periods.

Mama rested under their meager tree-bark shelter and gazed up at Totka as he pulled a blanket around her shoulders. He took special care of her, refusing to allow her to lift a hand for anything. It must not have escaped him that if Mama died of sickness Adela could hold it against him. And she might.

Opening the front of the blanket just enough for Mama's hand to slip through, he handed her a steaming wooden mug, then followed her line of sight to Adela who raised an acorn-filled hand in triumph.

Mama smiled, but it was Totka's nod of approval that warmed Adela clean through. It shouldn't mean so much to her, but she'd long ago admitted to herself she was a weak woman.

There was no forgetting how it felt to believe him dead, nor the relief at having him returned to her. And to her shame, in her moment of weakness, she'd allowed him liberties that had all the markings of what was good and right but that led to a ship that must never set sail.

She shouldn't rely on him for protection, strength, or love. That role was God's alone; although, she found it increasingly difficult to trust Him to fill those needs. It was an hourly battle, and she feared that with the next test—and there surely would be one—she would fail again, as she had at the pole, at the dance, on the bluff, in Totka's arms.

He hadn't touched her since that night, but she wasn't naive enough to think he'd changed his mind. While a portion of her was relieved he'd given her space, the other equally large portion longed for the intimacy they'd developed, modest though it might have been.

She deposited her acorns into her pouch and resumed foraging. When his familiar step sounded beside her, she continued combing the leaves and waited for him to address her.

"Have you found much?" He blocked the sun which did little to warm the earth. The arrows, a perpetual fan over his shoulder, were black against the washed-out sky, as was his face. His feather, not as brilliant as it once had been, stole the breeze and jostled the thin braid that held it captive.

The woodland was changing him. The same ornaments decorated his ears and arms and in one fashion or another he still took his ritual morning plunge, but something had shifted behind his eyes and he no longer laughed. His weapons had melded to his body, and he'd ceased shaving his head. Except for the tip by his ear, his crescent moon tattoo was no longer visible.

She handed him her pouch, and he hefted it for weight.

The grim smile he rewarded her with fell just shy of encouraging. "Enough for a decent meal for your mother."

"She has need of it."

Their eyes wandered to Mama who struggled to catch her breath through a fit of coughs. Adela almost went to her, but Lillian stepped up. The baby was taking Mama's strength, but Adela wouldn't put that fact to voice. It would do them no good for her to zing Totka with guilt over something he would not change.

He dug into his own bulging pouch, withdrew a handful of chestnuts, and deposited them into her own. "For you."

"But the children—" At the rebuke firming his lips, Adela quenched her protest.

"Walk with me." An abrupt stretch of the arm accompanied the command.

"Will you teach me to fish now?"

The creek offered little by way of sizeable fish, but most women came away with a small catch each day. How they did it without a net was something she'd been longing to know.

"Not today," was all he offered, his eyes ambling, his tone serious, his mind a hundred miles away.

The crunch of dead leaves filled the silence that spanned the time it took to put a screen of naked trees and brush between them and the camp. Without permission or indecision, he stole her hand from her side as if weeks hadn't passed since they'd touched.

Her stride faltered, her arm tensed. Should she withdraw?

He tightened his hold, taking the choice from her. If she objected strongly enough, he would release her, but his hand, though calloused, was warm, and she'd missed the feel of it, the connection it gave them. But in all honesty, despite his kindness, the man had no right to take any part of her, including her hand, and she would surely regret allowing him this liberty and herself this pleasure.

"I've never seen eyes the color of yours."

"The color of a turtle, my father says."

"The color of the Great Waters before a storm."

She plucked a vibrant green pine needle off a low-hanging branch, inhaled its tangy scent, and twirled it between her fingers. "I love the Great Waters. The sea birds. The salt on my skin."

"I will take you there, to Mobile. We will walk the beach and search for seashells, and I will make you a necklace of them." He said this as if they were not being hunted, as if hunger were a memory.

As if they had a future—a misguided notion if ever there was one. Her smile was subdued. "You have been to this beach in Mobile?"

"Once."

"When you loaded packhorses with weapons from the English?"

His steps ground to a quick halt, and he looked at her with as much shock as she'd yet seen him wear. A short laugh rocked his chest. "I'd convinced myself you were unaware of the cargo we carried north with us. But now that I know you, I shouldn't be surprised. Your sharp eye misses nothing."

"You should have killed me maybe?" She smirked, and he grunted.

"I would have sooner carried the muskets back to Mobile on my own shoulders. As clever as you are, you probably knew that as well."

The grin she withheld tugged at her lips. "Your eyes are windows."

"Singing Grass would agree with you." The fact clearly gave him no pleasure. "Once, several winters ago, I walked near the long snake with Leaping Waters. We were promised to one another. She was beautiful and kind, and I loved her so that I could hardly breathe when we were apart."

Adela squirmed inside, uncomfortable with talk of him loving another woman, even if it was Leaping Waters. She'd hardly spoken with the woman since the town had fled—they kept their paths far apart—but when she did, it was pleasant. Adela couldn't help but like her, which was a strange contradiction to the detail that Adela envied her even the memory of Totka's love.

A strange, shameful contradiction indeed.

"That day, we talked about our future," he continued. "Our lodge was nearly complete and the ground ready for planting. Within a few moons, I would offer the fruits of my hunt to Beaver as proof I could provide, after which her clan mother would free her to wed me."

Just as Adela was adjusting to the sudden switch in topics, the story stalled. "What happened between you?"

He looked toward the creek that gurgled at the foot of the slope they descended. Mist hung above it and stirred in the whisper of a breeze. "Before that moon arrived, I lost her to my cousin, and I have found no other woman worth pursuing. Until now." He stopped, and his roving eyes finally settled on her. "You know what you are to me."

Yes, of course she knew. He wanted her. Had spent a stockpile of days trying to win her. But, though she appreciated him, he was expending his efforts on the wrong woman. It must be so.

With a prayer for wisdom and strength, she swallowed and looked him in the eye. "I am glad Creator brought you to me, so I may know you, so we may speak of Him. But you should not pursue me. I . . . cannot be caught." With no small regret, she tugged against his hold until he loosened.

At his pursed lips, a bracing cold sheathed her from the inside out.

He remained silent for some time, but when he spoke, it was with increasing passion. "I am not called to be a White Stick or a medicine maker or to learn more about the white man's Creator. I am a Red Stick bred for war, and when I enter battle, whether for honor, blood vengeance, or for the woman I love, I do *not* lose. Only those whom I release from my sights will walk away unscathed or un*caught*. And you, Copper Woman, I do not plan to release!"

Dumbfounded, Adela put several feet of distance between them, powerless to unpaste her eyes from the zeal that hardened his features and transformed him into someone she'd rather forget.

The fort . . . the scalps . . .

She dragged breath into tightening lungs, making a wheezing sound. "My memories are sharp, Red Stick. You do not need to remind me of your remarkable skill in battle."

As though unleashed from hell, grisly memories flipped through her mind like a picture-book nightmare.

A child screaming for her mother.

The war cry that wouldn't stop.

He stood before her, hands affixed to her arms. His mouth moved, but all she heard was a single mind-splitting war cry and the rasp of air as it forced its way in and out of her throat.

She clapped her palms against her ears, but the hideous sights and sounds hunted her.

Elizabeth's last words.

The crackle and hiss of flames.

Lucy's lifeless eyes.

Unbidden, one after another, images flooded her mind. "God, I beg you. Make them go away." Tears filling her eyes warped Totka's face. "The Lord is good, a stronghold in the day of trouble. The Lord is good, the Lord is good."

He framed her head with claw-like fingers, and she studied his working lips until, at last, his voice penetrated the ringing din.

"You cannot run from me. Do you understand? Where you go, I will follow." Hadn't he always said that? "Even into the stinking swamp of your memories, I will find you! I will not leave you there to watch those you love die again and again."

The vehemence contorting his features equaled what she'd seen emerging from the fires of Fort Mims, except for one crucial difference — *this* ardor was forged not by bloodlust, but by passion.

For her.

Untamed and rare, it was a passion she'd never witnessed. Not in her father, nor in Phillip or Nokose, not in any man she'd known. Having it directed at her both terrified and entranced. The dual urges to bolt and cling to him made a stew of her mind.

"Do you hear me, Copper Woman? Answer."

Her airways relaxed, and her breath came easier. Her head moved in tense nods until she swallowed through the clog of tears. "But I see you still. Covered in blood" — her lids squeezed together, but the painted stripes on his cheeks remained — "and I cannot forget."

"You must forget."

Her eyes flew open. "I must *not* forget! To forget would be to betray my dead sister and the man I was to marry. I would betray them all!"

"And if you refuse to forget, you betray *yourself*, your own heart. Do you not?"

She couldn't lie to him. "I would never choose myself over them."

"Your path has been chosen for you. Open your eyes, Copper Woman, and see me for who I am. I am a man like any other, walking the warrior's path. To save my people, our land, our traditions! Though bloody, it is the path that brought me to you, and as long as I breathe, I will never regret walking it."

Her head wagged in broad strokes. "My path goes another way."

"You are wrong. Your path is *my* path, that of the Red Stick."

How could he say such a thing, make such a horrid comparison? "I am no Red Stick!" She wriggled free and backed away.

He followed. "You do not seek hair, but you belong to a Red Stick. My interests are now your interests — security, defense, war. Soon, you will accept that our paths have joined. They cannot be split."

"They can! Creator would not approve our union, and my father, if he lives, will split our paths with a single swift stroke."

His nostrils flared, and the swirl of tattoos on his neck quivered.

Had she convinced him to abandon his cause? The thought terrified her almost as much as the thought of letting her heart rule.

Fists clenching, he drew several lung-saturating breaths. Smokey air billowed from him. "I will die before *any* man takes you from me."

A nagging voice in her head told her to fall into his arms, to assure him he need fight no man for her, that she would go to him willingly. She silenced it.

"If I am to retain worth in the eyes of my people and my Jesus Creator, I must speak plain and stand firm." She must settle this. "You are the one who is wrong, Totka Hadjo. I am no Red Stick" — the ridiculous notion rode out on an edgy laugh — "and you'll not fight my father, or *any* man, to the death for want of me, a white woman and a slave."

As he neared, she locked her knees to avoid retreat into his arms. She would see this through.

He stopped when the radiating heat of his body warmed her exposed skin. A rapid pulse hammered the base of his neck. "Have I not yet proven it to you?"

"Proven . . . what?"

"You say my eyes are windows. See for yourself. Can you not find the truth in them?" He tipped her chin and held it in place until she gathered the courage to look him in the eye.

What she saw written there struck the air from her lungs. "The truth?" she eked out.

"A great love resides within me. For you, Copper Woman. And for you I would die ten deaths."

"No, I do not see—"

"You lie. Tell me you see it, or I will . . . "

His thumb rose from her chin to her lower lip and swept across its breadth.

"What will you do?" she whispered into his touch, not as afraid to know as she should be. Further evidence of her crippling weakness for him.

"Or I will do what I must to convince you."

On a shudder, she expelled a breath, barely able to stand the heat of his gaze, to make herself say what she must. "I . . . Yes, I believe it. I see it." If not in his eyes, then in his graveled voice, in the sear of his hand.

Gradually, his body relaxed as a wry smile set up. "I had so hoped your sharp eye would fail you this once."

She eased back and granted him a nervous chuckle, grateful they were back on more familiar grounds, yet not pleased with the result of their argument. Nothing had been achieved except a confirmation of her suspicions: he'd not changed his mind.

Without another word, he retook possession of her hand and

continued walking. Had he decided to let the issue go? What *was* the issue anyway? He'd never asked her a question or made any demand. It was probably for the best. She couldn't take much more — not without breaking down, one way or the other.

His stride was lighter, his expression more serene, and . . . Was that a smile curving his lips?

"Why are you happier now when we have argued?"

"Because, my little Red Stick, I am not the only one with windows for eyes."

A frown overtook her. What had he seen? Her weakness? Her will-draining fondness for him? Her debilitating attraction to him? God help her, she was drawn to him, but she dared not give up her heart. He was a Red Stick, a man who followed prophets proclaiming invincibility to flying lead. Whereas, she, a follower of Christ, was the cause of his crusade. But he'd told her she was far more than that. She was —

My little Red Stick . . . my, my, my . . .

Her heart thudded as her gaze zipped to her hand trapped in his.

You belong to a Red Stick. My interests are now your interests . . .

His interests?

Your path has been chosen for you.

Sweet Jesus, what had Nokose done?

Chapter 18

"Will you tell me how the women fish?" Adela asked Singing Grass who sat on a bed of leaves and pine needles and chopped a red coontie root.

She paused and passed a hand over her rounded belly. A smile slid up her face. "Not *show* you?"

Adela chuckled. "You are not fit to be fishing. But can you tell me how the others do it?"

"Fish sounds delicious. If you can catch it, I will cook it."

"Very well." Adela could almost taste the flakey, white meat. "How is it done?"

Her face reflected shock. "You do not expect me to reveal tribal secrets, do you?"

Adela's excitement wavered. Was the woman serious? She handed Singing Grass another root.

The woman took it, but couldn't hide the sparkle in her eye. She leaned in and whispered. "We use a magic plant."

"A plant? How?"

"Were you not listening? I said it is magic. We drop it into the water, and the fish swim into our hands."

Adela narrowed her eyes, and Singing Grass laughed.

"If only it were so simple, Sister." Totka ducked his head under the shelter and planted a kiss on Singing Grass' cheek.

"Well then, teach her yourself." She threw up her hands. "Take her. She is of little use to me anyway."

It hadn't taken much for her to draw her brother in from mending a hole in the roof of their simple pole-and-bark hut.

"You might be perceptive, but subtlety is not your strength," he said with all the dignity of a chief.

The woman's objective had become all too clear lately.

Singing Grass swatted him. "Be gone! And take this woman with you. She asks too many questions."

"Come, woman. You must catch dinner." Giving them a sideways smile, he took off in the opposite direction of the creek.

Adela rose to follow, but Singing Grass stopped her with a hand on her arm and spoke in a hush. "It's time you decide. If you will not be with him, then you cannot delay—tell him before he loses himself."

"I told him, two sleeps past, that he must not pursue me, that I cannot . . . " She hadn't said she couldn't love him because it wasn't true. But what *had* she said? She glanced behind her at the man in question.

Thumb hooked around the quiver strap crossing his chest, he waited for her.

"I told him that I cannot forget his part in the battle that took my sister's life. And so many others. I told him our paths are different, his and mine."

Singing Grass leaned forward, eagerness enlarging her eyes. "And? What did he say?"

"It's as if I never spoke."

A sharp, misty exhale burst from Singing Grass' nose. "Then it is too late. He will not be dissuaded, and either he will convince you to love him, or he will spend years in heartache." She took Adela's hand in a painful grip. "Try, Copper Woman. You are good for him, and your paths are not as different as they might appear. Try to love him."

"I did not say I could not learn to love him." Adela spoke at a measured pace. "Perhaps, in a way . . . I already do."

Singing Grass' eyes lit with expectancy.

"But he attacked my home. He killed my people. He carried their scalps. Would you wed a man who'd done such things to those you love?" It was a difficult question, but it begged asking.

Hope fizzled from Singing Grass, and she drooped. "I do not know. If I loved him enough, maybe . . . " After some contemplation, she hardened her jaw, collected the root, and chopped at a faster tempo. "We are not the same, you and me. I am no slave."

"Are you saying that as a captive I'm not free to choose?" Adela's heart thundered and tripped.

The knife ceased, and Singing Grass's eyes snapped up. "I did not say that. Muscogee women choose to whom they will bind their lives. Perhaps, in time, Nokose's clan mothers will accept you into Bear." The *swish-clip* of Singing Grass' blade resumed. "Before Nokose left, Totka spoke to him about you." The abrupt lift of her brow betrayed the focus of the discussion: Adela's future. With Totka.

Why would the men be speaking about her? Nokose himself had said the war would be over soon, and she would be a free woman again. Had Nokose lied to her those months ago, or was he simply perpetuating their charade? Either way, it was clear by Singing Grass' closed expression she would give no more answers.

Adela stood. "Thank you for warning me of this."

"Bah! It was not meant as a warning but as encouragement to open yourself to him." With a weighty sigh, the woman set aside her frustration and presented a tight, little smile. "The warning is this— take care with my brother. Once given, his love burns hot, and it does not die easy."

Adela already knew this about the man, and it was too late.

Heavy of heart, she arranged her face into what she hoped was a pleasant look and trotted to catch up with him. "The creek is behind us."

"Singing Grass said we need a magic plant. We might find it in the shade of those trees."

They roamed the woods for quite some time before he knelt and rummaged through the blanket of fallen leaves. He indicated a small shrub, then spoke a whispered prayer of thanks to the plant for its sacrifice.

"We use the root." He gave it a firm yank and exposed it's long, narrow end.

"The *magic* root." She grinned, but he was all seriousness.

"So my sister said, but you do not believe?"

"Naturally, I believe her. We'll put the plant in the water, and the fish will season themselves and jump into our fires."

Totka tipped his head back and laughed. It was a deep, warm sound, and it was beautiful. She tried to imagine him forcing her to wed him, but the thoughts wouldn't reconcile . . . until the image of him switched to that of the scalp-laden warrior, then to the man who had vowed to kill any other who took her from him.

That Totka might do any number of things to get what he'd set his mind on.

When he noticed she wasn't laughing, his smile faltered. "What's wrong?"

Should she ask? With a sigh, she realized she would get no rest until she had an answer. "Before Nokose left, did he . . . did you . . . make an arrangement that concerns me?"

Surprise, displeasure, and obstinacy took equal turns crossing his features. His jaw clenched. "Whom have you been speaking with to say such things?"

"You said I belong to a Red Stick, but that my interests are tied to you. Not Nokose. *You.*"

A shrug bumped his shoulder. "His interests, my interests—they are one." He moved to rise, but she stopped him with a touch.

"So it's not true?" Her pitch swung high with hope.

"And if I told you we have shaken on it, that you are mine already?" His face was a perfect mask of nothingness, windows closed.

Was he testing her? Or revealing what he'd already done?

Regardless, the truth remained the truth. "A man may own a woman's body, but her heart is not a *thing* to be bartered for or sold," she said softly, failing to ward off the sting of tears.

His study broke off. After he pulled out his knife, he busily sawed at the shrub's stalk. "I cannot speak of it, and I cannot abide this display of weakness. It has made too many appearances of late. Put away your tears, Copper Woman. They'll do you little good."

As though his knife bit into her heart instead of the root, she fisted the front of her blouse and methodically breathed through the pang of his censure.

"Your sister has come," he said without looking up.

"I'm pleased you two enjoy each other so much." Lillian spoke from just behind them.

Adela stood and used the distraction of brushing herself off to fit in several energetic blinks to eradicate her tears. "Is there something you need?"

"No, I'm here for something you need—a chaperone." She eyed Totka. "I don't trust him. Not where you're concerned."

"Do you realize he understands some English? You might apologize, seeing how he provides for you."

"It's he who should apologize." Lillian was never one to back down.

"Enough," Totka barked in Muskogee. "She comes with us." Faster than Adela would have thought possible, the man beat a path through the undergrowth in the direction of the creek.

Not trusting herself to speak kindly to her sister, Adela fell in step behind him.

Lillian's heavy footstep sounded at her back. Moody and discontented, she was more of a challenge to be around every day. Adela feared for her the way she blatantly glowered at everyone. Even Singing Grass, as kind as she was, was losing patience with her.

At the creek, Totka pointed out a small pool created in a deeper section of the slow-moving water. Someone had formed a semicircle of stones to trap water and, from the looks of it, fish.

Without his usual friendliness, he handed the root to Adela and instructed her to pound it between two rocks. He tied the mashed root to a stick and threw it into the deepest part of the pool. "We wait," he said and planted himself near Adela's feet.

Lillian propped her fists on her hips and huffed.

Adela tossed her a disapproving glance. She had no idea what he was doing either, but she chose to trust him.

Totka tugged on her skirt until she stiffly lowered herself beside him. "Forgive me," he said, his tone abrupt, his gaze riveted to the pool, except for a single flash to Lillian who examined them. "Your tears are not your weakness. They are mine."

While her chest constricted, he reclined on the grassy bank, arms crossed behind his head, eyes closed, mood unreadable.

"You are forgiven." She cleared her throat to rid it of the evidence of fresh tears—these brought on not by hurt but by a wave of unexpected affection. Heaven forbid she further weaken this quandary of a man.

Of all the men to belong to against her will, this was the one she would choose.

They lapsed into silence, and within a few minutes, first one, then two fish floated belly up to the water's surface.

She leapt to her feet and ran to the edge. "How wonderful!" She laughed and bounced on her toes. "What an excellent way to fish."

Totka joined her. By the gleam in his eyes, she sensed he'd hoped she would react this way. "You told my sister you would get the fish." He gestured at the water, challenge slanting his lips.

Adela beamed at him. "So I did." After she'd hurriedly kicked off her moccasins, peeled off her leggings, and hiked her skirt to her knees, she stepped into the frigid pool.

"Let him get the fish," Lillian said. "Mama would scold you good for showing your legs, Adela. You'll catch your death in that freezing water!"

Adela trudged toward the catch. She sucked in a breath as the cold water sloshed up her dress and wet her thighs. Scooping up a fish with one hand, she hurried on to the next, but an arrow reached it first, whizzing past and dunking the fish with a quiet splash.

By the time Adela swung around, Totka was already unstringing his bow, a swagger in his smirk.

Matching his smug look, she collected the speared fish, perused it, and clucked her tongue in disapproval. "You missed its eye entirely, but Little Warrior might give you lessons if you ask kindly." She trudged out of the water, and he met her at the edge to assist her up the rocky bank.

"Better if you ask. The boy would scale a barbed pole for you." The smile he shone down on her was subdued, but there was laughter in his eyes along with a dose of smolder. "As would I."

"Good to know. The two of you will make fine entertainment at the next stomp dance." She grinned, handed over their supper, and dried her legs with her skirt. Would there even be another stomp dance? It was hard to imagine life beyond the next meal much less beyond the war.

Totka's sober perusal of the fish suggested his thoughts ran the same course.

"What does the root have to make the fish die?" She plopped down and reached for her leggings.

"Poison, but it only stuns them."

"Ingenious," she said in English. "Don't you think Lillian? God created a poison to stun fish."

"Yes, marvelous. Let's go. I'm hungry."

As Adela slid her moccasins into place, Amadayh and a little girl emerged from the trees. Half-risen, Adela froze then straightened and attempted a smile, but the woman, cradling a pregnant belly, narrowed her eyes and hurried to the creek. The child skipped along beside her, black braids swinging across her back.

Totka prodded Adela on, but a shriek stopped them in their tracks.

The woman waved her arms and rattled off in Muskogee so fast, Adela struggled to keep up. Still, the woman's meaning was clear.

Totka interrupted her, his voice steady and smooth. "The pool belongs to everyone."

"Not to them!"

"They must eat too."

"Take them elsewhere to find food."

The girl, bone-thin, trained her eyes on the fish in Totka's hand.

Lillian took them from him and squatted in front of the child. "Are you hungry?" she asked in English.

Adela stepped up. "Lillian? What are you — ?"

"Translate for me."

She did.

The girl's large eyes brimmed.

Her mother hurried over, at first seeming as though she might pull the child away from Lillian but, after a blip of indecision, chose to lay a hand on the girl's back.

"Will you help us?" Lillian's voice was softer than Adela had heard in months, lacking the hard edge that had become so natural to her. "I'm looking for a person about your size to have these fish. They're a bit small for me. Will you take them so they don't spoil?"

"I can help you." A radiant smile shone through the child's unshed tears.

"Maddo." Lillian passed the fish to her.

Rolling a prayer of thanksgiving heavenward, Adela put her arm around Lillian's shoulder and, at Totka's nod, set out toward camp, leaving him behind to deal with the woman. "What prompted that?"

"The children — " Lillian's voice caught, and she gave a small cough. "The hunger in their eyes, I can't stand it."

"I know." Adela tipped her head to touch her sister's. "And we'll be fine, won't we, Lilly? We know how it's done, so we can catch more fish downstream."

"We'll have to create another dam in the freezing water."

Above them, the wind clacked bare tree branches against each other and spit old rainwater into their faces. "I don't look forward to it either, but we've always worked well together. Haven't we? It'll be done in no time."

Lillian threw her a sideways glance accompanied by a half-smile. "I thought that woman was going to pick up stones and finish what she started." She chuckled and shivered. "I imagined myself dragging your dead body back to Mama. It wasn't pretty."

"Totka wouldn't have let that happen."

Lillian looked dubious but said nothing. Instead, she gave Adela's waist a squeeze, making her heart smile and her feet step lighter. Her little sister tried to act tough, but she wasn't. She might be almost grown on the outside, but on the inside, she was little more than a frightened child.

Only a narrow ring of heat hung around the cook fire over which Adela and Rain Child worked. She scooted closer to it, but a bitter northern wind swept away most of its warmth. In her small pot bubbled the main meal of the day — a few Indian potatoes, a handful of parched corn. It was hardly enough to sustain them, and Mama and Singing Grass' children would get most of it.

"I'll put them in." Rain Child held out her grubby palms.

"What would I do without my helper?" Adela passed her a handful of wild onions. A little seasoning went a long way toward adding color to their drab existence.

Each day, they waited for word on how the war progressed only to lie on the frozen ground each night disappointed. Being several days' ride from any known village, they were completely isolated. But except for the threat of starvation, they were safe.

She grimaced at the keening emanating from Rabbit Clan across the camp. A warrior had returned the previous night, as they occasionally did. They came to bring news, provisions, hope. This time, hope seemed to have been missing from the delivery.

Nokose had yet to make an appearance from whatever front he

engaged in, but last they'd heard, he was alive and well.

As she did most days, Mama slept under their shelter with Speaks Sweetly, covered with their one bearskin. At night, her cough worsened, so during the day, she made up for the loss of sleep.

Despite its paltry appearance, the soup's fragrance teased Adela's nose. Hunger cramped her belly.

Lillian sidled up, hugging herself and shivering. "Is it almost ready?"

Adela nodded and raked fingers through Rain Child's hair as the girl stirred the onions into the soup. "You'll never guess who stopped me earlier to talk."

"I suppose I won't."

"Amadayh, the widow we met at the fishing hole."

Lillian looked at her askance. "Then why are you smiling?"

"Because it was quite pleasant. She invited me to come see her baby after she delivers."

"Copper Woman! Look what I've killed!" Little Warrior tore across the camp, holding high a dead opossum by its hairless tail.

Adela laughed and clapped her hands. "Well done, Little Warrior! Your blowgun keeps us in meat."

When he lobbed the floppy animal at Lillian's chest, she squealed, took up their laughter, and passed it like a hot potato to Adela who pitched it straight back to Little Warrior.

"Skinning a beast is a man's job. Hop to it."

He skipped back to his mother's booth, hollering as he went. "Prepare a spit, Copper Woman!"

"I will!"

"That child is always good for a laugh." Lillian chuckled, then brought her attention from Little Warrior's animated discussion with his mother to Adela. "So why would that widow want you to see her baby? I thought she hated you."

Adela squinted at Totka, reading his less-than-exuberant response to Little Warrior's accomplishment. Something wasn't quite right with him.

"Adela?"

"Hmm? Oh, not anymore, I suppose."

Lillian's eyes narrowed at Totka who left his knife and false smile with Little Warrior and made his way toward them. "Well, at least you don't have to keep looking over your shoulder."

Eyes blank, Totka stood before Adela's fire and watched it leap. A few small fish dangled from twine at his waist, but he made no mention of them. His shoulders lacked their usual square form, and he rubbed his thigh absentmindedly.

Lillian sidled up and tossed the contents of her cup onto the fire. It sizzled an objection.

Totka's responding hiss was louder, more startling. He smacked the cup out of her hand, then thrust himself between Adela and the fire, giving it his back, shielding her from Fire Spirit's eye.

Lillian gaped at Totka, horrified. "I forgot," she squeaked.

Water and Fire were opposites, never to mix. Singing Grass had once warned them of the consequences of this. Affliction, disease, misfortune. That was many months ago.

His entire frame tensed. "What were you thinking, you careless girl!"

Adela stroked his arm. "Totka, she simply forgot. It's not—"

He clobbered her mouth with his hand, eyes flashing at Lillian. "Excellent. Stand there and let the spirits get a good look at your foolish face. With any luck, you will spare your sister their wrath and take the full dose on yourself! There are some among us who would tie you flat to the ground and let Grandmother Sun scorch you for your disrespect."

Adela pulled his hand from her mouth. "She meant no harm! It is not our way to keep water and fire apart. No disrespect was intended. She's a forgetful girl, nothing more."

Lillian was in tears, shock draining her face of blood. Adela's own must resemble it.

At the slight softening of Totka's expression, she pressed on. "Is not Grandmother Sun wise enough to know the difference between disrespect and forgetfulness?"

His head dipped with a meager nod, then he studied Adela, looking her over, as though seeking signs of calamity.

She smiled up at him with as much confidence as she could muster. "No harm will befall us."

Gradually, he relaxed, released her arms, but remained a wall between her and the fire. He scanned the vicinity. Except for Mama and Speaks Sweetly in the lean-to, they were alone. "As sacrifice, the Bitter Eyes will eat nothing for four days. And she will thank me for it. White Stone would have let the sun have her."

More than once, he'd boasted of fearing nothing. When it came to death, she believed him, but she'd found he was afraid of two things. Losing her. And offending the spirits.

Adela's throat jerked with an abrupt swallow. "Maddo. I'll tell her. Later. For now, give her a task? The fish."

He untied the twine and tossed the fish at her sister's feet.

"He's crazy," Lillian said, backing away.

"Just dedicated and upset about something unrelated. Why don't you see what you can do with those?" She nodded to the fish and turned to Totka. "What troubles you? Apart from my sister."

He swiped a hand down his face and stared into the fire a long while before speaking softly, painfully. "Old Sharp Knife's soldiers slaughtered our warriors at Hillibee. They had no weapons. No tomahawks or muskets."

"Who had no weapons? The Hillibees?"

"The chiefs touched plume to paper, a paper with words of peace."

The scrape of fish being scaled filled her ears. "They surrendered after battle?"

"Before." His eyes glinted. "They made peace *before*. And there was no battle. Only slaughter!"

"What's wrong now, Adela?" Lillian asked from over the fish she cleaned.

"Wait, Lilly." Adela waved a dismissing hand, not taking her eyes from Totka. "I do not understand. The soldiers killed your people *after* peace was reached?"

"The warriors, yes." His voice fell dull and lifeless. "The women and children are taken captive; the talwa, burned."

She couldn't bring herself to believe it, and when he laid sad eyes on her, she knew guilt as though she'd committed the atrocity herself. A rank whiff of fish reached her nose. "You're sure? From whom did you hear this?"

With his chin, he pointed to the opposite side of camp. "Black Wolf was there. He tells me my father's brother is dead. His wife and children, gone."

She gazed in the direction of the keening, and a mixture of grief and fear stole over her. Would the women retaliate? Surely, they'd call for blood vengeance.

A glimpse of Lillian's big eyes and the skittish, erratic strokes of the scraping stone over the fish firmed Adela's backbone. "Their actions are inexcusable. Creator has seen their savagery. They'll be judged."

His hand fluttered up, as though to touch her, then fell back to dangle at his side. "The shame they bear is but a different color from that of my own people."

"Are we going to be overrun?" Lillian was standing now, the half-scaled fish forgotten.

Adela pasted on confidence. "No, Lilly. Nothing to worry about." She turned back to Totka, but his eyes and mind were elsewhere, focused on some unknown target beyond her.

"The conflict will reach us soon." One hand migrated to the club wedged into his sash, the other to the scar that troubled him. "If the Long Guns find us, you'll be spared, but I cannot speak so for their allies, the Long Hairs. In the heat of battle, Indians rarely show mercy."

"Then we will pray Creator hides us from them until this ugly war is spent."

"Pray, if it helps you sleep, but there's a good chance we will be found."

She swallowed hard. "Why are you telling me this?"

"Adela." Lillian's tone grew insistent. "Why are you upset? What did he do?"

They ignored her.

"Because you are strong enough to hear it and because you must be stronger yet for those in your care. And I'll not have you blind to what will happen if we are found. I will eagerly lay down my life, but I cannot promise it will keep you safe."

"You would fight? So few of you against so many? It's a battle you cannot win."

"Win or not, I have no choice but to fight. You know this." His clipped inflection told her to let it go, but she couldn't.

"I know nothing, except that if you fight—" Her throat clenched, and she forced a breath. "You will die."

Lillian stepped between them. "Stop brushing me off. It isn't *nothing*. Tell me wha—"

Totka snatched Lillian's elbow, and Adela's shoulders convulsed.

"Totka, no. She's frightened and asks only to understand."

He hauled Lillian back to the fish and jabbed a finger at the dirt. "Sit," he commanded in English.

Fists balled and arms stiff, Lillian returned his glare spark for spark. Whom did Lillian think she was baiting? Some untried brave?

"You've outmatched yourself, Lilly. Let me finish speaking with him. Then I'll fill you in."

With a huff, Lillian dropped to her backside.

Totka marched back to Adela, medicine bundle swaying, battle lines scoring his hunger-amplified features. It brought out the Red Stick and made Adela grateful she wasn't the subject of his wrath.

"My sister lacks no amount of nerve."

He snorted. "Your sister is a child who cannot tell friend from foe, and you, Copper Woman, have too quickly forgotten Hillabee if you believe I will surrender to the Long Guns."

"Hillabee was madness. It cannot happen again. Old Sharp Knife will not allow it."

"They will have their revenge for the attack on Mims' place, and I will not surrender."

At the unyielding set to his jaw, fear for his life clamped like a vise on her reason. "If you give your life needlessly, I will go to my grave cursing you for abandoning us!"

His brows pinched together, and he pressed in, aiming his disappointment with heart-crushing accuracy. "You threaten with curses the man who would spill his blood for you? Tell me it is love that makes such demands of me."

Adela rubbed damp palms over her belly and cast a sidelong glance at Singing Grass who'd arrived and hovered a short distance off, concern stretching her lips.

Was love the motivation? She shook her head. "It is fear speaking. Fear you will die a fruitless death."

Expelling a breath, he pulled away and rubbed his eyes with thumb and forefinger, weariness radiating from every part of him. "We are but a few warriors, and our task is greater than we are, but we'll not shrink from it."

Singing Grass spoke. "Brother, if you need, I will speak with her and —"

He raised a halting hand and a tired smile, then turned bloodshot eyes on Adela. "How could I live with myself if I surrender our innocents while my brothers raise the club and die by the hundreds?"

Her fingers dug into his forearm and gave it a hard shake. "You will surrender and *live* because if you do not, who will be left to father the next generation? Who will help us start over, clear the fields, rebuild burnt lodges, stock the rafters with smoked venison? Is that not why you were asked to stay? To preserve us?"

His mouth fell open, but he said nothing, only stared at her. Was she getting through to him?

She continued. "There is more than one way to accomplish such a thing! Giving your life would rob the Kossatis of a decent future."

Awe broadened his eyes. "You included yourself in our future."

Had she?

"Are you certain it is fear speaking? Because your words are the language of the heart."

As her last several statements replayed in her mind, her fingers sprang loose of him. She had indeed included herself in their future. How could she have when her mind hadn't processed the thought?

He invaded her space, stepping so close his moccasin bumped hers.

Like a fish near coontie root, she stared up at him, stunned, unmoving. The wind chilled her widened eyes and made them water.

Was that his hand resting on her hipbone, or did she only wish it were?

"It is *our* lodge you wish me to build, is it not? If I knew it was, I would value my life far more."

Heat swelled from her abdomen up through her chest, and she chastened her errant tongue even as a shiver of longing gripped her behind the neck.

His smooth cheek brushed hers as he leaned down and murmured in her ear. "Yes, Copper Woman, I will live for you and rebuild with you and father your children."

"Enough," Lillian snapped.

Heart pounding in her throat, Adela tried to take a hasty step away, but a steel clamp on her hip held her in place.

"We will settle this. Soon." The heat in his eye left no doubt as to his meaning.

Mama pushed up on her pallet and spoke quietly so as not to wake Speaks Sweetly. "Lillian, why are you upset?"

"Mama's awake, Adela. She needs you. *Now.*"

"Let her be, Lillian. I am not helpless." Mama coughed violently, contradicting herself.

The child stirred.

Adela tore away from Totka's grasp and on unsteady legs went to her mother. She rubbed Mama's back and with a shaky hand brushed the hair out of her face. "Get her some broth, Lilly."

Totka knelt by the fire and picked up cleaning the fish where Lillian had left off.

Lillian grabbed a bowl and filled it, distress dictating every abrupt move.

Mama's brows wrinkled as Lillian handed her the steaming vessel. "What's wrong? Is it the war?" she asked between sips.

"It's General Jackson," Adela said. "His men wiped out every warrior in Hillabee after they'd made offers of peace." Adela's voice dropped to a whisper. "Why would he do such a thing?"

Mama frowned. "I do not know, hija. It makes no sense."

Lillian threw her hands in the air. "Because they deserved it, that's why."

"But they weren't armed. They didn't fight back," Adela countered.

"Were we armed? Was Beth?"

"No, but one wrong doesn't justify another."

"*Chicas, por favor —*"

"These people obviously have no concept of right or wrong. Only murder, and the gorier the better!"

"Lilly!" Adela jumped to her feet. "You mustn't judge the nation by the actions of a few."

"Your sister is right, Lillian. We must—"

"A few?" she roared. "There were hundreds of them! Or have you been so wrapped up in *him* that you've already forgotten? Just like you've forgotten about Mama and me. Each day, she fights for life, and all you can think about is yourself. How dare you put him above Mama, above *me*?"

Astonished, Adela could do no more than blink.

Speaks Sweetly ran crying to her mother.

"Get a hold of yourself!" Mama said, but Lillian was too far gone.

"What's going through your mind, Adela? Do you actually think anything can come of this relationship?"

Adela stared at her, jaw slack.

"Answer me!" Lillian's hand was so swift Adela didn't know it had been launched until she felt its burn on her cheek.

Adela cried out and, when Lillian poised to strike again, she careened back.

From out of nowhere, Totka caught Lillian's raised hand and locked it above her head. With a single forceful move, he twisted her around to face him.

"She doesn't belong to you." Lillian spoke slowly, menacingly. "She will *never* be yours."

The flare in his eye said he'd received her message.

Adela stepped around her sister and settled a hand against his rigid side. "Totka," she said softly. "Free her."

"It is as I told you." His icy gaze was fixed on Lillian. "She is a foolish child. A few days under the sun might have served her well."

The defiance contorting Lillian's features faded.

He released her, and she took a few steps backward before her knees gave out and she sank to the ground.

Mama went to her side. "You went too far, *mi amor*. Adela does not deserve your anger."

Tears coming to perch on her lashes, Lillian seemed not to hear.

Adela moved to comfort her, but Totka pulled her away. "Let her calm herself. Your mother will speak reason to her. You will go with Singing Grass."

"Don't walk away with him, Adela." Lillian's voice broke with a sob. "Don't you dare leave me for him!"

It took all of Adela's will power to keep walking, and when she hesitated, Totka tightened his hold and firmed his stride.

"I'll be with Singing Grass, Mama," Adela called back.

"Adela. *Adela*." Lillian's angry voice reverberated through the clearing then absorbed into the wall of surrounding pine.

Unable to sleep, Adela leaned against a tree and peered into the surrounding darkness. The night's blackness was complete. In it, objects blended together, becoming indistinguishable and confusing, much like the thoughts swirling through her mind.

Lillian resented her, Mama's health teetered, and Totka maintained a precarious hold on restraint, waiting, she knew, for a single assenting nod or yielding look to take her to his lean-to.

Each day, each hour, was a new trial in withholding from him what he wanted. What *she* wanted.

He brought warmth to her soul that her bones hadn't felt in a season. The sight of his handsome, chiseled face had grown dear, and although he never pressured her, there existed a constant lure to share his bearskin, his heat.

And who could blame a slave what befell her during captivity?

How easy it would be to succumb to her deceitful heart, but to do so would be to fuse her fate with his. Theirs would be no frivolous affair but a lifelong commitment, and she couldn't bring herself to abandon her family, for as sure as she slipped into Totka's arms, she would slip out of theirs.

Knowing the danger, Adela had reduced the amount of time she spent with him, even going so far as to turn the other way when he came near. She missed his company, but it was for the best, regardless of what her heart told her.

Footsteps sounded from behind. The accompanying labored breathing gave her mother away.

"You should be resting, Mama," Adela said, but moved over to make room for her.

"How could I when you carry the weight of the world on your shoulders?" Mama's soft voice penetrated the darkness and the fog of Adela's thoughts.

Adela sighed. "Do I?"

"Maybe not the whole world, but a good bit of Mississippi Territory to be sure." A small cough escaped as she settled down and scooted close.

Adela thanked God that Mama's illness hadn't worsened over the last weeks. She knew it was the Lord alone who maintained her. There was no other explanation.

"It is Totka who fills your thoughts, no?"

Another sigh passed Adela's lips. "You should be under the blanket. It's too cold to be up without it."

Mama tucked her ice-cold hand under Adela's arm. "He loves you. You know?"

Adela glanced at the shadowy blur of her mother's face. "Yes, I know."

"And you return his love." It wasn't a question. And for good reason. "You understand that you are already his? That Nokose released you to him? The night he found you at . . . the pole."

Adela's heart stopped dead in its tracks. Typically, a woman's clan required a lodge be built for her and a crop raised. Clearly, the fact she was only a slave made that a moot requirement. "I suspected. How do you know?"

"Singing Grass told me a few weeks ago. Since, I have lived in fear he will force you to be his in every way. I tell myself he is a good man, but even good men have their weaknesses, and you, mi hija, are his."

All this time, her mother had shared Adela's fears, yet they hadn't spoken of it, choosing instead to live in isolated worry. "I feared that too for a while, but Totka has proven himself honorable and respectful of me. He wants my consent, and he knows I'll not give myself to a man who is not my husband before God."

"And . . . do you share beliefs in spiritual matters?"

The soft-spoken question kicked Adela's gut. "There's no reason to worry about such things now."

Mama's airy laugh ended in a sputter. "You would like to ignore this issue, but I would like to know, before . . . "

The way she said it struck a chord of fear. "Don't do it, Mama. Don't act like you won't be around to-to—" The lump in her throat cut her words short.

Mama pulled Adela's hand over her swollen midsection. A patter of little feet thumped inside bringing a bittersweet smile to Adela's face.

"The baby will need you."

Adela yanked her hand away. "No, Mama. I won't have you putting yourself in the grave. You're going to get through this," she whispered, trying desperately to control her emotions.

Mama appeared not to notice her distress. "When this war is over and you have found your father, the baby will need you."

Adela sobbed quietly, but her mother kept on. "Lillian is . . . is not herself, and I worry what may become of her. I will not make you promise, Adela, but I will ask you to consider . . . to consider the baby before making any decisions. It is a selfish thing I ask, but it is necessary."

"You're talking nonsense."

"It is a difficult thing, my dear girl." With trembling fingers, Mama touched Adela's cheek. "You have always been my brave girl. You must be brave *un poquito mas*, for Lilly, for the baby. Just a bit more, eh?"

She tugged Adela to her chest and cradled her head against it as if she were still a child.

Mama's lungs rattled and when her protruding bones dug into Adela's shoulder, Adela closed her mind to the thought that her mother might not make it through the winter, that Adela might be called on to be a mother before she'd become a wife, that God would demand yet another sacrifice.

That when He did, she would turn to Totka in her weakness and forever regret it.

Chapter 19

Big Spring Month (April)

otka checked Nokose's quiver. It was nowhere near full enough, but the time for making more was spent. His supply of powder and lead was also dishearteningly low. On the hunt for something with which to clean Nokose's musket, he opened one of the pouches strung at his waist and hesitated at the scrap of fabric crumpled at the bottom. It was a lifetime ago he'd torn it from his old shirt; another since it had been pressed back into his palm.

He closed the pouch, snatched his brother's rag instead, and commenced cleaning, pausing over two English markings etched into the stock. He'd always wondered what they meant, but Nokose had made it clear long ago he would not speak of it.

Totka should ask Copper Woman what they meant.

Nokose had been back among the People for a day. Tomorrow, he would leave again but not before he and Totka settled their business.

Singing Grass and their new daughter would go with him. Many wives, Leaping Waters included, were already at the Horse's Flat Foot, attending to their husbands' needs as the men fortified the Red Sticks' defensive position against Old Sharp Knife's advance.

Looking up from his cleaning, Totka locked eyes with his sister. She gave him a wistful smile.

307

Her devotion to her husband was admirable, but it should be Totka who went to battle, not Singing Grass.

He would go, except for those in his care. Not to meantion Old Grandfather's refusal to allow it. Totka's gaze wandered to Rain Child who made a talwa of sticks, then to Copper Woman who ground acorns against a stone beside her fire. Old Grandfather was right. The camp depended on him, and he could never leave them at the mercy of the forest and the enemy.

He could never leave Copper Woman at all.

It was hard enough that she kept her distance, adhering stringently to the vows she'd made to her Creator. But he, a man equally committed to his own truths, found it nearly impossible to fault her, which only heightened his frustration.

"Shine my musket any more and I'll kill ten men with its gleam alone." Nokose broke into Totka's train of thought.

Totka balled the rag, tossed it at Nokose, and offered what must seem a hollow smile. "Whatever works to finish this war."

"Have you met our father in battle?" Singing Grass asked.

"No, but it is rumored Big Warrior's men will oppose us at the Horse's Flat Foot. If it is true, Gray Hawk is sure to be there."

Nodding, she returned her attention to the fire.

Nokose had already been to the field, helping in the construction of what they hoped would be impenetrable breastworks.

He'd described the barricade as extending across the narrowest part of a small finger of land bordered on three sides by the Tallapoosa. It was there the Red Sticks prepared to ward off the Long Guns . . . or die in the attempt.

Totka didn't envy his brother the task nor the possibility he would come face-to-face with his wife's father. He passed Nokose the musket. "Tell me you have made my sister promise to leave before the battle begins."

On her way to the fussing baby, Singing Grass rolled her eyes his direction. "I know how to care for myself."

"Quiet, woman." Nokose playfully smacked her rump as she

passed him. "You'll leave when I say."

She swatted back, hitting air.

Totka chuckled. "How much longer until the Long Guns reach the field?"

"Old Sharp Knife's men are on the march as we speak, but the cannon and mud slow them. We have time."

Singing Grass soothed Totka's newest niece, then strapped her into the cradleboard and handed her to her father who was instantly transformed into a cooing mess.

Totka didn't judge him for acting the fool. From the moment he'd first held the little one in his arms, he'd fallen in love with her too.

Named for the times which had befallen them, Black Sky was nothing like her foreboding name. From the first, she'd gazed at him with trusting, unblinking eyes. The peace he found in them was the peace he'd yearned for his people, for his brother.

Yet again, Nokose had woken them all last night with blood curdling shrieks. It was the Shadows and their incessant clawing at the soul. Totka was certain of it. He knew that terror. It had taken some time to quiet the children and put the camp at ease.

This morning, Nokose woke tired and testy. Singing Grass soon mollified his temper, but Totka continued to worry.

"What nags at you? Apart from the battle."

"Galena spoke to him again last night." Fingers flying, Singing Grass wove strands of grass into what would soon be a blanket, an ancient art resurrected by dire need. "The woman does not know when to leave a thing be."

"Do not abuse her." A harsh chord twanged in Nokose's voice. "She means no harm."

Interest piqued, Totka leaned in. "What did she say?"

"She speaks of the god-man the whites claim to be a savior," Singing Grass replied. "Without him, she says, we all go to an evil place when we die." An angry yank on the strand she braided broke it in two. She scowled and picked up another to weave a repair. "After such talks, when Nokose sleeps, he finds only evil. Little wonder."

"Why do you not tell her to keep her tales to herself?" Totka asked.

Nokose scrubbed at his face with his hand. "My mind tells me the stories are nonsense, but my heart tells me to listen, to consider it. Why should her legends be any less true than ours?"

Thank the spirits no such thoughts had tormented Totka. But perhaps after he'd fought the Shadows as long as Nokose had . . .

As if in apology, Nokose shook his head. "It's the thought of death that makes me waiver from our mothers' teachings."

Tongue clicking, Singing Grass cast him a look out of the tops of her eyes, but Totka was intrigued by Nokose's confession. "Copper Woman speaks of the white man's Creator as well. While you're gone, I will learn what I can from her, then together, you and I can decide what to make of it. It's past time you let us all get a decent night's sleep." Totka grinned.

Nokose pondered Totka's offer for a moment and slapped him on the knee. "Do that. Upon my return, we will talk. You're certain she will speak to you of it?"

Copper Woman had put aside her root scraping to comfort Rain Child who was crying over a stick lodge Speaks Sweetly had destroyed. The woman's clothes were faded and her bones more pronounced, but the longer he knew her, the more beautiful she became. "No doubt. Until I confess belief in her god-man, she'll not consider binding herself to me."

Nokose wiggled his little finger into the center of Black Sky's tight fist, but at Totka's statement, his gaze popped up. "Oh? That creates trouble."

Withholding a grumble, Totka nodded. "As much as I love her, I cannot see giving up the old beloved path."

"Has she asked you to give it up or to add her beliefs to yours?"

Totka tugged his lower lip and considered the question. "She's asked that I learn from her sacred writings and that I trust the message of her Jesus Creator."

"It is not an unreasonable request. But for all her talk, she will bind herself to you. White women usually do not lay with men they do not intend to wed."

Black Sky took up fussing, and Singing Grass rolled her eyes at Nokose. "The woman is a stone. She has yet to crack."

Nokose gave an abrupt laugh. "You have not taken her yet?" he said over the infant's wail.

Copper Woman lifted her head, eyes as round as chestnuts.

"Keep your voice down, Brother."

"What are you waiting for?" Nokose reduced his volume minimally. "You've had *moons* with her. Why has she turned you down? Is it because she's a slave? If she were Beaver, she would feel more a part of the People. I'll bring it before my clan mothers. They spoke highly of her yesterday and might at last be agreeable."

"Very well, but she only needs more time. She will have me. Soon." He'd long grown weary of that word. One way or another, his weakness for this woman would eventually do him in.

Nokose turned a critical eye on his wife. "You said she would have him before I returned, that wedded or not, the deed would be done."

Shock heated Totka clear to his ear tips. "Together you plan my life for me from under the bearskin and think me too much a fool to notice?" He hissed the charge, aware of Copper Woman's rapt attention across the way.

Singing Grass sniffed at his indignation and addressed her husband. "My brother wants the woman's heart as well as her body. She is not a stack of pelts to be hunted and traded. This is complicated, unpredictable business." She snatched the baby from him, her lips protruding in a pout. Black Sky instantly quieted. "And Totka is right. Any day, she will move to his pallet. Her mother has not forbidden it. The war draws near its end, so it's time Totka learn the truth."

"Truth? What truth?"

Nokose heaved a great breath. "There is something you should know about these women."

Eyes glazed, Bitter Eyes methodically brushed her sleeping mother's hair, clueless she was being spoken of.

"Galena . . . " Nokose lowered his voice. "She was mother to me."

Totka's brows shot up. Nokose *did* have a story to tell.

"When I was a boy and orphaned, she and her husband took me in. Before they had children of their own they loved me like a son, but our people and our ways called to me. When I came of age, I left to find my clan, but Galena will always be my white mother."

Pieces of the puzzle began to click together in Totka's mind — the fort, the insistence on keeping a sick woman, on keeping all three, not for Nokose to own more slaves, but for Galena. Because he loved her.

Totka shook his head. How had he not known? He turned to find Copper Woman's inquisitive eyes on him — their brilliant green transfixing him even from this distance. Auburn strands licked her face like fire; a groove in each cheek deepened with her generous smile. She must not have heard much.

He smiled back unable to imagine life without her. "Why did Copper Woman not tell me?"

"I instructed her to bury the truth, to tell no one. If the wrong chief had learned that I sought to preserve my white heritage, that I cherished it . . . " There was no need to finish the thought. "I respect you too much to involve you in my deception."

Totka's smile was grim. "Did you know the mother would be at the fort?"

"No, but I looked for her just the same. The other two were unexpected burdens, but I doubt you feel now that I should have left them to die. At least not one of them." A wry smile tipped Nokose's mouth.

His brother had gone to much effort for his white mother, and Totka was proud to have had a hand in it — reluctant though he'd been.

Singing Grass swayed to put Black Sky to sleep. "The plan was always to take the women as slaves but to return them to their people as soon as possible, when anger had cooled and the time was right. But anger on both sides still runs hot, and you . . . " She spread an arm wide.

"Loved her."

"Indeed, you did. And what harm was there in letting you believe she was available? It gave you time to open your mind to the possibility of marriage and to convince her of the same. She might not be fully inclined just yet, but as my husband says, she is your perfect match."

Totka slashed fingers through his hair, uncertain whether to be grateful or irritated. "You gave her to me. We shook on it." The irritation was winning out. "But all along she's known she will be taken back to Tensaw, and you have known she was never yours to give."

"What have you lost?" Nokose asked. "No horse, no pelts. Nothing was traded for her. In short, I freed you to take her to wife or to bed her, if she was willing. It would seem she is not."

"She has much to overcome and requires a gentle hand." But Totka would not deny he'd frequently wondered whether she needed pressuring, whether a taste of him would nudge her over the brink. Doing so was as likely to push her further away.

Knowing she would not—*could* not—leave until the next blackberry month had given him a security he hadn't realized he treasured until it was removed from him. Now, they were telling him she might demand to leave sooner, and the thought wafted before him like a sour odor.

"No matter her choice," Nokose said, "if I do not come back, at war's end you must take my white mother and the Bitter Eyes to the settlements. If you do not, there will be no one." Not waiting for Totka's reply, Nokose called to Copper Woman. "Come. I would speak with you." He motioned her over.

As she sat on her knees before Nokose, she raised wary eyes to Totka. The evening chill tinged the tip of her nose pink; her cheeks and lips replicated the rosy hue, and in her otherwise pale face, her eyes shone large and vibrant and gave off the innocence and purity he'd come to cherish about her. Hers was a beautiful spirit—a spirit with the power to leave him.

Anxiety pummeled his gut, and he worked to grace her with a reassuring smile.

"I gave you to Totka some time ago." Nokose wasted no time. "He would take you to wife."

Her lips parted; her tongue darted over them. "I know."

"Why will you not have him?"

Totka knew why, but he was eager to hear her own it.

Her jaw moved, but no sound came out.

"Well?" Nokose prodded.

Singing Grass elbowed him in the side, and Totka snapped, "Give her a moment."

Nokose rubbed his ribs and glowered at them both. "Time she has had and lost. Tell us, Copper Woman, why will you not bind yourself to this fine warrior?"

As still as a fawn in hiding, hands folded in her lap, she studied an abstract point on Nokose's chest and said nothing.

Why would she not speak? Nokose was right—she'd had plenty of time to think on it.

"I know your father well enough to say he did not rear you to judge a man by the color of his skin." Nokose, sitting cross-legged, propped an elbow on his knee and leaned into it. "So what is the problem? Totka has saved you, fed you, protected you. And by the stricken look on his face, I see he has loved you. There is no one else for you here. Or in Tensaw, for that matter."

Slowly, she looked to Totka. What did she see in the window of his eyes? If she found the love Nokose spoke of, she couldn't possibly understand the depth of it.

"I am guilty of what Nokose accuses me. Stricken." He smiled and shrugged, then went sober. "And if you let me, I'll show you what it means to be cherished."

Her countenance relaxed and softened into a smile, and he knew she believed him and that on some level she returned his affection.

Hope sprang within him but was dashed by the sight of her sister approaching with their mother on her arm.

Copper Woman's serene expression vanished.

"What does he want?" Now that Lillian had arrived, the situation was certain to turn south.

Adela's mouth went dry while her eyes moistened. Deplorable tears!

She felt her weakness as keenly as she did the skirt balled inside her fists. It was large and tempting, and it was growing. Prayers for strength jumbled inside her spirit and, trapped by her desire for the man, never broke free.

Their mother clung to Lillian's arm until Singing Grass made a spot for her at the fire. "Is Nokose taking us home now?"

Singing Grass for once was silent.

"Not that I know of," Adela replied. "Another matter is being discussed. Totka asked me to marry him."

Lillian breathed hard through her nose. "May as well tell him no and get it over with."

Get it over with? As if Adela could dismiss with a word everything that Totka was to her.

"Hush, Lillian. It is her decision to make," Mama chided.

"Well, she obviously can't decide on her own. Look at her. She's actually thinking about it."

Adela flicked an imploring glance at Totka, unsure of what she expected him to do.

He turned to Nokose. "You should not allow the Bitter Eyes to poison her sister's ear. Make her leave."

Nokose cast an impassive eye at Singing Grass who bunched her lips and shook her head.

Lillian, oblivious to the parallel conversation, left their mother seated and took up a wide-footed stance beside Adela. "You can't possibly be considering this."

But she was—contrary to every sermon she'd preached to herself over the last weeks. Because she loved the man.

Wait, trust.

The whisper in her soul was subtle yet unmistakable. And it hadn't come from her own head because she wanted to do anything *but* wait.

Fingers in a knot, Adela awaited Nokose's ruling, longing for the peace Lillian's absence would bring.

He lifted a loose hand, palm in the air. "Since when are marriage arrangements made without female clan members present? My white mother and her dark-eyed daughter stay."

"Pfft!" Totka pushed off the ground. "This is no ordinary arrangement." He squatted beside Adela, placing her hand in his own and soothing out the kinks in her fingers. "Look at me."

She dared not.

A cough wracked her mother's frail body, and Adela winced.

Lillian stood on the opposite side of Adela. "Think of Beth and Phillip who loved you and who died, quite possibly, at that man's hand. Would you spit on their graves? Tell him no, Adela. *Tell* him."

Wait.

At least it wasn't a *no*.

"Do not listen to her, beloved." Totka's placid, steady voice was a balm. "She is bitter and shriveled inside and would have your beautiful spirit shrivel beside hers."

She closed her eyes and sucked air through her nose, breathing in the woodsy scent of him. "I can't, Lilly."

"You can't what?"

"I can't tell him . . . no." Tears pooled and dropped as she looked to her mother. "God help me, Mama, I want to be with him."

Her mother's shoulders sagged, but she managed a wobbly smile. "Of course, you do."

"It's either him or me." Lillian's eyes narrowed, and her pitch fell to a threatening level. "I won't be related to a Red Stick. Him or me, Adela. You decide." With a flip of her braid, she stomped into the waning day.

The pressure on her hand increased. Constrained hope shimmered just beneath the surface of Totka's reserved smile. How much had he understood?

She longed to tell him she loved him, but when she opened her mouth to do so, the Spirit spoke again.

Wait, trust.

Her jaw eased shut, and she bit her lip. She would wait. Until the Spirit gave her clear consent, she would wait.

Disappointment hunched Totka's posture, but he maintained his meager smile. "If you cannot say yes, do not answer. Think on it. There is time yet." He brought her fingers to his lips and murmured, "I would not have you come to me unless your arms are wide open. Until then, I will wait."

Chapter 20

Adela had known fatigue before but rarely like this. Doing well to place one sluggish foot in front of another, she let the moon guide her along the grassy riverbank.

It was night, but Adela had lost track of the hour. More than sleep, she needed to cleanse, to feel the cool river against her skin.

After two days of intense labor, Amadayh had given birth to a stillborn son. From the moment the woman knew there would be trouble, she'd sent for Adela.

Uncertain why she'd been called, Adela had stayed throughout the ordeal. She'd supported Amadayh when she'd pushed and wiped away her hair from her forehead when she'd rested. When it was over, Adela sat by her side and sang hymns until she fell into a fitful rest. Hours later, when the woman's grief gave way to a deep slumber, Adela slipped away.

She walked upriver a ways until the calm water and sandy riverbed gave way to large rocks that stretched from the bank to the one opposite. The river roared as, foaming and tumbling, it collided with the rocks.

Adela left her clothes on the last patch of grass then stepped into the water. Its frigid fingers crept up her legs as she waded deeper, allowing it to carry away the grime and sweat of the last two days. If only it could erase grief as easily. She dunked and scrubbed her scalp, then scurried back to the bank for her clothes.

Dressed again, she finger-combed her hair and watched moonbeams dance over the water's turbulent surface.

Memories carried her back to Tensaw and her childhood. Playing in the river with Papa and her sisters. Mama sitting on the bank in the shade, laughing and clapping as Adela submerged for the first time without fear. Totka emerging from the Alabama, black hair dripping, body glistening, every tattoo staring back at her.

Adela sighed, lay back, and let his image wander through her mind. The grass stirred in the warm breeze, the stars sang in harmony above her, and crickets chirped in praise to their Creator. She closed her eyes and let the sounds of the river lull her into sleep until someone spoke her name.

The sun played on the insides of her lids, and the stroke of a finger against her cheek coaxed her from a dreamless sleep. Against its tug, she opened her eyes to a blue sky and to Totka stretched out beside her, his head propped in his hand.

His brows furrowed into an intense line as his finger continued its trail down her cheek to the hollow of her neck.

Wide awake now, Adela bolted upright.

Totka chuckled. "I didn't mean to frighten you." He filled his fist with her loose hair and let the weight of his hand draw her down.

She followed the gentle tow and lay back with a sigh of resignation. Or was it utter weariness? Dark half-moons hung beneath her bloodshot eyes.

"I should not have woken you."

"Umm." Her lids drifted closed. "You deserve to be strung up by your toes." One crease of her mouth hooked upward.

"You can hang me next to Little Warrior."

"What has that little bug done this time?"

Contentment enveloped him like a warm breeze. What other woman outside his lineage knew and cared about the intricacies of Totka's life and loved ones? "Tossed my bow out into the river to see how far it would float."

Copper Woman's eyes flew open. "He did *what?*"

"My exact reaction." The brave had made great strides in his choices, but his curiosity still got the better of him from time to time. He was, after all, a boy of but six winters.

Flipping to her side, she mirrored his position, the side of her head cradled in the heel of her hand. "Well . . . " She dragged out the word while pointing to where his bow sat within easy reach. "How far did it go?"

Totka burst out with a snort. "Some distance. It became lodged in the half-sunken cypress down at the bend."

"Quite a trek for little legs. I take it you made him retrieve it?"

"Retrieve and repair, which is why it took me so long to realize you were missing. Your mother and Amadayh each thought you were with the other. I spent the better part of the noon hour finding your trail." The irritation of that hour bled into his tone. A shank of hair fell into his eyes, and he tossed his head.

"Did you think I'd run away?" She loosed a deep, throaty laugh and flicked the lock back across his eyes.

Another toss launched the hair back over his head. "Never occurred to me," he lied. Despite repeating to himself she would never leave her mother—never leave *him*—the possibility had continued to whirl through his gut, tightening it with each dizzying pass.

She'd had the courage to do it before . . .

"It's grown late. I need to go." She began to rise, but Totka stretched an arm across her shoulders to keep her planted.

"No need. Your mother is well. She believes you to be with Amadayh." At the inquisitive cock of her head, he elaborated. "There was no reason to worry her until I knew more."

"You're good to her." Her gaze swept him, head and chest,

with . . . was that desire prowling behind those florid eyes? "You are good to *me*." Her lashes drooped and lifted; her lower lip sucked in, a clear invitation—whether she intended it to be or not.

Instinctively, playing out a maneuver that, over moons of waiting, had teased his mind a thousand times, he reached for her and pulled her to him in an overarching embrace. He absorbed the swift, repetitive *hiss* of her breath, felt it swell and contract her ribs in rapid succession—his proximity directly responsible for both.

They'd been here once before, in a chamber made of grassy walls, and he knew without looking that her pulse tapped mercilessly at the little divot near the base of her throat. With his eyes latched onto hers, his finger found the spot.

Her heart pounded a frantic rhythm, but—except for the wreath of copper that framed her face and rustled in the breeze—she lay perfectly still, eyes round, a fawn under the nose of a hungry wolf. Didn't she know by now that he would never hurt her?

He eased down, testing her, and whispered against her ear. "Tell me you are not afraid."

Her breath came in a stuttered hiccup, tickling his neck. Chills coursed down his arms, and he tensed to keep the wolf in check.

"I fear only myself." Her voice was unusually thick. Was she crying?

He withdrew to investigate and collided with a fierce longing in her eyes—two pools of flawless trust. It was the sign he'd been waiting for, the undeniable confirmation that she wanted him.

Not allowing himself to think better of it, he swooped in. Tasting and searching, he trembled while groping for a measure of control, fearful of frightening her.

But she responded in eagerness, matched it even, tangled her fingers in his hair and latched him into place at her inquiring mouth.

He'd been right—all she'd needed was a little pressure. Why had he not done so sooner?

He rolled against her side, pinning her, feeling her form down the length of him. His blood ran fast; his skin prickled. Another minute and he would be too far gone to remember his name.

She uttered a soft moan into his mouth, then gasped and angled her chin up and away from him. "Totka."

"Hmm?" He flipped her hair out of the way and took advantage of her exposed throat, moving downward.

Her body stiffened, and although she hadn't moved so much as a finger's breadth, he felt her retreating, slipping away.

Would she be so heartless as to rebuff him now? "No. Do not ask it of me." A little more coaxing was all she needed. He moved into safer territory and laid a trail of kisses along her neck. "Is it a ceremony you require? It can be arranged. Today, if you wish," he spoke into the silky curve of her jaw, "but give me this time with you. Please."

Her spine hardened. "Totka . . . I cannot—"

He crushed her against him, expressing from her a breathy grunt. "Come back to me." He'd felt her tremble, heard her sigh; she wanted this as much as he did and couldn't possibly be strong enough to douse this inferno.

"Please!" She gripped his wandering hand, her nails biting.

He jerked back, stung. It seemed her strength knew no ends.

The distance he granted her managed only to boost her resolve. She shoved at his chest, then wriggled out from under him.

"What have you done to me?" He disgorged a gravely breath and flopped onto his back, splayed arms limp and spent.

"Forgive me. I-I shouldn't have . . . I should have stopped you sooner." Neck flushed, lips swollen, and hair a glorious, snarly mess, she pulled herself to a sitting position and adjusted her skewed blouse.

He seized a clump of his hair, pulled, focused on the burn of his scalp, glared at the cloudless blue expanse above him. "Why, *why*?"

"It was f-foolish of me to think . . . to let you believe for even a moment . . . Forgive me." Her voice broke.

The woman was contrite. Although the fact did little for his overheated body, it lessened his displeasure. He freed his scalp and stopped just shy of reaching for her.

With trembling fingers, she attempted to comb her mane into a semblance of order. "I did not know you would expect—" Her eyes skittered to him, over him, unveiling her unquenched thirst for more. Her throat convulsed. "I did not think you would ask for . . . all of me." A miniscule shrug tilted her shoulder, reminding him of her innocence. She was clueless to his misery.

"When a man has wanted a woman for ten moons, a kiss or two will not suffice."

Confusion filtered through her eyes. "Ten moons?"

"A full ten. Since the blackberry moon." He propped on one elbow and exhaled a lungful of air, not keen to recall every detail. "When you slew a wolf."

"When we *both* did."

Shame flooded him anew. He looked hastily away, hoping to hide it from her, but a tiny gasp whistling through her lips brought his eyes straight back.

Understanding flooded her study of him, created little creases between her brows. "Oh . . . " The sound was a groan of pain that echoed the one from the Wolf inside him. She reached to him, ran a soft thumb over the line of his jaw. "Totka, your totem animal, you . . . " A hum of sympathy came through her throat.

Prickles tormented his eyes, and he blinked. "You mustn't pity me." Or he would break before her. "I've been forgiven."

"Of course," she said, angling toward him. "But not properly thanked." Feather-light, her mouth brushed his cheek. It was the sweetest of caresses, yet most bitter in its brevity. "Maddo . . . beloved," she whispered against him, then drew back and searched his face. "Why? When I was your enemy. When you did not even know me? Why did you do it?"

He smiled then, warmed by a realization. "My spirit knew you well enough. For you are its other half."

Pink entered her cheeks, and his smile broadened. Her lack of objection spoke a wellspring of words. She knew as well as he that they each filled the other's hollow places. A lifetime of searching would never bring her another who could do the same. The dead Long Gun she'd called Phillip surely never would have.

"Before the wolves challenged me, I saw him," Totka said. "Your lover. When he touched you as only I should." He watched spellbound as she processed the knowledge that he'd been there, seen it all. That he knew there had been another. "It gives me some comfort to know I'm not the only male you have set at arm's length," he teased.

"You . . . saw us? Phillip and I?" The flush swamped her cheeks. "How? Why?"

"Did you think we would let you simply walk away? We had to know whether you would raise an alarm."

"I tried." Her voice went flat, as her mind took a three-day southerly journey. "He all but scoffed. Still, he was a good man. We were to be wed that day . . . He would not have been there otherwise. And now, he's dead." Abruptly, she rose and strode to the river's edge where she hugged herself, hunching.

He observed her a long while, allowing her to sort through everything he'd revealed before removing his moccasins and joining her. They examined the watery pebbles at their toes—hers creamy white; his, a shade lighter than the red sand. "He is gone, Copper Woman, but I'm here, alive and eager to love you."

"If you think my heart belongs to a ghost, you are mistaken." A genuine response and encouraging.

"Is it only the white man's Creator who restricts you, or has your sister soured you against me? I've heard of the needless rules white women inflict upon themselves before they wed. Is that what keeps you away? Help me understand." For he surely did not.

"My love for my sister is deep, but her displeasure alone is not enough to keep me from you."

It was her Creator then—ludicrous notion and too big to swallow. What Totka and Copper Woman shared was rare and beautiful. No spirit would forbid it.

Her tormented expression was a knife to his gut. Why did she inflict such cruelty on herself? He had undeniable evidence of her potential to burn hot, yet she insisted on rigidity.

He stared into the river and gnawed his lip, put out. Yet he was unwilling to condemn her and was slightly relieved it was only her spiritual beliefs that stood in the way. An annoyance, to be sure, but all things considered, it was a trifle matter.

No, that was not entirely true. They'd often spoken of her beliefs, and he would be wrong to say they were anything to her other than precious. At the remembrance, his confidence waned.

"Nokose Fixico spoke of your god-man the night he left."

"Oh?"

"I told him I would learn more, and when he returns, I will share what I think."

"You're a true brother to him." Pleasure and admiration elevated her pitch.

He took her chin and shortened the distance between them. His mouth descended to hers, anticipating the feel of her.

Her breast ceased mid-rise as her palm met his chest. "I've learned it is not wise to start what I cannot finish."

He lingered a moment at her mouth, then shut his lids and redirected to her forehead. "Then I will continue to wait." Voice husky, he gave her a crooked smile. "Though it slays me."

Chapter 21

*T*otka walked Adela back to the camp, so close his arm brushed on occasion with hers, and with each brush her pulse spiked and her grief deepened. But she didn't have time to dwell on his passion or the perfect contours of his chest because Lillian appeared around a bend in the path.

They'd not spoken in over two days—since the evening she'd given Adela an ultimatum. She might not like Adela's reasoning for spurning Totka's offer, but she should be relieved regardless.

When she caught sight of Adela, she lifted her skirt, and broke into a run.

Adela met her halfway. "What's wrong?"

Lillian tugged her arm, drawing her along. "It's Mama. She's in labor. Hurry!"

"It's too early. Are you sure?" Adela took off at a sprint.

Lillian kept pace beside her. "Yes, I'm sure! She's been at it for hours while you've been off doing who knows what."

They were at their mother's side within minutes.

Winded, Adela fell to her knees. "I'm here, Mama. I'm here."

Mama's sallow face was a poor representation of the lovely woman Adela knew her to be—emaciated, weather-beaten. She tried to lift her head, but it fell back with a *thunk*. "I knew she would find you."

"How much longer?"

"*Pronto, pronto.*"

Adela set about getting things in order when she noticed Kossati's women breaking camp. Arms full, they moved out and didn't look back. The shelters were left standing, the fires put out but smoking. Tension permeated the air like a fog of doom.

"Where are they going?" Adela asked.

"How am I supposed to know? No one talks to me," Lillian said.

Alongside White Stone, Singing Grass' children scooted at a snappy pace. Little Warrior looked back, concern marring his young features, but Adela had no time to comfort him.

"Lilly, have you fetched fresh water?"

"It's been kept near boiling."

"Tear a length of string from the blanket."

Adela adjusted Mama's position to make her more comfortable.

She groaned as another contraction assailed her. Lips trembling, she struggled for every breath.

Totka appeared beside Adela, club in hand. "Can she walk?"

"No. We will need your knife," she said in Muskogee, fearing to ask what evil lurked on the horizon.

When he handed it to her, his ashen face brought Adela a new level of dread.

Looking askance at Mama, he stood near Adela, coming closer than she would have expected of a warrior concerned for the power of his medicine. "We cannot stay."

"Leave me." Mama's voice was no stronger than a whisper. She gritted her teeth as another contraction seized her.

Adela stroked her hair. "Never, Mama."

"What's wrong?" Lillian voiced what Adela could not. "Ask him why everyone is leaving."

"Choctaw warriors were seen on the ridge, the far side." Totka's tone was ominous. "They come painted."

The name of the Muscogee's ancient enemy chilled Adela's blood. "They come for us?" Why would they care about half-starved women and children?

"I cannot be sure."

"How long before they arrive?"

"Not long enough."

"Take my sister and go." When she turned back to Mama, he took her about the arm in a pinching grasp and spun her back.

"You are not the one who decides."

"I will *not* leave my mother." Their gazes locked, each unrelenting.

His lips became a hard slash, and his grip became mortar, proving he had the final say. But he knew better than to demand she leave her mother. She'd warned him of this.

"Do not take me from her." An unexpected flood, tears overran her eyes.

Totka vacillated and released her with an angry huff. "I will regret this." He strung his bow, withdrew an arrow from his quiver, stroked its fletching into a sleek line, then stationed himself against a broad tree and scanned the woods.

She followed, glancing over her shoulder at Lillian and Mama. "What are you doing?"

Mama cried out, and a nerve twitched in Totka's jaw. "Your mother calls for you. Tell her she must be silent."

A new fear tore at her throat. He would not leave. And he would die for her, just as he'd declared — *for you I would die ten deaths!*

"No, you must leave. The Long Hairs are allies with the Americans. They'll not harm me."

"You are as ignorant of the Long Hairs as you are of the way of a man with a woman. I watched them kill my mother and grandmother. Trust me — they'll not hesitate to take your life."

She clawed at his sleeve, anger evaporating her tears. "You told me you would live for me. Remember your promise and go! What of the others? Go to them. Protect them!"

As though she were a biting gnat, he shrugged her off. "I can take my stand as easily here as on the run. If not more so. You have one hand of time. Use it well."

"And then?"

"And then we leave." One hour. He was giving her one hour. And then . . . ? "Merciful Jesus, give us a miracle."

Time stood still while Mama labored, but at last, Adela ripped a wide band of fabric from the bottom of her skirt and wrapped it around a squirming baby boy. Except for a few initial squeaks, he was silent. Reassuringly, the little chest rose and fell while his deep blue eyes squinted in curiosity at the world around him.

"I have a brother, Mama." Adela could scarcely get the words past the lump in her throat.

"I know, mi amor." It was but a whisper passed between lips paling with blood loss.

Adela laid him on their mother's chest, then lifted Mama's head so she could see him.

Tears stained her face as she murmured to him in Spanish and kissed his wet hair. "I am dying. Take him and leave me."

"No." Even as Adela denied it, the widening stain of red beneath Mama proved it true. "You're coming with us."

Totka took the baby from Mama and shoved him in Lillian's arms, then latched firm eyes to Adela. "It is past time."

"Carry her. Bring her with us!" she demanded, knowing full well, he wouldn't dare touch her.

Lillian whimpered at Mama's side.

"Go, Lilly," Mama pleaded. "For the baby."

Lillian wavered, then kissed her mother's cheek. "I love you, Mama. Be strong. Tell Beth . . . I'm still fighting." Before Mama could reply, Lillian was on her feet and gone.

From behind her, Totka clasped his hands to Adela's shoulder and shoved his mouth against her ear. "She will be dead before we make it to the creek, and if you stay another moment, we will die with her. We must go, *now!*"

Adela ignored him and took her mother's hand between her own. It was strikingly cold.

"A son," Mama said.

Tears dripped from Adela's chin as she leaned in to hear.

"I gave him . . . a son." A hint of a smile formed on her cracked lips, but her eyes began to flit aimlessly.

"I'm here, Mama. Don't leave me." She held Mama's face in her hands and pushed aside the thought that Choctaw warriors were minutes away.

"Take him to his Papa. *Busca a Dios,* Adela . . . seek God."

Totka's arms became a cincture that dragged Adela by the waist to her feet. Anguish rose from deep within, but before it could escape her, he clapped a hand over her mouth. "They are here. Run!"

Try as they might, her feet refused to obey. Totka took her weight and half carried her through the shrubs and briars at breakneck speed. Branches scratched at her face, but she couldn't see through her tears to avoid them.

A short distance in, her blinding fog lifted, and she saw Totka, jaw set and eyes pointed toward safety, loving her enough to hurt her.

She gathered her skirt into her arm and planted both feet.

Totka felt more than heard the Long Hairs fast closing in.

As surely as he'd seen them cresting the rise, they'd seen him. He'd been an imbecile not to drag Copper Woman away as soon as the child had been cut free. But hadn't he always known his weakness for her — and those woeful tears — would do him in?

She raced beside him now, matching his reckless stride, but he didn't trust her enough to let go her arm. Not after her earlier display. At least now he knew that when the Long Hairs slit his throat she would not leave him to die alone. Unless they got to her first.

The thought injected him with fresh speed. For once, the old wound in his thigh bowed to the urgency driving him, but Copper Woman could not. She stumbled, and her torso flung forward, yanking him down so that he doubled at the waist.

In the same instant, an arrow whistled above his ducking head. It *thwacked* against wood, and with his next step, he hurled himself to the forest floor, bringing Copper Woman down with him.

Their momentum carried them across a bed of treefall and moss and into a disorderly heap. Before they'd stopped rolling, he was back in an upright position—his first thought to his bow, still pasted to his hand; his second, to the arrows spilled out around him; his third, to a warrior loping toward them and rapidly eliminating the distance.

Totka had an arrow notched, drawn, and aimed downrange before Copper Woman untangled her limbs and lifted her head. "Stay down!" He stood on one knee beside her, seeking a target.

But the forest was still. Where had they gone? Were they flanking him? He broadened his scope.

"Show yourselves, Long Hair swine!"

His demand was returned with a silence so complete he knew they'd gotten the better of him. Any second he would feel the pierce of an arrow, and Copper Woman would be at the mercy of his enemy.

Well, they would not take him crouching down or panting like a woman. Slowly, he straightened his legs, his breath coming more even, more controlled.

"Totka!" His name rang out from the right.

Bowstring biting into his fingertips, he pivoted toward the sound but found only vacant woodland. "Who are you?"

"I am Gray Hawk, your father. I'm no Long Hair, and these Long Hairs with me are no swine." Grunts of agreement erupted from several points surrounding Totka.

His father? The voice was that of Gray Hawk, but . . . "My father is with Big Warrior at the Horse's Flat Foot."

"Put away your bow, my son." The voice's owner rose from

behind a fallen trunk.

It had been nigh on four seasons since Totka had seen the man—he was more gaunt and gray—but there was no doubt as to his identity.

"Father," Totka breathed the name, his bow lowering, the muscles in his arm grateful for the rest. His father wouldn't take his life, but the others he would never trust.

Copper Woman stood.

"Stay as you are," he said, sidestepping and backing against her, blocking her as best he could.

Gray Hawk began toward him. "My eyes rejoice at the sight of you."

Seven, no, eight warriors exposed themselves, four with the flowing mane of a Long Hair warrior, all with muskets drawn. His father had taken up arms with their enemy?

"I cannot say the same, for I'd rather not see you at all than see you with our enemy." Those who'd slaughtered his clanswomen. Did Gray Hawk have no memory of how his wife died?

"War is a confusing, bloody affair, but at its end, you will come to Tuskegee, and we will smoke the pipe. Today, though, you will leave the captive with me and be on your way."

"Why should I even speak with you? You're a traitor!" Anger burbled in his pit.

The clicks of several muskets being cocked whipped his bow back into place. He pointed the arrow's tip at the nearest man. "Copper Woman is mine, and you'll not take her."

"She is from Mims' place, yes?" his father said. "There will be a reward. Come, my son, let me help you. These others are thirsty for revenge, but they might be willing to exchange your life for the silver bits she will bring." Gray Hawk held his arm out, waiting to receive what he would never be given. "She is not yours to keep. Let her go."

Copper Woman's hand lighted on his shoulder. "It's a good offer. Save your life for another, more noble fight. Will you not entrust me to your father's care?"

Was she so eager to leave him? "No, I will *not*."

Gray Hawk's arm faltered. "She speaks our language?"

"She is no mere slave. We will be bound."

Gray Hawk rubbed his chin. "Has she chosen this path, or have you chosen it for her?"

"She loves me, Father. One day, she'll be the mother of your grandchildren. You will see."

Another warrior neared, a Long Hair *minko* by the crane feathers protruding from the silver band encircling his head. The chief addressed Gray Hawk in his **Muskogean** dialect. "If that is so, let the woman decide. She will tell us if what your Red Stick son says is true."

"And what of the reward?" another called.

The minko shrugged. "If she stays, Gray Hawk will provide the reward from his own purse—as a show of good will toward his son's new wife."

Totka balked. If there was a reward it would be a goodly sum, more than any one of them could pay. But Gray Hawk nodded without delay, and the taut bowstring in Totka's chest eased a fraction.

"If she leaves him," the minko continued, "I will return her to her people, collect the reward from them, and distribute it among these here. But first, we'll have our revenge on the lying Red Stick."

The familiar twitch in Gray Hawk's cheek belied his apprehension.

Totka sneered. "Do you think I do not know what you will do with her on the road to Tensaw? I will die before I let any man of you near her!"

"If he were telling the truth about her," another taunted, "he would not be afraid."

"Enough," Copper Woman snapped. "You yammer like old women!" She moved out from behind Totka so suddenly he had no time to lower his bow and swipe for her. Nor could he, with seven muskets aimed his way.

"Copper Woman, stop!" But she had already left him for his father. Bile leapt to his throat.

Gray Hawk, cheek in a spasm, eyed her like a plague.

An outburst of whoops and shrieks sent several birds flapping into the air. Two warriors moved in.

Copper Woman spun on them. "Stay your whoops and scalping knives! My father is a close friend of Old Sharp Knife. Touch Gray Hawk's son and the only reward you get will be a noose about your necks!"

Every man, including Totka, stared at her agape. It was possible her family had ties to Old Sharp Knife, but the rest was all bluster. Within minutes any one of them could have her auburn scalp dangling from his belt and neither her father nor Jackson would be the wiser.

Still, she held them in check—not with her connections but with her commanding air.

Totka stopped himself short of releasing an abrupt laugh. Who was this woman? Certainly not the one who a short while ago had been moldable clay between his hands, nor the one he'd lugged through undergrowth. No, this was the woman who'd offered water to a blood-drenched warrior, the one who'd fearlessly bathed before a cohort of battle-brazen Red Sticks.

This was the woman he'd fallen in love with, and as she faced his father, chin cocked and eyes still puffy from her bout with grief, he fell in love with her all over again.

"I will speak with you, Gray Hawk," she said. "After, I will go with your son."

Dizzying relief spurted through Totka's veins, and he locked his legs to keep from swaying.

Her brief, private exchange with his father ended with a swift, bold kiss to Gray Hawk's quivering cheek. She returned to Totka, and he wasted no time grabbing her hand and putting distance between them and his father's band.

When he was certain they were not being followed, he let her go and focused on finding her sister's tracks before night overtook them.

"What did you tell my father?"

It took her so long to respond that by the time she began, he'd forgotten his question. "I thanked him, and I asked him to bury my mother." Her voice broke, but he had no time to console her.

Was she thinking of the part Totka had played in her mother's death? But what was done was done. There was no changing it.

She said not another word as they doubled back and swept the ground near the abandoned camp. The first trail he found was that of a company of light-footed, sure-stepping warriors, a company numbering far greater than eight.

Keeping her a good distance from where her mother lay, he hastened his stride and soon found the girl's trail. It led away from the route the main body had taken and spread as wide and erratic as the Tombigbee. He pursued it and slowed when they reached a slope covered in waist-high ferns. Pointing to a tree, he motioned for her to sit.

Flushed and breathless, she obeyed.

His leg begged for the same treatment, but he ignored it and followed mewing sounds to the backside of a fallen log. He moved aside a bush and was greeted with a barrage of rocks and English.

Totka loosed the branches, and they bounced back into place. He turned to Copper Woman, a scowl affixed. "She is your crazed sister. You can get her out."

Without bothering to move, she spoke, and Bitter Eyes cried out.

"Keep her quiet." Totka scanned the trees behind them.

The bush shook as Bitter Eyes worked her way out. When she was on her feet, she handed the baby to Copper Woman and met Totka's heated gaze. Did he detect gratitude in her posture? Surely not.

Copper Woman came to him carrying the little bundle. "How can he sleep at a time like this?" She pulled back the blanket.

Totka broke his guard to examine the child.

His tiny lids had no lashes, and his fingers had nubs for nails. He was small, but seemed healthy—healthy enough to give a lusty cry and bring their enemy down on them. The faster they moved out, the better.

"We walk," he said and cut a new trail.

Circling wide to the west, he hoped to cross the Kossatis' trail and follow it north. Much later, he came upon it.

When the baby woke hungry, they stopped at a stream and dribbled water into his mouth. It helped little. Finally, he cried himself to sleep. Except for the snapping and crackling beneath their feet, there was silence again, and Totka breathed easier.

By the wee hours of the morning, there was still no sign of the Choctaw war party. Surely, they would have overtaken the villagers by now. Could they have been pursuing another goal? Totka would not risk slowing to find out.

An unnatural rustling sounded from ahead and set him on alert. Totka whistled and Long Arrow materialized from the shadows. They briefly clasped arms without comment, and a few strides later, Totka led Copper Woman and her siblings into an improvised camp.

Sleeping Kossatis scattered the ground. Not a fire had been lit, not a shelter erected.

As he stole through, several stirred and, recognizing him, shushed their frightened children. A dog growled, but was quickly silenced. An old woman whispered words of greeting to Totka, then raised a hand in acknowledgement to Copper Woman.

She signaled back and let out a heavy breath as if releasing a burden.

Totka guided them to a level plot. "Sleep here."

Seeming to understand, the Bitter Eyes dropped and curled into herself.

He held out his arms for the child. "Let me take him to Amadayh, then I'll be back." When he returned, he found Copper Woman and lay down beside her. He couldn't stay long—Long Arrow needed the company of his watchful eye.

"Amadayh took the baby?"

"As we knew she would. The child is in good hands, and Grandmother Sun is nearly upon us. Sleep while you can. I'll keep watch."

"It's good to be back among the People. I feel as though . . . I have come home." Her words jumbled together. "Are we safe now, Totka?" She sounded small and frail, all bravado spent.

"For now. Come. I'll hold you until you sleep."

She flipped to her other side and aligned herself flush against him.

He draped his arm over her and intertwined his fingers with hers. A weighty sigh left her lungs, and within a handful of breaths, she slept.

"When will you learn, my little Red Stick," he murmured against her hair, "that whenever you are with me, you are already home?"

Chapter 22

Mulberry Month (May)

Singing Grass stood before Adela, hair shorn, arms extended, and eyes glistening. In her hands lay an old musket with the initials Z. M. chiseled into the stock.

"Your father gave this to my husband when he left their home for Kossati." Singing Grass' lashes hung low.

Adela understood all too well the endless weight of mourning. Had Mama been gone only three weeks?

Yesterday morning, Singing Grass had broken Adela's cycle of mind-numbing grief by arriving from Tohopeka, the Horse's Flat Foot, with a cluster of widows and children and a party of warriors. Thirty-seven in all. Only one man, bloodied and barely alive, had come from that final, decisive battle. The others, having heard of Old Sharp Knife's sound thrashing, had straggled in from various fronts. Each wore the haunted face of the defeated.

To hear Singing Grass tell it, the Tohopeka breastwork was masterfully designed to partition, defend, repel. General Jackson's army hit it hard and fast, applying full fire from his double artillery. The wall thwarted the barrage, but the battle came at the Muscogees from every side, and with one-third fewer numbers than their foes, they could not withstand the assault.

No warrior surrendered. Not a one. Resilient, they ran, swinging the red club, to meet the enemy, then they bathed the field with their blood. Proof of their valor.

A thousand casualties, some were saying. A staggering number, and almost as staggering as the relief that Totka was not counted among them.

His cousin, Tall Bull, had escaped across the river. Though wounded, he'd taken Leaping Waters and fled to Florida with a small band of Red Sticks who refused to surrender.

Adela prayed Nokose's death had been swift, and that before his final breath he'd made his peace with God. The loss of him cut Totka deep. He'd spoken hardly a word since his sister came back into camp.

"My husband—" Singing Grass caught a sob and tried again. "My husband wished your father to have it back. May it kill no other white man."

Had many *had* it killed? Tentatively, Adela took the musket. "I will remember."

Seeming not to have heard, Singing Grass padded away.

Adela cradled the heavy weapon, imagining it in Papa's large, work-hardened hands. His eyes, crinkled with laughter, filled her mind along with a gut-twisting longing to fall into his arms, to confess that she'd failed Mama. Failed them all.

She dabbed at her moist nose. It could be he knew it already. If he was dead.

And their home? She spat out the thought it might have been destroyed. No, it stood waiting for her and Lillian, waiting for its new, young master.

Waiting, waiting . . . How long would it be required to wait? How long until peace was signed and Totka took them home to Tensaw? Then again, Kossati felt like home too. Or was it merely Totka who gave her that sense of belonging?

Heart heavy, she set the musket down and turned to Amadayh who suckled the baby and hummed an unfamiliar Native tune.

In her wild hair and tattered clothing, the woman was all smiles, thoroughly transformed. Mama would be pleased to know some small good had come from her death.

Death, so much death . . .

Adela and Lillian were no longer alone in their grief. It had touched every person in the camp, and the endless keening was wearing on Lillian's nerves, instilling in her a fear so irrational Adela worried she might do something imprudent.

Always jumpy, she kept a wary eye over her shoulder. Of what or whom she was afraid, Adela could only guess.

When Amadayh finished nursing, she passed the baby to Adela. "If he cries in the night, I'll come." She kissed his downy forehead. "He is strong and his name must be worthy of it."

Adela smiled. "True. It must." Although she didn't plan to be the one to name him. Papa would. If ever she found him . . .

The warring Red Sticks had been reduced to a few roving bands that were little threat to anyone. Soon, it would be safe enough to return. Nokose had given Totka the responsibility of taking them back, of helping them find Papa, but Adela feared he would be unwilling.

It being Lillian's night to care for the baby, she bundled him and lay down with him at her side.

The Kossatis' present encampment remained where Totka had come upon it after the Choctaw raid. No one cared to question why the enemy had ceased pursuit. But Adela knew—Gray Hawk was every bit as honorable as his Red Stick son. He'd not allowed the Choctaws to descend on his son's tribal talwa.

Before the sun had set that first full night after they'd fled, Totka had erected a shelter for Adela, Lillian, and the baby in their own corner of the woods; his sisters' he'd constructed a short distance off; he slept under the stars between the two.

As darkness overtook them, the camp quieted, and Adela slept until an urgent whisper dragged her awake. The fire had shrunk to a deep red glow; the hour was late.

She pushed herself upright and squinted to focus on the form of her sister rummaging about their small space. "What's wrong, Lilly? Is it the baby?"

"We've got to get out of here!"

"What are you talking about? Right now?"

"If we move fast, we can put good distance between us before they even know we're gone." Her trembling words came out rushed and almost unintelligible.

"Why are you rolling our blanket?" Adela's groggy brain refused to comprehend.

Lillian tugged on Adela's sleeve. "Come on! You're wasting time."

"Lilly, you're acting like the devil is after you. Calm down." Adela rose to stoke the fire.

"Don't!" Lillian snatched the stick from her hand. "They'll see us."

"We're safe here, Lilly. No one is going to hurt us." Adela spoke in slow, placating tones, scrambling for the reason Lillian might behave this way and for how to lure her out of it. "Come lay down. You're just tired." She tried to put her arm around her to guide her to their pallet, but Lillian pushed her away.

"I can't take it anymore." Her hands clapped over her ears. "Their crying and carrying on hasn't stopped for days. Listen to it!" She shouted the whisper, her voice raspy.

Fear zinged Adela's nerves. She glanced toward where Totka slept. Should she wake him? Would he know what to do? Mama would. So would Papa.

She stepped in front of Lillian to take her by the shoulders and halt her pacing. "I promise you no harm will come to us here."

"You say that because you don't see how they look at us. You're blind to it, but I swear they want revenge. They'll kill us while we sleep if we stay!"

They wouldn't. Because the McGirth women were no longer slaves. They were Beaver now, Lillian included. The clan mothers had approved the adoption before Nokose left.

Every Kossati knew it. Lillian knew it. She knew that their lives were now as dear to Beaver as that of their own children. If harm came to any one of them, Beaver Clan would retaliate in full.

Repeating the assurance would make no difference. Lillian didn't need the truth; she needed a sense of security. And these ten months of gradual decline told Adela that her sister wouldn't find it here. Not in her state of mind. There was only one place that would bring her peace.

"Take a deep breath and listen to me. I don't believe the Kossatis mean us any harm, but you're right about one thing." She assumed a confident tone. "It's time to go home. Not tonight, mind, but soon."

Lillian's shoulders relaxed as she expelled a deep, more controlled breath. "How soon?"

"There's the baby to think of, and we'll have to prepare. Maybe in a few —"

"I know where we are, Adela. *Exactly* where we are."

"What are you talking about?"

"Don't you recognize the old dock upriver? We passed it the evening of our second day out of the fort. The Indians set up camp in a field not far from it. You remember, right?" Level, calm, confident — Lillian spoke like her former self.

Not quite believing her sister had made an instantaneous recovery, Adela floundered for an answer. "No . . . I . . . wasn't paying much attention to where we were." She'd been consumed with Mama's health and Lillian's emotional state. But maybe Lillian hadn't been as frazzled as Adela had believed, and she'd always had a better handle on the woods than Adela.

"Well, *I* did. And I'm telling you, we're closer to home than we will be once we're taken back to Kossati. Home is four days' travel on foot. Maybe five since we'll have the baby to tend to. We'll let Amadayh go once we reach Fort Stoddart."

"Wait. Fort Stoddart? Let her go? Lilly, you're not making sense. Did you plan to prod Amadayh at musket-point all the way home?"

"Why not? We've had our share of prodding and abuse. It's time the tables were turned." And there it was. Her old reason-altering spite. "Let's go, Adela. Tonight."

Their brother grunted and squirmed in his bundle. They couldn't barrel into the wilds unprepared and unprotected. Hand to her chin, Adela paused to make as though she were considering it. "We'll find a better way. Let me speak to Totka in the morning. He'll take us."

"Lies, lies. He lies to you; you lie to yourself. Wake up, Adela. He's not taking you anywhere near Tensaw. The way he possesses you with every look, you may as well still be his captive."

With a hand-toss to the air, Adela snorted a scoff while inwardly shrinking at how close Lillian had struck at the heart of her own niggling fear. Totka would be more than reluctant to take them home.

"Besides," Lillian continued in a hush, "he's leaving in the morning for Kossati."

"What? That can't be."

"It's true. I heard him talking to Singing Grass late this evening."

Lillian understood Muskogee?

At Adela's stunned silence, Lillian emitted a soft chortle. "We've been with them almost a year. I've picked up more than you think."

"Maybe you have," she mollified, "but if he were leaving, he would have told me."

"Why would he when he intends to make you go with him? He won't let you out of his sight for a short trip to Kossati, never mind take you back to Tensaw. And I know what he intends to do with you on the trail. If you come back with your virtue, I'll be shocked. Do you see now why we have to leave toni—?"

"That's absurd!" Wind whipped in her ear as she pivoted on her heel.

"Where are you going?" Lillian hissed.

"To ask him myself."

A noisy tread lurched Totka from a light sleep. Moonlight outlined Copper Woman's curved silhouette, but there was nothing sensual about her strident approach.

Something was wrong.

She stopped in a secluded area a hard stone's throw from his pallet. He was still five paces out when she spoke. "Lillian tells me you are leaving for Kossati in the morning." Agitation rolled off her.

That was what this was about? Him leaving and not having told her yet? She was behaving like a petulant wife. How endearing—as was the glow of her pale hair under the power of the half-moon. Barely contained in the loose braid that hung over one shoulder, the wavy strands reflected the light in a soft glow.

"I planned to tell you in the morning."

"Do you intend to take me with you?"

"Do you want to go? I thought with your sister on edge and the baby being so new—"

"No, no. You were right to think I should stay for them. I only ask because Lillian said—" The shadow of her hand swiped the air between them. "Never mind what she said. She misunderstood. Or lied."

Likely both. He clicked his tongue. "You are surprised by this?"

"A little. For a moment she seemed so sure, so . . . stable. But it is no secret she's not well. Her mind is . . . confused. It is security she lacks, and she will not find it here. She needs our father, and our father needs his son. I wondered . . . "

Totka's heartbeat went sluggish. Cricket chirps magnified in his ear as she gathered her words and he waited and dreaded and wished she had come to him tonight with another more pleasurable request.

"Will you take us back, Totka? On your return from Kossati, will you escort us home?" Her soft-as-feathers voice shattered his heart. How could she love him—as he firmly believed she did, as she demonstrated in every look, every touch—yet ask such a thing of him?

He backed up a step. Although he'd anticipated the question, he still felt as shaken as a turtle shell rattle.

"Totka?"

No! he wanted to shout. *Never!*

Teeth grinding, he looked away, seeking composure beyond himself in the gentle spring breeze, in the cool glow of moonbeams, in the lungful of air scented with pungent humus.

They failed him. Pain built in the back of his throat.

He could never tell her that here, on Muscogee land, he had the upper hand, and he, *they*, could not afford to lose it. Once in Tensaw, she would be under the influence of her own people; she would be persuaded to see him as the enemy, a savage with no conscience and no future.

Only under one condition would he take her back to the white settlements.

The cup of his hand found her cheek. "Will you give me your word that you'll come back with me? To share my lodge and my life?"

"And will we share the same Creator?"

Why, why must she continue to pound the same enraging drum? The ache in his throat flared. "I curse the white nan's Creator for keeping you from me!"

The crickets went silent.

Copper Woman angled her face away from his touch. "I see." Her brief response carried a weight of sadness he couldn't comprehend.

"Will you not fight? Where has your warrior's spirit gone?" Had he slain it with his unfeeling retort?

"You've spoken your heart. There is nothing left to say. Travel safely. Goodbye, Totka." The airy kiss to his jaw took him by surprise as did her hasty withdrawal.

She'd taken two steps in the direction of her shelter before he regained function of his brain. Under no circumstances would they part this way. Several leaping steps flung him into her path. He grabbed her wrist. "It is your rejection that makes me angry. Not your beliefs."

"I understand. I do. Now, please, let me go."

"Never! Not like this."

She tugged against his iron hand and her bones clicked. She sucked a sharp breath, and he released her.

Both hands lifting in apology, he withdrew. What had gotten into him? He was no barbarian. Bitter Eyes would trumpet if she knew he'd mishandled her sister. And rightly so.

Torso slightly bent, she massaged her wrist. If a bruise formed, he would be ill.

"Copper Woman, I did not mean to—"

"Then why do you? Why do you hold on to me so fiercely?"

The question had nothing to do with her wrist, and the answer rode to him in an instant on the excruciating vision of Leaping Water rushing away, ridding herself of him for good. "Because I am not fool enough to make the same mistake twice."

"What mistake did you make? Was it with me?"

"Not yet. And *that* is what I plan to avoid."

At the inquisitive tilt of her head, he knew she would not let him dodge the telling.

He expelled a cumbersome breath, turned from her, and lifted his face to the moon which peeped around the jagged peak of an undulating pine. Dead needles prickled the soles of his bare feet as he let the years slough away and expose memories raw from overuse.

"A short time before Leaping Waters and I were to wed, while driving the Long Hairs off Muscogee land, I received a musket ball to the leg." Out of habit, he rubbed the muscle of his outer thigh just above the broken bone that never fully healed.

"It pains you still." Behind him, the crackle of her tread said she'd moved quite near. Would she snake her arms around his middle?

"Every day." He stood cold, alone.

"What of Leaping Waters?"

"For many sleeps, I was near death. When we knew I would live, I spent many moons regaining strength, then learning to walk again. In that time, Leaping Waters listened to the wrong counsel. She's always been weak-minded, unable to think for herself. Before I was fully healed, she sent me away from her."

It came then, Copper Woman's touch, in the center of his back, between the points of his shoulder blades, directly opposite his smarting heart. The contact was light and fleeting. But he would have expected no more from a woman riddled with the sort of fears Copper Woman battled.

"Then it was her mistake," she said, "not yours."

"The blame falls on my head. She was weak, afraid. Afraid I would not be able to provide or rise in the community. But she was wrong. In her fear, she chose the easy path over love. And I let her." The memory still choked him.

He'd argued her decision, but not hard enough. She'd walked away, and he—nursing wounded pride—had let her go.

In the break to regain composure, he heard nothing from behind, not a rustle, not a whisper of breath. He would think himself alone but for Copper Woman's warmth radiating through the worn fabric of his shirt.

If he slanted back, would she hold him? He took the surer method and turned a tight circle, bringing her breath within tickling distance of his neck. She didn't retreat, but neither did she lift her face to him. As stiff as a picket, she stared at the apex of his chest.

"I've seen unusual strength in you, Copper Woman, but the fear I saw in Leaping Waters, I see in you."

Her chin thrust upward. "I am *not* afraid."

"Aren't you? Is it not love that brings you in a fit temper to my pallet and fear that keeps you out of it? Fear of your own passion, fear of judgment from your family, from your Creator?"

Her head shook in wide arcs, and he curved his fingers around its base, stilling it. "But I am strong enough for both of us, and I will *not* make the same mistake twice. Do you understand what I tell you, beloved?"

The whites of her eyes shifted as she, at last, directed her gaze into his. "I do. Perfectly."

But did she really? Her drab, muted tone—dare he call it resigned?—left him unsettled. "Can you not see that I protect you from a choice you are sure to regret?"

As she turned her head aside, the bones of her neck rippled against his finger pads. Over the harsh winter, she'd grown thin, fragile. He'd done his best to keep food before her, but there had been far too many people to feed and far too little to offer.

Like a punch to the stomach he realized that in a few sleeps' time he could have her sitting before a decent meal in any number of Tensaw stockades. Yet he refused.

Guilt bit hard, but he pulled it out by the roots—not a soul in Creek country had avoided some form of suffering, but spring lay just the other side of tomorrow. The ground would yield fruit again.

Besides, there was Kossati yet to visit and the possibility of stores of food in its cellars. Odds were not completely against them that the Long Guns had spared the town a razing. Despite Old Grandfather's uncanny predictions.

Times would not always be so trying. He *would* provide for her.

"What of my sister and the baby?" She steered his thoughts back to their current dilemma. "Will you give her a choice, or is she tied to our fate?"

An excellent question. Copper Woman had been right about her siblings' needs, and he wasn't so unfeeling as to disregard them. "If you ask it of me, when I return from Kossati, I'll guide them to Tensaw. But know this, Copper Woman—it's a treacherous journey for a Red Stick. You would not be there to stop your sister from handing me over to the first Long Gun she sees. And you can be sure she'll not shed a tear when I'm swinging from the end of a rope."

She sighed. "I'd not thought of how dangerous it would be for you. You're right. You should not take them to Tensaw." Them, she had said *them*. Had he gotten through to her? "So, it is settled." She spoke as though drained; her posture slumped.

"Soon, when peace is reached. For now, you should sleep. No more worrying." He stroked her cheekbone with his thumb.

"And you have a hard road ahead tomorrow. How many sleeps will you be gone?"

The cool, wet track of her tears ran over the backs of his knuckles. Lids drifting closed, he savored the knowledge that she was no Leaping Waters, that she grieved the thought of him leaving. "Two. Only two."

"Then go." She collected a fistful of the shirt at his side. "The sooner you do, the sooner crops can be planted and the sooner rebuilding can begin." Her fingers trailed up his belly and settled in the valley of his chest where his heart's tattoo surged into a precarious rhythm.

This was a first. Apart from that one brush of a kiss, she'd never initiated any physical contact between them. How simple it would be to settle the matter of their future once and for all. Here, now. But he knew her well enough; she would leave him unsatisfied.

Regardless of what his brain knew, his body, of its own accord, drew itself toward her. "You will miss me?"

"Always," she whispered through thickness of tears, releasing his shirt to glide her arm up his back. Could she feel the energy he exerted to remain as he was? If so, she couldn't know how he longed to sate his appetite, how he endeavored to curb it, to keep his word.

The hand on his chest crept up his neck and into his hair where it applied gentle downward pressure. She rose on tiptoe and met his mouth halfway.

Her pliant lips tasted of salt and tenderness and a love so sweet it stung his lids and seeped into the corners of his eyes. Over a series of shallow breaths, she poured herself into him, communicating everything she refused to speak. Her message was at first bridled then insistent, followed closely by desperate to be heard.

She needn't have worried—he was listening and would all night if she had a notion, but he'd only just opened his ears when she disengaged herself and stole the wind from him.

His mouth instinctively pursued, but she was too quick and he, too disoriented. Dropping to the flats of her feet, she slithered out of his hold and made a clean and hurried break.

Beyond arm's reach, she stopped and, without looking back, spoke so quietly he strained to hear. "When you return, you will know where to find me."

Yes, he did. And he would.

Always.

Totka found Kossati in a deplorable state. Half burned, half overgrown it would require several seasons' worth of attention to return it to its original state. Together, they would make it happen.

The round house hadn't been touched, but all that remained of Singing Grass' summer lodge was three scorched beams and a blackened clay vessel. There was a chance, however, the seed maize in the storehouse had survived the fire.

Old Grandfather lived as did the sacred fire he'd refused to leave. Hope came in an assortment of shapes.

One being the form of a certain green-eyed woman who'd sent him off with a sweet message and all the incentive he needed to make quick work of his errand. After a cyclone tour of the talwa and after compiling a mental inventory of what required repair, he pointed Long Arrow's horse westward toward the encampment and kicked it into a canter.

After meeting with men to discuss the People's return, he entered the perimeter of their campsite with an eye toward Copper Woman's plot, but it was Singing Grass who, face stricken, raced to meet him as he dismounted.

"She has left, Totka!"

"Why are you shrieking? Who left?" She could not mean —

"Copper Woman! She's taken her siblings and gone from us." Her hands were clasped in a knot at her chest.

He scanned their little plot of earth. "You're wrong. She would not be so . . . " His nieces scampered around the trees. White Stone cradled Black Sky. Little Warrior dashed on spindly legs toward him.

Copper Woman's shelter was bare.

No sister. No baby. The Bitter Eyes never strayed from the hut.

The horse's reins fell swinging from his fingers. Whyever had he agreed to give her freedom, to make her Beaver?

"Forgive me, Brother. I could not stop her!"

An arrow of alarm struck his heart. He clutched his shirtfront almost expecting his fingers to collide with a protruding shaft.

"I tried, but what could I do? Nothing, but beg on your behalf, and I did. Except she would not listen! Not even Little Warrior could persuade her."

"Pawa, I told her it would make no difference." Little Warrior trailed him to Copper Woman's shelter. "Because you would find her, and she would be putting herself in danger for nothing. She's without a man to protect her, Pawa!"

The boy's fear was worming its way through Totka's blood like a vile poison.

At the shelter, her tattered woolen blanket sat folded, their three wooden bowls and cups stacked on top. He whisked it off the ground, sending the dishes flying, and spun back to Singing Grass. "Are you sure she has gone?"

"She would take nothing! Not even the cups. No gun powder. Only her father's musket and a striking flint. But Amadayh is with her. A small comfort."

Tongue a useless desert, he stared at his sister's anguish, at Little Warrior's fear, and tried to order his thoughts.

Copper Woman had left him. Left him!

With no guard against the damp of the long, dark forest nights.

And no way to protect herself. Only a useless musket.

The woman lacked no amount of bravery, but it would take a great deal more than that to ward off a pack of Red Sticks hungry for one last scalp. Not to mention the wolves.

The wolves . . .

He saw her again cast in the lantern's flickering orange halo, hatchet primed as she stared down the snarling beasts. The anxiety he'd felt then was child's play compared to now.

His jaw eked open, but no sound came through the crush of his throat.

Rain Child clambered up Totka's leg and clung to his back, nattering on about something Totka couldn't hear.

"Long Arrow would not go after her. Three less mouths to feed, he said. Little good he is to Beaver!"

"And Mother would not let me fetch you." Little Warrior's endearing attempt at manhood barely registered.

Chest hot with fear, Totka forced his brain to function, his mouth to obey. "When did she leave? How long ago?"

From her perch on Totka's back, Rain Child spoke into his ear. "Are you sad, Pawa?"

"Shortly after you left," Singing Grass said.

The tears. The kiss. Not a confirmation of love. A farewell.

His fist spasmed around the blanket's edge. "Did she tell you *why*?"

"Only that she would not have you risk your life by taking them south. She asked that I insist you not follow, but of course you must go after her, Brother. If you do not find her before she reaches Tensaw, she'll be lost to you forever." Singing Grass stood in his breathing space, hauling on his arm, telling him what he already knew.

When you return, you will know where to find me, she'd said.

Indeed, he did — in Tensaw. And he was not to go until he'd ceased cursing her Creator. She'd not said as much to Singing Grass, but she'd made it abundantly clear to him, not that he'd truly

353

listened.

Beaver or not, leaving wasn't her choice to make. He thought he'd made *that* abundantly clear. Apparently not because after a flagrant display of love, she'd left him. And she expected him to not go after her. Had she lost all good sense? After these many moons, did she not know him at all?

Fear swapped places with anger, then shoved its way back in for an equal share of his mind.

"Will you not go?" As gaunt and undernourished as the rest of them, Singing Grass looked up at him, a rebuke slanting her brow.

"And what of your needs? What of the children?"

"Plenty of men are returned from the war. We'll be cared for, and you'll be gone but a few sleeps. If you hurry."

Needing no more persuasion, he swiped Rain Child from his back and plunked her into her mother's arms, then stalked back to the horse, rolling the blanket as he went.

Singing Grass dogged his heels. "I've prepared a little something for your journey. Little Warrior, go fetch the wallet I put together for him." She took the bundle from Totka and tied it over the animal's hindquarters next to his own roll.

He leapt onto the horse's back. "Keep the food for the children. Tell Long Arrow he owes me further use of his horse. If he will not protect Beaver, his horse will."

"What of Kossati?"

"It is mostly ashes, but safe. Go home, Singing Grass. You will find your winter lodge intact. I'll be back. With Copper Woman. Then we will rebuild."

The horse pranced under his agitation.

Unfazed, Singing Grass leaned against his leg and reached to his arm. "Do not be angry at her. Your woman leaves because she carries a great responsibility. Be thankful she is strong enough to bear it."

"She is not my woman." Bitterness was an astringent brew to swallow.

She swatted his knee. "Not *yet*. Bring her home, and we'll rectify that. Do not doubt her love. Why else would she leave without you? She needs only time and patience."

His nostrils flared. "Both are in rather short supply." He veered the horse away from her. "Plant the seed maize from the storehouse. As to the rest, it will be a hard winter, but we will survive. All is not lost."

Only the better portion of his soul.

Chapter 23

*O*n her knees, Adela crouched low over the nest of grass-kindling she'd constructed and blew a gentle cord of air through puckered lips. The straw glowed and crackled, flaring into a youngling fire.

She settled back onto her calves and fed sticks to the flames as the aggravating buzz of thirsty mosquitoes descended. Three nights on the Wolf Trail without Singing Grass' bear grease to repel the beasts had been torment. "Of all the items to refuse to bring," she groused, smacking at her ear.

It had been a long, hard journey replete with hunger, exhaustion, and fear that they would encounter unsavory company at every turn, but under the circumstances, they'd done well for themselves. Except for a few squads of friendly Muscogees, they'd had the trail to themselves.

And not a white face to be seen. Either they were in hiding, in other quarters fighting straggling Red Sticks, or Lillian had led the women onto the wrong trail. There was also the possibility they were moving more slowly than anticipated and were still deep in Muscogee territory.

Either way, Lillian and Amadayh exuded confidence, so Adela waylaid her apprehensions and focused on maintaining the pace.

From the depths of the fathomless woods, a wolf took up a foreboding song and prickles rose along her spine. She exchanged a long look with Lillian, shoved another stick into the fire, and glanced around their little clearing.

With a crescent of bare, graduated hills to her back, the purpling forest ahead, and a trickle of a stream twelve paces away, she decided they couldn't have picked a more pleasant spot to rest.

All it lacked was Totka. And his bow arm.

There was no doubt in her mind that, despite her message, he would be on her trail by now. Her heart cringed. She knew full well she'd angered him, hurt him, set him on a frantic race to find her. But what else was she to have done?

Amadayah emerged from the woods and dumped an armful of sticks beside the fire, then squatted and hugged her legs. "The wolves are nearing."

"I heard. Once the fire grows strong, we'll take some and go together to get more wood."

Amadayah nodded. "We traveled hard today, but we'll not reach the white fort before he finds us." Her black eyes glittered with a smile. "I have known him my whole life, and I tell you the truth— you can run, but there is no hiding."

"He gave me no choice but to leave without him." Literally. "I have to get them home." She shot a glance at Lillian who rocked their little brother and gazed lovingly into his big blue eyes. "She's not well and needs our father," she whispered.

"I know. She is already better. With each sleep on the trail, she is less crazy." Amadayh grinned, then went serious. "Keep your eye on the northern horizon. He will be there soon. And when he scolds then kisses you, remember that not all women are so fortunate." A tear rimmed her lid and cascaded. She dashed it away, then used Adela's shoulder to push up, giving it a squeeze before returning to the trees for more wood.

Adela massaged her temples and closed her eyes against the burn of wood smoke, sleepless nights, and grief.

Heavens, how she missed him. Now that she knew the pain of separation, how would she ever be able to walk away from him for good?

He believed her weak, easily influenced, and he'd as much as told her he didn't trust her to choose the difficult, yet correct, path. What he didn't seem to understand was that she already had: she'd chosen Jesus and her pledge to Him. Tears stung at the memory of Totka's curse, but she banished them and used the energy instead to pray he might one day recognize Jesus as Creator, as well as the Water, Light, Rock, and Master of Breath all rolled into one Great Spirit.

In a very real way, Totka's was a legitimate concern. Her community — if any remained — would be hostile to him, not to mention the idea of *them*. Her own father might lead the charge.

"Adela." Lillian's urgent tone propelled Adela to her feet where she followed Lillian's big-eyed gaze to the hills.

A lone, mounted Indian stood stock-still at the crest of the far ridge. The horse's head drooped, but the man sat erect, his hair a tattered black flag, undulating behind him. The sun's last gleaming winked off a silver armband and toasted his bare body into a vibrant bronze visible even from this distance.

Never had a man been so beautiful, so daunting.

Strength began to drain from her limbs. Alternately yearning for and dreading his arrival, she banded her throat with her hand, and felt the pound of her heart's craggy pattering.

Unable to afford the weakness he accused her of, she determined to pull herself together before he arrived.

Lillian came to stand beside her. She tapped a nervous staccato on the baby's back. "Good gracious, he was fast."

An abrupt, shaky laugh broke free of Adela's throat. "That he was. I didn't figure on him catching up to us this far north in Creek country." His country.

The horse jerked into a canter, descended the slope, and sank behind the top of another hill.

"That man isn't quite human." The old high-pitched edge had crept back into Lillian's voice. "But man or spirit he's *not* taking us back. Either of us."

"Hush now, Lilly. We'll be home soon. He's come to escort us the rest of the way."

"You sound *so* confident." Lillian's lips turned.

She knew little of Adela's midnight conversation with him—only that she'd returned wet of cheek and resolute of mind. But Adela suspected her sister had put the pieces together.

"Go on back to the fire. Keep it blazing. I'll walk out to meet him."

Totka kept the horse at a lope until he was upon her. He wrenched a short rein, bending the horse's neck and destroying the sod with its hooves. The animal's lathered abdomen heaved; foam hung in long strings from its mouth.

Chest glimmering with sweat, Totka leveled a flat brown eye on her, equal amounts of choler and disappointment churning beneath his dignified bearing. The stubborn bent to his jaw didn't bode well for her—she was in for a tongue lashing.

Inwardly wilting, she hiked her chin to boost her nerve and bit her lip to withhold an apology. She wouldn't ask forgiveness for caring for her siblings or for fulfilling her dead mother's wishes.

He swung a leg over the horse's neck and landed with a muted grunt before her. His critical eye combed her, head to foot, before scrutinizing the campsite behind her, the creek, the Wolf Path some yards beyond.

A trio of wolves bayed, and Totka pitched his face toward the long roll of cottony mist that cozied up to the forest's blackening edge. Was he recalling another fear-filled night nearly a year past?

His breathing dropped from double-time to brisk to moderate, and still he said nothing.

Amadayh bustled over, chattering as she came. "What did I tell you, eh, Copper Woman? But he flew faster than even I imagined. And not a moment too soon. Go easy on her, Totka. Remember my throwing arm. I never miss." She nabbed the horse by the bridle and kept going, tossing words behind her. "I'll cool this poor beast, since the two of you have much to talk about."

Totka adjusted his quiver strap from the red line it had bored into his breast. He smelled of leather and toil and, except for the intimidating smolder in his eye, had the look of a man done in. He stood tilted, his good leg taking his weight. Moisture coated every part of him. Hair stuck to his back, but the long, frayed red feather twirled light and free in the muggy breeze.

Fear dug a knife into her belly. "You should not be here."

"Neither should you." Although quick, his retort lacked the expected heat.

When she opened her mouth to reply, he clapped two damp fingers over it.

"There is nothing left to say. It is enough that I've found you before the wolves or the Long Guns." He picked up the frazzled braid that hung over her shoulder and let it drop with a thud, lips twitching. "Although you look as though the wolves have already had a piece of you. And you've not slept."

The statement had the feel of a reprimand, but she wouldn't express regret for the consequences of her choices.

"Tonight, you'll sleep. Tomorrow, we reach the Claiborne fort before high sun."

"Claiborne?" As in General Claiborne?

"A new construction made during the winter. Audacious of them to build this far north, but" — he shrugged — "they have won the war, so who am I to judge their tactics?"

This meant saying goodbye that much sooner. "Point us to the gates, and we'll go on from there alone. It's not safe for you. They will know you had a hand at Mims' place." She blinked to sidetrack menacing tears and split a restless glance between his feather and the determination etching his mouth into a severe line.

Without preamble, he whisked out his knife, snagged the feather, and sliced his hair near the quill. The feather came away, and he held it upright between them, rolling the shaft between his fingers, studying the spinning feather.

Subtle grief rippled across his features; it scored a vertical line between his brows and sagged the corners of his mouth. What did that weather-worn feather tell him? She could almost see the images scrolling across the windows of his eyes: the loss of a noble yet hopeless cause, the destruction of his home, the doom of an ancient people strong of heart yet weaker in number than their foes.

She embraced herself to keep from comforting him and dooming her own cause.

He swiveled his arm at the elbow as though to release the feather and all that it represented.

"No!" She leaped on it, catching it as it caught the wind. "It will be safe with me." Immediately, she set to work plucking out the severed hair still bound by thread to the shaft.

How she had changed! From frightened frontier girl cowering under a shower of flaming Red Stick arrows, to Beaver Clan preserving the emblem of the Red Stick cause. But she couldn't stomach the sight of this man tossing to the wind everything he was, everything he'd sacrificed.

He crooked a finger and stroked the side of her chin. "My little Red Stick, vexing and brave."

She would guard his feather, but she was no Red Stick, and—blast the obstacles!—she was not his. But what use was there repeating it?

"Vexing, most certainly." She continued to pinch and release strands of black hair. "But it is yet to be seen whether I am brave." Only to be determined once she found the courage to send him away for good.

At Fort Claiborne's heavily guarded, closed gate, Adela stated their names and purpose. Before entry, Totka was required to leave his weapons with the soldiers—a demand he begrudgingly observed.

They were directed to proceed to the headquarters building at the far side of the crowded compound. The enclosed square acre teemed with people and the noxious odor of urine, manure, and fetid humanity, bringing to mind another fort, now a blackened skeleton. But, she told herself, this fort would not fall.

The war had been won.

Totka, back a ramrod, led the horse carrying Lillian, Amadayh, and the baby. Busily soaking it all in, Adela walked close beside him as they wound their way to the building flying the American flag. The site of the fifteen white stars flapping confidently from their pole stirred a long-forgotten place and began to unravel a gnarl within her that had grown so familiar she'd forgotten it existed.

They passed a kettle bubbling over a low fire, and the fleeting aroma of simmering meat beckoned. Hunger ripped through her gut, but she wouldn't stop for a bite until she'd spoken with the fort's commanding officer. Surely, if her father lived, someone here would know.

The back of Totka's hand bumped her thigh and released a flock of butterflies in her abdomen. In the fort's chaotic din, how was it she was aware of such a simple touch?

Over the short day's journey, they had found few moments to speak in private, but when they had, each one had been precious. He had questioned her about Jesus, demanding evidence of His existence and power, only to shake his head in frustration. She'd disapproved his denial of Jesus, and he'd disapproved her denial of the law-giving spirits.

Feeling inadequate, yet prayerful, Adela continued to speak her heart, as did he. But their beliefs were no more reconciled now than they'd been the day he'd stumbled over her in the field.

Through the overbearing heat of the afternoon sun, Adela felt Mama's icy hand tucked under her arm, as if that pitch-dark night enveloped them once again.

You must be brave un poquito mas . . . a little longer. Mama's words brushed her cheek, as real as if they'd just been spoken.

Oh, how Adela was trying!

A large-boned woman cut a path through the center of the expansive yard. Adela watched her progress and, as she neared, marveled at the crisp white of her apron and the spotless baby blue of her bonnet. The woman gawked back, and Adela glanced down at her own apparel—the stained, shabby Indian skirt, the stark pallor of her thin calves, six inches of which were visible beneath the ripped hem. Dried mud spatters covered her from her caked moccasins to her knees.

Totka was right. She looked awful.

His hand at her waist yanked her sideways into him in time to miss clipping the woman's shoulder as she sauntered past, a deprecatory look marring her puffed eyes.

"We are not dogs to be kicked under foot," Totka snapped in Muskogee. His curled lip sent a shock of panic through Adela. He looked positively menacing.

She hastily assessed their surroundings. Several men, soldiers among them, stood in a loose huddle, keeping a bead on Totka and speaking in private tones.

Adela pulled on Totka's arm, removing his hand from its white-knuckle grip on his empty sheath. She clasped his sweaty palm and donned a tense smile. "Wipe that snarl off your face and try to look pleasant."

"Adela, I don't like this place," Lillian called from atop the horse, apprehension warbling her voice.

"Sit tight, dear. We'll be at headquarters in a jiffy." It looked forever away.

Totka shook free of her and crammed the lead rope into her hand. "Take it, and stand clear of me. This will not end well."

A dozen steely-eyed men approached, and her breath quickened. "No, come back!" She lunged for him, missing. The horse pressed determinately on, pulling her with it. "Stay, Totka. I'll speak to them on your behalf!"

"Watch where you're going," Lillian called.

Adela skipped around a tent guy line and tugged the rope to steer the horse clear. "Whoa!" She halted the horse as group of soldiers surrounded Totka.

A burly redhead with a cleft chin jabbed him in the shoulder. "Look at the redskin, coming in here as bold as brass. A Red Stick if ever I saw one. And I've seen plenty—on the point of my bayonet!" His guffaw was echoed five times over.

Arms limp, hands loose, fingers twitching, Totka stared the man down.

"Leave him alone!" Adela dropped the horse's lead and pushed through onlookers toward the sidelines of the ring. "He's with me," she shouted, but no one paid her any mind.

"How can you tell he isn't one of the friendlies?" a Bluecoat asked.

"'Cause look at him. He's all skin and bones. Probably been hidin' away like the coward he is." The redhead shoved Totka in the shoulder, but he refused to bite.

"No, you're wrong!" Adela cried. Did a coward enter the enemy's camp without so much as a paring knife?

The growing crowd lengthened the distance between Adela and her chances of helping before the confrontation escalated.

"They're all cowards. Sneaking about, attacking on the sly."

"Stop this. Stop it right now!" She stood on tiptoe, but saw no more than the shoulders of those directly in front.

"I say we remind him who owns this country and string him up."

"No!" Adela screamed.

Cheers erupted and a scuffle broke out. Dust billowed into the air, blurring her already scanty view.

"You can't do that! Where's the commanding officer? Why won't anyone do anything?"

If God took Totka too, she wasn't sure she would have the strength to go on. She clawed at the backs of those standing in the outer ring and received an elbow to the belly. She stumbled backward as a conglomeration of grunts, taunts, and blows assailed her ears. Where was he? In the dirt?

"Someone, please, listen to me. You're making a mistake!"

A blue-coated soldier stepped from a door not five paces away and appraised the ruckus. Silver officer's epaulettes danced on his shoulders.

"Thank God!" Adela broke free of the mob and toppled against him.

He grabbed her by the elbow. "Hold up there, where are you —?"

"Please, stop them," she said, breathless. "I know him. He's done nothing wrong."

He took a slight step back to study her and thumbed his ear. Doubt bunched his lips.

"Do something!"

He hoisted his chin to assess the situation. Being quite tall, he had to have an accurate view of the fight. What was taking so long?

"You can vouch for that Indian?" Too slowly, he pulled his pistol from its holster and checked the priming.

"Yes, I told you, yes. Please, they'll kill him!"

"All right. Stand back." He raised his pistol and sent a ball into the air. The explosion hammered her ear.

Women screamed. Half the crowd cowered, others scampered toward cover, revealing the redhead and Totka in a brawl on the ground. An even fight.

Adela slumped against the doorpost, trembling.

Re-priming his pistol, the officer strode into the yard and lifted his voice in stern command. "On your feet, men."

A knot of thrashing legs, elbows, and knees, they kicked up dust as they rolled, neglecting the officer's order. Despite his larger size, the redhead didn't seem to be holding up against Totka's quick fist.

"Enough, private!"

Totka got in another solid punch to his opponent's eye before two bystanders seized his arms and hauled him up.

The officer planted himself between them, an imposing wall.

Palm to her chest, Adela recovered her breath, thankful for the officer whose presence kept her from throwing herself at the redhead and scratching his eyes out.

The man spit blood and pulled himself out of the dirt. One eye had already swollen shut. A laceration on his forehead oozed red. "We were just horsing around, sir."

"Private Malone, I've had about as much of your *horsing* as I can take. Report to Captain Everett for duty. You're on the picket line for the next twenty-four hours. Act up one more time, and it'll be a lashing."

The private gave his superior a weak salute. "Yes, sir." He gingerly collected his hat off the ground and shuffled to obey.

The officer holstered his newly loaded weapon and brandished a stiff finger at those detaining Totka. "Release him."

Totka jerked his arms out of their grasp and, blowing lungfuls of air, looked at the officer from slitted eyes. A muscle bunched in his jaw. Red dust coated him and muted the blue-black of his hair. His shirt was ripped down the front clear to his naval.

Instructing herself not to fall on him weeping, Adela went and with an unsteady hand swiped hair from his face to inspect him for injury.

He batted at her hand. "I am not hurt, woman."

Besides a trickle of blood from a split lip, she found him to be exactly as he claimed. "I thought you were being beaten to death." Her closing throat allowed for no more than a whisper. "Yet here you stand with nothing but a bloody lip. I should have known better."

The bunch in his jaw spasmed, then dissolved.

Adela shook her head in wonder—both at his resilience and at her reaction—and dabbed at his mouth with her fingers.

He angled his chin up and away. "It's nothing."

"Nothing?" she squeaked.

It was oh so much more than nothing. He could be lying in the red dirt, life draining from him—one murderous shot, one unseen, slicing blade was all it would have taken.

"This is no place for you! Why did you insist on coming?" She heard the desperation in her voice, felt it escalating but was helpless to stop it. "Why could you not have stayed hidden in the woods where it is safe?"

Bewildered, he cocked his head, and his earrings jangled. "How does a man abandon his own heart?"

There was no denying his love was a deep current, wide and unfaltering—so much so that she couldn't quite comprehend it. Although, after her own reaction just now, she was beginning to understand. Even so, her own love—a love she had yet to confess to him—paled in comparison.

Singing Grass's warning came back to her. *My brother's love burns hot . . . it does not die easy.*

"I suppose . . . I suppose it isn't possible." He'd said it before, many times, but she hadn't truly believed it until now.

What did that mean for them? After they'd found her father, Totka wouldn't stay. Singing Grass and the children needed him, and he wouldn't haul her back to Kossati against her will. Her father would never allow it.

Suddenly, Totka's adamant behavior, his refusal to let her choose, to let her leave Creek territory—all of it made perfect sense. Whatever control he might have had was stripped from him the moment they'd passed through Claiborne's gates. The one power left at his disposal was that of his love, and he wouldn't abandon it.

Wishing she still lived in the bliss of denial, she tried for a wobbly smile and fingered the floppy edges of his torn shirt. "This cannot be repaired. May as well destroy it."

"The Malone soldier owes me a shirt." His lips formed a bitter pucker as he removed an armband and tossed it to her.

She caught the ornament against her chest, then the second and, buffing one on her sleeve, turned to the officer who'd waited quietly while they spoke.

Posture erect, he gave her a sharp appraisal. "You speak Muskogee well for a white woman. At least I assume you're white under that Indian garb."

"I was white last I looked, but a bar of lye and a long bath have been in order for quite some time."

"I'm sure Mrs. Wheelie can arrange it."

"You're very kind to offer, Lieutenant . . . ?"

"Captain Dale."

"Pleased to meet you, Captain Dale." Adela dropped into a short curtsy—a ridiculous gesture coming from a woman looking every bit the wilderness she'd just emerged from. "My name is Adela McGirth. We're indebted to you for stepping in."

"Quite the contrary. I've been looking for an opportunity to knock some sense into Private Malone. It seems your . . . friend has saved me the trouble."

Adela handed an armband back to Totka. "This is Totka Hadjo. He's seen us safely here from the Kossati area." A simplistic description for all he'd been and done, for all he hoped to be . . .

Captain Dale extended his arm in typical Native greeting. "You are most welcome here," he said in flawless Muskogee.

One brow hiking, Totka tipped his head in acknowledgement and worked the silver over the bulge of his bare arm.

"Kossati?" The captain lapsed back into English. "That's a decent trek into Creek country. If I'm not mistaken, miss, you have a lively story to tell." He squinted a light-blue Saxon eye. "McGirth you said?"

"That's right, and my sister Lillian has our baby brother." Adela called to her. "Lilly, come meet the captain." Amadayh began guiding the horse to where they were while Adela turned back to Captain Dale. "We're on our way to Lake Tensaw. Our father is—"

"Zachariah McGirth?"

Adela's hand paused mid-extension, the second band hanging in the air between Totka and herself. "You know him?" He relieved her of it.

The captain's flat lips curved into somewhat of a smile. "Know him? The man fought by my side for nigh on half a year. He'll be beside himself when he sees you."

Adela's gaze shot to Lillian. "Did you hear? Papa's alive!" The sob and instant pool collecting between her sister's lids confirmed she had.

"It is good your father lives." Totka's voice was distant, the line spoken as though rehearsed. "It brings you joy and takes a death from my conscience."

Acutely aware of what this meant to him, Adela neared, reassurance ready in her extended hand—he knew she cared, didn't he?—but he evaded her by stooping to collect the discarded shirt. He wadded it into a ball. "Go to your sister. She needs you."

Somewhere beyond his calloused indifference, Lillian wept.

He gave Adela a little shove. "Go."

She moved to comply, but Captain Dale had already helped Lillian descend. "Come out of the sun," he said. "All of you. You look in need of a decent meal. I'll feed you, and you can tell me how it is you're still alive."

The captain led Lillian to a cot along the wall of his quarters. "There, now. Sit and cry a bit if it helps. You've been through quite an ordeal, I'm sure." He moved aside to allow Adela room to embrace her sister.

Totka threw his shirt onto the coals smoldering in the fireplace, then propped a forearm against the wall and watched flames ignite and devour the fabric. His lackluster face flashed with the flame's light, and Adela tightened her grip on Lillian to keep from going to him.

The captain drew another couple chairs up to his table. "I'll have one of the ladies prepare a meal and get you into some decent clothing. How about that bath after—?"

"Thank you all the same, Captain Dale," Adela broke in, "but we're eager to get home."

"You can go home, but you won't find McGirth there. Excuse me." He went to the open door, instructed a passing soldier to find Mrs. Wheelie, and turned back to Adela. "McGirth's been in Mobile for a while now. You'll find him at General Claiborne's place. Doing a bit of courier service, I heard."

"Oh." Adela sagged. Mobile was considerably farther than home. "Well then, we'd best be on our way. As soon as we take you up on your offer of food, that is. We're famished."

"You should rest, Miss McGirth. It's clear you're ready to drop. I'll send a dispatch and have your father here within the week."

Lillian sniffled, her eyes pleading. "But we can be there in two days by river. We've waited long enough. Adela, *please*."

"Another week does seem like an eternity," Adela agreed.

The captain rubbed his chin. "Yes, I imagine it does."

Within half an hour, they'd freshened up and were sitting down to biscuits and stewed beef. As the elderly Mrs. Wheelie fussed over them, Adela ate until her stomach protested.

Totka carried his dish to the entryway and ate looking out on the ever-moving compound. He stood four yards distant, but it may as well have been four miles.

Her heart cried, but wasn't it best they begin to cut ties now? *Yes*, she firmly told her whimpering heart, *it is*.

When they'd had their fill, Amadayh removed herself to a corner to nurse the baby, and Captain Dale asked to know the details of their ordeal. Not eager to dwell on it, Adela supplied rudimentary facts.

Considerate of her reticence, the captain regaled them with tales of their father's heroism, as well as the Red Sticks' fortitude and cunning.

Arms crossed and leaned against the door jam, Totka stood facing away seemingly uninterested in their talk, but Adela knew better. He understood more English than he let on, and he was far more interested in the battles he'd missed than she would ever be.

Did he anticipate a lynching? Was being close to her too confounded hard? Or was he plotting how to spirit her away? She wouldn't put any of them past him.

When Captain Dale had exhausted his overview of the war, Adela ventured to ask, "Were there any other survivors . . . at the fort?"

"Twenty-five or so," Captain Dale began, then his eyes widened.

"Come to think of it, your own servant made her way free of the pickets."

Lillian gasped. "Hester?"

The captain slapped his thigh. "The very one. Zachariah told me she was wounded but recovered nicely."

A smile stretched Adela's cheeks. "How wonderful! Anyone else we would know? And what of our house? Was it burned?"

"No, no. Rest assured. I imagine it remains much the way you left it."

The way she'd left it . . . with Papa. Who was alive and completely unaware they were too.

"You've been gracious to offer us your quarters for the afternoon, Captain." As she spoke, Adela stood and stretched out her hand.

He enclosed it between his own. "The pleasure was all mine, I can assure you. You won't stay and recuperate?"

"Thank you, but there's plenty of sunlight left. We should be going."

Totka pushed off the door. "Will you trade, Captain? The horse for a dugout."

Captain Dale clapped Totka on the shoulder and saw it done.

Chapter 24

The cypress dugout rocked and dipped into Mobile waters to the beat of a chilled, flesh-stinging rain. The lively river sometimes broke over the bow threatening to tip them.

Muscles cramping, Totka plunged the paddle blade into the choppy, black river with ever-increasing strength, eager to get the women and baby out of the brutal weather. When the skies unleashed their fury, Totka should have made for the shore, but the women had begged to press on, and being so close to their destination, he'd decided to allow it. He wondered now, whether they regretted their request.

Bitter Eyes crouched at the far end of the vessel bailing water with cupped palms. Amadayh was behind her; she paddled opposite Totka, pressed to keep up with his more powerful strokes. Copper Woman sat nearest him, hunched over the boy, using her body as a shield. It didn't stop him from squalling.

The child didn't know how good he had it. It? He had *her*. And would, until Totka convinced Copper Woman otherwise. He knew it as surely as the hail pelting his naked back.

It was right that Copper Woman wished to care for her brother. She was the next best thing to a mother. But she could not be in two places at once, and put alongside the helpless infant—and a jealous, demanding Creator—Totka was only the man she loved.

These facts, however, would not stop him from trying to convince her to return with him. But time with her was at a premium. Singing Grass would be looking for him soon, and rightly.

Old Grandfather had given him a grave task; Totka should be scouring the Kossati forest for timber and deer. The spring sun had long since warmed the ground and burnt through the time of planting. The first crop of maize should already have reached the height of his knee, yet Totka wasn't even certain their compromised seed would germinate.

He had but a handful of sunrises with Copper Woman, and he would use each one to persuade her that it was no great shame to leave her brother's upbringing to her sister. The boy wouldn't suffer under the younger one's keeping. So long as he did not choose to love a Muscogee woman . . .

Dusk overcame them but could not blot out the white oyster shell bank that broke out of the trees along the long snake's northern edge. Beyond the bank, lay a wide stretch of miry lowlands, and somewhere in the abysmal gray beyond that, the town Mobile. Dead ahead, with its pilings and wooden beams punctuating the water at perfect intervals, a scant fisherman's quay traversed the mudflats and jutted across their path.

Totka recalled it from his visit a full year prior. It would do.

He swept the blade of his paddle out toward the bow, cutting sharply toward shore, narrowly avoiding a broach, and directing the vessel up the bank next to dock. As soon as the underbelly scraped bottom, Bitter Eyes leaped out and was buried to her ankles in water. She sloshed ahead, then hopped on bare feet across the shells and climbed the stairs to the boardwalk that traversed the expanse of muck separating them from the town.

They caught up to her at a fishermen's shack where she argued with an old angler who reeked of his occupation and refused to let them pass. McGirth's musket in hand, Totka ducked his head between his shoulders and waited with Amadayh and the angry baby as Adela joined the discussion.

She made as much progress as her sister.

Indians, it seemed, were as welcome in Mobile as they were in the Claiborne stockade. That two in their party were white did not appear to register with the man. Adela was permitted to write a message sending for McGirth.

Totka directed the women under the narrow lip of the shack's roof; nearby, lay a heap of discarded tarp. Rainwater skidded off its oiled surface. He picked it up, and several rats scurried for new cover. By the time he'd tossed it over the huddle of women, the baby, already suckling, had ceased his protest. Totka handed one corner to Bitter Eyes. The other he held over Copper Woman who reemerged into the downpour to hug his neck and shout a *maddo* in his ear.

He'd done as he promised. He'd returned the sister and brother. McGirth was on his way.

With a hand to Copper Woman's lower back, he peered down onto the beach to the dugout, which was almost invisible through the blinding rain and darkening sky. How simple it would be to scoop this woman up and flee.

The plan played out in a flash of lunacy —

Bitter Eyes would raise an alarm, but the angler would do nothing. McGirth would pursue, but he would be too slow.

Paddling upstream in this swift current? A nightmare. But Totka could land the craft beyond the town. Send it back, floating upside down. Capsizing and drowning was not a farfetched idea. The rain would obliterate their tracks in moments.

So simple. So impossible.

Copper Woman would hate him, and he would hate himself for hurting her.

The choice would have to be hers. He was powerless, unable even to beg; she would go nowhere until she'd seen her father. But after . . . Maybe *then* she would consider it.

As his last chance at controlling the outcome poured through his fingers, he satisfied himself with a watery kiss to her temple, tucked her back under the tarp, and adjusted it around her.

He moved to the opposite side of the walkway, stared into the drenched horizon, and let the rain buffet him until the boardwalk vibrated with a man's heavy tread. A form materialized out of the murk. The man was of no great height, but as broad as a bear, he would be a beast to tangle with. A wide-brimmed hat obscured his features, but Copper Woman recognized him.

She darted out from under the tarp and ran, stopping short of him.

Through the drumming cold wet, Totka heard nothing and saw little. Only two silhouettes, the smaller disappearing into the shadow of the larger.

Totka turned his back to the scene and gripped the rail. Let them call him a coward. He couldn't watch. There was no escaping the cries of wonder penetrating the weather.

Against his will, his heart softened and his mouth curved. Personal druthers aside, it was a good thing, this reunion—a gift for his beloved and a beautiful ending to a painful episode in their lives. Splinters bit into his palms as joy and grief wreaked havoc on his insides.

When he found it within himself to look back, they were moving away, vanishing into the vision-dimming torrent. Totka stared at the spot they'd occupied, empty now. As empty as the hollow place in his chest.

His legs refused to move until Copper Woman reappeared, trotting toward him, skirt plastered to her legs, hair to her face and neck. "What are you doing?" she hollered, taking him by the hand. "Do you enjoy getting a beating?" She laughed and urged him to follow. "Come meet my father."

He went with her but controlled the speed, keeping them at a walk. "Get the baby indoors first. Go to them. These moments belong to you. I'll follow and meet your father later."

She gave him a squeeze, and when the others came within sight, she dashed ahead. McGirth, occupied with shielding the baby with his hat, had yet to notice Totka.

Copper Woman entwined her arm with McGirth's and just that effortlessly removed herself from Totka's care and reentered her father's.

As Captain Dale had said, McGirth had taken up residence with General Ferdinand Claiborne, the man responsible for the defeat and plunder of Holy Ground, the man who'd cornered Red Eagle on a bluff overlooking the Alabama. But Red Eagle had outwitted him and leaped, horse and all, into the mighty long snake. He reached the other side without ever having lost his seat. Such was the prowess and courage of the Muscogee.

Little good it had done them.

Feeling much the half-drowned cat, Totka stood in a shadowed corner of the white chief's kitchen, an outbuilding constructed solely for preparing food. Amadayh beside him, they created a lake on the planked floor.

McGirth, child in arms, straddled a stool before the wide hearth. A black woman coaxed the fire into a ferocious blaze. Another rubbed Copper Woman head to foot with a blanket, then left it draped over her shoulders before moving on to the sister. Copper Woman knelt before her father and helped the man peel the sodden wraps from the infant's wrinkled, pink body.

He bawled, McGirth gushed silly noises, and Copper Woman laughed and cried in the same breath.

Bitter Eyes slumped against her father, shivering and sniveling, those ever-present, unchecked tears creating a mess of her nose.

The general's rotund wife bustled over to Totka and Amadayh. Her frilly white cap bobbed shadows over her rosy cheeks. She released a barrage of English, then shook her head and reduced it to two words. Food or clothes — which to receive first appeared to be the question.

Amadayh opted for dry clothes; Totka, for whatever aromatic delight steamed in the pot over the fire. Amadayh was ushered out while Totka was nudged toward a bench at the table where a heaping bowl was placed before him. He dug into the vegetables and beans, all else fading away. As he started to feel his humanity returning, Copper Woman spoke his name.

When he looked up, he found McGirth had risen and now studied Totka, his expression a turbulent sea of . . . What was it? Anger? Anguish? Certainly not kindness.

Unshed tears amplified Copper Woman's eyes. She retained her father's arm and urgently, yet quietly, spoke something Totka couldn't hear over the fire's crackle, the sister's sobs, the cook's clattering. Unfazed, McGirth passed his son to the Bitter Eyes who left with a consoling Mrs. Claiborne as he and Copper Woman approached the table.

Expansive of chest, immense of fist, and narrow of eye, McGirth presented an imposing figure. "You were there?" He bit out the words in Muskogee, his voice rough, his tone accosting.

Stomach forgotten, Totka found his feet, grateful for the advantage his height afforded. And for the tomahawk cradled in the loop on his belt. Reminding himself he desired to wed this man's daughter, he loosened his stance and slackened the tension in his jaw. "I was."

The two servants remaining in the room ceased their noise-making and stood at attention, ready to flee.

The blanket cocooning Copper Woman spilled to the floor as she followed. "Father, let me finish."

"Tell me, Red Stick, that you had no hand in the slaughter of innocents so that I do not feel compelled to kill the man who brought my daughters back to me."

There was no need to specify which slaughter. Something about this man brought to mind every kill, every scalp. A hideous, black thing, shame descended. But why? Totka'd had no part in the killing of women and children. He had no reason to regret a battle expertly won.

He banished the remorse, along with the urge to avert his eyes from the pain that scored crevices into McGirth's brow. "I entered Mims' fort alongside my brother Nokose Fixico. We killed many Long Guns, but the only women we touched were yours."

"Why? What have you done with them these moons? Why did you not bring them to me immediately? What reason could you have to take them with you!" Anger colored McGirth's neck a crimson hue. His quaking arm jerked, and Totka braced himself.

"To save us!" Copper Woman wedged herself between them, one arm warding off her father's advance, the other slung back against Totka's stomach. "Only to save us, Father. And Nokose Fixico was . . . " Her voice went from fervent to gentle; her posture drooped. "He was the boy, Sanota, before receiving a warrior's name. Upon sight of Mother in the fort, he had compassion on her. On us all."

McGirth's eyes—Copper Woman's own vibrant green—flickered surprise, then understanding, all fire sizzling out. His arm went limp. "Sanota . . . yes. He would save his white mother. He was always a good boy. Nokose Fixico, you say? Crazy Bear, a good name. And where is he now?"

When Copper Woman shot a sorrowful look up to Totka, he supplied, "His bones rot at the Horse's Flat Foot."

The news dealt McGirth a blow that sent his hand to his forehead and silenced him. After a span, he said, "My first son. Such a good boy he was. Another despicable loss." His voice broke.

"A good man, as well," Totka said, feeling the loss afresh. "A fine warrior. He believed as I did, that the Red Stick cause was destined to fail but noble enough to die for."

McGirth lifted an uncompromising gaze. "And kill for."

True, even now. Totka's chin sank in a deliberate nod.

"Yet you saved my wife and daughters alive from the fort."

Totka would not lie. "It was Nokose's doing."

Copper Woman shook her head. "Only at first. We would not be here today but for this man. To tell you everything Totka has done for us would be a story days in the making. He saved my—our lives many times over."

"Is that so?" McGirth searched Totka hard for an answer, but Totka would not take praise where it was not due.

"It was no great thing I did." Any man would do the same and more for a brother, for the woman he loved.

"My daughter believes it was, and if she said you saved her life many times over, then you did. Which means I am in your debt many times over."

Totka collected the musket from where he'd propped it against the wall and offered it to McGirth. "I place your daughters back into your care."

Copper Woman laid a hand on McGirth's arm. "It's your old musket, Father. From Nokose. Do you remember it? See, your etching is there."

McGirth grasped the weapon. "Yes, I see. He gave it to you?"

"Singing Grass brought it back from the Horseshoe," Copper Woman continued. "Nokose asked her to give it to you."

McGirth ran a finger over the marks that represented his name. He took Totka's shoulder in a crushing grip and clapped a hand to his neck, giving it a stiff-armed shake. "How can I repay you? You have but to ask, and if it is in my power, I will give it to you."

If the man had sprouted wings and levitated, Totka wouldn't have been more surprised. But McGirth would soon regret—and retract—his generosity. "My need is great. Are you certain you would make such a gesture?"

Eyes growing large, Copper Woman sucked a tiny, sharp breath, but her father spread wide his hands as though offering all of himself. "And why not, when you have given back to me all that I hold dear?"

"I ask for a portion of what I've returned. This here, your copper-haired daughter. Above all else, she is what I want."

Chapter 25

Blackberry Month (June)

Lavender-scented suds rose to Adela's chin as she sank into Mrs. Claiborne's tub. She sighed as a young slave poured another bucket of steaming water in at her feet. "It feels wonderful. I believe I have half a year's worth of dirt to scrub off me."

"You be wantin' another bucket of water, missy?"

"Maybe in a little while."

"I'll be back." She left Adela to soak.

Sinking beneath the water, Adela massaged her scalp. Reluctantly, the soot and grime released its hold. The warmth relaxed her and loosened the kinks in her muscles. As they eased, she came up for breath, finally beginning to feel her old self again. She soaked until her toes shriveled, wondering whether Totka was doing the same in the small outbuilding her father occupied.

It was a wonder Papa had opened his quarters, considering Totka's bold, request—a request coming far sooner than Adela had imagined it would. Her father's offer had also been unexpected, and Totka was never one to let an opportunity slip by.

Morose, Totka hadn't spoken two words since Papa had refused him, but Papa'd hardly had a chance to adjust to Adela being alive before being asked to give her up again. To his credit, he'd played the part of a gentleman and refused politely, appearing not entirely shocked at the request, though he couldn't have foreseen it.

Despite her insistence that Totka retire for the evening, as she'd eaten, he'd sat with her, as stiff and distant as a bodyguard. After, he'd seen her to the narrow staircase leading to the upper guest chamber, all the while saying nothing.

Maybe a warm bath and a good night's rest would lure him out of this austere bent. She prayed it did. After all they'd been through and in light of everything they meant to each other, parting from him on less than amicable terms might crush her and incapacitate her for the job she was leaving him to do—that of raising her little brother.

The next morning, as she slipped a green calico dress over her head, she breathed in the scent of the fabric. It smelled of spring. She fingered the filigree collar, reminding herself to thank Mrs. Claiborne for finding it for her. The townsfolk had been more than eager to help the returned captives.

Adela worked her hair into a single, long plait, coiled it about her head, and pinned it in place. Feeling like a new woman, she went in search of Totka and her father.

Entering the parlor, she stopped short. "Doctor Holmes! You're alive!" She threw her arms around his wrinkled neck.

The doctor rubbed little circles into her back. "That I am, child. I suppose God has more in store for the two of us." His laugh broadened Adela's smile.

"How did you manage to escape?"

"A few of us, including Hester, got out through a hole we cut in the picket. We ran like the dickens. Most were"—he cleared his throat—"cut down, but I made it to the lake. I found a concealed hollow beneath a fallen cypress, just big enough for these old bones."

"We were on the lake side of the fort, but I don't recall seeing you. Our paths must not have crossed."

Lillian entered the room, hair shinning almost black, her cheeks, immaculate and rosy. She held the baby over her shoulder with a possessive hand flat on his tiny back. Totka appeared behind her, and she moved to let him pass. With a wary glance Totka's direction, she engaged the doctor in casual dialog.

Adela's and Totka's eyes aligned.

The sides of his head were freshly shaven, his crescent moon, stark and boldly displayed. Her fingers itched to outline it, to curl around the back of his neck and pull him down for a kiss that obliterated the unease in his restive eyes, but those days were behind them.

The lack of his bow and quiver stood out to her like vibrant red war paint. A weapon shouldn't make a man, but without his bow, Totka seemed half present. Judging from his alert posture, he felt the loss of it too.

But he had to know that no harm would come to him here. He was an honored guest in this house, and why shouldn't he be? He'd returned two of the McGirth women. The fact he'd also brought home his fair share of scalps had been addressed and put aside.

The Claibornes had treated him kindly, supplying him with the clothes he wore: a loose white long-shirt that ruffled along the deep V of its collar and vividly contrasted the bronze of his skin, an indigo sash that punctuated the shirt at the hips, and buckskin trousers. If he'd been offered shoes, he turned them down for his moccasins, as worn as they were.

Adela curled her toes inside her own moccasins and greeted him with a smile.

Rigid, he briefly inspected her—hair, dress, and hair again— before drawing his lips into a hard slash. With a finger, he moved aside the lace curtain to his left and peered out onto the street.

She touched the ring of her braid. It was neat and in its place. Was he upset at her for not supporting his ill-timed request? He had to have known she wouldn't. Pride piqued, she bore a hole into his broad, inflexible back. Maybe he wouldn't have such a hard time abandoning his heart after all . . .

Adela forced herself to join Lillian's conversation with the doctor. "And you walked to safety? How long did it take?"

Dr. Holmes drummed his ample belly. "It took me a week to reach civilization, and I about starved in the process. Thought I would run into Red Sticks for sure, but they weren't interested in an old man like me, or maybe I'm too sneaky for them." The doctor laughed at his wit.

Lillian's laugher joined his. "Didn't you know, Doctor? We have our very own Red Stick. I'm sure he has an opinion."

Adela felt the blood drain from her face. "Lilly, hold your—"

"Well, Totka? Would you be interested in Doctor Holmes' scalp?"

Except for the pulse surging in Adela's ears, silence descended around her.

Totka didn't so much as twitch, but the taut sinews in his neck told her he hadn't missed Lillian's question.

At last, Dr. Holmes sputtered a nervous chuckle. "Is he a . . . was he there? At the . . . ? Oh my. Isn't this unusual?" He tugged on his vest and straightened his cuffs. "Never mind, because here I am. Fit as a fiddle. No life is taken without God's say-so, isn't that right?"

Hands clasped behind his back, Totka turned at the waist and gave the doctor a penetrating look.

Dr. Holmes flushed pink. "Is there something I can help you with, sir?"

Totka broke his stare and turned back to the window. "Tell the man I admire his cunning and endurance," he said in Muskogee, his tone even yet not quite friendly.

Adela relayed the message and added, "And please forgive my sister, Doctor. She hasn't learned to control her tongue."

Lillian elongated her jaw, working it to the side. "Yes, forgive me, Doctor Holmes. I tend to talk first and think later." Fabricating dignity, she strode for the exit. The even staccato of her shoes led to a slamming door.

Adela jolted.

"The mind is a delicate thing." Dr. Holmes lowered his voice. "Not as easily repaired as the body. Give her time. Now that brother of yours is a fine, healthy lad, if ever I saw one!"

Adela leapt at the change in subject. "Isn't he beautiful? A true gift."

The door reopened and Papa entered. "What's wrong with Lillian?"

Street forgotten, Totka turned and crossed his arms. The action accentuated the heavy rise and fall of his chest and added to his already intimidating height. He filled the room with an overbearing presence and that unique, wild flare of Native confidence she'd become so familiar with.

When her father caught Totka's piercing gaze, he angled himself to meet it face-on.

Unhurried, Totka veered his line of sight to Adela. Along the way, it mellowed so that it fell softly on her. In it, she found the man she loved, the one who'd pressed her palm to his breast and told her with a single word he was giving her his heart.

To perdition with the contentment blossoming on her face!

Instead of returning it, Totka's eye left her for Papa. Was Adela seeing things, or did their silent exchange hold an undercurrent of challenge? What had transpired between them since the night before?

She hastened to Papa's side and placed a tender kiss on his weathered cheek. "Lillian's a little out of sorts, but it's nothing time won't fix. Have you thought on a name for the baby?"

Her father wasn't to be distracted. His blue-green eyes took her in. "My sweet Adela . . . " His knuckles grazed her cheek, and he transitioned into Muskogee. "You are as beautiful as always. It feels almost as though you had never been taken from me." As his calloused thumb stroked her jaw, his gaze shifted back to Totka and darkened. "But you are back now. Back to stay."

In his tattoos and copper skin, Totka did not belong in this white man's fancy room, waiting for the call to eat his fine food while

Kossatis emerged from the wilderness like wary animals and sat down to nothing in their bowls.

He made an X of his arms and reminded himself he was a warrior and the son of a noble people. It didn't keep at bay the longing to accompany Amadayh to the kitchen to eat with the other hired help and slaves. He would if not for Copper Woman.

She had yet to arrive from her room, but he knew what he would see when she entered—a thing of grace and beauty, stalwart yet fragile, familiar yet altogether unrecognizable.

This evening marked the third since they'd arrived in Mobile. Each one had brought a new level of agony as she'd transformed from shredded refugee into someone he didn't know.

"Mister, er, Totka," Claiborne's wife compelled his attention from the door. A squat pillar of wave upon wave of ruffles, she stood beside him, chin tipped considerably upward to compensate for their difference in stature. "You leave . . . tomorrow . . . your home?"

He picked up just enough to follow her question. "Tomorrow. With the sun."

A new wet nurse had been found for the boy, so Totka could no longer justify delaying their return.

The woman's gloved fingers embraced his arm, and her ruddy cheeks rounded with a smile. Her mouth moved, but, though Totka gave the appearance of polite attention, he had tuned his senses to the door.

Copper Woman entered and with her a cross-breeze that undulated her gown. It encompassed Totka with a delicate floral scent before clacking a painting that hung against the wall and driving the flimsy curtain through the open window into the twilight.

Claiborne's wife gave a little cry and rushed to slam the window shut, leaving Totka relative privacy in which to agonize over the vision being denied him.

A pale-yellow gown hugged Copper Woman's curves and dropped from her ribcage in flowing, formless waves of delicate fabric that forced him to rely on his stores of memory to recall the form hidden beneath. Matching the green of her eyes, a simple ribbon bisected her throat and drew his gaze downward to the scooped neckline that exposed the delicate bones laid out like an invitation at the base of her throat.

Her eyes, large, bright, and green, danced around the room until they found his and, smiling, made a home. Splashes of warmth colored the apples of her cheeks, and she set out toward him.

She was lovely, as usual. His only criticism, her bound hair pinned in a fashion intended only for married women, as though she'd already moved on, already been claimed by another. And hadn't she been? By her father?

As though to prove his point, the man intercepted her before she reached Totka. Lacing her arm through his, he escorted her out so quickly the glance she flung behind her missed Totka entirely.

The white chief offered his arm to Bitter Eyes, and the mistress of the house tittered and latched onto Totka's elbow. Feeling much the snared rabbit, he worked at an appropriate facial expression, failing miserably until he imagined how Nokose might guffaw at the unlikely scene.

Appropriate or not, by the time he'd reached the dining room, he'd achieved a crooked smile.

Copper Woman was seated opposite him—not the gift it should have been since looking at her had become more torture than pleasure. She noted his half-smirk and raised her brow in question.

"Just imagining what Nokose might say of my being here," he said.

"Ah, that *is* an amusing thought." She leaned over her plate and spoke conspiratorially. "Now, imagine Rain Child and all those ruffles." With a subtle tilt of her head toward Claiborne's wife, she gave a tiny snort. "She would bury her hands in them."

Totka's smirk doubled. "Or crawl under them."

A neat cough hid the bubble of laughter that shook her shoulders. Another cough, this one from McGirth two chairs over, sobered her in a flash. All mirth gone, she feigned interest in Claiborne's wife who prattled on about Totka hadn't a clue what.

Why did she insist on pretending she belonged here? She could return to her Tensaw life, and she could shut Totka out of it, but it would do her no good. She and Totka were attached at the soul, and no amount of false indifference would change that.

Totka aside, the Muscogee way of life had become an indelible part of who she was, and he had the proof. At the hem of that expensive, impractical fabric, she still wore the moccasins he'd made. She might arrange her hair in the white fashion, but her feet told another tale.

He rested his elbows on the table, bumping his plate against his glass, then slanted toward her and spoke under his breath. "Why do you wear your hair bound in such a manner?"

Although her gaze remained fixed on Claiborne's wife, her mouth bunched into an attractive little pucker. His toes found hers beneath the table and stroked them, noting every joint through the thin layers of deer hide.

Her back went bowstring-rigid a heartbeat before she shot him a glance barbed with a flaming tip.

Scorched, Totka withdrew and snatched the white cloth that was folded into a triangle on his plate. He gave it a brisk shake to unfold it but froze when her foot nudged his.

Instead of offering the apologetic look he anticipated, she gave a quick shake of her head. Along with the sudden, complete silence at the table, it told him he'd broken one of their table rules. What? What was he supposed to know? She flicked her eyes toward the head of the table.

The general? He had yet to touch his cloth. Was that the problem?

Suppressing a grunt, Totka dropped the fabric in an untidy heap onto his plate, after which the general closed his eyes and broke into a prayer. All heads bowed except Totka's and McGirth's.

Neck bent, Copper Woman exposed her crown to the candlelight, setting the rope of her braid aglow like a golden wreath. How much better it would look unconfined! His fingers itched to rectify it.

Anywhere but here, he would.

The oration continued at length, the only movement coming from two chairs over. Totka felt the burn of McGirth's censure a good while before deigning the man a leisurely gander. But the prayer was completed, and their visual exchange was thwarted. Shame too, because Totka had seen not fatherly indignation as he'd expected, but something else entirely. Anxiety? No, that couldn't be right.

The general shook out his cloth. Others followed suit, and the dinner proceeded.

Claiborne entertained them with a narrative of when he was a boy. Dishes clinked, silver sparkled, and laughter sprinkled the air — all of it wearing on Totka's spent nerves.

At the story's conclusion, Copper Woman set her fork against the side of her plate, laughed, and lightly clapped her hands, but the creases of her mouth were held a bit too stiffly.

Totka scowled at the pretense. At the ridiculous formality.

Oblivious, she launched into her own story.

All eyes riveted to her, giving Totka license to stare. Not at the enchanting glisten of her moist lips nor their hypnotic movement. No, it was the flutter of her hands, the way she gingerly dabbed the corner of her mouth, how only her wrists settled on the table's edge. Her cultured manner both awed and appalled him.

But they didn't fool him. Hers was a charade. All of it. Did no one else see that beneath the refinement was a woman screaming to be free? Free of her familial obligations and rigid ideals? Was he the only one to notice the shadow of the lightest gray that swathed her eyes?

His brief survey of the table told him he was. That is, until it landed on Bitter Eyes who was ready for him with a simper. Yes, she must be quite pleased with the situation. She had her sister exactly where she wanted her. And Totka where she wanted *him* — back on the road to Kossati. Alone.

He lobbed the gesture back at her, grabbed his glass, and tossed its contents to the back of his throat.

Copper Woman's story continued, but it grew more painful to

watch her trying to be someone she was not. Old Grandfather had spoken truth, but the ache he'd prophesied was too much, it carved too deep.

Totka focused on Copper Woman's tale. It was that of another time—a time before she knew him when laughter was abundant, as she would have them believe it was now in her eyes. But when he left tomorrow, she would no longer be laughing.

His brain spun as he struggled to follow her English. It galled, pushing him beyond patience. He set the glass back down with an angry *clunk*.

In the middle of a word, Copper Woman paused, her lips still parted.

"Stop pretending you are this—this *person*." He indicated toward her with a flattened hand.

All eyes swiveled to him, while Copper Woman's wounded gaze bore a chasm into his heart. But she didn't show confusion, nor did she contradict him.

Totka's chair squealed across the floor as he rose. He tore his eyes from her and turned to her father, continuing in Muskogee. "Zachariah McGirth, thank this great chief for his hospitality toward his enemy, but I will no longer burden him with my savage company. As planned, I leave at first light."

Copper Woman was on her feet in a flash. The other men rose with her.

"Do not go." The tremble in her voice was controlled yet discernible. And so, the façade fell, revealing her for who she was.

He quirked a brow. "From the table or from your life?"

Moisture filled her rounded eyes, and he steeled himself against it. She began to rotate to her father, but Totka anticipated it.

"Look at *me*. Not him!" He regained her sight, skittish though it was, and it broke his heart. He planted his palms on the table. "Why this fear, Copper Woman? Did I not say I am strong enough for the both of us?"

"Papa," Bitter Eyes spoke, but Totka drove urgently on.

"You must decide. Will you continue this game, or will you bind yourself to me and return to your true home?"

"You have said enough!" McGirth interrupted. "Don't answer him, Adela." Livid, he strode to the door, his footfall rattling silver against porcelain. "Totka Hadjo, I will have a private word with you."

Copper Woman sank into her chair as though her knees had given way. Clucking like a mother hen, Claiborne's wife went to her.

"I will go with your father, but you and I, we have not finished our talk." Totka waited until he'd received Copper Woman's slight nod before he followed McGirth into the rear enclosed yard where the man turned on him.

"Was my answer regarding my daughter not clear?"

"It was."

"And yet you persist in this futile pursuit! I am greatly in your debt, but I will not allow you to manipulate her into binding herself to you or to exclude me from decisions regarding her welfare or her future. In the presence of our hosts no less!"

McGirth was right. By all accounts, Totka had overstepped his bounds. He filled his lungs with the humid, salty air and let it eek out. "Forgive my rudeness, but be at ease. Our hosts know only that the wild red man under their roof has bad behavior and a harsh tongue. And that you have brought him under submission."

"Have I?"

Totka widened his stance and folded his arms. "You have not."

McGirth threw up his hands and stormed the length of the high, stone wall hemming the garden. He'd not reached the end when he swung around and stalked back. "There must be something you need. Money, seed, livestock? What do want of me?" Was that an edge of desperation propelling his bribe? If it was, it could mean only one thing—he didn't have the power over Copper Woman he would like Totka to believe he had. Why was that? She adored this man, honored him, had abandoned Totka and risked great danger to find him.

Nightfall had cooled the air, but Totka's blood was up. Perspiration dampened his shirt. "Do not insult me! Of course I have need of all those things, but my heart cannot be bought. And there is *no* obstacle that will keep me from Copper Woman. I will lose her only to death."

"Is that what it will take?" The half-lit night couldn't obscure McGirth's tightening fist or the subtle forward shift of his posture.

In a slow, deliberate movement, Totka uncrossed his arms and let them rest at his sides. He wouldn't fight his beloved's father. "I am Muscogee. Not afraid to die." His only fear was living without her.

"Not a soul would question it." This was most definitely a desperate man. A man who knew he would lose his daughter. Again.

There came a strange stab of pity to Totka's chest. He weeded it out, giving place to hope. "Only your daughter."

As though struck, McGirth backed off and fell silent.

"It is beneath you to threaten me."

"Hardly. The war is not yet over. You are my enemy, an all-but-defeated Red Stick." His words, though lackluster, held truth that hit their mark and bored a hole into Totka's pride. "Do you not care for her wellbeing?" McGirth continued. "I take no offense at the color of your skin, but your actions place a foul mark on your head, and you have nothing to offer but a destroyed talwa and a hopeless future."

There they were again, those ugly details. In Kossati there would be hunger, much labor, endless derision from those on the outside. There would be suffering and— No! He wouldn't entertain a defeatist spirit.

He lifted his jaw a degree to counteract the doubt ruffling his confidence. "The next year will be a trying one, but we will recover. Together."

"Not with my daughter!"

"Like it or not, she is Muscogee—Beaver Clan and worthy of it. There is a warrior's heart in her, brave and loyal. She should not waste it on tea and dainty food, and she should not give it to any other man whose love will inevitably be weaker than mine. Weaker than she deserves."

"A warrior's heart?" McGirth's head jutted backwards. "Not my Adela."

If he believed that, either he didn't know his daughter as he should, or Totka had brought out the warrior's heart in her, for he had seen it right off. Bold and bright, it had stared back at him from the meadow's floor. "Did you know she killed a Talladega warrior? Drove the blade through his spine, straight to the hilt." Nokose had witnessed it, and Totka had seen the evidence of it on her hands.

Zachariah flinched. Good. Let him be shocked. His daughter was no ordinary white woman. She'd had a father and an adopted brother to teach her to admire the Muscogees long before Totka had schooled her in their customs. She was Muscogee at heart, and it was time McGirth knew it.

"And on the long journey, she rivaled any number of warriors with her resilience. Through pain and hunger and fear, she did not wilt or beg, and she did not cry."

"Is this true? My poor child."

Totka barely processed the interruption. The need to speak of her, to make this man understand the passion he had for her and why, drove the telling from him. "In Kossati, she was knocked from a horse with a stone to the head. It could have killed her. I—" His throat went hoarse, but he pushed the words out. "I thought it had. But she is *strong*. Strong enough to forgive the woman who hurt her. Strong enough to survive the slave pole. Strong enough to put aside her own longings for the love of her sister, the same who threatened to disown her."

McGirth held up a hand. "Please, no more. I cannot—"

"And when her mother lay bleeding out and painted Long Hair warriors neared, Copper Woman refused to leave her."

Hands to the sides of his head, McGirth spun away with a howl that softened Totka's tone.

"They surrounded us, intent on taking my life. But she cowed them—not with bow or blade but with words. Because she is a *warrior."* His little Red Stick. "And she fights for those she loves."

The only person she would not fight for was herself.

Spent, Totka let the night surround them with its perfect calm. All was still except for insect song and the soft roar of the not-too-distant long snake.

At last, McGirth spoke, even and quiet. "I hardly know of whom you speak. You are not describing the daughter I knew, or the one I have been with these last sleeps. She is . . . much changed. Stronger, yes. But also, weak. I see weariness in her—little wonder. And she is. . . " He seemed to be searching. "Conflicted. Grieving. She is in no state to make decisions that will impact her life, and you are wrong to press her for an answer she is incapable of giving."

When it came to her own needs, she *was* weak. Hadn't Totka seen it himself long ago? Accused her of it even? He, too, had witnessed the war playing out behind her eyes. Firsthand, he'd experienced her complete inability to make certain decisions. Namely, regarding him. But depriving her of her source of strength would do her no good, and Totka refused to believe there was any source for her greater than himself. "I agree with what you say, but her weakness and grief will deepen when I am gone."

McGirth turned back to him then, but he seemed smaller somehow. "Do not think I'm blind to the power you have over her. Should you ask her again tonight, she is likely to succumb to your wishes. But tell me—would you have her go with you for *her* good, or for your own?"

The question was a war club blow. It thrust the air from Totka's lungs and left his mouth hanging. Under his watch, Galena had died and Copper Woman had not thrived—not in the physical sense—nor was there any hope that conditions would improve soon.

"I think we can agree," McGirth said, "that this place, where there is no hunger or uncertainty, is the best for her."

"You speak true, but what good is a full belly when the chest is empty?" He had experienced both and would take hunger over loss any day. "Tonight, I'll speak with her again. She understands the sacrifices and risks. Should she choose to be my woman and come away with me, will you forbid her?"

"I forbid that you *ask*, not that it will do any good. It can safely be said you would rather stop breathing than stop pursuing my . . . Copper Woman. And, yes, I forbid that she leave. But . . . " He ran a hand over his face. "I'll not lock her away if she decides that is what she wants."

Truly?

"Adela must be allowed to make her own choice. A man cannot force a woman to do anything *and* retain her love. And my daughter's love is most precious to me."

Wasn't that what Totka had tried to do—force Copper Woman to stay with him until she saw reason? It hadn't worked in his favor. McGirth was proving a wise sort and more willing to release his daughter than Totka had believed possible. There was still one more hurdle to be leapt.

"And what of your son? Who would rear him with Copper Woman gone?"

"A strange question. One she's put to you as an impediment to binding herself to you?" McGirth proceeded as though knowing Totka wouldn't answer. "The child would do better under her care than her sister's."

"Clearly," Totka snipped out, irritated at the mere mention of the darker sister's inadequacies. Revealing that now would be to paddle backwards. He tempered his breathing and began again. "But that should not be an obstacle to her happiness."

Hands behind him, McGirth rocked back on his heels. Totka could almost hear the cogs turning in his mind. "Agreed. We would manage without her."

"I will tell her you said so."

"No. I ask that you not speak with her of it. Not of the child nor of marriage nor of leaving. Not tonight. Not tomorrow." The request was made so humbly, so quietly and slowly, Totka couldn't be angry. Only curious as to the thought process behind the request, for there had to be one.

"If not tomorrow, then . . . when?"

"Go back to your people, Totka. Reestablish yourself. Build a home. Plant maize and celebrate the Green Corn. Fill your storehouse and crib. At the next blackberry moon, return and ask her again whether she will go with you."

It was a sensible request. Totka hated it.

The Muscogee marriage process required a lodge be built and meat be presented as proof he could fill the role expected of him. Only then would a woman be released to a man. That could be accomplished in a few moons. Four seasons was excessive. A snort and brisk shake of the head conveyed the sentiment.

"Four seasons. It is all I ask." All? As though four seasons were a small space of time. "Give her that time to find herself again. To grieve and heal."

"And, you hope, to forget me."

McGirth placed a heavy hand on Totka's shoulder. "As you said, Adela is loyal. If the love you share is genuine, it will endure the trial, and you will have had time to prepare a home worthy of her." His sudden tenderness could almost be construed into fatherly affection. "If her love is fleeting, she'll have had time to recognize it."

"It is *not* fleeting."

"Prove it. Come back this time next summer, and if she chooses to return to your talwa, she will go with my blessing. If you ask her again tonight, tomorrow, or return any time before the next blackberry moon"—the hand clamped down; all tenderness gone—"I'll fight you for her. And let there be no mistake, Red Stick, you will not win."

Still in her dinner gown, Adela perched on the sill of the tiny window of her unlit chamber and watched Totka watch the moon.

He stood fist to mouth, elbow resting on a folded arm, as still as she'd ever seen him. She didn't need daylight to note the stoop of his shoulders.

After he and her father had left the dinner table, Adela hadn't had the strength to continue in polite company. *Stop pretending, stop pretending, stop . . .* Totka's accusation continued to reverberate. Until that moment, she hadn't realized she was pretending. She'd simply been trying to convince herself she could live in civilization again. Without him.

She also hadn't realized until that moment that he knew her so well. Tonight, he knew her better than she knew herself. Which only intensified the sting and the desperation to learn to carry on without him.

Shortly after, she'd excused herself and, stationed at the window, watched the exchange below. The sill's edge had numbed her leg long before her father had left Totka standing as he was now, pensive and . . . Yes, resigned.

Whatever the men had spoken of had not had a favorable outcome. Not for Totka.

She'd always known he would leave without her. But now, judging by his posture, he knew it too.

Her fingers went to her bodice and outlined the long center ridge of the feather hidden beneath the folds. "Totka, my Red Stick." She tried the words out on a whisper. They fit nicely around her tongue, but they were gone now, and he hadn't heard them.

A quiver began in her belly and grew until her insides became a gelatinous stew. Pulse racing and palms sweating, she beat back nausea. A familiar feeling, this fear. But fear of what?

No more pretending, Copper Woman. She knew of what. Fear that he'd finally given up on her. Or had been forced to.

But if he had, he was justified—she'd given him little reason to continue pursuit.

Bathed in shadow and defeat, he looked small and forlorn, as though a falling pine needle might shatter him. He'd never looked small to her, not once, and as the image took form in her mind, she despised it, wanted it ripped out, wanted it replaced with the man who would pursue her until she was strong enough to be caught.

Below her room, dinner continued, her father's baritone now mingling with the muffled conversation. It would be another long while before they put away their wine and their whist and scuttled off to bed.

On Indian's feet, she padded silently down the stairs and out the backdoor. The night hit her like a damp blanket, and the door clicked shut behind her. Not pausing to weigh her actions, nor caring, she collected her gown's hem from the sandy grass and jogged to the far side where Totka remained as she'd seen him from the window.

His back was to her, but no doubt he knew it was she who approached. Even so, he stayed as he was until she used his back to stop herself.

Arms flung about him, she ran her hands up his chest to his shoulders, appreciating their breadth, his height and strength. He was not small. He was not weak. He was Muscogee, a Red Stick. Not afraid of pain or death. Only of separation.

Flexing her arms, she culled the gap between them and pressed her cheek to the ridges of his spine, drinking in his aroma so familiar to her now: bear grease, leather, toil, confidence. If self-surety were a scent, it would be his. Had it been only a year since she'd first taken in that scent?

The muscles of his chest expanded and receded with a great breath; in her ear, the wind of it whispered through his lungs, and his heart beat strong and regular, steadying her frantic mind.

He covered her hands still capping his shoulders. "You should go into the house, Copper Woman." It wasn't a reprimand but recognition of the delicacy of a white woman's reputation and the risk she ran of losing it. Which confirmed he knew she would stay, and he would not.

"Let them think what they will. I could not stand to see you here alone looking so . . . lost." She wouldn't insult him with her initial assessment.

"But I am not lost. I am here." He unhooked her and rotated within the cage of her arms, then peered down on her. How had she even entertained the thought he was small?

Lightly, his fingers probed her head, walked along the groove of her plait, and paused to dig. A pin slid from its mooring, then another. "Perhaps, my little Red Stick, here among the whites with their ruffles and lace and their peculiar manners" — the rope of her hair slipped and thudded against her back — "perhaps you are the one who is lost?"

A heavy breath tugged downward the corners of her mouth. "Maybe you're right." Although at that moment, with him working to unravel her hair, she felt anything but lost. "Maybe I will feel differently once I've returned to my father's home, but here I am only confused."

Amid the distraction of his hands in her hair, she sensed more than saw the nod he offered. "Which is why I'll not return for twelve moons."

She took in the news with a mixture of relief and chagrin. "It's a long time." But he *would* return. He'd not given up on her.

"Too long for my liking." He gentled through a snag that tweaked her scalp. "But there is wisdom in it. It was your father's request, and I'll abide by it to win his blessing."

That her father would give his blessing at all — even a year from now — was surprising. No doubt, he saw in Totka that man she did. That he was loyal and brave and good. And that he was good for *her*.

Totka set her away from him, then forked both hands through her hair to shake it out. He tipped his head to the side. "Much better."

"If I had known you are partial to it down, I would not have put it up."

He harrumphed. "With me, you have always worn it down, as an unmarried woman should. If you had not been so happy to put aside Muscogee ways, perhaps I would've spoken of it."

"I cannot unpeel my white skin, and nothing about this makes me happy." She flattened her palm, tiny and pale, against his, long and brown, and lifted them to chest level. "We are quite different, you and I."

His fingers threaded through hers and contracted. "Our differences will not keep us apart."

Oh, but they could. She relaxed her hand and arm, but he held them aloft. "Do not ignore my concerns, Totka. There is my brother to consider and—"

"We'll not speak of your brother again. Not for another four seasons. Much will happen in that time."

"Fair enough. And what of my Creator?"

"Your Creator is not my own, so he cannot keep you from me."

"Yes, He can do—"

A firm yank on her hand bounced her into the wall of him where he trapped her with an arm at the small of her back. "No, he cannot. When I am gone, you will know the pain of separation. And when I return, we will be bound." The usual determination hardened his voice.

"He *can* keep us apart, if He wishes. Until you truly believe that, save us both the heartache and do not come back." She pushed against his rigid chest, but when he didn't budge, she slumped. Pushing him away had only ever lengthened the stride of his pursuit.

Changing tack, she allowed a moment of silence to calm herself, planted a tiny kiss on his chin, and whispered against it. "I love you, Big Warrior Totka Hadjo."

The arm about her tightened. He released her hand to support the back of her head as she looked up at him. "Are you certain? It is the first I've heard it."

"I should have said it long ago, for it is true. I've often wondered if it has been true since your arrow stopped the wolf." She shook her head. "But that's not possible."

"The seed was sown that night." There it was again, that certainty of his that both soothed her spirit and disturbed her pulse.

"Looking back, I think I always knew I would love you."

"Even at Mims' place?"

"No." She frowned and looked away. "Not then." When he rubbed her back, she rapped his chest with a forefinger. "But I was not afraid of you."

"That, I believe. You never feared me. Not as you should have." He gazed off into the gloom somewhere beyond her, chin cocked as though his pride had been wounded.

Smiling, she pulled his feather from her bodice. "And why, my daunting Red Stick"—she tickled his neck with the feather's tip—"should I fear the other half of my soul?"

He snatched the feather and released it to the wind. "And what does a woman do with the other half of the soul she does not fear?" As he pulled her up on her tiptoes, his mouth descended. "She leaves him."

"She loves him. Shall I show you how much?"

Pride discarded, he fitted his mouth to hers, and let her do to him exactly as she'd offered. She kissed him the way she knew he wanted, the way he'd kissed her by the river when he'd sent her spinning, the way she'd wanted to do ever since: hard, greedily, insistent, driven not by thought but by need and desperation. Desperation to brand herself onto him with a burn that would outlast the year.

By the time she broke away, out of breath and quavering, her lips throbbed as though her heart had taken up residence within them. His breath was hot against her ear, and the skin of his back was slick against her nails. When had her hands climbed beneath his shirt? She withdrew, smoothing it back into place.

He leaned the side of his head against hers while his fingers, ensnared in her hair, massaged her scalp. "You are good at that. Too good perhaps."

"My love speaks for itself. It is deep and fixed, like a hot coal beneath my ribs that I cannot escape. That I do not *want* to escape. But as deep as it goes and as immoveable as is it, my Creator abides deeper yet. And just as I do not want to part from you, I *cannot* part from Him or his teachings. It is impossible. Do you understand what

I'm telling you?"

He pulled back to look at her, and she ached a little with the loss of him. "You are saying you love me, but you love the white man's Creator more. That you'll not have me unless I abandon my mother's teachings for that of your sacred writings."

"Abandon? Not at all." She freed a sigh. "I am asking you to go back to Kossati and search for Him. He's promised He will show Himself to those who seek Him. Call on my Jesus Creator, and see if He does not answer. Did you not promise as much to Nokose, your brother?" She presented the question with slight goading.

Totka loosed a low, disbelieving laugh that rumbled clear through her. "You know where to strike a man." His thumb drew a line down her jaw, then back and forth over her lower lip. The calluses from his bowstring snagged against her, bringing to mind the wolf's yelp, the vibrating shafts, the many ways he'd loved her.

She kissed his thumb and rested her face in the palm of his hand.

"Very well, Copper Woman. I accept your challenge."

The night became fuzzy with unshed tears. He would leave, but he would continue to search. "He is faithful, Totka. I promise. Seek Him, and He will find you." Wet trickled from her eyes.

He pulled his hand from her cheek and dug into his pouch, then wiped her face with a soft cloth. "One day, your tears will be the end of me."

She sniffled and laughed. "Then I'll save them for when you are gone."

He pressed the frayed cloth into her palm, then enclosed her fingers over it. There was no need to wonder what it was or why he'd given it back to her. With one last sniff, she tucked the scrap into her bodice where the feather had been, happy the place was filled again.

He turned her around and pulled her flush against him. Finger stretched toward the sliver of new moon, he spoke into her hair. "When the next blackberry moon is just so, I will meet you in the glade where I first loved you. We will talk again of your Creator, and when we are through, I will make you mine."

Epilogue

August 1814

Adela stretched her legs out in front of her and leaned her head back against the trunk of the tree that stood watch outside their kitchen. It had been the perfect day for a picnic—sunny and warm with a mild breeze quite abnormal for August.

It was difficult to be indoors. The house was too silent. The busy creaks and groans of the floorboards and door hinges had diminished, as if the structure were observing a time of silence in honor of the deceased, so when Lillian suggested they eat outdoors, Adela had jumped at the idea.

The hour passed pleasantly enough, almost as though Lillian's threat to disown her had never happened. Almost.

"Wasn't it precious, Lilly?" Adela asked. "His first smile."

Lulled by the songbirds above, their brother Charlie slept on their picnic blanket, milky drool seeping from the corner of his mouth. He had taken to bottled goat's milk with some hesitation, but now he thrived.

Lillian nodded. "Mama should have been here to see it."

Adela caught the tinge of bitterness in her sister's voice, but she said nothing. Lillian continued to sink in a quagmire of hate. How long until she gave it up?

Sometimes, Adela thought what Lillian really wanted was a good spanking. Barring that, a good talking to. Beth would have told her to grow up and move on. She would have said life was too short to spend it wallowing. It was what Lillian needed to hear, but Adela couldn't bring herself to say it. Not the way Beth would have. *She needs time and our prayers*, Adela repeated to herself daily.

After all, it had only been two months since Totka had escorted them to Mobile. Adela had made an intentional choice to look beyond their suffering. Grieving still, yes, but moving forward, choosing to forgive — to love.

Loving had not been hard for Adela, not with Totka offering his so freely. She often wondered if she might not have bounced back so quickly had his love not been there to fill in the holes her loved ones left behind.

Her mind drifted, as it usually did with every thought of him — which felt like every moment of every day. The ache for him had numbed a bit as the days ticked by, far too slowly, but it never left. It was an arrow lodged between her ribs that only he could extract — nine months, twelve days, and a few hours — and oh, she prayed that he could, that God would show Himself real to Totka.

Memories poured over her, hounded her — his lilting voice humming in her ear; his hand a vice on her arm, dragging her through the cane, through the forest, away from rescue, away from certain death; his perseverance; his passion; his promise — each memory sweet. Even the tough ones.

A smile worked its way over her mouth as she smoothed her apron pocket just to feel the thickness of the snippet of fabric inside it.

"He has Papa's nose," Lillian's voice broke in.

Adela's eyes popped open. "Who?"

"Who do you think? Totka?" She pointed a tense finger at the sleeping baby. "Charlie, of course."

"Oh. Well . . . yes, I suppose he does. He also has Papa's eyes and hair." Adela's eyes and hair.

Papa was all smiles all the time. Although he had yet to open up about it, he'd had a difficult row to hoe following the massacre. Stories swirled of his fearless trek through Creek country to inform General Jackson of the assault on Fort Mims, of his tireless pursuit of the enemy, of his reckless heroism and his utter despondency. It had taken much blood to satiate his desire for revenge, and once he'd gotten his fill, he'd been left dry and desolate, inspired only by the occasional need for a courier to run a dangerous path through the wilderness.

The Lord had rewarded him, Papa claimed, despite his many failures, and his transformation was a beacon of hope for a devastated community. The McGirths had found a happy ending, cracked though it was.

"I feel about like Charlie." Lillian yawned. "I think I'll take him in and lie down with him."

"Good idea. I'll clean up here and follow you in."

Lillian picked up the baby and tilted him toward Adela. "Give me kisses, Sissy," she said in a silly voice.

Adela chuckled, enjoying a brief glimpse of the old Lillian. "Sweet dreams, little man," she crooned and planted a kiss on his pudgy cheek.

The two made their way to the house, and Adela began collecting the remnants of their lunch. Hester came out and took the utensils from her.

"You look plumb wore out, Missy Adela. I got this here. You go on and have yourself a rest."

"I feel better than I have in months, Hester. You just don't want me touching your dishes." Adela passed her a toothy grin, and Hester responded with a playful swat.

"*My* dishes. Soon you'll be sayin' I own the house, too." She swung her dishtowel toward the kitchen as she spoke.

Adela snatched the cloth from her and popped her with it on the rump. Hester shrieked and the two tugged at the towel until Hester plopped down beside her, spilling the wooden utensils onto the grass.

"Good," Adela said, linking arms with the woman. "Leave those and sit with me a spell."

Hester snorted. "I ain't got time to be gabbing. That floor in there ain't gonna scrub itself."

"Life's too precious to be so busy." Hester wavered, so Adela pressed on. "Just for a minute. Then I'll scrub the floor myself."

"I'll sit with ya, but I won't have you scrubbin' my floors."

"*Your* floors?" Adela gave the older woman a sideways smile and bumped shoulders with her. They laughed, and Hester threw an arm about Adela.

She leaned her head on Hester's shoulder and sighed deeply. "I missed you, Hester."

She patted Adela's knee and spoke in a broken voice. "It's good to hear them words. This house was silent as a tomb for longer than I care to recall. The angel of death stole the joy from this place, but God done brought it back."

"Hester?" Adela asked, fearful to broach the subject they all skirted.

"Hmm?"

"What was it like for you . . . in the fort?"

The woman didn't hesitate to respond. "About the closest to hell I ever care to come."

"Were you afraid?"

"You better believe it! I know where my eternal home is, but the pain it was gonna take to get me there, now, that was something to be fearin'."

"I know what you mean. We might have come out alive, but I ended up hurt anyway . . . when Beth died. Then Mama. Now Lillian . . . "

"The death of someone we love be the worst kind of pain."

They fell silent for a moment, but Adela couldn't resist the urge to speak of another she'd lost. "I saw Phillip die. Right before me, he—" She swallowed. "I tried to save him, but it was no use. There were too many." And Totka was too swift, too engrossed in battle.

"I knew you was gonna speak of the man sooner or later."

Adela didn't expect the world to blur with tears or to feel the lump forming in her throat. He had been a good man. He'd been good to *her*. Good enough to die for her.

"Did you . . . did you see him too . . . at the end?" The last word came out on a squeak from between trembling lips.

Hester stared at the ground and nibbled on her lower lip. "Phillip come out of that hole in the picket right behind me." She spoke as if replaying it in her mind. "I was shot and would have fallen if it weren't for the good Doctor Holmes runnin' by my side. Phillip and his brother, Captain Bailey, the both of them took on the redskins so this here woman could get to the cane." She pressed her lips into a tight line. Her chin quivered as she struggled against tears.

Adela didn't recall seeing any of the others. Only Phillip, parrying, slashing, falling.

"The captain he . . . he got belly shot. About broke my heart seein' him go down. I couldn't bear to see Phillip go too, so I ran. I ran into the canebrake all the way to the deep water. That was when God put that dugout right there before my eyes so I couldn't miss it."

Adela wiped her wet cheeks with the back of her hand as the horrifying scene played out before her mind's eye. "He shouldn't have been there. He'd come for me. To get me out. He shouldn't have died."

They sat in silence for some time while Adela processed all she'd learned since coming home, until a thought struck and sent a shiver down her spine. "Papa said Phillip wasn't found among the dead, and since he died outside the fort his body wouldn't have burned. He couldn't have been one of the . . . unidentifiable. Why didn't they find him?"

Hester arranged her lips into a ball. "What are you sayin', child?"

Adela's question neared the absurd, but it was worth asking. "Do you think there's a chance he's still alive?"

Hester bunched her brows and shook her head. "It been over a year, Missy Adela, and we ain't heard nothin'. Where would he have been all this time? Captive, like you?"

"I didn't see him, but there were several large parties. If he was with another . . . " Something Totka once said came back to her. The Muscogees took male captives for only one reason. If they'd taken Phillip, he'd been tortured and slain long ago. "Oh, God, please no." Why had she pursued this line of thought?

Hester's face reflected the horror gripping Adela's throat. Emphatically, she wagged her head. "It was three days before them soldiers got to burying the dead. Think of the wolves. Any wild animal could of—" Hester cut off the gruesome thought, which was a sight better than the previous. She peered into Adela's water-logged eyes. "Why you thinking this way? You ain't feeling guilty is you?"

Taken aback, Adela considered Hester's question. "You mean about Phillip dying because he came for me? Yes, always."

"You ain't got no call beatin' yourself up. 'Bout his death or 'bout lettin' love in when it come calling—no matter the past. You know I love that sister of yours, but Lilly, she done shut love *out*. No ma'am, it be better what you done . . . loving that Red Stick how you do."

Adela gasped. "I never said I loved him." She'd spoken of him but no more than she'd spoken of Singing Grass or Nokose or the children. At least she'd tried not to.

Hester's laugh enveloped Adela like a warm embrace. "It be written all over that pretty face."

A blush crept up Adela's neck, and she fidgeted inside her apron pocket, her fingers stroking a tattered edge of the remnant. "I do love him. So much it hurts. Right here." She touched the place the arrow was buried. "But I told him I have a responsibility to my family and that I couldn't be with a man who rejected my Jesus, but he's coming back for me anyway."

"I believe it. He'd be as dumb as an ox not to come after you. And I pray he does. You deserve a dollop of happiness." Hester stood and stretched her back.

"When he comes back, I'm afraid we'll both end up with nothing but broken hearts. He said he'll seek God as I asked, but I'm not sure he understands how serious I am about the matter. And how could I leave baby Charlie?"

"Where your faith be, girl? You thinkin' God can't turn a man's heart? Work out a few measly details? Look at you sittin' here alive, pretty as a picture with your hair all glowin'. I ain't never gonna doubt the power of God again, not after seein' what He can do!"

Adela threw her hands up and laughed. "All right! All right, you win."

Arms filled with dirty dishes, Hester marched toward the house, hollering as she went. "You bet I'm right. Now, get on up. My dirty floors are callin' your name."

"I'll be right in," Adela replied and rested her head against the rough bark behind her. Her mind wandered to the last time she'd sat just so under a tree. Mama had been beside her then, frail yet stronger than Adela hoped to ever be.

Mama was with Jesus, and Adela was a different person. They all were.

And Totka was . . .

She glanced down at the swatch of his shirt in her hand. It often made it there without her knowing it.

Totka was as near as a thought away.

Yes, she would have faith, and she would trust. Totka had yet to let her down.

If he said he would seek her Jesus — wherever that might lead — he would. If he said he would be in the meadow at the next blackberry moon, he would. And Adela would meet him there, heart wide open. The moment couldn't come soon enough.

War had flipped the world upside down, producing broken homes with uncertain days ahead. Still, Adela couldn't help but believe her future was ripe with hope, just waiting for the picking.

Thank you for reading!
If you enjoyed Totka and his Copper Woman,
please consider leaving a review at an online venue.

Turn the page to learn more about *The Red Feather*
and to see what's ahead for the characters in
The Sacred Writings...

Beneath
the
BLACKBERRY
MOON

PART 2
The Sacred Writings

APRIL W GARDNER
Creek Country Saga

The Sacred Writings
Beneath the Blackberry Moon, book 2

Big Warrior Totka Hadjo enters his toughest battles yet — the fight for love, the invasion of fear, and the inescapable ashes of each.

The war has ended, and now, Totka Hadjo must endure eleven moons and twenty-six sleeps without his beloved Copper Woman. But he has a two-fold task to keep him occupied: establish a lodge deserving of her and challenge her Jesus Creator to a vision, to prove his existence.

Totka leaves the whites' settlements with Copper Woman's holy book, an object with medicine strong enough to keep at bay the hounding ghosts of his unavenged ancestors. But the sacred writings cannot restrain the Bluecoat who has returned from the dead, the one who first owned her heart. From the far reaches of the Muscogee Confederacy, Totka is powerless to stop the onslaught of events that conspires to take his beloved from him forever.

Leaping Waters, Totka's old passion, is a constant presence he cannot escape, but she might be able to unlock the spiritual mysteries found in the holy book. While he wades through the confusing symbols, the Choctaws, his ancient enemy, are determined to seize prime Muscogee hunting lands. In the process, they aggravate wounds that might never heal and expose him to a truth too bitter to swallow.

Denial and revenge go down much easier.

AVAILBLE FOR PURCHASE

To be notified when a new book is out and to receive the occasional sale notification, visit **www.aprilgardner.com** and subscribe to April's newsletter.

April W Gardner

APRIL W GARDNER writes Christian historical romance with a focus on our Southeastern Native Tribes. She is a copyeditor, military wife, and mother of two who lives in South Texas. In no particular order, April dreams of owning a horse, learning a third language, and visiting all the national parks.

Enjoy these other books by April

HISTORICAL ROMANCE

Creek Country Saga:
The Red Feather
The Sacred Writings
The Ebony Cloak
The Untold Stories (supplemental reading, e-book only)
Bitter Eyes No More
Love the War Woman
Finding Pretty Wolf (2020)

Standalone:
Beautiful in His Sight

CO-AUTHORED
Better than Fiction (women's fiction/historical romance)

Contact:
Facebook: April.Gardner1
Website: AprilGardner.com
Email: aprilgardnerwrites@gmail.com

Author's Notes

In the wee hours of a sleepless night in 1999 the Lord brought to mind Chief Red Eagle, the inspiration behind this book. (My lineage is connected to him through his father's brother.) That night, as images of his fearless leap filled my thoughts, I found myself wishing his story and that of his people were told in novel form. And so, the dream began.

Sometime later, I came across a sketch of Zachariah McGirth's experience at Fort Mims. His family's triumphant story provided the skeleton for this novel. The following is the true account of the McGirth's miraculous survival:

The McGirths were a family of ten — seven daughters and one son. During the massacre, all were taken as slaves, minus Zachariah's only son who died at the fort.

The orphan boy, Sanota (whom I gave the warrior's name Nokose Fixico) was raised to manhood by the McGirths. He later returned to live with his people. During the attack on the fort, he came upon Mrs. Vicey McGirth (a relative of Chief Red Eagle) and her children and took them under the pretense of acquiring slaves.

Just as in my story, Zachariah had left that morning to check on his farm only to return later that day with his slave, Caesar, to find the place a heap of burning rubble. He was the first to come upon the gruesome scene.

Sanota hid the McGirths in the woods and hunted for them the duration of the war. One day, he announced he would fight at the Horseshoe Bend, and if he did not return, they must make their way south toward safety. This they did on their own.

While believing his family dead, Zachariah became known as one of the few men brazen enough to carry expresses through enemy country. That is, until an unexpected and joyous reunion with his family on a Mobile dock in March of 1814.

While visiting the site of Fort Mims in 2007, I learned that during the excavation of the fort's only well, archeologists found an ax head with the initials "Z. M." pinged into the iron. Historians surmise it belonged to Zachariah McGirth, but how exactly it got there was my privilege to imagine.

All other elements regarding these characters and the events in their lives happened on these pages alone.

Other characters from history books are the eldest three Bailey brothers, though I changed some of their given names. Major Beasley's slovenly leadership and death, the slave at the whipping post, Mrs. Bailey (to include her bold skewering of the cowardly soldier) and Hester's and Dr. Holmes' heroic escapes also color the pages of American history books.

Other actual historical figures include Captain Dale, Peter McQueen, and Josiah Francis. For more on these figures, please see **Cast of Characters** below. Josiah's story will be told in upcoming novels, beginning with *Bitter Eyes No More* (released Feb. 2017). Tragically, the massacre at Hillabee is a fact that history "experts" have often glazed over.

The comet and earthquake alluded to that influenced many Creek to believe the prophets actually occurred. It is recorded that the British knew the faithful comet would appear. They revealed this to Tecumseh in hopes he might use it to sway the Creeks to fight against the Americans. It worked.

While it is not known what became of the McGirth's after the war, we do know that Chief Red Eagle (Billy Weatherford) became friends with General Andrew Jackson. Weatherford settled down on a farm in southern Mobile County not far from the site of Fort Mims. As his father before him, he prospered breeding fine horses. While believed by some to be a traitor to his people, others, including many whites, held him in high regard. By the time of his death in 1824, locals described him as being "brave and honorable and possessing a strong native sense."

While researching for this novel, I developed a profound awe for the Natives of our country, once theirs alone. *Beneath the Blackberry Moon* tells of the beginning of the end of the noble Creeks and their mighty confederacy. In it, I attempted to be fair to both sides giving logical motives to seemingly illogical actions, such as the unbridled attack on Fort Mims. I pray I accomplished this task.

I tried to stay as accurate as possible to Creek culture, history, and spiritual beliefs. Happily, I have two amazing people to thank for any cultural accuracy that I attained: Edna Peirce Dixon and Ghost Dancer, a true Alabama Red Stick. Without them, *The Red Feather* would be a sad little stew of errors! Each, with selfless love and dedication, invested more time and attention to this project than a thousand thank-yous can touch. They were gracious with my ignorance and my imagination, which (as imaginations tend to do) roamed freely. In some cases, to aid the storyline, I purposefully veered off track.

Totka's red feather is one such instance. To my knowledge, the Red Sticks didn't wear red feathers as a sign of their attachment to the faction. The red war club (sticks) had long been a symbol of the Red Sticks, not the feather.

Also, at various times in a warrior's life his name would change completely. I retained the first portion of Totka's name for reader ease. And because I couldn't imagine calling him anything else!

The timeline of the historical events was fudged to allow for the events in my fictional characters' lives. For the actual timeline, please see **Creek War Timeline** below.

Beneath the Blackberry Moon: the Red Feather touches only the beginning of Creek woes. The tribe's story continues to unravel as seen through the eyes of Totka, Adela, and others in book two, *The Sacred Writings* and book three, *The Ebony Cloak*. Lillian's romance and discovery of God's mercy and grace can be found in *Drawn by the*

The Red Feather

Frost Moon: Bitter Eyes No More. Tall Bull's story, *Love War Woman*, is due for release in late 2017.

It's my prayer that through the lives of these characters you will not only have experienced a portion of our forgotten heritage but also have developed a well-placed respect for this land's first inhabitants.

I pray you will be encouraged to hold fast to the faith during whatever trials the Lord sees fit to pass your way.

We are troubled on every side, yet not distressed; we are perplexed, but not in despair, Persecuted, but not forsaken; cast down, but not destroyed; For all things are for your sakes, that the abundant grace might through the thanksgiving of many redound to the glory of God. For which cause we faint not; but though our outward man perish, yet the inward man is renewed day by day. For our light affliction, which is but for a moment, worketh for us a far more exceeding and eternal weight of glory.

II Cor. 4:8, 9, 15-16

~April W Gardner

To learn more about the Creek Indians, the settlers of Creek country, or the Creek War, please visit me on the web at: **aprilgardner.com**.

Book Club Discussion Questions

1. Do you agree with Adela's decision to reject Totka because he didn't share her faith? Why or why not?
2. What would you have done in her place?
3. Do you think Adela and Galena could have done anything differently to help Lillian through her grief?
4. Were the Red Sticks justified in their war?
5. Do you blame Nokose and Totka for their part in the assault on Fort Mims? Why or why not?
6. Was Adela foolish or courageous for loving a man who was so "wrong" for her?
7. America's past with her Natives isn't attractive. In regards to the Muscogee and what you've learned about them through this novel, what do you think could have been done differently by either nation to avoid the Creek War?
8. Do you think Phillip is still alive? Why do you suppose Adela was curious to know?
9. Compare the reactions of both nations to the following events:
   * The massacre at Fort Mims by Native Americans.
   * The massacre at Hillabee Town by General White's soldiers.
10. What portion of Muscogee history, culture, or spiritual beliefs revealed in *The Red Feather* did you enjoy learning about the most?

Cast of Historical Figures

Please note that while I enjoy using and following history as closely as possible, I made the characters—even the historical figures—as I wanted them to be. I try not to misrepresent history, but I always put the fiction first.

Major Daniel Beasley

Commander of the garrison at Fort Mims who ignored reports of Red Stick sightings and neglected to make proper preparations for an attack. He died while trying to close the fort's gate and was one of the first casualties in the assault.

General Ferdinand Claiborne

Commander of the Mississippi Territory militia. He was sent to Tensaw in the summer of 1813 and led the first organized offensive after the Battle of Fort Mims. His troops destroyed the Red Sticks' supposedly impregnable Holy Ground, the location of Red Eagle's famous leap from the bluff. After the war, he returned to his plantation in Natchez, Mississippi Territory where he died in 1815 due to health issues stemming from the hardships of the Creek War.

Captain Sam Dale

Sam Dale's is a little-known name that should rival that of Davy Crockett and Sam Houston. All three fought during the Creek War, but Captain Dale saw the most action. He fought the Battle of Burnt Corn and participated in the campaign against Holy Ground, but he is most known for his famous canoe fight in which he and two others killed nine Red Sticks in hand-to-hand combat while straddling two canoes floating down the Alabama River. (As told in *Beneath the Blackberry Moon: the Untold Stories*)

Josiah Francis

One of the most notable Red Stick prophets, Francis was the son of a white trader and a Creek woman. He claimed to have been rendered blind by his prophetic visions. After a miraculous healing, he became the most ardent of the Creek prophets. He played a significant role in the construction of Holy Ground. After the war, he worked with the English and Spanish to renew the Red Stick cause. General Andrew Jackson considered Francis his worst enemy during the Creek War, and in April 1818 was finally victorious over him. Josiah Francis died in 1818 by order of Old Sharp Knife.

General Andrew Jackson

Jackson served as major general of the Tennessee militia during the Creek War. He led several campaigns against the Red Sticks, and their defeat is due in large part to his frontier experience and dogged persistence. Through the Treaty of Fort Jackson, he secured millions of acres of Creek land for the United States. Shortly after, the capture of Pensacola and the victory at the Battle of New Orleans earned him a name that would eventually lead him to the White House in 1829.

Peter McQueen

A mixed-blood, McQueen led the Battle of Burnt Corn and participated in the destruction of Fort Mims. After refusing to sign the Treaty of Fort Jackson, he fled to Spanish Florida where he continued to resist American intrusion into Creek territory.

Zachariah McGirth

Son of a British commander from the Revolutionary War, Zachariah grew up in Creek country and married a half-Creek woman named Vicey. He became a wealthy planter in the Tensaw region of Mississippi Territory and narrowly escaped the Battle of Fort Mims by being absent the day of the attack. Believing his wife and children dead, Zachariah became overridden by grief and employed himself the duration of the Creek War by riding as courier between his settlements and Georgia when no one else could be found brave enough to go. Learn more about the fictional McGirths' story in *Beneath the Blackberry Moon* books 2 and 3, *The Sacred Writings* and *The Ebony Cloak*.

Samuel Mims

Trader and ferryboat operator, Sam Mims owned the largest home in the Tensaw settlements. Because of its size and centralized location, his home was frequently used to host social events. Its use as the site for a fort was the natural choice. He died during the battle.

Creek War Timeline

Fall 1811. Tecumseh arrives from the north to preach his vision of joining tribes and nations to stand against white encroachment.

June 1812. United States declares war on Great Britain.

Spring 1813. Civil war breaks out in Creek Confederacy.

May 1813. Red Sticks make several trips to Pensacola to purchase weapons from the Spanish.

July 27, 1813. Battle of Burnt Corn.

August 30, 1813. Battle of Fort Mims.

November 18, 1813. Hillabee Massacre.

March 27, 1814. Battle of Horseshoe Bend (Horse's Flat Foot).

August 9, 1814. Treaty of Fort Jackson signed, surrendering millions of acres of Creek land to the United States.

*Although only four are touched on here, there were fourteen notable conflicts of the Creek War.

Glossary

Acadians: descendants of 17th-century French colonists who were exiled from Canada by the British. Those who settled in Louisiana become known as Cajuns.

Alabama: Roll Tide! (Couldn't help myself.)

Alabama Town: a town of my creation based off a tribe that still exists, the Alabamas. Ancient Alabamas lived in seven towns near the location of my fictional Kossati. Alabama Indians were *not* Muscogee but a separate tribe of the Muskogean linguistic group and part of the confederacy. They were closely related to the Koasatis (see Kossati) and more distantly to the Choctaws.

Beloved Men: old war leaders retired from battle but venerated in council.

Blood Vengeance: among the topmost legal principle of Southeastern Indians of the time. If a person was killed, it was the responsibility of his male clansmen, under guidance of the clan mothers, to retaliate in equal manner. The purpose being to restore balance in the clans.

Bluecoat: soldiers in the United States Army. So named because of their blue wool coatees. For this era, my creation.

Breechcloth: a long rectangular piece of animal hide or cloth that was brought up between the legs and under a belt at the waist. The ends hung like a flap over the belt in front and behind. Worn as outerwear by men and sometimes as underwear by women.

Broken Days: counting sticks bundled together to keep track of the passage of time. They were distributed to towns to mark the approach of special events such as battle or ceremony.

Chokofa: circular townhouse found in the ceremonial centers of some towns. Used in cold or inclement weather in a manner similar to the town square.

Chunkey: a variety of hoop and pole game in which a stone was rolled and sticks were thrown to the location the player believed the stone will land.

Clan: a category of people who believed themselves to be blood relatives, even if untraceable. Clan permission, authority, and protection were often called upon. The blood law fell on clan shoulders. Clan structure and responsibilities extended across the confederacy so that a member of Deer Clan would expect to be received as a family in any Deer Clan home in any town. Clans were associated with particular animals and natural phenomenon, the care of which they were often responsible. Deer Clan elders, for example, would monitor proper hunting in proper season.

Cock Fletch: the fletch of an arrow that varies in color from the other two. Often points down when nocked on the bowstring.

Couch: used for sitting and sleeping. Couches were arranged along the wall, raised two-three feet off the ground, made of saplings and cane, and covered with split-cane mats and animal skins.

Creek Confederacy: formed by survivors of the devastation wrought by 16th-century Spanish expeditions. The Muscogee were the strongest tribe at the time, and over the course of one hundred plus years, accepted refugee tribes under the umbrella of their protection.

At its peak, it was so mighty George Washington treated the confederacy on a level of respect equal to that of France and Britain. The Creek War of 1813-14 began its decline.

Creek countrymen: sons of European traders and Creek women who grew up in Creek country yet lived slightly apart in a blended lifestyle.

Darkening Land: the spirit world; where a soul goes after death; located in the west. Also called Spirit Land, or the Haven of Souls.

Earth Spirit: female; one of the four law-giving elements. Takes forms such as soil, rock, and Corn Woman who is the embodiment of the spirit and from whose body corn originated. Also called Mother Earth.

East, Sacred: one of four sacred cardinal directions; associated with the Sun Spirit, the sacred fire, life, and success.

Elder Brother: 1. a title of honor. Elder brothers were supposed to be kind and protective toward their younger brothers. **2.** A woman's brother was her closest blood relative, and in some ways closer to her than her husband. Their relationship carried over to her children. In place of their father, an elder brother taught her sons much of what they needed to know to be men. In the absence of an elder brother, a younger brother filled the role.

Federal Road: a U.S. postal route bisecting Creek country. It linked trading establishments and became a route for pioneers passing through to lands in the west. The road became a point of disturbance between Creeks and Americans.

Five Civilized Tribes: consisted of Creeks, Seminoles, Chickasaws, Choctaws, and Cherokees. So named by George Washington in his "plan for civilization."

Fire Spirit: male; assistant to the Sun Spirit.

Flageolet: a simple wind instrument made of cane.

Four, Sacred: a "magic" number that is expressive of the Creek belief system. Their *four* can be understood in a rough comparison to the Christian *three* for the Holy Trinity.

Four-day Journey: the number of days it was believed to take for a soul to journey to the darkening land.

Go to Water: ritualistic bathing done all year at dawn to overcome pollution and increase longevity.

Grand Council, 1811: the annual Creek grand council in which Shawnee-Creek Tecumseh arrived from the north with a plea for all tribes to join forces against the whites. There is debate on whether he preached peace or violence, but regardless, it was the spark that eventually enflamed the Creeks to civil war.

Great Warrior: the warrior selected led the town in war. He arranged ball games with Great Warriors from other towns and carried out the will of the micco.

Healing Song: a formula chanted or sung over a patient with the intent of engaging his spirit, restoring the correct flow of energy, and returning him to full health.

Herbal Warriors: the spiritual role of herbs as they work to heal a person's body.

Hunting Dreams: instead of saying "good night," the Creeks said, "I go to hunt a dream."

Ibofanga: neither male nor female; was above all and was the unifying principle of the spirit world. Ibofanga was the impersonal Creative Force. It created and set in motion laws that govern the universe. Every element of nature had a part of Ibofanga residing inside it. Its counterpart was the Chaotic Force, represented by such beings as the tie-snake.

Knower: an individual with spiritual and psychological wisdom who also possessed second sight. A knower could foretell death and interpret dreams, among other things. A knower diagnosed but did not cure illness. Not to be confused with medicine maker.

Kossati: a town of my creation based off of a Muskogean tribe that still exists, the Koasatis. Ancient Koasatis lived in two towns very near the location of my fictional Kossati both bearing the name Wetumpka. Big Wetumpka was situated on the site of present-day Wetumpka, Alabama. Koasati Indians were *not* Muscogee but a tribe of the Muskogean linguistic group and part of the confederacy. They were closely related to the Alabama.

Lineage: a Creek's closest blood relatives, specifically those who lived together in the same family settlement. The Creek social system was organized as follows: individual, lineage, clan, town. The Creeks were a matrilineal society, meaning their blood (and clan) was traced through the women. Although a man was involved in his children's lives, he was not their blood relative nor was he ultimately responsible for their upbringing.

Little Brother of War: stickball. Defined as such because of its violent nature and its use as a substitute for war.

Long Guns: Indian term for white settlers. My creation.

Long Hairs: extinct Muskogee term for Choctaws. The Choctaws originally wore their hair long and unshaven. By the historic period (the story's setting), warriors had begun to shave their heads in a manner similar to the Creeks, but I revived the term to add flavor.

Long Snake: a term I borrowed from the Cherokee's river deity.

Lower Towns: all Muskogean towns established along the Chattahoochee and Flint Rivers and their tributaries. Being geographically closer to Georgia colonists, the Lower Towns had easier access to trade goods. Because of that, they became dependent on the whites and were supportive of keeping peace with whites and assimilating their cultures. Many Lower Towns allied with the Americans during the Creek War. See Upper Towns.

Lunar Retreat: the time during menstruation when a woman was to stay separate in a designated moon lodge. Her latent power during that time would weaken a man. To break a lunar retreat rule was to commit a crime similar in nature to adultery or even murder.

Maddo: thank you (Muskogee language).

Master of Breath: see Wind Spirit.

Medicine: Creeks' equivalent to our terms "magic" or "power." Bad medicine was used by witches. Examples of good medicine were herbal warriors or healing songs. Medicine could also be neither good nor bad. A woman's medicine during menstruation was powerful but not bad, so long as it was properly handled.

Medicine Bundle: small items wrapped in a package and worn by warriors for spiritual protection. Items varied from individual to individual but each held special significance to that warrior.

Medicine Maker: men who were trained diseases and healing herbs. Valued for their knowledge, not for any innate power they might have.

Micco, talwa: town chief. There were many levels of micco in both civil and military roles. This particular title was political.

Milledgeville: capital of Georgia from 1804-1868.

Minko: chief. Choctaw language.

Mississippi Territory: an organized incorporated territory of the United States that existed from 1798-1817 and was comprised of present-day Alabama and Mississippi.

Moon Lodge: a place set apart for women.

Muscogees: an indigenous people who once dominated the Southeast. They occupied land from the Atlantic coast to central Alabama and were the founders of the Creek Confederacy. Also known as the Creeks.

Muskogee: language spoken by the Creeks and Seminoles.

Muskogean: indigenous languages originating in Southeastern United States. They consist of many dialects which are divided into two regions. East—Creek and Seminole (Muskogee), plus four others. West—Chickasaw and Choctaw.

North, Sacred: one of four sacred cardinal directions; associated with cold, trouble, and defeat.

Old Beloved Path: tribal traditions handed down by elders generation after generation.

Order of Things: natural law that encompasses ecological principles. A way of doing things to promote harmony, show reverence for law-giving elements, and to avoid their displeasure.

Owl: an ill-omen, a witch on the wing.

Pawa: maternal uncle. A pawa oversaw the discipline and training of his sisters' sons. See elder brother. (Muskogee language.)

Peace Town: a sanctuary where no violence could take place. Places of refuge for runaway slaves, the homeless, bands in conflict, and lawbreakers. The peace was enforced by Red Sticks.

People of the Point: Muskogee term for Seminole Indians. So called because of the peninsula (Florida) they lived on.

Red Sticks: 1. one of two social labels available to Creek men (Red Sticks/White Sticks). Red Sticks were known for courage, strength, alertness, physical skills. They held leadership roles in warfare, security, and law enforcement. So called because of the red war club, the symbol of war. **2.** During the Creek War, the term "Red Stick" took on new meaning for the white settlers. For the duration of the war, a Red Stick was a Creek warrior who opposed the Americans; however, many warriors of the white persuasion shared their views and fought alongside them.

Red War Club: symbol of war. Before the musket, it was the preferred hand-to-hand combat weapon. To call men to battle, a red war club was raised in the square.

Regular Army: soldiers under the direction and pay of the federal government. Contrast with militiamen, who were volunteers organized by state.

Roach: a stiff crest of hair running down the middle of the head. Also called a Mohawk.

Sacred Fire: the principle symbol of purity. Sun's representative on earth. Believed to report evil to the Sun who would dispense punishment. Found in each town's square and chokofa.

Scratching: a practice used to train for hardiness, to purify, to seek spiritual knowing, and to invoke the spirit of the individual's totem animal. A sharp, four-pointed instrument was raked across the chest, back, arms, legs. Depending on gender, age, and purpose, scratches varied from simply breaking the skin to creating wounds that bled and left scars.

Shadows: ghosts, evil spirits. The term is my invention, although the Muskogees did believe that ghosts of bodies improperly buried or those of ancestors whose deaths were not avenged could haunt a man. The Muskogees before Christian influence did not have a "good Creator" or an evil counterpart such as Satan. Their concept of "evil" was one of chaos.

Sight, a: as far as one could see. Rough equivalent to our mile.

Single-pole Ball Game: played by men and women together around a pole up to fifty feet tall. A player who succeeded in hitting an object on the pole with a ball earned points. Men used stickball sticks; women used hands.

Slave Pole: a pole stationed in the town square to which slaves and captives were tied and often tortured. By the historic period (the story's setting), slave poles were no longer in use. I brought them back into use to serve the story's purpose. However, during the

Creek War, soldiers *did* come across Red Stick towns (see Red Sticks definition 2) that featured red poles adorned with scalps.

Sleeps: the marking of days or the passage of time. One sleep equals one day.

Sofkee: a thin gruel made of cornmeal or rice. Cooked with wood-ash lye and often eaten after being left to sour.

South, Sacred: one of four sacred cardinal directions; associated with warmth, peace, and happiness

Standing Militia: the most reliable units of militia (volunteer soldiers). They were well-equipped (at their own expense), organized, and met annually to train.

Stickball: a violent team sport resembling lacrosse in which a set of cupped sticks were used to lob a ball against a pole or between two poles that formed a goal. Used as training for battle and sometimes used as a substitute for war. Also called the little brother of war.

Stomp Dance: intertribal celebrations or social events. As with most every Creek event, stomp dances were religious in nature and, through ritual, blended the four law-giving elements in a reverential way.

Sun Spirit: female; one of the four law-giving elements. Source of all light and life. Also known as Grandmother Sun.

Tafia: a cheap trade rum, the primary liquor consumed by the Southeastern Indians of the 18th and 19th centuries.

Talwa: a Creek community. Muskogee language.

Tippling House: an establishment in which liquors are sold in small quantities.

The Floridas: the combination name given the two regions of Florida (West Florida and East Florida) which existed during the setting of this book. In 1813, both were owned by Spain. Also called Las Floridas.

This World: the middle world of the Indian three-world cosmos. The place Indians lived.

Tie-snake: believed to be powerful snakes that crawled up on land to drag victims under water.

Under World: the lowest of the Indian three-world cosmos. Existed below the earth and water. Epitomized chaos.

Upper Towns: all Muskogean towns established along the Alabama River, its branches (the Coosa and Tallapoosa), and their tributaries. Being sheltered from the Georgia colonists by geographic distance, the Upper Towns were more staunchly traditional. Because of that, they resisted assimilation and fought to retain their way of life. Many Upper Towns put out the red war club against the Americans and their allies during the Creek War. See Lower Towns.

Upper World: the highest of the Indian three-world cosmos. Existed above the sky. Epitomized order.

Warriors' House: the communal lodge where warriors met for council, purification, and to plot warfare.

Water Spirit: female; one of the four law-giving elements. Takes the form of rivers, lakes, rain, mist, streams, and the ocean.

West, Sacred: one of four sacred cardinal directions; associated with the Moon Spirit, souls of the dead, and death.

White Sticks: 1. one of two social labels available to Creek men. White Sticks were known for reasonability, patience, mediation skills, scientific knowledge. Their roles included medicine maker, civil duties, diplomacy, ensuring of peace. **2.** During the Creek War, the term "White Stick" took on new meaning. For the duration of the war a White Stick was a Creek warrior who allied with the Americans; however, many warriors of the red persuasion shared their views and fought alongside them.

White Drink: an herbal tea brewed for ceremonial purposes. It was consumed in large quantities in the council square and had a stimulating effect similar to excessive quantities of coffee. It often caused vomiting, which was done outside the square and was said to empty the body of impurities (alcohol) and ensure a clear mind. Called black drink by the Anglos.

Widow: required to mourn four years. During that time she was to crop her hair (representing a severing of accumulated memories) and not care for it. She was to dress unattractively and sleep over her husband's grave.

Wind Clan: the most prestigious clan. Specialized in predicting weather.

Wind Spirit: male; one of the four law-giving elements. Also called Master of Breath and Hesagedemesse. Assistant to Ibofanga. Controled energy links of all living things. Took and gave life.

Winters: the span of a year. My creation. The Creek year began in late summer at the Green Corn Festival.

Witch: any person who is heartlessly evil as to be beyond forgiveness. A witch sought the demise of others to add the deceased person's life to the span of his own.

Yatika: speaker, orator (Muskogee language). Every talwa had a yatika who was well-versed in the nuances of the many Muskogean dialects. Typically, a micco did not make public speeches. This job fell to the yatika who knew the micco's mind and used his oratory talents to convey the micco's (and the council's) wishes.

Made in the USA
Las Vegas, NV
31 May 2022

49616527R00256